Also by Carol Cassella

Oxygen

healer

CAROL WILEY CASSELLA

Simon & Schuster

NEW YORK
LONDON
TORONTO
SYDNEY

SIMON & SCHUSTER
1230 Avenue of the Americas
New York, NY 10020

First Simon & Schuster hardcover edition September 2010

SIMON & SCHUSTER and colophon are registered
trademarks of Simon & Schuster, Inc.

For information about special discounts for bulk purchases,
please contact Simon & Schuster Special Sales at
1-866-506-1949 or business@simonandschuster.com

The Simon & Schuster Speakers Bureau can bring authors
to your live event. For more information or to book an event,
contact the Simon & Schuster Speakers Bureau at
1-866-248-3049 or visit our website at www.simonspeakers.com.

Manufactured in the United States of America

1   3   5   7   9   10   8   6   4   2

Library of Congress Cataloging-in-Publication Data

Cassella, Carol Wiley.
Healer / Carol Wiley Cassella
p. cm.
1. Single women—Fiction. 2. Anesthesiologists—Fiction.
3. Seattle (Wash.)—Fiction.
PS3603.A8684 O99 2008
813'.622   2007037542
ISBN 978-1-4165-5612-1
ISBN 978-1-4391-8040-2 (ebook)

For Kathie and Ray, who showed me
what marriage can be

healer

· 1 ·

The body is a miracle, the way it heals. A factory of survival and self-repair. As soon as flesh is cut, cells spontaneously begin to divide and knit themselves into a protective scar. A million new organic bonds bridge the broken space, with no judgment passed on the method of injury. In her residency, Claire had treated a trauma patient who'd felt only one quick tug, looked down at her severed hand and wondered to whom on earth it might belong; even pain can be stunned into silence by the imperative to live.

As many years as it has been, Claire still understands the human body. She understands the involuntary mechanics of healing. But how an injured marriage heals—that remains a mystery.

This house feels so cold. Claire's fingers had been a shocking white from the knuckles to the tips after she stripped off her gloves when they finished unloading the U-Haul a few hours ago. She should be somewhat warmer by now, indoors, but it's as if the cold has worked its way into her core and radiates outward, chilling the room. They haven't been out to the house since summer, and dust coats every surface; seed-shaped mouse droppings dot the sofa cushions and countertops. The pallid light seeping through the windows seems too weak to hold color; everything in the room is muted to a shade of gray.

Jory sits on a cardboard box with her arms hugged across her stomach, her hair draped around her shoulders. "When is Dad getting here?" she asks.

"Between business trips. He'll come as soon as he can." Claire says this calmly, soothingly, the way she tries to say everything to Jory these days; announcing breakfast cereal choices and packing instructions as if they were salves, verbal Vicodin or Xanax. She kneels to open the door on the cast-iron woodstove and crumples newspaper between broken sticks, watching Jory without watching. Hunting for other emotions behind her sullen anger. Claire strikes a match, shelters it inside her cupped palm until it burns plump and dependable, touches it to an edge of newsprint and a week of stock quotes flames into hot orange light. The smoke stings her eyes, she squints and closes the thick glass door, toggles the metal lever of the damper until the sluggish air inside the chimney rouses and twists silver-gray tendrils up into the night.

Jory is quiet for a while, then says, almost accusingly, "We don't have very much wood."

Claire flinches, hears it as, *"Fathers build fires, mothers only turn up thermostats,"* wants to retort that they have a lot less of everything they are used to, thanks to her husband. "We have plenty of wood out in the shed," she answers. "I should teach you how to get the stove going."

Jory ignores her, tucking her hands between her knees and turning toward the windows so that all Claire sees is the fall of gold hair.

"It's a good woodstove," Claire continues. The Realtor had told them that, hadn't he? She hadn't really cared at the time; they'd never expected to sleep here in winter. "I'll call the furnace man tomorrow. And Dad can bring some space heaters when he comes."

"School starts tomorrow," Jory says. Claire chucks bits of wood onto the conflagrant pile and slams the stove door before they can spill out. "School starts tomorrow," Jory repeats, taunting her now.

Claire looks up and answers her, for the first time today, in the voice of an equal. "It will be all right. There's a school in Hallum if we stay very long." She sees Jory's stony expression and adds, "Or you can homeschool if you want. Whatever you want."

Jory seems to grow smaller, as if she would clench herself into a tight ball. Her face is locked inside her crossed arms so that her voice is barely audible. "I want to go back."

Claire sits on the ash-covered hearth and stares at the burning cinders tumbling against the glass like small animals scrambling to escape an inferno. "Well. There is no going back. Not yet." The words come out as stern as a slap, not what she'd intended; she clenches her teeth at the sound. But other words still burn inside her head, words she chokes before she can hurt the people she loves—a litany of all they can't go back to: no private school, no ballet lessons, no abiding trust that tomorrow will be the same or better than today. Not even the leeway to haggle for a fair offer on their lakeside home in Seattle.

It seems a perverse joke, Claire thinks, that after years of saving and insuring it had not been a fire or flood or disease that brought their world down. It wasn't global warming or terrorism, no collapsing levies or tsunamis—none of the headline threats that had spurred her to re-stock their Rubbermaid emergency boxes and stash wads of cash in suit jacket pockets at the back of the closet. Instead, for Claire and Addison and Jory, it felt quite personal, like a precisely-placed bomb destroying only *their* lives, leaving their neighbors and friends to stand unscathed and sympathetically gawking.

Claire had discovered the first hint of their ruination smoldering in a declined Visa credit card on a Christmas shopping trip with Jory, buying, of all the ironic possibilities, a twelve dollar collapsible umbrella. She'd left a message on Addison's cell phone warning him that their credit card number had been hacked, thinking the problem lay with the bank or the computer system. Surely they had been wronged by some outside force.

The daylight has almost faded but she doesn't want to leave the fire even to turn on the light. *It is easier with Addison away.* The thought darts across the surface of Claire's subconscious with the speed of an endangered bird. Jory is staring down at the scarred pine floor, oblivious to her mother's distress. Claire can keep up a front for Jory—mothering teaches you that from the first reassuring smile you give your toddler after a tumble. But if Addison were here he would see through Claire, she is sure. He would see her doubt and then the doubt could become real—could become the edge of the splitting maul. It almost makes her want their life here to be too difficult without him. If they can make it alone, just Jory and her, what unites their family except the tenuous hold of memories?

Jory is shivering and Claire hunts around for a box that might hold sweaters. She rips packing tape off cartons of china and shoes and bedding, the gritty sound of tearing cardboard almost welcome in the face of Jory's determined silence. In the third box Claire finds some of Addison's ancient high school track sweatshirts protectively folded around candlesticks and vases and a favorite Waterford bowl. She tosses a sweatshirt to Jory and pulls another one over her own head, cinching the hood close around her face, smelling something familiar in the thick cotton: a musty hint of old wood, or even, she imagines, Addison's gym locker, the indelible perfume of his adolescent sweat. She lines the fragile crystal pieces along the mantelpiece, dusting the bowl with her sleeve before she sets it down.

"Why are you unpacking that stuff?" Jory asks through her cloak of hair.

"No reason to leave everything in storage." Claire unwraps a serving platter, searching her emotional reserves for some way to mitigate the desolation she hears in her daughter's voice. "They're pretty, aren't they? We might as well enjoy them while we're here."

"They'll just get dirty. Or broken."

"Your grandmother gave us this plate, right before you were born." Claire looks at her distorted image in the silver, imagines her own mother sitting down for dinner with them in this drafty room, pursing her lips as she serves herself slices of tomato or fruit tart while Claire tries to explain why they've moved. "Put it on the table for me, please?"

Jory doesn't move. Claire sets the platter on top of another unopened box and stands up, brushes the ash off her blue jeans. "Let's go into town for dinner."

Without looking at her, Jory says, "I thought we couldn't afford to eat out anymore."

"We can't." Claire pats her pockets and kicks aside the newspapers scattered beside the woodbin. "Where did I leave my keys?"

· · ·

Food helps. The cheaper and greasier the better, sometimes. Over a cheeseburger Jory starts to talk again: a conversation about hair straighteners—what *is* the ideal width of the irons? Can eyelash curlers really pull out your lashes? And ballet, of course, her friends at the dance school and what they think of the recital piece. Maybe she could get new pointe shoes mailed to her, since there is no place to buy them in this itsy town.

Claire has begun to view adolescence as a compartmentalized, re-volving door. Openings flash by into different sectors of her daughter's life and the trick is to stand close at hand, poised and ready to jump in. There is a time-warping aspect to it: a flash forward to Jory at eighteen, competent and hopeful; a glimpse back to Jory at eight, vocal, with fresh, uninhibited awe.

Claire pushes her French fries across the Formica table toward her daughter and rests her chin on interlaced hands. "We'll drive back to Seattle when you need new toe shoes. It's not so far if the passes are clear. We can make a weekend of it now and then. Get your friends together." She doesn't bring up the fact that there is no ballet school in Hallum Valley. "Once the furniture comes how about you invite some friends over here?"

"Like, to do what?"

"Ski. Hike. Mountain bike." Claire eats another French fry, stalling to come up with something teenage girls might actually enjoy in Hal-lum. "I don't know. What do you want to do?"

"Go to the movies. Shop. Hang out in the mall. *Nothing* we can do here." Jory drifts into silence again. "Speaking of, where am I supposed to sleep tonight?"

"Were we speaking of that? Just share with me tonight." The house is minimally furnished with a sofa they'd bought at a yard sale last sum-mer, a set of folding metal chairs and a dining table. But until the mov-ing truck arrives they have only the old double bed they'd squeezed into the U-Haul with some smaller boxes. "We'll be warmer that way." She expects Jory to balk at this suggestion, but instead her face softens, as if she's been relieved of an unexpressed burden. It occurs to Claire that it is the very mattress Jory was conceived upon.

The waitress brings the check over and asks if they want any dessert. Claire orders two ice creams and a coffee only to postpone looking at the bill. Every penny of it will be borrowed; they are borrowing to pay interest on borrowed money. What's another ice cream? Jory slides the plastic binder that holds the check toward herself and flips it open to see the total, then slaps it shut again and pushes it back to her mother. "Let's say Dad finds a new investor next week. Can we buy our house back?" She flashes the comic grin that has always signaled she is near the edge, ready to snatch her feelings back at the slightest threat and turn everything into a joke.

Claire does her best to smile. Her mouth turns up, she can force that, but she can't seem to make the rest of her face—her exhausted eyes, her knotted brows—go along. She wants to ask Jory how much she's overheard behind closed doors, what rumors she's picked up at school beyond the explanations Addison and Claire have given her. And at the same time Claire doesn't want to know. She doesn't have the heart to reassure Jory, yet again, that the *family* is the house, and thus it will go wherever *they* go and can never be sold or lost. But as if graced by a moment of precocious instinct, Jory averts her gaze from her mother's face, suddenly intent on drawing faces in her melted ice cream. "We'll find a better house this time. You get your pick of rooms," Claire says. Jory lets out one short laugh without looking up and Claire can't tell if she appreciates this effort at optimism or is scoffing at her mother's simplification.

"So," Jory says after a deep sigh, her tone altogether new, as if the prior sentences had been spoken by other people in some other place. "What are you doing tomorrow?"

"Unpacking. Dusting. Want to help?"

"No," Jory answers, rocking back on her chair.

"Great! I get to decorate your room, then?" Claire asks, hungry for her own ice cream again.

"I thought I'd just paint bull's-eyes around the spots of mildew on the walls. So what are you doing after you unpack?"

"After *we* unpack?" Claire picks up her spoon and pulls the sweet thick cream onto her tongue, a simple pleasure. Any topic feels easy to her now. "I might start looking for a job."

"A *job*?" Jory sounds dumbfounded, and the front legs of the chair slam onto the concrete floor. "Doing what?"

Claire cocks her head at Jory's incredulity, gives her a moment to backpedal before she answers, "Being a doctor. What else? Should I try to earn money as a professional mother?"

Jory considers this. She looks at her mother appraisingly, and a flash of the eighteen-year-old whips by. "I can't see you as a doctor." Claire shrugs and spoons a lump of ice cream into her coffee, watches the ivory whirl blend to an even chocolate hue. Jory's snorts—the fourteen-year-old returns. "I mean, I know you're a doctor. But you've, like, probably forgotten everything by now. I mean, how long has it been since you actually took care of a patient?"

"Well, how old are you?"

"Fourteen. And three months. And thirteen days," Jory answers after a moment's calculation.

"Okay. It's been fourteen years, six months, and twenty days since I saw a patient," Claire answers, remembering those last weeks in bed, unsuccessfully willing her own uterus to hold quiet and nurture Jory's wispy lungs one more day, one more hour, to inch her over the line of survival. All Claire's years of medical training would have felt absurdly pointless if the final price paid was losing this life inside her.

"God. Please don't make me the first guinea pig," Jory says. "So, are you going to wear a white coat and all?"

"I don't know. Is that what makes somebody a doctor?"

Jory is quiet for a moment. She studies her mother with a skeptical look on her face that makes Claire feel oddly insecure. Or maybe it isn't skepticism—maybe it's embarrassment. Is she embarrassed to think about her mother seeing actual patients, possibly her own classmates, if indeed she deigns to attend school in Hallum?

Claire shifts uncomfortably in her seat and fingers the handle of her coffee cup. Then she tucks her hands between her knees and leans across the table confidentially, "Maybe you can help me write a résumé. Know how?" Jory shakes her head but sucks in her bottom lip, probably considering the opportunities she might wrangle out of this offer.

Claire plunges on. "You could help me practice my interview. Or at least figure out what to wear."

Jory picks up her Coke and holds the cold glass in hands cloaked by the stretched out sleeves of her high-necked sweater. It is a Renaissance look that suits her, thinks Claire, harmonizes with her waist-length hair and her pale skin—Juliet debating Paris's proposal of marriage. Portia contemplating mercy. Or would the fouled fortunes in the Boehning household twist her into mad Ophelia?

"Well, whatever you do, don't wear red. You know that red suit you have? You should ditch that suit, Mom. Sorry," she adds in inauthentic apology.

"My black one okay?"

Jory shrugs and tips her glass up for the last sip of Coke, sucks out a ring of melting ice to encircle her folded tongue. "Caw ah fith yo heh?" Claire frowns, confused, and Jory swallows the ice. "Can I fix your hair?"

"What do you suggest?" Claire rakes her fingers through her hair.

"Bangs. To hide your wrinkles. And color the gray."

"Do I have that much gray?" Claire had skipped her last hair appointment knowing what the bill would be, a childishly vengeful part of her imagining Addison marking their months of duress as he watched her hair grow out.

"Since Christmas you do. It actually looks kind of good on you, but nobody wants to hire somebody who's old." Jory postures for the anticipated lecture; a stilted confidence wavers in her eyes.

But Claire feels part of herself drain away, as if her core has suddenly shrunk inside her skin. Right now she has no stomach to cope with the fact that age can be an asset for a physician—*if* it comes with experience and credentials. She stands up. "Let's go," she says, shoving her arms into her coat.

Jory hesitates, her groundwork shifting beneath her. "I didn't mean . . ."

"It's all right. I just need to get the fire going or the house will be too cold tonight."

· 2 ·

The fire is stone dead by the time they get home, no smoke at all from the chimney and the living room windows forbiddingly black. Claire wishes she'd left a light on, some beacon at the end of the long winding drive down through sagebrush and aspen to the house. The reflection of starlight off snow is the only illumination, an isolation that is more appealing when Addison is with them, when they have come to the country only to find respite from the city. She hands her cell phone over the car seat. "Call Dad. He's probably back at his hotel by now." She listens to Jory's end of the conversation, overblown descriptions of unloading the U-Haul and the two of them wrangling the mattress up the narrow staircase, when will he get the Internet going so she can check her Facebook, what color she intends to paint her room here. He is never left waiting for the door to swing open on some pocket of her inner life. Claire parks and takes another two boxes out of the trunk, then knocks on the rear window of the car to get Jory to come inside.

"Hey, how did your meeting go?" she asks her husband when Jory finally relinquishes the phone. She tries, as always these days, to ask such a simple question as if their fate didn't depend on it.

"Good. Pretty good."

"*Pretty* good?" She pins one of the boxes between her hip and the wall of the house while she unlocks the door. Jory is huddled behind her, jumping from foot to foot to keep warm.

"What can I say? There are a lot of labs working on anti-angiogenesis drugs. I set up meetings with two companies next month."

"So no contract talk." Claire bites her lip, reminding herself again not to start every one of their conversations with a question about his work, pinning too much hope on an answer she knows she won't hear yet.

"Nobody wants to commit right now, Claire. Even the giants are feeling the credit squeeze."

She steps inside the house and slides the heavy box to the floor, presses her forehead against the closed door and clenches her jaw against the cold. "It's down to seventeen tonight. They're saying it'll go below zero next week. I'm calling the furnace guy again tomorrow. We can't get it above fifty-five without the woodstove."

"Do everything you can to get him to repair this one."

She hates the ominously sober note in his voice, the implication that he needed to tell her that. Every conversation seems to circle back to money, the vortex sucking them down faster than they can swim. She takes a breath and tries another stroke. "Is your hotel nice? Bring me some good soap if they have any."

"It's fine. I'm at the Sheraton. The conference in Chicago is at the Drake, but I might just stay at the airport."

Claire sits down at the dining room table still wearing her coat and runs her fingers through her hair, pulling it back from her brow and massaging her scalp. "Addison. Just stay where the meeting is. Half the deals get done in the bar anyway—you always say that." She slumps deeper in her chair and picks at the caked debris caught in the grooved tabletop. "I might try to type up a résumé tonight." She says it bluntly, too tired to fake the cheerleader.

Addison chuckles as if this were a joke, but when Claire doesn't respond he adds, "We can hold out another few months. You don't really want to try this, do you?"

Now Claire laughs, so loud Jory's face pops up over the back of the sofa. Claire drops her voice. "I just paid eighteen percent interest on a cheeseburger!" Out of the blue she remembers the going-away party her closest friends threw for her, organized at the last minute because Claire hadn't had the nerve to tell anyone they were leaving Seattle until after the house had sold. They had brought her feminine, indulgent gifts—bath salts and brass boxes of herbal tea and a coupon for a spa day; baked casseroles she could freeze for the drive over the mountains. It had all been quite lovely until one of them asked how Addison was handling the disappointing news about his study drug and the others fell awkwardly silent. Her friend Anna, married to Addison's biggest investor, had finally rescued the moment by joking that Addison could earn a million faster than Wall Street could lose it. But Claire hadn't been able to get her spirits up again, their gifts now feeling like more unpayable debts.

Addison clears his throat and she can almost feel him grip the phone, swerving back toward a calmer discourse. "So. You guys okay there? You've got enough wood, I hope. Be sure to let the Hendlers know we're in the house—they'll call the police if they see smoke."

"Yeah. I'm getting great at building fires. Bring some space heaters out next weekend though, would you? And mousetraps."

"Sure. They're on my list." He sounds relieved to be given this purposeful assignment, so easily accomplished. She knows he will dictate a reminder note to himself as soon as they hang up—he has always loved making lists of tasks just so he can cross them off. She had caught him, on more than one occasion, writing down chores he had already finished. Once she had figured out her own birthday gift—her Audi—when she saw the checked-off reminder to call the insurance company.

Claire gets up and walks to a dark corner of the kitchen while Jory crouches by the woodstove crumpling paper into balls and sorting through the woodbox for smaller pieces. The kitchen sink smells of mildew; she turns on the hot water faucet to flush the drain. "Addison? Do you think, I mean, did you get the feeling anybody at the meeting has heard about why the review board shut the study down? Is that why you're not getting new investment money?"

She hears him take a deep breath and almost wishes she could snatch the question back. "No. I don't think so. That should be protected as proprietary information; nobody's legally allowed to talk about it. Not even Rick Alperts."

Claire wraps her arms more tightly around herself, shivering inside her down coat. "You haven't run into him at any of the conferences, have you? Would he take that chance?" It is a ridiculous question. Rick is fueled by risk. But somehow it's easier when they turn together against him, make Rick their living and breathing common enemy.

"I heard he's back in California. People know we ran out of time—ran out of money—but nobody knows the details."

"So you're pretty sure he hasn't talked to *Nature* or the *Wall Street Journal*?"

He laughs, but she can hear the tension in it. Even so his laugh still relaxes her, as it always has, skips her past the last months to remind her that one stupid gamble should not be allowed to ruin love. "No. Not yet, anyway. Sleep tight tonight, okay? I'll see you Saturday," he says.

On Wednesday morning she hangs her black suit at one end of the shower and turns the handle all the way to hot, hoping steam will erase the creases pressed into the material after being packed in a box for three weeks. She forgets about the blouse, though, and once she finds it, crammed into another box with silk scarves and lingerie, she has to button the suit jacket up to the top to hide the wrinkles. Dress shoes are in some other huge container, somewhere, labeled on one side or another with thick black marker MOM'S CLOSET. Around two in the morning on the last day before they had to be out of the house she had given up on neatness and begun pitching her wardrobe into any half-filled moving crate, most of them not yet delivered. She dives headfirst into the most likely container, its sides bulging with the weight of personal adornments, and comes up with a single black leather high heel. The other one turns up two boxes later beneath a clock radio, a Ziploc bag of perfumes and three Tumi handbags.

"Now your hair's a wreck." Jory stands in the doorway, swallowed inside Addison's thick bathrobe, black circles of mascara bleeding under her eyes.

"Well. Matches my clothes, then. Dad forgot his bathrobe, huh?"

Jory shrugs and picks up a brush from the table, stands in front of her mother and lightly sweeps the tangles off her forehead, training locks of hair around the curve of her fingers. "Stand up. Turn around. You look okay. Not like a doctor. But okay."

"Yeah, well, who needs nice clothes when you wear a white coat all day, anyway. You all right here alone for a few hours? There's oatmeal. And a pizza in the freezer. I'll go to the store tonight."

"I'd be better if you'd gotten a TV hooked up," Jory says, brushing her own hair now, winding the mass into a silken tower on her head and posing with the brush at her lips like a bristling microphone.

"At least we got the computer going. There's a box of DVDs under the chair. I think we need some kind of dish for the Internet." She props a full-length mirror against the wall, Jory now splay-legged on the bed behind her. It has been weeks since Claire wore anything except blue jeans and a sweatshirt, and the suit feels cut for a different woman. She smoothes the fabric over her abdomen and turns to see herself from another angle. The fit, she decides, is not the problem.

"So this suit's all right?"

Jory rolls over on her back and stares at the ceiling. "Sure."

Claire walks to the bed and leans over to fill Jory's view. "I'm just talking to people at the hospital, Jory. We'll probably be back in Seattle before I have to take a job. Okay? Don't just eat chips and soda for lunch. Something with some protein in it. You should be able to call me on my cell phone. I'm pretty sure the signal reaches there."

She picks up her Coach briefcase—perhaps the third use since she bought it ten years ago. Inside are the résumés she and Jory had worked all yesterday to create. Jory had gone to the town library to download templates, and pulled adjectives out of the air so the short facts of Claire's relevant history might fill at least three quarters of a page. She has xeroxed copies of her medical degree, internship certificate and license tucked into the inner pocket of the briefcase as well. No one will ask to see them today, unless they take her for a complete charlatan. But they make her feel authenticated. She kisses Jory on the cheek and walks on tiptoes out to the car so her slender sharp heels will not break through the thin ice.

· 3 ·

There are three medical clinics in Hallum Valley
and one hospital capable of minor orthopedics, low-risk deliveries, ap-
pendectomies and a rare exploratory laparotomy if the weather is too
bad to get to a city. A ninety-minute drive gets you to Wenatchee, where
almost any medical or surgical problem can be patched up. There are
plenty of opportunities for a doctor to work. She tells herself this again,
much as she did twenty years ago. Economies may rise and fall, wars
can be won or lost, ruling powers conquer and be conquered in turn,
and people will still need doctors. The size of the city shouldn't matter.
Health should be the equalizer of all human beings.

Claire had used this consolation to justify taking out her medical
school loans; used it to fortify herself in the middle of the night when
she groped for something stable and safe in the scary liminal zone of
young adulthood while her mother railed on her to figure out a way to
support herself. She would train herself in the art of healing—because
no one could take that away from her. Security she could pack and
carry in the protected space of her mind. Forever. So it had seemed, at
least, when she was young and did not understand that one bad decision made in the middle of the night could leech away even the most
fervent self-confidence.

The Sunrise Bakery is ten miles from their land—eight down small
county roads and two more down the highway—almost as quiet as the

14

back roads at this time of year. She parks the Audi in a pond of muddy slush, grips the door rim and pivots on the thin leather sole of a single pointed toe in order to plant one shoe on solid ground, soaking the other foot in a grimy melt of plowed snow.

It is a small place; six tables and a single booth, a big window lined with loose panes that rattle at every gust of wind. She waits for her coffee and looks around the room; a few retired couples reading the newspaper, two women in fleece vests talking in the corner, their hats still snugged down over their ears. One of them glances at her shoes and bites back a smile. Claire smiles at her and pays for the coffee. Then she steps through the slush again and drives home, changes into black jeans and snow boots, and drives across the mountain pass to the hospital.

Hallum had nearly turned into a ghost town three decades ago, shrinking with each graduating batch of offspring. Mining and timbering and farming had all been played out and the few made rich had moved on. Then Reaganomics seemed to manifest, and the golden spout of technology trickled money down in buckets, in tubs, in pools, in lakes. Hallum survived by cultivating two classes, the servers and the served, both sliding along the Teflon interface of tourist dollars. Thirty-year-olds dressed in REI vests and biking shorts bought second and third homes and then flat-out retired in search of the raw Northwest. They paved Issaquah and North Bend and Cle Elum and kept on, drove east in hybrid SUVs all the way across the Cascades to Hallum Valley, land the planet seemed to have held in waiting until superfluous income could inflate its only dependable commodity: breathtaking natural beauty. Stock options and initial public offerings were converted to five-bedroom log homes with solar panels and gasoline generators.

And so the town survived, flush and crowded on holidays and in summertime, sparse and quiet the rest of the year. Shops opened along the three-block main street; tractor dealers converted to mountain bike sales, feed stores put in stainless shelves stocked with whole-wheat pasta and imported olive oils. Even the Sunrise bought a Gaggia espresso machine and hired a barista. In a town where the split between the haves and the have-nots was once measured by the rust on one's pickup, a new paradigm of "normal" had settled like invisible gas. Now the split fell between those with more money than a man could fathom and those who served them. Caught in the middle were the people who sold their dirt-dry farms with those breathtaking views or their family-owned businesses that catered to ranchers and orchardists, and then sat and watched as prices rose and rents rose and their money ran out.

Claire and Addison had bought their house here a few years after Addison sold his first biotech company, Eugena. Their friends all had second homes; it seemed almost logical to invest in the place they loved vacationing. But she had never considered how it would feel to have a Hallum PO box be her sole address. It colors her view of the small town as she drives through, as if the skin of it had been turned inside out. The simplicity of the clapboard-sided buildings, the wood rail fences, the absence of stoplights and neon and malls. All of it felt more puni-tive than peaceful when it came without choice.

The road follows the river, black as oil where it slides between its frozen banks, a contest between cold progress and solid ice. Small brown birds hover and light on straws of aspen chewed raw by the deer; a few horses stand inside a muddy pen, each with a rear fetlock cocked and ears low against their heads, as if resigned to be annoyed by the sharp wind all winter long. She thinks about Addison. She pictures him in some Hilton or Fairmont, in his silk and cashmere Barneys suit, get-ting ready for drinks and dinner while she runs the tank nearly empty in hopes of finding a cheaper gas station farther down the road. It's almost funny that he'd made millions discovering a simple way to di-agnose a deadly disease—ovarian cancer—a fortune built on bad news. And then all of it lost on the precipice of a cure. Ironic enough to be almost funny.

Sawtooth County Hospital is half an hour away over a shallow mountain pass between two neighboring valleys. It is surprisingly modern, but then what was she expecting? A line of double-wide trailers jury-rigged with a laboratory and X-ray machine? A log cabin with electricity and scrub sinks? In all the years they've been coming to Hallum they have never needed medical care beyond what Claire could piece together from her own first-aid kit; all she has verified has been the assurance they could be airlifted back to Seattle.

She follows signs to the back of the building near the emergency room entrance and parks in a visitors' lot next to two ambulances. There is a helicopter landing pad to her left, and beyond that are rolling fields that climb and climb into hills and then into mountains spotted with dense green stands of ponderosa pine. At the lower elevations the shadows lace the snow blue on the undulating slopes. The tops of the peaks disappear into flat, gray clouds.

The lobby of the emergency room is uncharacteristically calm, at least compared to the inner-city public hospitals of her residency. An old man leans forward on his chair with his hands pressed against his eyes; his younger friend or son reads a newspaper to him, jumping from headline to headline as if he took no real interest in any of them. A few whining children squirm in their mothers' laps, a few more squall behind shut doors, struggling against stitches or tetanus injections or close inspection of ears and throats. The triage nurse asks Claire if she is a new drug rep, and brightens when Claire answers that she's a new doctor in town, hoping to meet the medical staff. The nurse doesn't react to the self-conscious note Claire hears in her own voice and points the way to the offices down a hallway. The chief of medicine has taken the day off to go ice fishing, the woman says, but there should be a secretary around who can let her know his schedule.

The newly cleaned carpets smell of disinfectant vaguely camouflaged as citrus. The walls are covered in a shiny washable plastic; the chairs and love seats with industrial upholstery, all their colors muted to an unnatural hue by the fluorescent lighting. And the chill—hospitals are never warm. She remembers working call shifts, roaming the nearly empty halls of Harborview Hospital at three and four in the morning with a blanket wrapped around her like one of the homeless souls she doctored. She could be blindfolded and know the function and purpose of this building. It leaves her feeling even more out of place, an uninvited guest in a house she used to own. She should scrawl a name tag declaring her purpose here: "No, not a patient. Not a visitor. I'm one of you, an insider. I've just forgotten where I left the doctor in me."

She puts her briefcase on a chair and pulls out one of her résumés. The top two-thirds encompassed ten and a half years of her life, from college until she left her residency three months before graduation. All she sees is the empty space at the bottom of the page; she would have to write a book to fill in that blank. It's the details she's left *off* that critically define her, she thinks. Everything had crowded together at the end. That last terrible call night working in the emergency room; patients were waiting eight, ten, twelve hours and both of her interns were busy in the trauma room. There hadn't been time to listen to every complaint as carefully as she should. She had been overwhelmed. She didn't learn the consequences of her triage decision until days later. She can hear her adviser's voice as clearly in this lobby right now as she'd heard it in his office fourteen and a half years ago: "Every doctor makes mistakes. Medical instinct, that sense that someone's sicker than they look, that's not in a book, Claire. It takes years of experience. Take a day or two off. Get some rest."

But the next day her uterus began the slow process of expulsion, doing the proper work of labor at the improper time. Jory was delivered almost three months early and Claire began the weeks of vigil in the neonatal ICU, willing the power of her mind and her love to do what her body could not: keep Jory alive. She remembers being enraged at fate, at God, at her corporeal self for its failure. There had been moments in the middle of the night, watching Jory's doctors and nurses struggle, when Claire was certain this was punishment for her missed diagnosis. What part of it all had kept her from going back to finish her residency? She didn't know. She had let the course of life make her decision.

She puts the résumés back in her case and snaps the lock shut. She should leave, she decides. It is a waste of everyone's time to pretend she could take a job here; that she's come for any grander purpose, if she drills her conscience, than to goad Addison, to prove that she will not stand by helpless. She looks around to orient herself, wanting to get to her car without going back through the emergency room. A woman with silver-streaked hair and a navy blue sweater buttoned tight over her white nurse's dress walks out of the bathroom at the end of the hallway and fixes Claire in her focus, strides toward her with so much authority Claire wonders what rule she could have broken. The idea of explaining herself to this woman—to anyone—suddenly feels overwhelming. She opens her mouth to ask what the visiting hours are and the nurse halts in front of her. "They're all at lunch."

"I'm sorry?" Claire says.

"If you're here to see any of the docs, they're all in the cafeteria. Chief is out today." She pauses just long enough to see Claire nod, then takes hold of her arm and marches across the lobby into a small, brightly lit cafeteria.

At a long rectangular table six or seven people laugh and talk, breaking into each other's words like they spend so much time together they don't filter their conversation around manners anymore, dive straight in for the punch line. Every other table seems sober in contrast.

The navy-sweatered nurse says, "Thursday's burrito day. Nobody goes out. People from town drive over just for lunch on Thursdays. I'm Marti. I didn't catch your name. How should I introduce you?"

"Claire. Claire Boehning."

"Ms. Boehning, meet our staff docs. And a few interlopers. One good look and you'll decide to stay healthy. Jim, they want to know if you need contrast on that CT. Can I get you a cup of coffee?" she asks, turning back to Claire.

Thank God she had changed her clothes. There are five men and two women at the table, dressed in jeans, khakis, lined fleece shirts; not a white coat among them. Not . . . *doctorly,* she thinks. But the last time she had lived and worked in the world of medicine she had been in academics, where rank and role were clearly and constantly defined. They are all within ten or so years of her age, all but one—a tall, white-haired man well past retirement age. One of the youngest, a puff-cheeked fellow with a chin cleft, reaches out to shake her hand. "Have a seat. Don't let these guys scare you. Z. Make room for her." The elderly man scoots his chair and Claire slides into a seat at the end of the table. A plate of tortillas sits in the middle and she wonders if Jory has eaten.

Marti brings her a cup of coffee and sits at the other end of the long table. "So you're looking for a job."

Claire smiles, glad not to be the first to say it. "Do I look unemployed?" Her voice comes out higher than normal; she tries to relax her throat.

"Nobody around here carries a briefcase unless they're selling something, and we know all the reps. Are you a nurse?"

"A doctor. We just moved here. My family." She pauses a beat. "My daughter and I."

"How old is your daughter?" asks one of the women.

"Jory's fourteen. We moved out from Seattle last week. But we've owned property here for a few years, on Northridge Road—outside Hallum."

"Where on Northridge?" This from the man two down, a gaunt blond with bangs cut perfectly straight across his forehead as if he'd done them at home with sewing scissors, his voice melodic enough to mitigate his stern face.

"About eight miles out. There's an old homestead there, with an apple orchard."

"Oh, you're at the Blackstock homestead. Is that right? That's a nice piece. I bike around there. What are you going to do with the house? I'm Steven Perry, by the way. Surgery." He stands up to stretch over the others and shake her hand.

Claire nods and takes a sip of her coffee, a quick flash of their tabled house plans pushed out of her mind. "Yeah. We feel lucky to own it."

"What's your specialty?"

"Family practice." She says it calmly enough, knowing the answer implies all the things she isn't—board certified and experienced. "We aren't sure how long we'll be living here yet, but I thought I'd introduce myself. Find out who might be looking for help if we stay." She starts to add more, but leaves it open-ended, shrugging her shoulders in a quick half apology. They introduce themselves then, going around the table with names and specialties she tries to memorize but finds no space for, too preoccupied with guessing what she might have to explain next.

"You should stop by Kit's place, south of town along the river road," a pediatrician named Jenna says. "She's been busy. I don't know if she's advertising, but I can call her up." She turns to Marti. "Richardson just hired a nurse practitioner, so he's probably stretched. What about Alton?"

Marti shrugs. "Maybe. He says he's losing so much money he's thinking of moving to Wenatchee. He's a bald-faced, cheapskate liar, though." And she laughs. "Z? How about you? Aren't you ever going to retire?" Marti looks across at the white-haired man next to Claire. She has assumed, with his silent, observing passivity, that he is a part of this gathering only through social history, quiet, perhaps, with the winding down of age. Only after Marti singles him out does he introduce himself. "Dan Zelaya." His hand is rough as a rancher's, the hand of a man who uses his body more than his mind to earn a living; the joints stiff and knotty but firm in grip. He wears a string tie and a white pearl-snap shirt—a neat row of enameled buttons with little silver rings around them and blue embroidered trim work. All that is missing, Claire thinks, is a cowboy hat.

Marti gets more enthusiastic as she goes on. "Dan, you've been running the busiest clinic in the valley with one nurse and a box of old Band-Aids. Hire this woman and take Evelyn to Arizona for the winter."

The table erupts with laughter, though Claire can't tell if it is about the pecuniary limits of his clinic or the idea of heading south. Dan winks at her and lifts a large felt cowboy hat off the seat next to him; his long, angular fingers close over the entire crown with room to spare. The hat has the same silver snakeskin rope around the brim that encircles his neck, silver-tipped tassels that click when he settles it over his white hair. "Never get her house fixed up if she works with me." Then he stands up, taller than she had expected, and takes his leave.

Steven pulls a prescription pad out of his shirt pocket and writes down names and directions for Claire. The table slowly empties; even Marti finally excuses herself to return to the ward. Claire finishes her coffee and watches the patients leaving their own tables, plays a game of guessing their diseases, stopping short of trying to recall differentials and treatments. She has danced this initial foray into Hallum's medical universe nimbly, she decides, diverting any details about why they had left Seattle. And never once had she reached into her briefcase to pull out her makeshift résumé.

· 4 ·

Jory is asleep when Claire finally gets home, though it is past three. She is the elongated mound buried under three down comforters piled on the double bed, the quiet breath in the otherwise still room. Claire stands in the doorway after a brief survey of the clutter throughout the house—identical to the clutter left behind that morning. Jory has slept her day away in the certainty that one of the adults in her world will carry her steadily on to the next milepost.

But Claire needs to move around, the best diversion she's found so far. She hunts in the closets until she finds a small electric fan and props it in front of the woodstove to draw the meager heat deeper into the room. Corrugated boxes are stacked on the peeling kitchen counters, shoved up against the walls and piled at the bottom of the stairs waiting to be carried up, and these are only a fraction of what was packed onto the moving van. Most are labeled with a room that doesn't exist here: Mom's study, walk-in closet, library, guest powder room, butler's pantry, media room.

This house has no such discretionary rooms. It is a single tall box divided into four spaces, two bedrooms sharing a bathroom upstairs, and one large living room and a small kitchen down. There is another box, too, a utility alcove and tiny toilet stall shunted underneath a low shed roof adjacent to the kitchen—probably added in the forties when the house was finally electrified. Last spring break Claire let Jory and her friends paint all the kitchen cabinet doors in enameled reds and blues and yellows—the only vibrant colors in the house.

There is a large porch running along the front, with the broken remains of decorative wooden corner pieces at the joints between post and beam, resembling quartered wagon wheels. Four wide plank steps drop down to the land, which spreads in liquid undulations across eighty acres until it dives five or six hundred feet to the valley floor. Back when this county was first developed, first taken from the Indians, people probably considered the entire ranch their dwelling, at least seasonally. Back when the interior of a house afforded little more than protection from wind and rain.

There is a barn, too—the kind people stop to take photographs of on leisurely Sunday drives with no destination in mind. It is useless, really, but for nostalgia—it lists so much Claire has warned Jory not to play inside it alone for fear that it might collapse in the least wind. And beyond the aspen groves there is even a shallow stream that empties into a dredged cattle pond clean enough for swimming in the summer, when the earth blisters and the grass is so dry it sounds like the rustle of snake skins.

They had looked for property in the Okanogan area for more than two years, driven over a thousand square miles east of the Cascades. Addison seemed to have some particular vision in mind, a cutout that necessitated an exact fit, a missing piece for his entree into the privileged world. He wanted something bold, the seed for a family dynasty. Claire teased that he'd watched too many episodes of *Dallas* as a kid. But at least once a month they drove over the mountain passes to wind through the valleys and along the rivers that fed the Columbia.

Addison had finally found this place on a solo trip, a weekend Claire and Jory had stayed in Seattle for a ballet rehearsal. Claire knew the minute she answered his phone call that they would own it— Addison was ready to write the check, a cash-out deal. Claire didn't even see it until after she'd signed the papers, a fact she now takes as a bitter example of how freely, even gladly, she had given up asking where their money went. The supply had seemed endless.

The house had been built at least ninety years ago, directly over a burned-down homestead cabin, one of the first in the region. In its time it must have been quite the showcase, with indoor plumbing and a second story, sunk into a broad sweep of Idaho fescue; the original vegetable garden had long ago wasted to a scar of Barnaby and mustard tumbleweed that delineated the plowed rectangle as clearly as any deer fence. This land was so different from the rainy west side of the Cascades; with barely enough water to scrape by, the native bunch grasses reliably succumbed to opportunistic weeds anyplace the soil was disturbed. An apple orchard had been planted in an atypical era of heavier rains, and the trees, long gone to ruin, watched over the house like an audience of craggy old men. Jory said they looked like the wickedly enchanted trees in *The Wizard of Oz,* ready to throw rotting apples at these invading city folk.

The house had seemed familiar to Claire somehow, from the very first time they bumped down the winding, overgrown driveway. The cracked windows, the knob and tube wiring, the peeling wood siding, the very fact that it had lain untouched for so many decades conjured for her both possibility and reminiscence. She had walked through the chilly rooms trying to imagine the family that built this home—the Blackstocks—back when the land could be had for nothing; imagined how hard they must have worked these fields until too many years of drought forced down the harsh truths about dry-land farming. The ranch had been leased for cattle grazing after that, but the Realtor had no record of anyone else inhabiting the house. Claire wondered if there had been children, more than one; whether it was purely the shifting of climate and crop that drove them out, or if divorce or disease and death had emptied the house. It felt important, somehow, to believe that it had been abandoned because the settlers had moved on to good and hopeful things, that the bones and dust here remembered more joy than capitulation.

Claire takes a Costco-sized pack of Clorox wipes out from the box labeled CLEANING SUPPLIES, and starts scrubbing the counters and cabinet shelves, sweeping flecks of insect wings and mouse droppings into a garbage bag. She crouches to pull a package of paper towels from behind the steel P trap under the sink and abruptly scrambles backward, striking her head on the bottom of the counter when a mouse skitters across her hand and disappears through a gap in the cabinet panels.

The smell is overwhelming, the sour, yellow odor of mouse urine. The shrink-wrap around the paper towels has been gnawed into a ragged hole, and the towels themselves shredded into a cushioned nest of fluff and excrement. Three naked, fetal mice blindly claw the exposed air that was a safe universe only seconds ago. She crouches, breathes through the sweet wool of her sweater sleeve, trying to remember the incubation time for hantavirus. They would have to be alive, of course, she thinks. No longer than the end of her smallest finger, the color of a new pencil eraser. She gets to her knees and hunts out the plastic dustpan, angles it beneath the pipes to scoop up the infant mice. One rolls ahead of the flange, risks being crushed against the wall, and she uses the soft edge of a sponge to flip it gently into the pan, gives herself a minute to accept that she is going to jettison them into the snow.

She carries them far enough from the house so they will be invisible from the windows, but rather than fling the weightless contents out to scatter wherever gravity carries them, she deposits them gently, even considers burying them. It might be faster that way. The low sun angle shadows every wind-driven gully as deep as a cavern.

Coming back in she stamps the ice off her boots and turns to shut the door behind her, stifling a gasp when she discovers Jory standing there, wrapped like a winter bride in one of the white down comforters.

"What were you doing out there?" Jory asks.

Claire brushes her hair back, careful not to touch her own face with her contaminated hands. "Nothing. I'm cleaning." She rests the dustpan against the wall. "I thought you were sleeping."

Jory is silent, and Claire leans forward to kiss her forehead. "I've gotta get to the store. What do you want for dinner?"

Her habits are still city habits; running to Whole Foods for a single meal, expecting to find the flaked salt and saffron stems and arborio rice for the dish she's craving. In Hallum it is eleven miles to the Food Pavilion where she settles for Morton Salt, McCormick curry powder and Uncle Ben's. But there are advantages, too, she decides, to the rural truths of living out here. This store is amply stocked with mousetraps and poisons.

Claire stacks her cart with enough groceries to get them through the week. She buys all the basics—spices and oils and vinegars, coffee and flour and sugar and tea bags—too tired to remember if she packed the contents of her kitchen cabinets into the U-Haul or left them behind for the moving truck. The cart becomes so laden it threatens to careen at any subtle slant in the floor. When there is little room left she goes to the far corner and studies the choices for ridding their home of the rodents who have run freely for the last decade or more. There are all sorts of contraptions and devices—a whole science of extermination. There are those that trap and kill through starvation and thirst, those that quickly electrocute, those that flavor poison as nourishment for mothers to take back to their babies; and the Havaharts, for the softhearted souls who want to believe that throwing them out in the snow is not equally fatal. She puts two Havaharts on top of the food and heads to the checkout stand, but thinks again about the distance to town and the knot on the back of her head. She asks the clerk to wait while she runs back to grab a box of d-CON.

Hallum has folded up for the night. Other than the lone bar at the other end of town, the grocery store is the last business to close. Strings of tiny white Christmas lights are still draped around a few gift store windows, the single streetlight at the end of the block shines on empty parking spaces and deserted sidewalks—no theater, no neon, no cruising teenagers marking territory with booming music.

A fine mist has crystallized into a stinging cold. Her gloves lie on the front seat; she can see them through the window. By the time she's packed the groceries into the trunk her fingertips have gone so numb she can't puzzle the key into the front door slot, and every passing locked-out second makes her hands stiffer, clumsier, winds her up in frustration until she wants to kick the door.

"*Señora?*"

Claire jumps when she hears the voice, sucks in a draft of freezing air so quick and deep it burns and her keys fall into the snow underneath the car. A woman is standing in the gutter only a few feet from the car, dark-haired and darkly clothed enough to be nearly invisible in the icy fog. Claire's heart pounds so hard she is startled into confusion.

The woman awkwardly backs up onto the sidewalk, nearly slipping on the icy lip of the curb, *"Discúlpame. Sorry!"*

There is such a sincere apology in her tone Claire doesn't need the translation. The voice is small—or rather, from a small person—and when Claire calms down enough to focus she can see the woman is compacting her slight body into a stanchion against the freezing night wind, her arms locked around herself. She is dressed in a buttoned-up cardigan and jeans. A knit cap, pulled low over her hair, and mittens are the only hint of seasonable clothing. Claire starts to ask her if she needs help, but the habits of the city rise up before logic and she looks down the block and behind her into the street, which is swallowed up by the night only a dozen yards from the store lights. A single set of taillights is just turning the corner. "Do you need something?" Claire asks. The woman shakes her head, seems almost embarrassed by the question. Claire glances another time over her shoulder and bends down to retrieve her keys. She unlocks her door and tosses her purse onto the seat beside her gloves, standing between the open door and the safe interior of her car. The store is closing—banks of fluorescent lights shut down in a series along the ceiling, from back to front, until only the glow of freezer cases and the green flickering of the registers show through the glass doors. The staff must have left through the back door. "They're closed," Claire says, then feels silly for stating the obvious. "Do you speak English?" The woman shrugs her shoulders. *"Habla inglés?"*

The woman untucks one bare hand from beneath the other arm and holds her thumb and forefinger an inch apart. "I study."

Claire looks up the street again. "Do you have a ride? A place to stay?" She searches her foreign vocabulary and pops up with a word for *house*. *"Un maison?"* French—what closet of her mind had that come from? She rummages her memory again, more strategically. *"Casa. Una casa?"* she asks, moving her finger in a little stirring motion she hopes will translate to "nearby."

The woman's eyes—remarkably large for her face—brighten, and she nods quickly. She leans down and picks up a canvas pack, holds it up briefly in front of Claire to confirm she has a purpose and destination. Then she hitches one strap over her shoulder and starts to walk down the street, stepping cautiously in the narrow track of icy foot-prints compacted between storefronts and curb. Claire watches her for a minute, uneasy and considering, until her cell phone rings and Jory tells her the house is freezing and she can't get the fire started.

The woman is at the end of the block when Claire passes her in the car. She stops and rolls down the passenger window, waits until the woman is close enough to hear her. "*Señora?*" Claire holds up a heavy red plaid lumberman's jacket Addison used to wear in college. Jory had dragged it out of the closet to wrap around her feet and left it on the floor of the backseat. "*Por usted.*" The woman seems hesitant to approach, and Claire realizes that she herself is now the suspicious one. She drapes the jacket halfway through the window so it's easier to reach and puts the car into Park, the heater blasting onto her aching hands. "*Por favor.*" She keeps smiling at the woman, wants to urge her to just take the jacket, finally, so she can go home. The ice crystals are beginning to turn to snow; lacy white wafers drift onto the hood of the car and dissolve into clear beads. At last the woman steps off the sidewalk and puts her hand on the wool, now flecked with snowflakes. Claire broadens her smile, ready to close the window and leave. But still the woman hesitates. "*Sí, por usted,*" Claire encourages, trying not to sound impatient.

At last the woman folds the jacket into her arms and leans down so her face is fully visible through the open window. "Thank you. Thank you. I will care for it for you." The ungainly phrase comes out in a heavy Spanish accent, like that of someone who might have studied the language but rarely pronounces the words. It draws Claire's atten-tion, this solemn acceptance of responsibility for a piece of clothing Claire would have given to Goodwill the next time she cleaned out the car. And something she sees in this woman's remarkable eyes, too. Thanks, surely, is there, but her obvious gratitude—and obvious need for a coat—is clearly tinged with shame. With a small wave, the woman turns away and begins climbing the steeper street that heads to the few residential blocks before the town disperses into fields and orchards and forest. At the top of the hill she disappears into the unilluminated night, still carrying the jacket in her arms.

· 5 ·

Indeed, the house is freezing. It doesn't help that
the bathroom window upstairs has been left open for who knows how
many hours, probably after Jory tried to clear the room of steam. Her
underwear and T-shirt are soaking in a pool of suds beside the bathtub.
Her hair is still wet and turbaned in a towel, and she is wrapped in both
Claire's and Addison's velour bathrobes, reminding Claire of the way
Jory would sweep through the house at the age of seven or eight, playing queen in a plastic gold crown and just such an oversized bathrobe.
That was only six years ago. Turn around and it's gone.

"Did you ever get dressed today?" Claire asks, dumping the wet
clothes in a laundry basket.

"What? In case my friends came by?" Claire returns the look without a word, and Jory drops it with a noncommittal shrug.

The kitchen is exactly the same as Claire left it, except for the
Cheerios stuck to the sides of an empty cereal bowl. She's too tired to
cook, or at least too tired to be imaginative about it. She puts a plate
of sausages in the microwave, which she serves up with sliced jack
cheese and apples and a bowl of roasted almonds. Jory sits grimly in
front of her plate as if saying a silent, sullen grace. "What's the matter?" Claire asks.

"I thought you were buying dinner."

"This is actually very nutritious if you think about it. A little un-
orthodox, maybe, but it's got all the food groups." Claire studies the

29

table for a minute and gets up to scrounge through the refrigerator. She comes back with a bag of washed spinach and opens it into a bowl, picking out a few darkly rotting leaves. "There. Balanced meal."

"Where is Dad, anyway?"

Claire glances at her watch. "Landing in Chicago. I'm sure he'll call."

Jory peels the translucent casing off the sausage and coils it at the edge of her plate. "What's in Chicago?"

"Another meeting. People who might want to help him get his lab running again." Claire reaches across the table and folds the sausage skin into a napkin. "We've talked about this, honey. He doesn't like having to travel so much. He'd rather be here. With you." Jory flicks her eyes at Claire. "With *us*."

They eat in silence after that. Claire finally opens the newspaper, unfolding it noisily across half the table just to disguise the sound of Jory's chewing, which she seems to be intentionally exaggerating. Jory picks at the denuded sausage and the cheese, then gets up to serve herself a bowl of ice cream. "They were still alive, weren't they?"

Claire looks up over the newspaper and shakes her head once. "I beg your pardon?"

"When you threw them into the snow. They were still alive."

Claire pushes the paper aside and presses her fingertips against her closed eyes, presses until the blackness is flecked with tiny purple dots. "Sweetie. Mice carry diseases. We can't let them breed under the sink."

Jory smacks the back of her spoon against the surface of her ice cream, slamming it into a mushy vanilla pond. "It's worse that way. Doing it halfway like that. You should either save them or kill them."

She swallows a spoonful of ice cream like it's gristle. Claire can tell she is trying not to cry. A hot wave floods up from Claire's stomach, makes her want to dig the damn mice out of the snow and revive their pitiful frozen souls. "Well, maybe their mother found them out there. And they say freezing isn't a bad way to die." *Did she really just say that?* Jory is stone-cold silent, wrapping all her anger into this cause. "Okay," Claire starts over. "You're right. I was a chicken about it." The towel twisted around Jory's hair has slipped to one side and she holds her head at a slant to keep it balanced, finally jerks the wet mass of cloth onto the floor. A strand of damp hair trails through her ice cream. Claire clears her throat. "We could get a pet. A cat."

Jory might as well be deaf for all the response she offers, but Claire sees the tension curving her lower lip, the eyes fixed on her bowl.

"Like, a barn cat. Only we'll keep him inside. We wouldn't even have to feed him." That remark finally starts the tears down Jory's cheeks. Terrible as she feels, Claire prefers this to the stalemate. "Well, you *wanted* a cat when we were in Seattle. I thought it would make you happy!"

"Get a cat? And you're looking for a job? How long are we staying out here?"

She looks so miserable Claire is ready to forgive the dumped clothes and open window and filthy kitchen. She walks around the table and squats with her hand on Jory's sleeve. "Oh, baby. I can't give you a number. It's just till Dad gets things back on track with his company."

"You keep saying that. You and Dad both, since we sold the house. But you never say how long that will take. I mean, look at this place!"

Claire rubs her daughter's back but feels her spine stiffen even through the two bathrobes, a twitch of withdrawal she tries to respect, accepting that this house looks different to all of them now that it is their only home. "I can't tell you how long. Who knows, maybe Dad found an investor at the meeting today—it could happen anytime. And I'm just exploring the jobs out here. It's all going to work out, sweetie. It's temporary. I promise."

And a mother always, always keeps her promises. So the mark has been set, the cards laid out. It cheers her up, in a way, as if such a promise had the power of all round-bellied maternal goddesses behind it. How many blind leaps into optimism mothers offer their children. And maybe that was part of the reason things usually did work out all right. Maybe the endgame attributed to fate could be bent by the collective will of mothers—there was a thought to play with, though it made it hard to figure out how anybody could possibly wage a war under that cosmic plan.

She sends Jory upstairs with the laptop and a DVD and unpacks the groceries, almost enjoying the fresh start to the kitchen. Yes, the spices are only the cheapest, sealed up in their clear plastic bottles with their red plastic caps, not the little tins of polished silver with hand-lettered labels she used to buy at DeLaurenti. But they are all fresh. The cabinets are uncluttered, as minimalist as the days of her first apartment with Addison, when they would spread a beach towel in front of the wall heater and eat cheese and crackers and popcorn and peel a whole box of mandarin oranges with a bottle of the cheapest wine, and enjoy it all just fine. Just fine.

She scrubs each shelf before arranging the items in neat rows, sweeps years of dust out from behind the refrigerator along with the remnants of the mouse nest, imagining this kitchen with new appliances and countertops and slate floors. It's the perfect setting for soapstone, this antiquated kitchen. Maybe they should put in an Aga stove.

They had already sketched out plans for a remodel, even hired an architect at one point years ago. He and Addison had turned the practicalities of design into a philosophical art—debating the "vernacular references" of the farmhouse lines, the "cultural history" imparted by dormers versus hip roofs. Addison reveled in the house-to-be, blind to the existing buckled floors and ruptured gutters, the deflowered bouquets of sprung wires. It was the planner in him. The dreamer. Claire understood that better than he ever would. Addison was happier in the creative adventure than in any finished house. And where would the world be without dreamers? Especially the world of science. Back in the Stone Age. Still depending on witch hazel and poultices. Claire was fine with letting him conspire and doodle and walk through imaginary configurations. In fact, until this week they'd spent all their vacations to Hallum at one of the local resorts, visiting their property only to scruff around in the orchard hunting deer antlers and the translucent sheddings of snakes, collecting the small sour apples in autumn for pies they never baked.

Claire had always been more intrigued by the land than the remodel, craving the escape it promised from their overscheduled lives. They already had more house than they needed in Seattle, she'd said. Room enough for all three to get lost in, intersecting through an intercom or a meal grabbed between carpools and Addison's long days at the lab. And then he had started work on vascumab, became hypnotized by his certainty that this drug, his very own invented molecule, would turn cancer treatment end over end. He had finally let the architect go until they had time to spare.

Looking around the room now, it's obvious to Claire that the most prudent decision would be to tear the whole house down and start over. Still, it's disquieting to think about condemning so much history to a landfill; an insult to the family that slaved to build it—the Blackstocks, whoever they were. Almost funny to realize that several generations of living, all the birthing and loving and arguing, even the dying, could be fully played out in one spot, yet the only lasting memory seemed to be their name.

Her cell phone rings—a riff from Eric Clapton's "Layla" that Addison had plugged in to signal his calls. His voice sounds bright, and combined with her current magical optimism she opens with a retelling of the day that makes it all fun, the way she knows they will look back on it in a year or two. "I'm thinking I should put some shredded newspaper in the Havahart traps so the mice can stay warm till we dump them out in the woods." He laughs at this. Claire ducks behind the kitchen wall so Jory won't figure out they find humor in her compassion. She can see his full mouth lift his already boyish features into the uninhibited hilarity of a kid. He has always been able to make her laugh before any dispute grew too hot to control, at least until these last few months. But since the night he told her the truth, all of it, about the drug study data and the money, a few of their arguments have been caustic enough to leave scars. "So how's the Drake? Is the bathtub nice and deep?"

"Built for two!" he answers. "Wish you were with me. How did you like the hospital?"

"Well, that's quite a segue!" Claire jokes. "I don't know. Nice enough. The doctors I met seemed nice. If we stay here long enough to get sick I'd feel okay going to some of them." She pauses, expecting a comeback. "I was glad nobody asked to see my résumé, though. It's hard to even introduce myself as a doctor, you know?"

He's quiet for a moment, then answers, "Yeah. I know."

Claire had expected him to contest her insecurity, bolster her. She laughs anyway, unwilling to let the conversation turn negative. "Sure you know! You have to carry your résumé in a two-inch binder." She opens the refrigerator while she talks and studies the fresh contents—there is something deeply reassuring in knowing they could survive a week or more in a blizzard now. She pours milk into a mug and dumps in two tablespoons of chocolate, adds a third and sticks it in the microwave. Addison seems to be waiting, as if he could see all of this. "I should have been a pediatrician. Maybe the board would give me credit for raising Jory and I could get certified." She expects a chuckle at least, and wonders for a minute if they're still connected.

"Yeah," he answers at last, in a resigned tone, and even though she knows he does not mean it, she hears it as a stinging reminder of how far she's fallen from medicine.

Her mood darkens. She takes a gulp of hot chocolate and tries to start over. "It must be freezing up there. Have you seen the list of who's coming to the meeting? Stock market went up today—a little. Maybe you should treat everybody to a hot buttered rum or two and then just slip a blank check in front of them."

"There's an idea."

"Oh, I have a better one. I thought of this in the car today—start talking about all the symptoms of colon cancer and pick out the guy who looks the most nervous. You'd get both an investor and a customer—just like that guy with the cure for baldness." She waits through another minute of silence and shakes the phone, looks at the handset as if his face might appear in the shining black plastic. "Addison? Are you still there? I'm just trying to cheer you up."

She waits again, and finally hears him say, "I don't know how I'm going to pay our health insurance bill this month."

Now Claire is silent. She puts the hot chocolate down, acutely aware of how still the room is, how still a winter night is. "You mean, you don't know which account to pay it from?"

When he finally answers she is more frightened by his tone than his words—the vacancy in his voice. "Nash's investment was split, do you remember? Half for drug development and half to be paid when the review board, the IRB, approved the phase one human trials." Nash. Married to Anna, Claire's best friend. He'd bet twenty million dollars on vascumab, ten of it lost now, but ten still on the table, leverage Addison could play to attract new investors.

"And? He's still in, right? I thought he promised you he was still in until you could repeat the animal trials and go back to the review board."

"It's a problem of timing—"

She interrupts him, doesn't have the patience for another lecture about venture capital risk or equity positions or stock options. "Maybe . . . I don't know . . . maybe we have to borrow against the retirement plan. I mean, the accountant said that was possible, right?"

When they had discussed this, the most dire contingency plan, Addison had always stonewalled on risking that much of their future. It was the only asset left besides this land and this house. She hears the faintest sound through the phone, a low hum that couldn't be Addison, it sounds more mechanical than human. Suddenly she is back at the Gap store in downtown Seattle crowded against the counter by impatient Christmas shoppers, trying to explain to the flustered clerk why her denied Visa charge for a twelve-dollar umbrella has to be a fluke. "What have you done?"

"We were so close, Claire. Weeks from IRB approval and Nash's second check. I couldn't let it fall apart. I had to bridge the gap."

"What are you saying to me?" Claire feels like a gaping hole has broken through her middle. Standing perfectly still, she tips off balance and grabs for the counter. "It's impossible to take out your whole retirement fund. It isn't legal."

Addison's voice sounds like it's coming from another planet, bleeding with humiliation, but oddly detached, too. Like he's talking about someone else's life. "I rolled it over. I transferred the money. The law allows you ninety days between withdrawal and deposit." Claire is sitting on the floor though she doesn't remember sliding down the wall. She tries to talk but nothing comes out.

Addison goes on, "Nash said he'd back me up if there were a delay.

I had to keep the lab going—I had salaries to pay. It didn't feel like a choice."

Claire coughs and chokes out, "And then Nash changed his mind, didn't he?"

There is a long pause before Addison answers. "He heard about Rick and the animal data. He's got a business to run, Claire. It's not a question of friendship."

Claire's lips are tingling. "And now we are at day ninety-one and you can't pay back the retirement fund. Is that what you're telling me?"

When Addison does not refute her, in fact, does not answer her at all, she hangs up the phone without another word.

· 6 ·

Jory is tucked into a fetal curl against Claire by morning, the sunken center of the old mattress a trapped pool of heat in the cold room. Claire kisses her cheek and stuffs her own still-warm pillow against Jory's back before she slips out of bed to dress. Her face looks gray in the mirror; she had barely slept. She checks the furnace, thrumming steadily and yet the room couldn't be more than 60 degrees. She mounds a pyramid of paper and kindling and small logs in the cold stove, sets the butane lighter on top for Jory to use, then goes back upstairs to tape a note to the bathroom mirror, signs it with a lipsticked heart.

Claire drives to the biggest clinic in town, a low brick building huddled beside the river. The gravel parking lot holds four or five cars, Subarus and four-wheel-drive pickups, cars suited to the valley's deep snow and spring slush. She had not felt nervous on the drive here, had felt, in fact, a blinding, determined confidence storming out of her anger. A furious resolve not to talk to Addison until she had a job. But suddenly she wishes she'd called ahead, or asked Jenna, the pediatrician she'd met at the hospital, to call ahead for her. What was she thinking? That the county is so starved for doctors she can barge out of the blue into a busy physician's office hours? That because she shared the letters *MD* behind her name she had some invisible privilege?

The receptionist asks for her name and insurance card, and Claire says she hasn't actually come to see the doctor. Well, yes, she *has* come to see Kit, to see the doctor, but not as a patient. She takes a breath and starts over. She is looking for a job.

"Are you a nurse?"

"No, I'm a doctor. I just moved here."

The woman behind the desk pauses, and then leans across the counter. "Can you wait a bit? She's backed up right now, but I'll tell her you're here. She may not think she needs any help, but I'm the one who makes out her schedule."

Kit Halpern has a single thick chestnut braid dangling over her shoulder alongside the curving black tube of her stethoscope. She has close-trimmed, unpolished fingernails and her white coat hangs open over khaki pants and a plain navy turtleneck. She wears no makeup; looks like a woman who probably doesn't consider makeup a smart use of her time. Claire pictures her getting dressed early every morning, putting on the same clothes she'd worn the day before if they are passably clean, braiding her dark hair with memorized motions, not a glance in the mirror. Threads of gray are woven through the braid—she is probably older than Claire by five or six years. There is an assertiveness in the lines at the corners of her mouth, and the direct gaze of her clear gray eyes suggests the comfort of compassionate authority.

Claire waits while Kit dictates a chart note. The facing wall is covered with degrees and certificates—it looks like she's stuck them in whatever cheap ready-made frame best fit the paper, more a convention than a point of pride. Claire scans the bookcases for photographs—Kit on a horse, Kit with three wolfish-looking dogs. No Kit husband. No Kit children. She tries to imagine herself owning that side of this desk, its labeled plastic trays stacked high with her own patients' medical charts. She still remembers all the secrets a chart can tell, the pain nobody talks about: marital infidelities that shed light on genital sores, the unconfessed alcohol that explains a distressed liver. The averted gaze of teenagers who squirm about falling grades and missed curfews and the smell of pot in their hair, young enough to believe they invented sin. *And how would the Boehning financial disaster be diagnosed? What tabbed section of the chart would hide their secret?* She tries to remember if there is a blood test to measure stress hormones.

She catches Kit watching her and blushes. "Candace, my receptionist, says I should hire you. But maybe I should ask you if you're looking for a job first?" Beyond the half-open office door a nurse walks a patient down the hall; another two exam rooms have red flags calling for Kit as loud as alarms.

"I *am* looking for a job. I'm sorry I didn't call you first, to make an appointment."

"Oh, don't worry about that. You'll find Hallum's pretty casual. In a year you'll recognize everyone on the street—which is a bit of a problem when you're a doctor here. I get almost as many consultations in the grocery store as I do in the office. Where did you go to medical school?"

"University of Washington." Claire reaches into her briefcase and pulls out one of the résumés. "I want to tell you up front . . . I haven't worked in a long time. Not since I had my daughter. But I've tried to keep current. My license is up-to-date. And I read the journals. I know that's not the same as treating patients, but I was thinking maybe I could start working almost as an apprentice. On a reduced pay scale." She sounds nervous, talking too fast. It isn't Kit that puts her on edge, it's this job. It's realizing this is a job she might like, this is a doctor she'd like to learn from, to work with. She holds the résumé in her lap for a minute, looking at its open white spaces wishing a sheer force of will could tack on those last few months and that critical piece of paper. Then she puts on a determined smile and hands it over.

Kit swivels back in her chair, reading. Claire concentrates on relaxing the muscles of her forehead. What's there is good, might even be considered impressive. She'd coauthored three papers while she was in her internship, one in *JAMA*. She'd made Alpha Omega Alpha, had been a star of her internship class. She was elected chief resident, but had to drop that when she went on bed rest. Her references are well-known names in academic medicine, even though some have already retired. Jory had done a great job with the layout. Claire was kind of amazed she'd known that much about fonts and formatting. If she'd ever been that thorough with her homework she'd have made the honor roll.

She watches Kit's eyes move down the single sheet of bond paper in her hands, and spots the precise moment Kit recognizes the problem. The narrow crease between Kit's dark eyebrows deepens and she looks up, puzzled. "You didn't finish your residency?"

Claire sits up straighter. "No. I couldn't. I had some trouble with my pregnancy. I had to go on bed rest at twenty-six weeks. Then Jory—my daughter—needed a lot of medical care for a couple of years. And then . . ." She lets her eyes rest on a leafless tree shivering outside the office window where an empty bird's nest is buffeted in the wind. She lifts one shoulder and lets it drop again. "No. I never finished."

"So, you're not board certified?"

"I couldn't take the boards. I was short the required hours." That answer is obvious to both of them, but saying it aloud feels like some kind of justified penance. The whole room seems to sigh, and Claire sees Kit's shoulders sag. She knows, then, that she would have gotten the job. She could have worked with this admirable woman and nurtured her own medical practice alongside her.

Kit folds her arms across the résumé on her desk. She looks almost as disappointed as Claire, which, for some reason, makes the rejection harder. "It's not me," Kit says. "It's the insurance. My malpractice insurance would never take you. Well, that's not really fair. They would take you at a higher rate. I can't afford to hire you if you're not board certified."

Claire's face goes hot, embarrassing her even more. She should have told Kit outright, before she even sat down. She feels like a liar, telling everyone at the hospital, and Kit, too, that she is a family practitioner. She is a doctor of nothing. All that work, all those years of school, and she had quit before she got the final official stamp. In a profession that demanded the gold seals that were only doled out with the last handshake on the graduation stage, she had blown it.

Claire tightens her fingers around the leather binding of the steering wheel until her wedding ring bites into her flesh. She feels diminished by the verbalization of the years she's been away from the practice of medicine—personally diminished, as if it subtracted from her value as a human being to say the double digit aloud and admit that she's never earned back the fortune her education cost her parents and the state. She should paste a picture of Jory at the bottom of her résumé where the missing months of training should be—Jory's, at least, was one life she knew she had saved.

The wind whips at her car and the low gray clouds blur onto the snowy horizon scratched by black lines of bare cottonwood and willow. Maybe she has no right to try to be a doctor again. Really *be* a doctor— place her hands on someone else's naked skin in search of a diagnosis, ask questions of strangers she wouldn't expect them to answer to their spouse. Maybe she'd given up that privilege when she dropped out of her residency in premature labor, and then never gone back after Jory was born. She had trained for six and a half years preparing to take care of thousands of people—tens of thousands of people over the working years of her life. And then she had given it up in order to take care of one. She had walked away without even admitting it was a conscious decision, forever couching it as a temporary pause. If there was to be only this one child, who had seemed both sturdier and more vulnerable with each of the four failed pregnancies that followed, then Claire would not hire out any part of motherhood. She would prove to the universe the mistake it had made in giving her only one chance. At least that was the most palatable reason she could live with. And by the time she had gotten up the courage to go back, there was so much money she could walk away for good.

But now there was no money. Now she had no choice.

· 7 ·

It takes only two more days to burn through the possibilities for an uncertified, inexperienced doctor to earn a paycheck anywhere near Hallum Valley. Claire makes appointments with three other private clinics near town, stopping last at Hale Richardson's. He is sixty-four, "almost busy enough for a second doc," until he sees Claire's résumé. He is nice about it, as the others were. By the time he walks her to her car she feels worse for him than herself, he looks so uncomfortable. "Sure you want to stay in Hallum? Might have better luck in a bigger market."

Claire folds her résumé into a square small enough to fit in her pocket. "My husband lost his job. It was quicker to sell our house in Seattle than the place out here." Hale has the kind of face that makes her want to go on, to explain that it was a bit more than a lost job. It was an entire company. A fortune, in fact. Overnight. Their whole life gambled away on a single blip of disputed data. Instead she shakes Hale's hand. "You've been very kind. Keep an ear out for me. If you hear of anyone desperate enough to hire me . . ." He laughs with her and Claire gets in her car, waving as she pulls onto the road before he can counter.

The weather is turning worse; a hostile tease of cold, as if nature were whispering its warning to take shelter. When they had come here for ski vacations such a turn was always exciting. She and Jory would stand by the enormous open log fires in the big resort lodge, and Jory would check at the front desk every hour to see if the passes

42

were closed, hoping for an excuse to miss a day of school. They would call room service for extra down comforters and hot chocolate, and snuggle in the deep window seats watching the black night turn white with whipping snow, a surge of alarmed exhilaration every time the lights flickered. When you can pay for so much protection from the elements, the threat becomes a game. She turns the heat up in the car and leaves a message for Jory, who, despite three calls in a row, will not pick up the phone.

There is only one more place within any reasonable radius, a free clinic advertised with one line in the classifieds, on a street somewhere south of the warehouses. She stops at the highway debating whether to even bother, then turns south, away from home. The grid of Hallum is so small the roads quickly untangle into long reaches down fence lines that bulge against the weight of snow. Deer stand with their backsides to the wind, nipping at the brush and young trees, which skew at angles through the drifts, having survived the deep cold only to be destroyed by the winter-starved herds. The road is clear for the most part, though each heave of wind stirs up a snowy ghost before the car. It's a little disorienting, with the clouds so low they hide the mountains and the diffuse light of late afternoon washed evenly across the sky.

She comes around a low hill and a distant line of trees marks the river to give her some bearing, but the only visible buildings are a few scattered ranch houses and barns. She must still be four or five miles outside of town; it is an area well beyond the usual tourist loop. Farther on, a cluster of concrete blocks squats between this road and the highway—a metal fabricator, a lumber yard, a tractor repair barn—the working industry that churns gritty and resolute behind the ski shops and gift galleries.

At the entrance to the driveways she sees a white sign with a bright red cross painted above two words: CLINIC and CLINICA. The building itself looks identical to its industrial neighbors, coldly functional, cheerless but for the yellow light brightening a row of high windows. She would wonder if she'd truly arrived at a medical facility—one for humans—but for the sign above the glass door. She puts the car into reverse and starts to back out of the lot, then brakes again, scans the empty yard and parks beside the wheelchair ramp leading up to the entrance. What harm is there in talking to them? Maybe they could give her a lead? And then there is the harsher truth she's just starting to face: she has been turned down by every other clinic in this town.

The waiting room is less bleak than the building. The mint green walls are lined with molded plastic chairs stamped out in sun-faded primary colors. Seven are occupied. A couple of teenaged girls, one wearing a skimpy tank top, are huddled over a Hollywood gossip magazine. The rest of the patients are Hispanic, and Claire feels their eyes on her as she walks up to the reception desk in her knee-length down coat carrying her leather briefcase. There is a swinging gate that separates the waiting area from what must be exam rooms and offices; it looks deserted, with only a single light at the far end of the hallway and all the doors shut.

The woman behind the front desk is also Hispanic, young and round faced with smooth hair parted in a perfect line down the middle of her scalp and pulled into a tight black ponytail. She is typing data into an ancient computer—a bulky CRT box that blocks Claire's view of her body. Claire starts to introduce herself but the woman holds her hand up as a stop sign without even glancing up, then jumps into a stream of animated Spanish. Claire is about to stop her when she notices the telephone headset. She puts her briefcase on a chair and waits, studying the posters thumbtacked to the walls: YOUR CHILD'S DEVELOPMENT, DIABETES CAN HURT YOU WITHOUT HURTING, ARE YOU SAFE IN YOUR OWN HOME? Most are in Spanish.

A children's area is set up in one corner, miniature plastic chairs tucked under a wooden table holding a wire maze dotted with sliding colored beads. When Jory was three she had caught her foot on just such a toy and bitten down so hard on her tongue they had rushed her to the local emergency room with blood spilling from her lips. Claire had been too panicked to think of any first aid at home, not even ice.

"Can I help you?" The first English words she's heard in this room make her turn back to the desk, but the woman is still focused on the computer screen. After a minute, though, she says it again, now taking off the headset and fixing Claire with a mildly impatient look.

By now Claire has changed her mind about coming in the door at all, feels, in fact, an overwhelming desire to be soaking in a hot bath-tub—and not the pitted tank waiting for her at the house. She wants her old tub. The capacious, milky-white oval with the sloping back and the brass waterfall spout that somebody else is now paying a mortgage on. She shakes her head at the receptionist, ready to duck out and leave when someone starts toward her down the hallway. Lit from behind he looks Ichabod-ish, tall and slightly stooped with lanky limbs and a long torso. But as he crosses the threshold of light she sees his face and her mood abruptly changes. It's the doctor from the hospital—the old cowboy. God, she didn't even realize she'd filed him under such a nickname, but there it is, presenting itself so spontaneously she breaks into a smile.

There is an angularity about Dan Zelaya that begs a question of heritage—Native American, maybe, or Middle Eastern—his name obviously Hispanic; white hair that defies classification except as el-derly human being, aging along a final common pathway. A mixture, surely, judging by his skin tone and the blue cast in his dark eyes, and his name. He straightens up some when he sees her, bringing his heels together as if he might make a small bow. He has on that same string tie he was wearing at the hospital. She starts to introduce herself to him again, but he gets there first, introducing her to Anita, the receptionist, who stands up to shake her hand. Now Claire sees that she is well into a pregnancy.

Dan opens the gate and starts back down the hallway as if it is un-derstood she will follow him. He has a long stride and she has to skip a step to catch up. He leads her back to a large room with two exam tables covered in crisp white paper. A couple of stainless steel Mayo stands are pushed against the wall, there are a red crash cart and an EKG machine that clearly predates the digital age, a cast cart, a plastic case of sutures. It must be their urgent care room. "How'd you find me?" Dan asks her.

"I got a bit lost," she answers. He breaks into a wry smile at this and Claire shakes her head. "Oh, I didn't mean it like that! I've been visiting all the clinics in the area."

He waves his hand in front of his face, brushing aside manners. "I like it better the first way. Everybody who comes in here is either lost or getting close. Anybody hire you yet?"

Claire is about to give him the optimistic spin she's been rehearsing for Jory, but shrugs, worn out on selling herself. "Nope. Nothing. Want a copy of my résumé? I have plenty left."

He presses his lips into an uninspiring taut line and shakes his head. "Wish I could even think about it." They talk for only a few minutes before Anita raps on the open doorjamb and calls Dan into the hall with a spatter of scolding Spanish. A flash of color moving behind Anita's shoulder catches Claire's attention, a red and cream plaid so familiar she starts toward the door. It's Addison's jacket, the one she had handed through the window of her car a few nights ago. The woman wearing it—it must be her—is swallowed by the bulky coat, could be a child it dwarfs her so, a ruff of black curls rolling just above the collar line like fur trim. Claire starts to call out to her, wondering if she is ill, was possibly ill that night, but she has already moved out of sight.

Dan sees the startled look on her face and smiles. "Anita is happiest when she's boxing me into line. Running late again." He offers Claire his hand. "Keep at it. There're a lot of sick people here who don't have a doctor. Trust me on that one." He points out the rear exit that leads to the parking lot and follows Addison's jacket into the exam room.

Claire takes a minute to look around the urgent care room, wishing she had the funds and the business sense to set up her own clinic, be her own boss, who could scoff at her half-page résumé and give herself a big fat raise. She considers leaving a résumé on the counter for Dan to discover after she's gone, but decides it would, at best, cause pointless guilt in someone she already likes.

It looks like he has set it up on a shoestring, this place. But sufficient, she decides. Probably sufficient to take care of most people's needs. There is something inspiring about recognizing that Dan must make most of his diagnoses based on physical exams—the stuff she'd been taught in basic science and introductory medical school classes and then quickly put secondary to CT scans and MRIs and cardiac catheterizations. You got a better grade when you could stuff the workup and formal presentation of a patient with solid numbers, something more quantifiable than the subjective description of what you'd heard through your stethoscope. Every medical intern learned that lesson the first time they were raked over the coals for not knowing the blood calcium level to a decimal point.

She hikes her purse over her shoulder and is almost out the door when she notices a plaque nailed onto the wall: URGENT CARE ROOM FUNDED WITH A GENEROUS DONATION FROM RONALD S. WALKER. She sets her briefcase down and looks more closely at the brass square, runs her finger over the name. In one of those moments where the world seems to shrink she remembers a charity fund-raiser she had attended only three or four years ago at the Fairmont in Seattle, hosted by Ron Walker. She knows him. Well, she doesn't really *know* him. But she's met him. Come to think of it, it was for some medical charity fund—maybe this clinic.

They had gone with Rick Alperts and his wife, Lilly, only a few months after Addison had hired Rick. They had seemed so young to Claire. They weren't, really—only younger by eight or so years—but they were young to the glitzy biotech world that Addison and Claire were already becoming a little jaded toward. Addison had bought a table for the lab, treating all his bright young recruits to a glimpse of the gold that beckoned alongside the reward of saved lives. Rick had met another avid biker that night, and bid six thousand dollars on a custom-built bicycle and a group trip along the Tour de France route. Claire had sat next to Lilly. She clearly remembers telling Lilly about the sale of Eugena, how Addison had brought the signed paperwork back to the hotel that night with a bottle of French champagne, tied about the neck with a ribbon knotted through a two-carat diamond solitaire—her belated engagement ring. He had dumped a box of lavender bath foam into the tub and climbed in with her, made Claire open the envelope right there dressed in nothing but a froth of scented bubbles, made her read the astonishing numbers out loud.

It almost turns her stomach to think of it now, the way Lilly kept looking at Addison. How she had asked Claire to tell the story over again, the glitz and gold eclipsing everything else Addison was working for.

After the study fell apart and Addison told Claire about the disputed lab results—data Rick still insisted were anomalous—she had asked Addison if giving Rick a share in the company might have been the root of it. Would things have been different without the promise of such a payoff? But Addison had heatedly countered that no drug is perfectly clean. Every drug study contains gray zones, where judgment and experience ultimately have to define what is fact and what is irrelevant variance at the diminishing ends of a bell curve. He had talked as if the margins of scientific theory could build a new house around their family. As always, when he defended Rick, it had deteriorated into a tearful impasse they both had to walk away from. Now she often wondered if Addison was subconsciously atoning for his own delay in reporting the missing data to the review board; his refusal to blame Rick seemed nearly irrational.

She and Addison had bought a week in the Galapagos at Walker's auction that night. She already knew that Ron Walker had investments out here in Hallum—Walker Orchards, the landmark hillside of apple and cherry trees south of town, thousands of them standing in meticulously groomed parallel rows, their pink and white blossoms so lush in spring that weekend traffic slowed with rubbernecking tourists. Its sprawling stone house was practically a symbol of Hallum's agricultural history. Walker didn't live there, but she remembered talking to him about Hallum at the fund-raiser. They'd actually been talking about wine at the time, and Addison had said he'd always dreamed about getting a vineyard going on the east side someday, when he had time. Walker said he'd gone in for apples instead, "breaking the Gen X trend," though he was older than both of them by at least a decade. She can practically feel her brain cross-linking the threads—tagging the Walker from Seattle with the Walker who owned the orchard and the Walker named on this plaque. So, who knows? she asks herself, turning once to scan the meager equipment in this room. Maybe that ancient EKG machine was bought with the check they wrote for that trip. She can't help thinking about what they might do with that twelve thousand dollars if they still had it today.

· 8 ·

The predicted snow hovers and teases until she is almost home and then, like an enormous down pillow, the weight of such nearly weightless particles breaks and spills silently from the clouds. She punches in the number for the house and waits for Jory to answer, hangs up and hits Redial until Jory's petulant "Hello" puts a halt to Claire's imagined fires or falls.

"Did you eat anything? There's leftover hamburger in the fridge. Can you heat that up?" Jory exhales into the telephone, only enough to confirm that she is alive and whole. "I should be home in half an hour. Or so. Is the furnace working okay? You're not cold, are you?"

"I hate hamburger."

"Well, cook some eggs, then. Or mac and cheese. It's starting to snow pretty hard, so don't worry if it takes me a while to get back. Did Daddy call?" Claire waits for some response until she hears the double blip of lost reception.

The driveway is nearly impassable by the time she gets home; the car slithers and skids down the last steep turn. Proof again, she thinks, that snow tires might help you go but they weren't much good at helping you stop. Jory is eating Chunky chicken noodle soup out of the can with a huge glass of chocolate milk. Claire pulls a chair next to her; Jory seems determined not to acknowledge her.

"Hey," Claire says.

After a long, chilly minute Jory clips, "Hey, yourself."

Claire leans forward on her crossed arms, close enough to break the seal of her daughter's exclusive space, waiting to see if she'll be allowed to stay. "I was gone a long time. I'm sorry."

There is no response to this but a slight, magnetic pull toward her mother instead of away. Claire tilts her face until her temple rests on Jory's shoulder, awaits the yield as her daughter relaxes. "Are you still hungry?" Jory shrugs. "We could have a popcorn and movie night." Claire starts up the stairs. "Give me a minute. I'm freezing."

She strips her clothes onto the bathroom floor and puts on her robe, then dumps a whole box of bath salts, Anna's gift from the going-away party, into the skim of rising water dyeing it an iridescent blue-green. She's been saving them, planning to share a bath with Addison as a celebration when they move back into some decent home with some decent bathtub. But the truth about life, she is deciding, exactly at this moment, in fact, is that you never know what lies around the corner. She's just sold off a closet of clothes she's barely worn, books she's never read, a cellar of wine that was getting more valuable by the day. So she will soak in this tub alone and imagine Addison, perhaps soaking at this very moment in the Drake's deep, marble-lined tub, a billion tiny bubbles fizzing in the coils of his chest hair.

The water is still cold when she tests it. "Jory," she calls down from the bathroom. "I'm not getting any hot water. Did you take a long shower or something?"

Jory walks to the bottom of the stairwell and looks up, her hair tangled down the front of her robe. She looks so childlike from this vantage that Claire feels her throat constrict. "No. The stove stopped working, too."

Claire comes back to the kitchen and turns on the burner, sniffs the air for gas. "Oh God. We must be out of propane." She turns the knob on and off again, then looks at Jory. "You didn't smell anything funny, did you? Did the stove just stop while you were cooking?"

"I was cold. I had the stove on to keep the kitchen warm."

"You're kidding me. Tell me you're kidding me." Jory stands quietly in the middle of the room before almost imperceptibly shaking her head.

Claire raises the window in the kitchen and throws open the front door. "Jory—you can't heat the house with an unvented stove! You want to die of carbon monoxide poisoning? Were you just not thinking?" But then she sees the hurt look on Jory's face. Their house in Seattle had radiant floor heat, a remote-controlled gas fireplace, stayed a cozy 70 degrees in every season.

Claire goes to her, wraps her arms around her daughter's slight shoulders and feels her shudder once, smells the sweet coconut rinse in her hair. "It's okay. I'll check the second tank; it might still have some gas. It's all gonna be okay, babe."

But after a half hour in the knee-deep snow holding the flashlight in her mouth while she tries to pry the housing off the second tank she slogs back into the house, her hands aching. She piles wood into the stove and heats up a Cup Noodles in the microwave, holding the Styrofoam in her palms and watching her fingertips go from white to pink to red. The soup tastes frighteningly good—salty and starchy and thoroughly preserved. Jory is at the computer now, hypnotized inside her digital social life. Claire walks up behind her and scans the status posts scrolling down the screen, abbreviated quips about parties and ski trips and clothes. All Seattle friends. Nothing on the screen written by Jory herself. As if she is spying on the world taken away. Claire kisses the top of her head. "Come to bed soon, will you?"

She goes upstairs to the bedroom they are sharing—temporarily, she reminds herself. Until Addison finds an investor. Until Addison sells his molecule. Until Claire can support them all. She drains the cold turquoise water out of the tub and washes her face and underarms with Wet Ones before climbing in bed, waiting for Jory to join her, deciding to worry about it all tomorrow.

But her dreams wake her before midnight. Dreams of falling from ripped-open airplanes, dreams of the solid earth breaking apart and swallowing her house, dreams of misshapen, hooded figures. She rolls onto her back to stare at the ceiling, listening to the skitter of mice inside the walls, counting Jory's regular, even breaths. This is not cancer, she tells herself. No one is dying here. I have my mind, my hands, the will to earn a living. I have Jory, my sweet, contentious, adolescently self-centered Jory. And Addison. I have Addison.

She gives up on sleep, and slips out of bed to check the thermostat again. The overhead light illuminates a pale circle in the living room floor she's never noticed before, where some mysterious repetitive motion has worn the varnish away. A rocking chair perhaps, or some former resident's dog turning circles before settling. She stands at the front window looking across the field to the valley, discernible only as deeper black under a slightly paler sky at the limit of sight. The sky has cleared. The new snow is a vast, unmarred crystal sheet.

There is a small cupboard beneath the staircase packed with abandoned goods they'd poked through when they first bought the house, disjointed bits of history too worthless to sell but too cool to throw away, including a few oddly matched snowshoes. The Realtor had used them to show the place to clients in winter when the drive was left unplowed. It's obvious these are from an earlier generation—wood and cord and leather instead of the high-tech metal and nylon designs Claire has seen racked beside skis and snowboards in sports stores. She untangles two similar enough to pass as a pair, carries them to the door and slips her bare feet into her damp fleece-lined boots, stuffs the bulky sleeves of her bathrobe into Addison's down coat. Then she steps outside, straps the webbed snowshoes on and awkwardly sets out across the field toward a rim of rising moon.

If you headed north from this exact spot with the right gear and enough stamina you could walk clear across the Canadian border and never hit a fence. Who knew, maybe all the way to the arctic circle. They've spent so many of their vacations to Hallum at the resort, playing tennis or swimming or ice skating, that they have explored few of the trails carving through the adjacent state lands and traversing the Pasayten Wilderness. She has a momentary image of a backpacker pulling out a passport and converting money at a border crossing. But of course it is all woods and mountains out there, the odds a million to one you'd see a patrol.

The snow absorbs all sound and reflects all light; the silence is profound. It hammers inside her skull with her pulse and is, at the same time, as expansive as the star-studded sky. And the cold. A cold that can embrace you—kiss you into death. Her body warms as she pushes farther across the field; she finds a pace of exertion that matches her reserves, a comforting rhythm in the crunch of the web and frame on new snow, the regular huff of her breath. Nothing else.

She misses Addison, mad as she still is. But if he were with her they would be arguing, after that last horrible phone call. That's the thing about a marriage—even a good marriage. It's so easy to spread your own blame around, pin half your own bad choices onto somebody else. And if Addison has told her lies, or maybe fairer to say "withheld truths," didn't that fit patterns they'd both carved into their marriage from the day she quit her own career?

The night Addison told her what had happened at the lab and what had happened to the money—how fast the cascade had snowballed from "putting some skin into his lab, a personal investment," to drowning debt—she was the first to say they should sell their home. A house couldn't bleed, couldn't cry. It would shelter and swaddle the next family as comfortably as it had theirs. Thank God they *could* sell it to pay off the debt. She had consumed her anger by moving forward, pouring so much optimistic fuel into the planning and packing and sorting that any lurking spark of rage blew out as she flew on to the next task. It had taken her months, maybe not until last night, to realize that she couldn't allow her mind to linger. Because then she might discover how much or how little she would ever be able to forgive.

She sleeps late the next morning, wakes in a curled pocket of warmth with Jory's legs sprawled diagonally across the bed, every breath a puff of smoke. As she is heading for the shower she remembers the propane, wonders where the money will come from if they have to fill the big tank. She puts on layers of clothes to trudge out to the barn where it takes her half an hour of clanking through rusted tools and car parts to find a wrench, her hands too numb to use it now. When she comes through the front door she discovers the reason for the worn patch of flooring she had noticed the night before; Jory is spinning pirouettes on her toe shoes in the corner of the living room, her gold hair in a wild sweep. Her skin is taut against the muscles of her straightened leg, defiantly brimming with time and possibility; no damage yet to be undone.

God, her body is half a woman's now. More than that.

She must have been up for a while; one of the boxes Claire pulled out of the cupboard with the snowshoes last night has been opened and the contents are haphazardly spread over the floor and sofa cushions—glass medicine jars, a tin box of school track medals, a single moth-eaten, button-up high heel, framed photographs and drawings all wavy and spotted with water damage. Claire clears a place on the couch and watches Jory spin her way right through the floorboards. Once she's warm again Claire puts her soaking boots back on and high-steps into the same deep snow prints she had made last night, climbs onto a cinder block and hammers at the propane connector until she is sweating in her parka—all the more desperate for a bath. Finally she boils a jar of water in the microwave and pours it over the encrusted mechanism, then cracks it free with the wrench.

When she comes back inside this time Jory is sitting on a folding metal chair facing the window; the skinny wires of her iPod earbuds snake up her neck and nestle like white parasites in her ears. She is playing an invisible set of drums in the air, rocking out with her legs splayed wide for balance. "The water should be hot again soon," Claire says, cranking her boots off from the heels. "I'll have to put the chains on to get the car up the driveway."

Jory doesn't turn around. Claire comes up behind her, can hear the music even with the earbuds plugged tight to Jory's auditory canals. "It's too loud," Claire says, then plucks one out and puts her mouth where the parasite had been planted. "Too loud! You'll wreck your hearing. You're listening to Sting?"

Jory shrugs. "Beats that Withers guy with all the 'I knows,' whoever he was." She pulls the wire out of her mother's hands but turns the volume down. "It's Dad's iPod. I can't find mine, and I know I packed it with my hair straightener. I bet he's got my iPod. You'd think he would have noticed it's pink. Some guy called for you."

"Who?" Claire asks.

"Don somebody."

"I don't know anybody named Don. Did you write it down? Why don't you ever write messages down?"

"Why don't you hook up the answering machine? Maybe it was Dan. Weird last name. Doctor Dan."

Claire stands in front of her, takes the iPod out of her hand and turns it off. "A doctor called for me? And you didn't write it down? I'm looking for a job, Jory. Think. What was his name? Did he say which clinic?"

"Z. Zihautanejo. Zenia. Zinzanni. Z something."

"Zelaya? Dan Zelaya?"

"That's it!" She takes the iPod back and heads up to the shower.

"Did he leave a number?" Claire calls up the stairs, but all she hears is the rhythm of "Magic, magic, magic," hammered out on the sink with the wooden shanks of Jory's toe shoes.

· 9 ·

The next morning Claire wakes Jory at seven with a tray of fresh pancakes covered in butter and syrup, brought to her bedside. Jory slams her pillow over her head and groans. "You can bring a pillow and blanket in the car, but you have to come," Claire says.

"Why? You're the one who wants a job."

Claire leaves the tray on a chair and walks out, turning back from the doorway to say, "Sometimes 'want' has nothing to do with it. Get dressed. We're going to look at the school on the way back from town." She closes the door just as the pillow hits the wall beside it.

It takes forty-five minutes to untangle the snow chains and wrestle them onto the tires. The snow has settled overnight; a fine crust sparkles over the surface and gives with each step, as if she were the first person to walk this corner of the world. Ice crystals sting the rim of her nostrils. She waits outside for Jory, arrested by the blindingly white field. The marks from her snowshoes have blurred into wide teardrop-shaped shadows, and an evenly staggered line of pierced holes track her eyes to a mule deer beyond the orchard. It is a blue and white world this morning.

Jory refuses to put on her shoes. Claire watches her walk across the icy driveway in bare feet and considers how long it might take to generate frostbite. She storms back into the house to grab Jory's muddy snow boots and throw them on the passenger floor side. They drive to town in silence.

Dan unlocks the clinic door wearing a scuffed leather workman's jacket, blue jeans and the same boots he'd been wearing both times she's seen him. As he steps back inside he sees Jory in the backseat of the car and invites Claire to bring her in for some hot chocolate, but Claire promises him that her daughter is happier wrapped inside her blankets trying to sleep.

He flicks on lights behind the desk—they are the only two people here, apparently. She starts to ask him about his message yesterday, but the phone rings and he picks it up, talking in fluent Spanish pronounced with so little accent—not even an attempt, really, no trilled rs or blunted vs—that Claire can almost understand him. She had taken two years of college Spanish, but when she and Addison spent ten days on the coast of Spain after a European pharmaceutical meeting she'd relied on an electronic translator. She could read enough to get them through restaurants and museums and castles, but the dialect and speed of native speakers, their words rippling along without a breath between them, laced with slang, had totally stumped her. Addison learned just enough to assure their guides and concierges that his wife spoke fluent Spanish, and then he'd stand aside with crossed arms, his face bulging and flushed with choked laughter while Claire tried to stop the incomprehensible flurry of words. The memory makes her wish he were here to applaud her translation of Dan's bland Spanish. And then, just as suddenly, she remembers sitting in her kitchen two months ago trying to help their housekeeper, Consuela, understand why, through no fault of her own, she no longer had a job.

Dan hangs up and waves her through the swinging gate into a hallway lined with four identical exam rooms. Opposite these is the urgent care room she'd seen the other day. There is also a pharmacy—or at least a large closet lined with shelves stocked with generic drugs and pharmaceutical samples—and what must have once been a bathroom, now converted into a rudimentary laboratory with a microscope and centrifuge.

"We still do our own gram stains now and then. Remember how?" Claire looks at him expecting a laugh, certain he must be kidding. "No matter." He leads her into one of the exam rooms and pulls out drawers holding culture swabs, speculums, guaiac cards, sterile lancets, cotton four-by-fours and gloves. He fans out various colored lab slips and order forms and shows her where to mark the diagnosis and name and billing code. "Not that we get paid for much of it."

She tries to concentrate on everything he tells her, tries to be interested in how the ancient lab equipment works, and the donated slit lamp and glucometer. They don't have any pharmacist, he says, but the drug companies give them meds through the SHARE program, which the clinic doles out on a sliding scale—in other words, pretty much free. He shows her stocks of splints and bandages and plaster casting mix, how to thread the paper roll into the EKG machine, how to wrap electrical tape around the broken leads when they fault.

He has a way about him of leading without looking back, as if his agenda were understood without any need for explanation. It isn't an ego-driven assuredness like she'd experienced so often in medical school, or even with Addison's colleagues. More like a placid acceptance that paths have been laid out for all of us and there is no point beating about for alternatives. Initially she thinks Jory must have taken some specific message from him last night that she forgot to relay, that he had called her back to finish the interrupted tour, or encourage her help with fund-raising. But even with his scarce eye contact, his look of being immersed in some question too immense to tackle in conversation, she finds the urge to pin his motives down quiet inside her, a readiness to let this unfold as it will.

After twenty minutes or more he stands at an alcove kitchenette between the pharmacy and lab and pours two cups of coffee from the Mr. Coffee parked next to the microwave. "It'll boil your teeth down. Want some creamer?"

She takes a sip and her lips involuntarily purse. "It's fine. Nice and hot."

He leans against the wall and crosses one boot over the other. There is no finish on the leather anymore—they seem a part of his own skin, they are so thoroughly worn. He swirls his cup, watching the surface, in no hurry to wrap up whatever he believes he has started.

A door closes in the front room, a computer is booted up, Claire tries another sip of the coffee. Dan glances toward the gate that separates patients and caregivers and clears his throat, "You already have a lab coat? I never wear white myself. But I've got extra in the closet."

"Are you hiring me?" The note of incredulity in her voice makes it sound like she's joking. And it feels that way to her—as if it might hurt less if she makes the joke first.

"I need you to start today, if you can."

"Today?" She hesitates, thinking about Jory out in the car, the moving van supposed to show up any day. And then a more uncomfortable thought: wondering if this is the job she wants, recognizing a twinge of dismay at giving up the career she'd never really started in the first place. Then slamming back into the truth: this is the only job she can get. "No," she answers. "Tomorrow. I can start tomorrow. I don't have a lab coat. I'll borrow one, if that's okay." Dan opens a closet and pulls out a coat, turns it to look at the front, swaps it out for another and holds it out for her to put on. The breast pocket is embroidered with the name Dr. E. Zelaya. "Your wife?" Claire asks.

Dan nods. "She's retired now. Volunteers from time to time. She'll like you. Put your papers there on the desk and we'll get them run through the administrative bullshit. The pay is lousy compared to what you're used to, I expect."

Claire holds the envelope with her résumés in her hands. "I'm not used to any pay at all," she says, looking at his eyes to see if she should hand back the coat. "I haven't worked as a doctor in fourteen years."

He nods slowly, moves his tongue around inside his mouth searching for some foreign particle or just a moment to react. "Any secrets I have to know about?"

She hesitates, wondering how he would react if she told him everything. He shifts his gaze to some point beside her, as if to give her a moment of privacy; his thick eyebrows are white with only a thin spatter of black hairs. "I'm not board certified. I'm licensed, but I'm not certified. It could affect your insurance."

"These patients don't sue. They need a doctor. Got a DEA?"

"It's expired."

"I'll write the scripts until you get the paperwork in. Do you want to know your salary?"

Claire starts to answer him and stops, bites the inside of her lip. "Is it negotiable?"

"Nope. Not now."

"Then tell me later. I want the job."

Despite Claire's promise that they will only drive by the school, stop just long enough to pick up registration forms, Jory remains barefoot and determined to stay put in the backseat. She steadfastly averts her eyes while Claire drives in a slow circle around the single-storied building.

"It doesn't look so bad," Claire says. There are two tennis courts, buried under snow and ice. The building itself is relatively new, with square and rectangular windows set at skewed angles in the stone walls, as if to promise some degree of humor will find its place in the school day. Jory slumps deeper in the backseat while Claire goes in to introduce herself and get the papers. It isn't the patriarchic redbrick establishment that her private school in Seattle is, to be sure. But with a graduating class of thirty-two, maybe Jory can find a place for herself here.

She reaches the entrance just as the bell rings. Classroom doors slam open and students turn the hallways into a five-minute party. She flattens herself against the wall and watches, mentally inserting Jory into the mix. Jory, with her taste for Juicy Couture and skinny jeans mixed in with all this fleece and worn denim. But they look like nice kids to Claire. A janitor rolls open a floor-to-ceiling door that runs on a track in front of the lunchroom; groups immediately crowd at the round and rectangular tables. Claire imagines Jory looking for one vacant seat on her first day and feels a clench of recollected adolescent trauma.

Before she leaves the office she grabs fliers about the after-school clubs: the Nordic ski team, the rodeo club, the theater program. Nothing for dance. Claire asks the school secretary: there is a woman who teaches jazz in her home, but Hallum, as Claire already knew, has no ballet studio.

On the way home Claire turns the heat up twice before she real-izes Jory has the rear window open and is scattering fragments of all the brochures and bulletins into the snow along the side of the high-way; her secret trail of crumbs that might eventually lead her back to someplace she cares about. Claire bites back a tirade about littering and shuts off the radio, starts talking about what electives Jory can take. They'll shop for some new school clothes; maybe it's time she gets her own cell phone. "Baby, I know it's hard. And scary. You'll make friends here. I promise. We should be back in Seattle by next fall."

But by the time they leave the highway Claire has quit probing for some path into Jory's hurt soul. The small space inside the car grates with her anger.

There are fresh tire tracks at the top of the long driveway down to the house. "Jory, somebody's here. Oh, no! What if it's the moving van? They were supposed to call first!" She looks in the mirror to see Jory's reaction—she is totally absorbed in writing looping versions of her signature on the window in the fog of her breath. But when they see Addison's Lexus parked where it had obviously slid down the last ten feet of the road, Jory screams. She is out of the car, hopping red-footed through the snow until he picks her up in his arms. His eternal child. A fist grips Claire's chest, something scary-close to tears that she can't promptly attach to joy or surprise. Something else altogether.

She waits until the other two untangle. "Hey. Which airplane did you drop out of?" With Jory watching, Claire goes to Addison and loosely wraps her arms around his waist. She stands still, feels the cold silkiness of his parka against her cheek and waits for his scent to come back to her, slow to uncoil in the icy air. When she is ready to pull back enough to look at his face he holds her fast. Not demanding, not beg-ging. Asking, she concludes. Asking her to move on.

"I couldn't find my key," he says, in a tone of chagrin that is big enough to make Jory wrap her arms around him again.

"I thought you were the movers when I saw the tracks." Jory flashes a look at her and Claire adds, "I mean, we're happier it's you! And I'm sure they would have just driven right back to Seattle if we weren't here."

She puts a hand over her eyes. "Oh God. Come in. You must be frozen." She unlocks the house—wondering, actually, why she had bothered to lock it in the first place, as if the deer or coyotes were a threat.

Jory consumes her father. That is the word that comes to Claire's mind—*consumes.* She *adsorbs* herself into his presence with an energy Claire hasn't gotten from her in weeks. When Jory was two or three she had gone through a phase of coming into their bedroom every night, almost always right at two o'clock, as if she could tell the time. She was so small she had to hoist herself into their bed, where she would slide neatly between them, tense and wide awake with the exhilaration of her trespass. They were usually too tired to carry her back; and there had been so many months when every premature breath had felt perilous that the ease of cuddling until they all three seemed to breathe in unison still surprised Claire. Eventually they just bought a king-sized bed.

Claire occupies herself with dinner, scrounging through what had seemed like such a well-stocked refrigerator to come up with something more meallike than she and Jory usually eat. She starts boiling water for pasta and chopping cloves of garlic. The kitchen grows warm with steam, the window above the sink sweats into a gray glaze, softer than the black block of sky.

Addison comes in and stands behind her while she splits the pods open with the flat side of the knife blade. "You cut Chicago short?"

He starts to say something, then seems to change his mind and starts again. "It wasn't the right meeting. Better to concentrate on Los Angeles next week."

Claire nods. "Meaning what? Too many people already knew?"

He doesn't answer her and she has to think, carefully, for a minute about how much she wants to say so early in this unexpected visit. "Can you get out the olive oil? Top shelf."

Halfway through dinner Jory excuses herself to watch TV, coming down from the flirtatious high her father has ignited. Claire picks at her spaghetti, finally pushes it away and folds her arms on the table. "Did she tell you yet?"

"Tell me what?"

"I got a job."

Addison puts his fork down and stares at her. When he says nothing after another moment Claire raises her eyebrows. "A job. I got a job."

"Doing what?"

She tilts her head, giving him a minute to retract his question before she finally answers, "At a clinic. I start tomorrow."

"Claire. You don't have to—"

She cuts him off. "How do I not have to do this?" She picks up her plate and silver and walks into the kitchen. "I kind of like having health insurance. Must be the doctor in me. I don't think it comes with a retirement plan, unfortunately."

"Ah! God." He sets his elbows on the table and presses the heels of his hands against his eyes. "I shouldn't have told you that."

She drops the plates in the sink so hard one chips. "No. You could have waited until one of us ended up in the emergency room and let me find out then. There are some things, just maybe, it's better to learn from your spouse than a Gap store clerk."

As if she had a sixth sense, Jory dances into the kitchen asking for ice cream. Claire gets out bowls while Addison fills the sink with hot soapy water, and their forced felicity over dessert eventually feels real enough to turn away from the anger.

They play a round of Life, another of Clue, and then Claire piles two comforters and pillows on the couch. "I have to go to sleep, guys. You can toss for who gets the other half of the bed." She can see from Addison's fallen face that he'd forgotten they were short on beds until the moving truck comes. She kisses Jory's cheek, and Addison's lips— lingering just long enough to let him know that she does prefer the felicity to the argument. But when she wakes up at six to go in for her first day of work, Jory is in bed beside her.

· 10 ·

In the second year of residency every doctor-in-training
was set up with a fledgling clinic practice one afternoon each week.
In many ways these four or five hours out of the eighty- or ninety-
hour work week were the only ones that resembled the life they would
lead after they graduated, caring for average ambulatory patients with
average ambulatory problems. Their hospital work was more exciting. Almost always. To be admitted to a hospital, patients had to be
so thoroughly diseased or traumatized there was no option to send
them ambulating right back to their homes. The only real difference
between their resident's clinic and the private practice most of them
were headed for was that all the patients were poor, uninsured, and
had no other doctor to call. When their pain or breathlessness or swollen joints became unbearable they would start in the emergency room,
waiting hours to be questioned and examined by student doctors who
sporadically excused themselves to consult a small library of textbooks
in the cramped office behind the triage desk. After enough inspection
of cavities and orifices and blood and X-rays for the residents to reach
a plausible diagnosis, the patients were discharged with instructions
printed out on a half sheet and stapled to the bill they couldn't pay:
"Take all your pills, watch for swelling and redness, change your dressing twice a day, follow up with your physician." Thus, in rotating order,
the doctorless were matched up with the doctor trainees who needed
living and breathing specimens to learn their trade. It was a nicely sym-

biotic arrangement, on paper. But it will be different here in Hallum, at Dan's clinic, Claire thinks. Her patients will have a choice. They will choose her. They will want her. She will have time for them.

She parks the Audi near the clinic steps and opens the door, then shuts it again and scrounges through her purse for a brush and her lipstick. When she angles the rearview mirror toward her face she is almost startled by the nervous look in her eyes. Who wanted to be treated by a nervous doctor? A dark shape cuts across the window and she nearly jumps to the other side of the front seat. Then Anita bends low enough to look inside the car. She smiles and jangles her key ring, apparently assuming Claire has already discovered the front door is still locked.

As soon as Claire is out of the car Anita starts telling her how many patients they have scheduled for the day, which ones will be no-shows (because yesterday was payday), and which ones will bring their whole family in without an appointment (because whenever they can get a ride to the clinic they pile grandma and all the babies into the truck to see Dr. Zelaya without even considering how tired he gets at this age), and which ones will show up just as she's trying to lock the doors tonight, but this time she is *not* going to be softhearted about it. Her feet get too swollen by the end of the day to put up with these delinquents.

"When is your baby due?" Claire asks her.

"Not soon enough! I'm only four months. But it's number three. No more belly muscles, I guess. I pooched out really quick this time. I washed your coat for you."

She points to Evelyn Zelaya's newly ironed white coat on a hanger just beyond the waiting room, drops her bag onto the floor behind the desk and begins turning on lights and the computer. "You know how to make coffee, right? I hope better than Dr. Z."

Dan comes in the back door ten minutes later. He asks her just to shadow him for the first few days. A weight lifts when she realizes she won't have to tell anyone she is their new doctor. Not yet, anyway. He introduces her to the patients as his "colleague." They look at her, then shift their eyes back to Dan for some confirmation of trust before they smile or nod and allow her to melt into the background. She stands tucked into the corner behind the exam room door—her starched coat with the false name embroidered on it, her hands rigid in the empty pockets—and tries to pick out words she understands. *Dolor, sangre, sarpullido, pastillas, pinchazo* . . . She tries to piece caught words and phrases into symptoms or cures, tries to work them into questions she will need to ask some patient within a few days, if Dan doesn't change his mind about her. In medical school she had learned a fair bit of Spanish at the public hospital. Even Seattle, as far as you could get from Mexico, had a densely woven Hispanic world populating the apartments and row houses of Beacon Hill and the Central District.

A little after nine the back door slams open, sending a shiver along the wall and a gust of snow across the mat. "You're late," Dan calls out without looking up from the medical chart he's making notes in.

"I'm early. This the new doctor?" Frida, the clinic's nurse, is a compact woman with skin the color of brown eggshells, who wears her black hair twisted up in a hot-pink bandana, socks and sandals on her feet despite eighteen inches of snow. She flashes a stunningly toothy smile at Claire and from then on acts as if they've worked together for years. Claire finds the sense of being taken for granted enormously reassuring. "How'd he get you suckered into this job?" Frida asks, shaking more snow off her coat onto the floor and pouring herself a cup of coffee. "He must not have told you what it pays, that's for sure."

Claire glances at Dan, who has not lifted his eyes from the chart. She sees the corner of his mouth twitch, and when she looks back at Frida she's laughing. "You should give her a raise just for making a decent pot of coffee."

Claire still hasn't asked about the salary; she is forty-three years old, and this is the first time she has worked for a paycheck other than the assigned and nonnegotiable stipend of a resident. She hardly knows *what* to ask, as if she has any option. Her main financial goal is to make sure Dan doesn't regret his offer.

By the time he pauses for their lunch—peanut butter and jelly sandwiches and peeled grapefruit—Claire is too numbed by her own ignorance to be hungry. She had scribbled a few notes on the sly in the first few patients' rooms, worried that if Dan caught her he would slap up against how embarrassingly inexperienced she is. It feels like the medical journals she's been reading for the last decade are little more than movies trying to imitate real life.

At the end of this first day she gives herself a competency test. She stands against the closed exam room door of the only patient still left in the clinic and imagines herself one step ahead of everything she sees and hears, translating the words she understands and anticipating Dan's next move, which question he will ask, what physical exam he'll do, what blood test he'll order. She gives herself a score of 55 on a sliding scale weighted by the language barrier. Clearly failing.

Dan looks exhausted, a sallow shadow darkening the pockets under his eyes. Claire tries to apologize for all her questions, her fumbling, her inadequate Spanish, how she has slowed his pace and kept them all here past six. He stares fixedly at her while she talks until she runs out of words, at which point he squints his eyes, deepening the sharp groove that runs in the narrow space between his brows, and leans a notch closer, almost broodingly serious. "You're not planning to quit on me, are you?" She shakes her head. And then he laughs, all the lines in his face breaking a new way. "Well, then. I'll head home. Frida's in the back—she can lock up."

After she says good night Claire walks toward the front entrance, where she'd parked eleven long hours ago, the waiting room now lit only by the single streetlamp at the edge of the parking lot, a diffuse fluorescent gloom. She thinks, for a moment, that Anita must have left a radio on, but as soon as she nears the swinging gate at the end of the hall she recognizes the voice of a patient seen two hours earlier, a young woman from Guatemala who's just started at Walker's Orchards, come in with a complaint of headaches. Her back is turned when Claire enters the waiting room. She's reading the symptoms of diabetes out loud from a poster on the wall. At Claire's approach, she says, "*Ah, Miguela. Mira. Es la mujer.*" Then, holding open her small bag of drug samples: "*¿Cuántas puedo tomar cada día?*"

Claire is more startled when another woman's voice comes from near the desk, behind her. "*Oh, bien. Doctora,* you have in Spanish?" Claire looks inside the bag and takes out one of the boxes—the directions are only in English. Dan must have been tired, to have forgotten the translation. She writes them on a blank sheet of printer paper and says the words out loud, hoping she'll be able to tell from the woman's reaction that her simple Spanish is clear: *"Una pastill cada mañana, y una pastill de la noche. Claro? Dos cada día."*

"En la noche," the woman standing behind her says, and Claire looks at her closely for the first time; a small woman, maybe thirty-five or so, a little young to be the patient's mother. Suddenly Claire recognizes her. It's the woman from the grocery store; the one she had glimpsed here at the clinic the first day she visited. She feels a rush of relief to see that the woman appears well. Claire hadn't noticed her eyes before, underneath the knit cap she'd worn. They are almost too large for her petite face, accented by stark brows that arch toward her temples like wings, Claire thinks; the silhouette of a soaring bird.

Claire holds out her hand, feeling almost like she's run into some old school friend, surprisingly happy to stumble on some link in Hallum that doesn't ache of her former life clashing with this new one. *"¡Señora! Cómo está?"* The woman glances at her friend and back to Claire, in a puzzle. "The jacket," Claire exclaims, trying to come up with the Spanish words. "At the grocery store. *Chaqueta.*" At last her face breaks open into recognition and she smiles, darts over to the coat rack and pulls off Addison's red and cream plaid wool lumberman's jacket.

"Sí, sí. Muchas gracias, señora. So warm." Claire remembers her voice now, too, the English words heavily accented, as if she has learned them from a book with almost no verbal practice.

"So you have a friend here?" Claire makes the circling dance with her finger again, this time indicating the two women. *"¿Amigos?"*

"Amigas," she corrects, but shakes her head. *"Sólo estoy ayudando a ella esta noche.* Only helping." With that she turns to the younger woman and asks her something before they both put on their coats. "Thank you, *doctora.*"

"De nada," Claire answers. Just before she locks the door after them she asks, *"¿Cómo se llama?* Your name? What is your name?"

The woman is all but hidden inside Addison's jacket; its masculine bulk makes her look unusually vulnerable, but she reaches out her hand and takes Claire's with an assuredness uncommon among the patients she's met today. It is as small as Jory's. "Miguela. Miguela Ruiz."

Claire raps on the bathroom door but Addison doesn't hear her over the running water, and his voice—"Stairway to Heaven" in falsetto. She goes inside and closes the door, sits on the toilet seat. It's comforting in the small steamy room, tinted with the scent of pine soap and the creamy smell of his shaving cream. Addison pulls the shower curtain back. "Hey! How was it?"

"Exhausting. Humiliating." She unbuttons her sweater and twists her hair up off her neck. "Between you and me? I feel lost."

He shuts off the water and pulls a towel from the shower curtain rod. "Well, it's a totally new experience for you, Claire. You haven't practiced medicine in fourteen years. How could you *not* feel lost?" He steps over the side of the tub with the towel wrapped around the soft bulge at his waist. He is heavier since he's been on the road, eating fast food and convention dinners. Ordering the extra martinis that might close the deal.

"I thought I'd kept up better than this. I don't know, I guess I was reading too many articles about the latest angiotensin receptor blockers and not enough about parasites and vitamin deficiencies."

"Buy some new books—primary care stuff. You'll catch up."

She thinks about it for a minute. What possible image could she give him to bridge the gap between his concept of what a doctor is and this job. "I don't know where to read about how I'm supposed to treat diabetes when the patient lives in a trailer with twelve other men. How do you keep a supply of clean syringes and refrigerated insulin?" She raises her hands to make a point and then lets them drop back into her lap. "I don't even understand their language. I'm not sure I won't end up doing more harm than good."

Addison sits on the side of the tub and picks her hand up in his. His face is flushed and damp, erasing all the tiny lines that might show his age. Where does he hide his stress? "Do you want to go back to Seattle?" he asks. "You didn't even try to find a job there."

She plummets into the memory of her last lunch date with Anna at Chez Shea in Pike Place Market, the big arched window haloed with a wreath of Christmas lights. Anna. Married to Nash. She remembers joking with Anna about playing Ma on *Little House on the Prairie* in Hallum for a few months until Addison had time to repeat the animal trials and start another application for the human phase tests. Wishing she were allowed to say more, to tell Anna about Rick Alperts's role in the fiasco, so she could stomp out the look of pity and doubt in Anna's eyes. "Well," Anna had said as she hugged Claire good-bye at her car door, "it's all good." Claire had wanted to lash out at her when she said it, and at the same time couldn't blame her at all. Because it always *had* been good. For all of them. In one generation they had forgotten how heartless the universe could be.

A short, sarcastic laugh escapes her and she asks Addison, "If none of the clinics *here* would hire me without my boards, who would hire me in Seattle? Besides, we can live on half as much in Hallum. At least we own this dump." She sees him take a breath and then quickly shut his mouth. "Sorry. This 'graceful vintage home.'" His head falls forward at this. She takes the sharp edge off her voice and leans closer to him. "I *am* sorry. I'm just tired." Drops of water have collected on his earlobes, suspended like jewels. Claire reaches up and touches one, breaks the surface tension so it runs down her finger. "You're wearing diamond earrings."

He looks at her, gripping the hand he still holds. "Speaking of, where is your ring?"

"Locked in the filing cabinet. Filed under 'D'—either for 'diamond' or 'debt,' I haven't decided. Felt funny wearing that ring to the clinic. It could buy a whole house in Mexico." Addison nods. He looks so sad to her. So forlorn. She wants to forget every heated accusation and every splintered trust—hear them once, discuss them once, and forget them. But how do you do that? Why is it so hard to give Addison the same unconditional love she gives Jory? Is the heart for such absolute forgiveness granted only through childbirth? Instead, as always, any rub between the place they had been and the place they have arrived brings a curtain down between them. Claire is unwilling to turn from it this time. "I should sell the ring, Addison. It's not like it was my real engagement ring. Buy me another one when you find an investor."

He looks straight at her again, grips her hands so tight it hurts. "Please. Hang in there with me—a few more months."

"I will. I am." She says softly, feeling the sting of tears. "I'm trying."

He scans her face, and she sees him looking for something there that she wants him to find. "Yeah." He says after a minute. "Yeah. I know you're trying."

And she *is* trying, although the enemy dismantling their union is not always clear to her, leaves her wondering, sometimes, exactly what she is fighting. It is not about the loss of money, surely. She had fallen in love with Addison long before he was rich.

They'd met during her first clinical month in medical school, in the Harborview emergency room. "Initiation by fire," the dean had editorialized with a wry smile when he read out her assignment. Addison had materialized out of the generally invisible cleanup crew in the aftermath of a multifatality car accident—materialized like a ghost in his orderly's floppy white pants and tunic.

She was trying to write out admission orders for a patient with a hip fracture who'd been shunted to the back hall while the living were sorted from the dead. Her resident, Andy Keets, had whipped a blank order form out of a drawer behind the nursing desk and paused for a full two and a half minutes in his own scut work to bark out the orders she should use for a routine admission. Keets was a sharp, burly, aspiring surgeon who could be a comic guardian or a pitiless drill sergeant to his novitiate medical students, depending on whether he'd been allowed to wield a scalpel in the operating room or demoted to holding retractors. He terrified her. She'd scribbled the orders down in the little notebook she kept in a pocket of her short white coat, but she'd misplaced the book in the scuffle of the trauma room. Now she was lost in the middle of the sequence, somewhere between "Diagnosis" and "Vital Signs."

Her pen hovered above the paper. She picked up the phone to page Keets, then hung up; it was safer to scrounge around among the blood-soaked drapes looking for her notes than to catch him in a foul mood. It was three AM. Her eyes were so tired her contact lenses felt like they were glued to her corneas, and the missing orders drifted from her memory like weeds on a tide.

She heard someone talking and jumped, realized she'd nodded off at the desk. God, she'd drooled onto the page and "Diagnosis" now bled into a faint blue pool.

"IV." It was Addison, sitting on a parked gurney next to her sleeping patient, watching her write—and sleep. Claire wiped the corner of her mouth and stared at him.

"You have to say what kind of IV fluid to run. What do you want? Normal saline, D-five-W, lactated Ringer's?"

She felt oddly insulted that an orderly would try to tell her how to admit a hospital patient. She knew she ranked low as a third-year medical student, but she'd rather have Keets chew her out than let a janitor see how lost she was in this foreign world that was supposedly her career. But the very next thought that skittered across her fatigued brain was *He won't age very well, but he looks so young now that won't matter for decades.*

He jutted his chin toward the paperwork. "Keets tell you the mnemonic?"

Now she was flustered, as if some mortal flaw in her intelligence were being exposed to someone that mattered. She started to stand up, ready to transport her patient up to the orthopedic floor by herself and figure out the orders there. She'd copy them from some other chart if she had to.

Addison hopped off the gurney and grabbed a pen and a clean order sheet from the desk drawer, and started writing capital letters down the left margin. "ADCVANDISSLD. *A: Admit* to floor. What floor's she going to? Ortho, right?" Claire nodded. "*D: Diet.* Is she going for a hip pinning in the morning? So she's NPO. *C: Condition.*" He glanced over at the rickety woman snoring lightly into her oxygen mask after a dose of morphine, her pulse oximeter flashing 97 percent. "Stable." He moved closer, stood just behind Claire so that she felt the warmth from his body, saw the way his forearm flexed as he scribbled down the page. He reached the final *D* and wrote "*Date?*"

Claire looked up at him. "What do you mean? Date of discharge? I don't know yet."

"No. I mean you and me. A date?"

He couldn't have timed it more perfectly, which proved to be an inherent, uncanny sense he had about the world, or at least the world of biochemistry. A second sight that made him millions until he focused too far. At that instant the elevator doors opened and Keets strode over to the desk. "Why is the hip still down here? I need you in trauma two."

Claire snatched the pen away from Addison. "I wasn't sure I got the orders right. You want to look at them?"

"Boehning, help her out, man." Keets jerked a thumb at Addison, "Not even a doc and he's smarter than any of you pitiful grunts."

Hospital orderly work was only one of the menial jobs that had interrupted Addison's education. He had a tuition scholarship to Harvard, but after his father lost his last bet Addison didn't get any help from home. He'd gone door to door through Newton and Beacon Hill and Back Bay with a bucket and mop, washing windows all summer to pay for books and food. One year he'd cleaned cadaver tanks in the medical school anatomy lab. Claire didn't know about it until Addison's mother told her. She figured he'd kept it a secret because he was embarrassed, but when she discreetly asked him how he could stand it, Addison was nonplussed. "I had to get through school. I needed work I could do around my class schedule."

He spent three years at Harvard working every weekend and holiday on a farm in the Berkshires, bunking in a half-restored schoolhouse out in the middle of a rotting apple orchard with trees gone as spiny as crabs. It was the one job he'd really enjoyed. He'd made a nightly ritual of lying in a fallow field until he counted three falling stars. In wintertime he would haul out an aluminum recliner, the nylon webbing busted through at the seat, and wedge it into the snow. Focused. Waiting. Uncompromising.

He told Claire about the farm on their first date, the very last *D* in ADCVANDISSLD. So she had taken him home with her after dinner, shoved all the blankets from her bed through a small window onto the roof of her apartment and lain for the first time in the hollow of his shoulder, arrested, astounded by the perfect fit of herself against him. He had teased her through the lyrics of Chapin and Dylan and Waites, counted out Bill Withers's twenty-seven "I Knows" for the first time, like a premonition. They had watched the sky for hours, Claire undeterred by the obscuring lights of Capitol Hill and downtown Seattle, until three perfect stars fell. Three perfect stars that eventually led to a perfect family of three. Jory, Claire and Addison. Falling.

· 11 ·

On her fourth day, Dan puts a patient's chart in Claire's hands and points to the first exam room. "Think you're ready?"

She wants to blindly assure him that this is the moment she's been looking forward to—it is, after all, such optimistic hubris that had defined the best and brightest in medical training, herself included. But the falseness of it catches, and all she can say is, "Does she speak English?"

"Anita can translate when she's not checking people in. You can buttonhole Frida or me between patients. You aren't working alone."

Claire opens the thin chart, as much to buy time as to get information. Dan watches her for a minute, then steps into the cramped office they all share and comes back with a stethoscope. He drapes it over her shoulders and says, "You look ready enough to me. Have at her."

Elena Ynez, a twenty-two-year-old woman, is sitting on the end of the exam table. She has put her blue gown on backward, so the opening gapes in front, exposing part of her breasts and abdomen. Claire introduces herself and pulls another gown out of the drawer, holding it open so Elena can slide her arms through the slits. A toddler clings to Elena's leg; she takes one wobbly step and slips to the floor, tipping over the waste can. The crash makes her face twist and she sucks in a deep breath, ready to wail. Claire unwraps a wooden tongue depressor and draws a puppet's face on one end, waggling it in front of the baby until she forgets the whang of dented metal and crawls over to grasp the toy. "*¿Cómo se llama su niña?*"

The woman smiles and a gold-rimmed tooth gleams in the front of her mouth. She answers in rapid Spanish, gesturing at the baby and laughing, going on for sentence after sentence with barely a pause. The only word Claire thinks she understands is *blanca,* which may be the child's name, or the color of Claire's coat, or perhaps the snow, or the mountains she had crossed coming north from Mexico. Claire smiles and lifts one finger in the air. "*Momentito, por favor.*" She steps into the hallway and waits until Frida appears. With an apologetic plea Claire pulls her into the exam room.

Frida ends up doing almost everything except the brief abdominal exam, walking Claire through translated questions, helping her find the urine specimen cups, showing her how to spin down a test tube of the cloudy yellow fluid and prepare a microscope slide. Claire's only contribution is the confirmation of white blood cells floating in the magnified droplet and a prescription for Bactrim, which Frida finds for her on the shelves of their small pharmacy. That and a happily distracted baby. Claire stands out of the way in the closet-sized room while Frida hunts for the Spanish language label to tape onto the bottle. "Don't we have to send it out for a culture?"

Frida opens an under-the-counter incubator and pulls out an agar plate of culture media. "We start with this. If it's something other than *E. coli* we send it out. You can at least tell if it's resistant to sulfa in a couple of days. You've made a culture smear before, right?"

Claire gives her a tight grin. "Sure. In my first year of medical school. You don't send it to the lab?"

Frida laughs. "We have a lab. And we use the hospital lab. We just don't have any money. This isn't the medicine you learned in your Seattle private hospitals."

"It's not even the medicine I learned at the public hospital."

Frida unwraps a sterile wire loop, dips the end into the test tube and draws a wide S down the center of the gel. She carefully places the lid on top without touching the rim and puts it back in the incubator. She is about to walk out to see the next waiting patient when she stops; Claire can almost see her consciously rein in her perpetually frenetic pace, sweep her eyes over Claire's face and hair, appraising. "Dan's needed help for a long time. I don't know what made him finally cave in to that fact." She presses her lips tight for a second and goes on. "It's not an easy job."

Claire nods, wondering if she wants Frida to finish the thought still working its way forward.

"You expect you'll be staying in Hallum?" The gold and bronze glints in Frida's eyes darken a little when she says this—not in any offensive way, Claire thinks. More an honest reflection on the energy everybody here is putting into making this, her role here, work.

Claire feels her face flush, stumbling over the obvious fact that the chaos in her own life could infect everyone she tangles up with along the road home—wherever home ends up being. "Well, I guess you could say we're in transition right now." She is about to tell Frida how deeply grateful she is for this job and scoot out from under the harder question, can almost sense Frida is expecting such evasion, poised to pull back and define their relationship through it. Claire pauses, decides without conscious thought to say exactly what she is thinking. "I don't know how long we'll be here. But I won't leave you in the lurch. I promise."

Frida presses her lips tight once more and then beams her enormous smile onto Claire. "Well. Glad that we have that out of the way."

Over the next weeks Claire feels like the practice of medicine is a language she once knew fluently, but which has now receded so deep into the corners of her memory she only vaguely understands it, no longer speaks it. Symptoms, terms, signs and syndromes rush back to her after examining a patient and slip away a second later, leaving her tongue-tied in front of Dan—all the parallel but imprecise words proving inadequate. She is only beginning to recognize what most doctors discover while still in their twenties: the gap between theory and truth is wider than it looks. You can pass a test with honors in medical school, but patients do not come with multiple-choice bubbles lined up below their complaints. The possible diagnoses must be winnowed out of hundreds floating in the thin air of recalled symptoms and diseases. It is perspective, in the big picture of life and death, that medical school can only get you *ready* to learn. The relativity of outcome that patients need, more than anything, can only be learned through years of experience.

So she discusses every patient with Dan. She presents cases as if she is back in medical school, sounding as stilted and awkward as when she presented to attendings in her early clinical training. "This is a thirty-seven-year-old Hispanic female, G8P6AB2 with a history of gestational diabetes presenting with polyuria and a positive pregnancy test, LMP approximately four months ago." "A seventy-six-year-old Hispanic male, status post-MI times two, with a history of poorly controlled hypertension and medical noncompliance presenting with new onset occipital headaches and photophobia." "This sixteen-year-old Caucasian female was in apparently good health until January twenty-third, when she developed intermittent lower abdominal pain associated with purulent vaginal discharge."

Dan listens with his slow, serious nod, his eyes focused at a point near her feet. His expression seems simultaneously distracted by some imponderable internal question he finds mildly amusing and intently focused on Claire's descriptions. He Socratically asks her opinion about the most likely diagnosis or her first treatment choice. And when she outlines her differential and the blood work or CT scan or MRI that might distinguish them, he looks up and his eyes narrow, just a bit, a half-worked grin playing at the edges of his mouth. "And let's say you order this thousand-dollar MRI, or the three hundred dollars of lab work, what do you anticipate they're going to show you?" After she answers, no matter what she answers: "How would you treat him if you couldn't get that test?" And, after a few more guiding questions: "What would you guess the harm to be in trying that treatment first? Then, if he's no better, then we choose one test."

"But you'll end up treating the wrong thing, at least part of the time."

"You will. And the first rule is 'Do no harm.' But the second rule, in this clinic, is 'Money wasted is lives lost.' We have funds, and we have patients, and if we run out of funds somebody farther down the line gets no care."

Anita, who manages the accounts, is blunt about the budget. "I should just make it up every day—fake names and fake insurance. Fake social security numbers paying real enough tax dollars to the U.S. government and we don't see a dime of it! The only thing you can count on by closing time is that we lost more money." When Claire offered to help her with the books she had rolled her eyes. "You want to help me? Go take care of my kids. Go clean my house. Go yank the beer bottle out of my good-for-nothing husband's mouth." But then she had burst out laughing and patted her expanding abdomen. "Pregnant ladies get to say whatever they want."

Claire borrows textbooks from the donated library Dan keeps on a shelf above their desks. After a rushed dinner, Addison and Jory play cards, or Jory improvises dance steps to Addison's music (everything from Miles Davis and Nina Simone to Michael Jackson), while Claire studies, sometimes stuffing her ears with foam in order to concentrate over their noise. She focuses on diseases she'd only memorized for tests in school. Now she sees patients who carry inside them the medical legacy of the Third World, nourished in poverty, neglect and misguided folklore. From their rural villages and crowded slums they bring the parasites that thrive in their swine and river water, the viruses that multiply in their mosquitoes and lakes, the bacteria that bloom on their fruits and vegetables. They harbor the remnants of measles and mumps, the threat of tetanus and meningitis, the stalled growth of protein and iodine and vitamin deficiencies.

Mixed in with the migrants are America's working poor, too rich for Medicaid and too broke to buy insurance, who've ferreted out how forgiving Dan's sliding scale can be. At least their problems don't have to be filtered through a translator, leaving her to wonder—as she does with the Spanish speakers—why the words Anita says don't match the look of pain or humiliation on her patient's face.

Procedures are even worse. She can't relearn those from a textbook.

"Patient in room two needs some labs drawn, can you get it?" Dan asks her at the end of a day after Frida has already gone home.

Claire starts to say, "Of course." She has drawn pints of blood, gallons of blood. Fourteen years ago. Is it a skill like riding a bike? Does one forget? He must see her blanch; the narrow crease ditches between his brows and he grabs a yellow paper gown from a box Anita has placed beside the door. "Put this on. This, too." He hands her a white mask and pulls one over his own mouth. "Chest X-ray looks like TB."

He opens the door after a sharp rap and leans against the exam table, one lanky leg propped on the stepstool. He is limber for his age—Claire guesses he's at least seventy-five, though the high desert sun out here steals years from anyone who doesn't relentlessly shield himself. The paper mask looped by thin elastic bands behind his ears appears nearly inconsequential on such an imposing man, as if his height and composure could wither the potency of any stray bacterium hitching a ride on flecks of sputum.

An elderly woman sits on one of the plastic bucket chairs. Her skin is the color of the unpolished copper cookware that used to hang above Claire's Wolf range—not gold, not brown, not bronze, but some mottled blend of harvest hues, more an armor than a living organ. She has a knotted braid of gray hair at the nape of her neck, and when she smiles at Dan, Claire sees more pink flesh of gum than ivory of teeth. Her granddaughter, a child of four or five, squats on her heels in the corner of the room.

Dan addresses the old woman in his blunt Spanish, asks her something about a Saturday night escapade; she laughs and calls him her *novio*. She fumbles in a colorful woven shopping bag and pulls out two bananas and several caramel-colored blocks wrapped in waxed paper, wagging one of the bananas at Claire until she comes over and takes it. Dan makes much of the gift and holds her dry, arthritic hands in his own.

There is a moment of transition then. *"Con permiso,"* he says, turns one palm up and lays the first two fingers of his right hand longitudinally along her radial pulse while he counts with his head bowed, as if he could hear her heart through his touch.

Claire watches, wishing she could make herself invisible. The woman wears a faded black housedress with a pattern of dots, belted at the waist with a length of nylon cord, and over that a loose-knit cardigan. Her breasts sink onto her lap with the weight of generations and the labor of her life. Her shoes are bent over at the back and her heels, leather thick and cracked, scrape against the floor. After a moment Dan turns to Claire and introduces her to Maria Solano. The woman takes her hands and clasps them together as if she were praying, murmurs something indecipherable. Her clouded eyes scan Claire's face, taking in her hair and her earrings, staring at the pleated paper over her mouth until she slips one elastic band off her ear just long enough for the woman to see her full smile. She reaches up and strokes Claire's cheek with the tough palm of her hand, says something to Dan that makes him laugh. He takes a pink plastic emesis basin from the cabinet over the sink. "Draw a CBC, liver panel and creatinine. I'm next door if you need me."

The basin holds three glass vials with different-colored rubber stoppers, a butterfly needle, tubing and a tourniquet. The woman smiles. Claire smiles back from behind the mask, then raises her eyebrows to intensify whatever eyes alone can express. The child clutches a Cheetos bag between her chest and folded knees and watches the scene wordlessly. Claire smiles at her, too, but the girl's face looks frozen, either because she is shy, or totally absorbed with trying to figure out the mask. Without moving her eyes she plucks an electric orange Cheeto out of the foil bag and pops it in her mouth, shedding dust like bright pollen down her chin and shirt. Her grandmother breaks the spell with chattering Spanish, pulls a Kleenex from deep within her cleavage and passes it toward the child. Claire grabs a paper towel for the girl instead. "¿Más limpia?" she says, forgetting the word for germs. The old woman beams and nods, though Claire suspects she would do the same regardless of what Claire told her.

Then she turns back to Claire and pushes up her sleeve, offering the soft flesh and fine blue veins at the crux of her right arm for the tourniquet and needle. "Aquí, mira, Doctora. No tengo miedo." She smiles and stares at her exposed bare arm, seeming to will the flow of blood.

Claire slips the tourniquet around the pendulous bulk above her elbow and seats herself on a footstool, legs planted square and firm. She searches for the words for 'Make a fist,' but only those for 'hand' and 'tight' come to her, so she emulates the motion and the old woman copies, nodding and watching for the veins to balloon.

Claire also watches. She taps the antecubital fold with the ball of her first finger, flicks the nail of her middle finger against the woman's skin where it creases like a worn flannel sheet. She rubs hard over the surface with an alcohol-soaked pad. Nothing appears.

"*Aquí es una pequeña vena. Casi aquí. No se preocupe,*" the woman says, scratching at an invisible rivulet of blood.

Claire slips on latex gloves and readies the needle, swabs once more with the alcohol wipe. Then she holds her breath and pierces the skin with the razored bevel. She gently pulls the plunger on the small syringe and watches for the flash of red. Nothing. She withdraws and reangles and pierces again. And then again. The woman doesn't move, but Claire feels her arm tense and then relax as she overcomes an instinct to flinch.

"Maybe your hand is better. *Tal vez en su mano,*" Claire says, keeping her voice easy. She snaps off the tourniquet and ties it lower on the woman's forearm. Serpentine veins rise across the dorsum of her hand, swollen with the back pressure of blood. These should be easy, visible and close beneath the surface of her splotched skin. Claire stretches new gloves over her perspiring hands; again, alcohol is swabbed, a fresh needle and syringe prepared. The woman watches her veins fill, points to one with her scarred index finger. "*Esta es la más grande, verdad?*" she says, and thumps it as if assessing melons in a vendor's stall.

Claire's needle pierces the skin again, tougher here than at the antecubital fossa; the vein slips away from the probing surgical steel like a lithe snake, loose and untethered. Suddenly there is a flash of red in the clear tubing and she teases back the plunger on the syringe, advances the needle a millimeter more. The flow stops. A dark purple welt oozes through the subcutaneous tissues and the map of veins disappears below a tender bruise. Claire pulls the needle out and presses a woven cotton pad over the wound until the blood stops spreading.

The woman leans across her bounteous lap so that her face is quite close. She squeezes her eyes shut and whispers, consolingly, "*Lo siento, chica.*" Then she pats Claire's knee, lifts her other arm onto the fold-out table and rolls up her sleeve, ready for Claire to try again.

"*Espérame,* okay?" Claire says, and tapes a bandage over the puncture, drops the needles into the red sharps disposal box and stands up. The little girl stays crouched in the corner of the exam room, her eyes brown and deep as lakes.

Claire goes down the short hallway until she hears Dan's voice in a closed exam room; a red flag lets her know he's busy with a patient. She lifts her hand to knock but hesitates, reluctant to interrupt, trying to think of a way to tell him that she can't draw blood from a vein the size of a fat spring worm. She considers going back alone to try one more time, but the thought of putting that tolerant woman through more blind sticks is worse than any look on Dan's face. As if he'd heard her poised fist, Dan swings the door open until it bumps up against his metal chair. He holds a clipboard with a history and physical form on his lap. Through the half-opened doorway she sees a woman's feet, small, tucked into black ballet flats—the drugstore kind—like a pair of small black birds.

"I'm sorry to interrupt. Do you have a minute?" Claire says, her voice filled with humiliation.

"No blood, huh?" Dan says, scraping the legs of the chair against the floor to push it away from the door. "Remind me when we get our next million dollars to build bigger exam rooms, would you?"

She grimaces. "I don't know. If you keep me on staff you might have to put the money into a phlebotomist."

"¡Nueva doctora, una mujer por usted!" he says to his patient, a girl of seventeen or eighteen who is changing back into her clothes. She smiles and immediately opens a conversation Claire can't understand.

They are at Señora Solano's door when Claire turns around and catches Dan standing still with his hand over his abdomen.

"Did you eat anything today?" The question pops out of Claire just as she would have asked Jory, almost mixing up her caretaking roles. "You don't have to stay. I can try again. It's already after six."

Claire can see he's worn out, but he smiles and says, "What? Did my wife call to put you up to that?" He raps on the door of the exam room where Señora Solano waits with her sleeve still rolled up and positioned on the foldout table. He pulls a string of glittery pony stickers out of his pocket, loops it around the little girl's upstretched hand and squats down to whisper some joke in Spanish; the child stares open-mouthed and then animatedly tells Dan something about a *caballo* and busies herself pasting stickers onto the front of her shirt.

And then Dan teaches Claire how to draw blood, as she had been taught in her earliest clinical rotation in medical school eighteen years ago, while the old woman smiles and chatters to him in Spanish. He labels the three velvet-red vials and translates for Claire. "She's worried about you. Said you started going a little pale on her. Told me I should feed you a good dinner." He winks. "Looks like we've both got people watching out for us."

"Let me lock up tonight. Go on home," Claire says after they are back in the office. All three desks, lined up against one wall of the cramped room, are stacked with charts and lab reports and medical journals. Frida and Dan's desks are the worst, the piled folders a testament to their productivity. Or popularity, Claire can't help thinking. Claire's desk, wedged into the corner after they had lifted one short filing cabinet on top of another to make room, has its own growing stacks—most of the folders still pristine and thin since Anita gives her the youngest, newest, and, therefore, usually healthiest patients. It still looks so temporary compared to Dan's and Frida's. Anonymous. None of the photographs and coffee mugs sitting like glass islands in oceans of paper. None of the Mexican *milagros* and woven *ojo de Dioses* they've both strung from thumbtacks and drawer pulls.

Dan rubs his eyes. "Well. If you're okay with that."

"Very okay. But I need a key."

He smiles at this and she sees that look he gets, where she's tapped into some secret he's kept wrangled up inside until the right snare catches and pulls it forth. "Still not quitting, huh? I thought you weren't ever going to ask for it. Now I guess you're going to want to know your salary, too. Should I hold on to the key till you hear it?"

Dan leaves out the back door twenty minutes later. The salary is lower than she'd hoped—and she had not hoped for much. But she suspects at least part of it has been shaved from what he takes home himself. She takes her key ring out of her purse and drives a ballpoint pen between the spiraled circles to wedge in her new clinic key. It's funny that a couple of inches of stamped metal makes her feel so included, like she's been taught the clinic's secret handshake. But the new key won't easily fit on the crowded ring; not until she takes off the four keys that had opened and locked the many doors and garages to her Seattle house. She lines them up on her palm. She could send the keys back to the Realtor to give to the people who bought their home, it would be a nice gesture, but the locks have probably already been changed. They are worth nothing to anyone now. She walks out the clinic's back door to the dumpster behind the building and drops all four keys into the dank and humid vat of waste.

· 12 ·

"Your mother called," Addison says.

"Ah. Gretta," Claire says, dropping onto the couch still packed into her down coat, hat, gloves and boots. "Why don't you ever start the woodstove?"

"'Ah'? That's all you can say? Here. Taste this." Addison holds a wooden spoon over his cupped palm, tempting her into the kitchen like one might lure a stray animal. "Tell me if it needs more garlic."

Claire dips a finger into the red sauce and licks it, suddenly starved. "It's great. So is this your new job?"

He turns away, putting the rest of the contents in his mouth and *hmmm*ing in a satisfied voice, but Claire can tell he is miffed. She rests her head against his back, feels the rocking of his shoulders as he stirs, waits for the gentle push back toward her to know they can drop this one. It is slow to come. "I sent her an e-mail a few weeks ago," Claire says. "Told her it would be too muddy to visit until June and her Ferragamos would be wrecked, but by summer the remodel should be finished and she can have her own bathroom." She pauses, waits for a signal. Nothing. "And who knows? By then Pfizer could be your new best friend."

After a slow, cool moment, the press of her cheek into his back, he edges back toward her, her joke a bridge across the place they don't examine. It is always one of them giving, one of them relinquishing, she thinks. But never both. Never together.

She hugs him with a single fleeting clasp and goes up to change into her bathrobe and slippers, plays one round of "Answer Ten Questions and Find Out What Food You Are" with Jory, a link from some Seattle friend. Jory is a ripe persimmon. Claire an artichoke. Addison serves them all spaghetti.

At dinner Jory seems electrified, zinging through a backlog of gossip about people she hasn't seen in more than a month: who had started driver's ed, who had gotten the ballet lead, who had pierced the most remote corner of their body. It is as if her own uncertain future is so scary it's pushing her in reverse.

Claire flashes a look across the table, watches Jory coiling noodles around her fork with intense concentration. She rests her fingers lightly on her husband's arm. "Did you show Dad the school stuff we picked up?"

Jory shakes her head, furrows her eyebrows without lifting her gaze from her food. "May I be excused, please?"

"You're done? You didn't eat much."

Jory shrugs. "It was good. I'm just not hungry." She carries her plate to the sink and swirls it quickly under the water before dropping it in the dish rack. Even from the table Claire can see it is still streaked with tomato sauce.

Before bed Claire asks Addison, "Did you talk to her about it? She's less defensive with you. She has to go. It's already three weeks into the semester." They are both sitting on the rim of the tub, trying to keep their voices low enough not to carry through the thin walls. Where did parents talk to each other for all the centuries entire families lived in one room? God, for that matter, how did they couple enough to have more than the first few children?

"She thinks if she enrolls here it means we're never going back." He says it in a nearly defeated voice. Claire doesn't even want the replay of the conversation Addison and Jory must have had.

"There are some things a fourteen-year-old doesn't get to choose." They hear the computer shutting down in the living room and stop talking for a minute. "When is your next meeting?" Claire finally asks.

"I have to be in San Francisco Friday afternoon."

"So she'll be alone until I get home from the clinic. Six thirty or seven. An oncology meeting?"

Addison brightens up a little, and Claire feels the small rush of hope she is learning to dread, learning that the safest space has been compressed into the single step from this moment to the next. "It's a venture capitalist meeting. Some big names—big biopharm investors."

Claire nods, scraping off a blot of dried toothpaste from her bathrobe. "You won't be here when the moving truck comes, then?"

"I can't miss this meeting. All I need is one big investor. If I have that, I can go to a bank for more. Nash would probably come back in, too. As soon as we repeat the animal trials everything could fall in place."

"Assuming the mouse data comes back normal this time."

"Yes. Assuming that. And I think it will. I'm still convinced those results were a fluke." Claire feels his eyes on her but doesn't look at him. "It could happen quickly, Claire. Everything could turn around."

"Well," she answers, brushing white flecks off the lap of her robe, "not quite everything."

At the end of clinic the next day Frida waves her into the back office. She drops a white cardboard box in the middle of Claire's desk, pasted all over with the superhero and baby animal stickers they hand out to pediatric patients.

"What is it?"

"What does it look like? It's a graduation present." She leans against the wall with her hands jammed into her coat pockets. Her black curls spiral out of her lemon yellow headband like party streamers.

"Graduation?"

"Three weeks and you haven't quit—not that I don't see you think about it now and then."

"Only when Anita gives me three rooms at the same time with no translator." Claire lifts the lid and takes out a Dove dark chocolate bar and a pocket Spanish–English dictionary. She laughs, "Hah! Reading my mind again!"

"I thought you needed one you could hide in your coat."

"Yeah. Maybe it will osmose straight into my brain. Thank you." She leans over and gives Frida a spontaneous hug.

Frida returns the hug, one armed and one beat late, as if it surprised her. She tucks her chin down and Claire can tell that she's a little embarrassed, but a little pleased, too. "So what do you think? Is it getting easier?"

"I'm not sure yet. I'm kind of afraid I have just enough knowledge to be dangerous." She rather wishes Frida would burst out laughing at this but continues without a blink. "It's *me* who should be thanking you guys."

"Is your husband still in town?" Frida asks.

"He's trying to get Jory organized for school today. We're about to give her the ultimatum."

Frida seems to turn this fact over a few times, maybe just trying to imagine this absentee father shopping for school clothes. "Hmm. She'll be happier once she knows some other kids." She pushes away from the wall with the sole of her foot and pulls the strap of her purse over her shoulder. "Buy you a cup of coffee on your way home?"

Claire shakes her head. "I can't drink coffee after noon—keeps me awake."

"Great. I'll buy you a beer."

No one answers at the house, so she calls Addison's cell phone, thinking they have probably driven into town. But when he doesn't answer that, either, Claire calls the house again. At last Jory picks up, sounding almost giddy and thoroughly annoyed at having to stop whatever she is doing to pick up the phone.

"Why are you laughing?" Claire asks.

"We're playing Pictionary."

"It's that funny?"

"Dad made a new rule." She starts giggling again. "You have to draw all the pictures holding the pencil in your mouth."

I should have thought of that, Claire thinks. The last time she spent an entire evening without speaking to me. "Okay, honey. Well, tell him

I'll be home in an hour. Start some dinner would you? Hugs and kisses." But Jory has hung up some seconds before.

Frida has already snared a table and ordered two glasses of beer by the time Claire gets to the bar. "I figured you were in a hurry. Took the liberty," Frida says.

The minute she sits down Claire feels completely spent, an almost pleasurable sense of having been thoroughly worked, like a sauna after a long run. "I feel like I just got off a night on call in the ER."

"Did you even eat lunch today? Dan almost never does, lately. He's losing weight." Frida twists her yellow bandana off and wraps it around her wrist, her hair gradually loosens around her face. "But you can tell you're catching up with it, can't you? I mean, you were great today!"

Claire shrugs, but can't help smiling at the compliment. Just those few words and she feels brighter. The beer comes and she takes a small sip, worrying she'll be asleep at the table if she finishes the glass. "I think every patient I saw asked me for an antibiotic. Even the skin rashes."

"Have you spent any time in rural Mexico?" Frida asks.

Claire raises her eyebrows and smiles. "Does Cancun count?"

"Only if you followed your waiter or maid back to their house in the barrio. Most village pharmacies stock about four drugs of any consequence: Amoxicillin, Septra, maybe Cipro if they're lucky. That and ibuprofen. Antibiotics are the only medicine they've ever seen save a life." She puts her beer down and strips off her sweater, only a neon orange tank top underneath. Her arms are surprisingly muscular, her shoulders broad and well grooved in the triangles where her deltoids and biceps intersect. In her fleeces she looks almost stout, but now Claire sees there is little fat on her.

Frida is the daughter of a black mother and white father who had married in the early seventies, convinced the racial divide would soon be obsolete. They had lived in a commune in the Texas hill country until it disintegrated, and then moved to central Mexico near San Miguel de Allende. At some point their altruism had merged with the benefits of capitalism and now they ran a spa that was often photographed in *Travel + Leisure* or *Town & Country*, though a percentage of proceeds funded a local charity. Claire had asked her once if her name was derived from Frida Kahlo, but Frida said she shortened it from her given name, Freedom, after she started nursing school back in Boston, hating the obligation of such a noun. Now that Claire is getting to know her, that seems like a perfect analogy for her personality— the bleeding-heart optimist blended with the coolheaded pragmatist. Enormously giving, up to the point it stopped being fun. It is making for an easy friendship, Claire thinks, not having to waste any time with social charades, which Frida has a tendency to throw her head back and laugh at—the broad, rolling sound of it as big as her broad smile.

Claire pours a handful of salty pretzels into her hand and asks Frida, "Are you worried about Dan? He seems pretty tough."

"I love worrying about Dan. That's my biggest contribution to the clinic. You know why he started this place, right?"

Claire pushes the bowl of pretzels toward Frida. "He told me some about where the money comes from."

"That's the *how*, not the *why*." Frida pours her beer into a glass mug, angling it steeply along the side with the practice of a former waitress or bartender. Claire comments on it and she laughs. "Got through school courtesy of The Cask and Flagon." She takes a sip and settles back in her chair. "He won't tell you unless you ask him. His mother lost a whole family crossing the border during the Depression. Three kids and a husband."

"Dan's father?"

"No, no. She married Dan's dad a few years later—in California, I think. Dan didn't even know she'd had another family until he was grown up."

"What happened?"

"They were coming across from Sonora. A whole group. In the middle of the desert her husband was bitten by a snake and couldn't keep up. They told her she could stay with him or leave and save her kids. So she sent the children on ahead with another family and stayed with her husband, thinking he might get better overnight. But he didn't. She ended up walking for three days, until somebody found her, half dead." Frida leans closer. "She never saw her kids again." She squares her wide shoulders and settles back. "She ended up in LA with Dan's father. They never let Dan speak Spanish growing up—which is why his accent is so lousy. I think Evelyn taught him."

"Is she Hispanic?"

"Evelyn? Evelyn is everything." Frida laughs. "She's white. But she sees the world differently. Like she was born nowhere. Or everywhere. He and Evelyn started the clinic about fifteen years ago with money they raised in a bake sale."

Claire stops chewing and narrows her eyes. "A bake sale? You're kidding."

"I am not kidding. A bake sale and guilt. They twisted the arms of every rancher, orchardist, restaurant and hotel owner between here and the Canadian border—everybody who was making a profit on migrant labor—to put this clinic together. The other docs in town do a little pro bono, but the nearest state-run public clinic is seventy miles away. Across a pass that's closed half the winter." She lifts her shoulders once, as if that's the best she can do with the story in brief. "This clinic is Dan's *mission*."

"How big a donor is Ron Walker? I saw the plaque with his name."

"Big. The biggest. But others, too. And some grants. Dan gets another doc in now and then. But you have to do this job because you love it. And it's hard to keep working for love when you want to buy a house and have a few kids. Especially since land prices here have tripled."

Claire looks away; her eyes light on the skin of her own folded hands, turning red and chapped in this hard climate. She wonders if Frida is still trying to figure out what Claire is doing here. Frida leans over her crossed arms and scans Claire's flushed cheeks. "It's okay. You don't have to tell me how you landed here. Not that I wouldn't love to hear." She raises her eyebrows in a little wave with a conspiratorial smile on her face, like she is giving Claire an opportunity to do something good for herself she just hasn't tried yet. When Claire doesn't say anything Frida sits back again and shakes her head. "My mother always told me I should quit entertaining myself by messing with other people's minds."

Claire presses her lips together, then stretches them into a tepid smile. "I don't know. My mind might improve with some messing these days. And my own mom would probably agree." She takes a drink from her beer, enjoying the bite of it at the back of her throat. "It's not really that complicated," she says, then puts her glass down and rakes her hair back from her face, clenching her fingers into her scalp. She looks at Frida to gauge how much she is up for—the story seems so clear in her mind until she tries to track down the beginning. "Okay. That's a lie." She smiles and shakes her hair loose again. "It's actually very complicated. But the gist is that Addison is in research. Biopharm stuff. Twelve years ago he designed a blood test for ovarian cancer and started a small biotech company—Eugena."

"A blood test for cancer. So I could have, like, one poke, and find out if I have ovarian cancer?"

Claire nods. "One poke. Before it's ever metastasized. When surgery could cure you. It's still too expensive to be used as a screening test, but in a few years it might be part of a routine chemistry panel. It made the cover of *Newsweek*. Lots of hoopla. So, anyway. He sold Eugena two years later."

Frida settles back in her chair with her beer glass resting on her abdomen, clearly ready to hear as much as Claire is willing to tell. "Something tells me he sold it for a lot of money."

"Yeah." Claire smiles and raises her glass to her mouth, but puts it down again before she takes a sip. "Yeah. It was a lot. Kind of made it easy not to go back and finish my residency."

Frida waits through a minute of silence before she nudges Claire to go on. "And then?"

"And then we bought our land here, planning to build a new house. And then Addison came up with a *new* idea. A cancer drug. One of the VEGFR-2 drugs. Heard of them?"

Frida looks across the room as if the answer might magically appear on the specials board. "Vaguely. Fill me in."

They're antiangiogenesis drugs. They inhibit blood vessel growth in cancers, so they kill the cancer without killing all the other tissues. Cure you without all the horrible side effects. At least theoretically. Lots of promise in the lab but lots of disappointments in real patients. The usual."

"Don't tell me," Frida says, flagging the waitress for two more beers. "He figured out the problem nobody else saw."

Claire lets out half a sigh, half a laugh and lifts her chin. "He's a smart boy, my Addison. It was all the buzz." She starts in on her second beer, aware that this is the first time she has talked about vascumab, Addison's drug, with anyone other than him—inherently poisoned conversations that clarified nothing. Resolved nothing. Now, here, she could offer her own version. Uncontested. No broken web of trust tearing at every word.

"Out to save the world, huh?" Frida says.

Claire's face flinches briefly before she smiles again. "I guess if you're already rich and brilliant, you might as well save the world, too."

"So what happened?"

"He put the money he got for Eugena into a new lab. Brought other investors in, too." She scoots nearer the edge of her chair remembering the liquid flow of credit offered once Addison had assembled his stellar team. "It takes an unbelievable amount of money to design and produce a drug. Unbelievable. Half a billion dollars, easy. And the whole process—the designing, the applications, the testing—it's years before you earn a dime. And you're in a race against a dozen other labs working on the same class of drugs. It's a huge risk." Frida is listening with wide eyes, looks like she is either appreciative or entertained by Claire's passion on the subject. "But Addison wanted to fund it with a small group so he'd have more control. The goal was to prove the drug worked in early phase studies and license it to a big pharma company, let them carry it to market. Two companies were already talking to him. He hired some of the best people in the field—lured away the lead scientist from another lab in California that was working on a related drug. Everybody was given a share in the company—everybody stood to make a fortune if it succeeded." She pauses, considering where the line for libel could be drawn in a small town bar, in a conversation with a friend. "Anyway. They'd already applied to start the first tests in volunteers—phase one trials—when Addison discovered a possible liver reaction in some of the animals." She stops. It would take her the rest of the night to explain all the unanswered questions tangled in that single sentence. Now she wishes she'd cut the whole story to one line: "Some mice got sick and then we went broke."

"Well," she finally goes on, "I'll cut to the chase. He had to pull the application at the last minute." Frida seems to recognize Claire doesn't want to say much more; Frida's face looks softer, fuller, easing a fixed tension around her eyes that Claire hadn't noticed until right now.

"And you lost everything along with it," Frida says.

"He had some loans called. It got ugly pretty fast. And, well, there you go. Or here we are, I should say."

Frida smiles at this, but there is painful compassion behind it. "So we don't get a cure for cancer, then?"

Claire tilts her head to one side and tries to look optimistic. "He's hoping he can run the animal studies again. He thinks it was an error in the data. It really was a great idea. Or is. It really might save a lot of lives."

"So why would one error shut down the whole lab?"

Claire feels her smile stiffen again. "It wasn't so much the error itself. It was the way it was handled." She lifts her beer, hoping Frida will let her talk about something else now. "Onward and upward. Or backward. Didn't somebody once say 'Fading gentry is the leading edge of a revolution?'"

"I don't know, did they?"

"Well. They should have. So, cheers to the revolution." Claire raises her mug in a falsely gallant toast. "At least Dan gets another doctor out of it, assuming I'm more a help to him than a liability."

The bar is filling up, all the locals who've finished work, and gone home and finished dinner, now meeting up with friends. Someone catches Frida's eye and waves, then another. There seems to be a friendly acceptance of the general lack of anonymity in this town; it makes Claire aware that she hasn't crossed over yet. She feels Frida watching her and almost wishes she could have told her more. On the other hand, she thinks, there is no better place to find privacy than in anonymity.

· 13 ·

By the time Claire gets in her car it's after ten. Flakes of snow bat at her windshield. Out of the blue she remembers a cliché about Eskimos having thirteen different words for snow. That had never made any sense to her before they moved out here.

Addison is probably asleep by now. He has the kind of brain that can unwind right in the middle of *the* organic chemistry puzzle that just might tag the next decoded gene. Once, when they were hot-in-love-dating she had asked him what he was thinking about. Only a young woman would ask that of a man, she knows now. The question came at that stage when their bodies were almost electrically interdependent and there were few censored thoughts. But she wanted to hear about the never-shared part of himself—learn some secret that would irrevocably bind them. And she wanted him, too, to plead for her own secrets, because for every thought she voiced, a thousand more hummed under their conversation.

"Nothing," he had said. "I'm thinking nothing." At first she felt shut out, and then freshly inspired to make him trust the fortress this new love felt like. And then, long after he'd fallen asleep, she felt disappointment. Maybe his deepest interior was more a void than a universe. Either way, it was the first spark of understanding that even in this fathom of union, two people were still two people.

Now, after fifteen years of marriage, she understands that some of what Addison thinks is impossible to explain. At least in any comprehensible human language. She imagines it as infinitesimally small particles of blinding light zinging from one neuronal synapse to another, mapping out biochemical puzzles he didn't even know he was tackling.

She knows it leaves him feeling disconnected sometimes. Lonely even. Driving through the darkness with the windshield wipers flapping away at the snow, she plays with a vivid memory of Addison coming home from the lab well after midnight, years ago. Claire, half asleep, was hanging over the side of Jory's crib trying to keep a pacifier lodged in her squalling mouth. He'd walked into the room with such a vacant stare she'd been jolted back into the moment, worried he'd stumbled home after too many drinks or bashed his head in a car accident. She'd left Jory to go to him. "What's wrong? You look—I don't know—like you're in shock."

She could practically watch his brain shooting signals out to his tongue, trying to shape his insight into vocalized tones, his eyes scanning the horizon of the room and his mouth half a smile. Finally he'd gotten out the best he could: "Right now—until I go back to the lab tomorrow—I am the only person on the planet who knows what I've just discovered." He looked right at her then, and she could tell he wished there were some possible way to transfer what he was feeling to her own experience, because it was going to forever separate them. He was in a time and space that was transforming not just his life's work, but his whole perspective on the universe and his purpose within it—and he wanted to bring her with him. But that was impossible. Impossible. He took her hands in his own, gripped them right up against his chest. "Not just the only *living* person, I'm the only person ever. *Ever.*"

She remembers it all now, every detail of that night that she'd almost forgotten. The way he smelled like the rain, the blue light from the clock washing over his face in the dark room, the give of the bed as he lay her down, Jory now soundly sleeping. He turned the words he couldn't find into his body, moving and seeking and wanting and probing and penetrating in a way his mind would never be able to—the closest they could be.

They had made a baby that night, the first in a series of incomplete fusings of body and soul. She didn't know, when she lost that accidental life, that every future conscious, desperate try would fail, too; and so when the spotting had started, the cramping taken hold, she had cried, but not with the yawning despair that would come with the others. Every pregnancy that followed Jory was a celebration, even after they both learned they should protect their hearts. And every loss broke them wide open with grief. When Claire couldn't bear it anymore she'd had her tubes tied. But almost as hard as giving up her own hope was the fear that she had failed him somehow, that her uterus was too weak to create the family he wanted so badly. It was years before she realized her loss mattered more to him than his own.

She starts to cry with the memory of it—for the part of Addison she will *never* be able to know, and for the children that never got to breathe, and even for the fact that her body could not accomplish that miracle anymore.

His discovery in the lab that night had culminated in Eugena, and within a decade Eugena would most likely save a thousand lives. More.

The only light downstairs comes from the computer screen; the illuminated clutter and lingering odors give Claire a good guess about Addison and Jory's evening: the damp floor below their dripping coats and the piles of snowballs mounded in pyramids just beyond the porch, the monstrous box of CDs from Addison's car next to Jory's iPod, the smell of brownies. They have left one for her, neatly wrapped in plastic on a saucer—the only tidy thing in the house. She is at least appeased by their graciously sparing her a corner piece, and she could entertain herself believing they had left the pan out on the counter only so that she could scrape up the hard crumbs she is fond of. She fills it with hot water to soak and walks around the couch to turn off the computer.

"Hey. Have fun?" Addison rubs his hand over his face and props himself up on an elbow.

"Couldn't get her to give up the bed, huh?" Claire asks, sitting on the edge of the cushions.

"Not worth the struggle. The movers called. They'll be here day after tomorrow."

Claire nods. "The day you leave."

He is awake now; sitting up in his boxer shorts, he pulls the down throw around his bare shoulders. "I have to leave tomorrow. Early."

"You're kidding. What changed?"

"One of the people I want to meet with can only see me tomorrow afternoon."

She doesn't say anything for a while, both of them sitting side by side listening to the wind shake snow from the trees. Finally: "We haven't talked about much."

"Well, I guess nothing has really changed."

"Yeah," Claire answers wistfully, thinking that the problem was really that *everything* had changed, and that was more impossible to talk about than nothing. "Is this guy very promising, do you think?" Addison does a little dance with his shoulders, which tells her as much as she wants to know about it.

"Addison, do you remember Ron Walker? He hosted the fundraiser we went to at the Fairmont a few years ago. Where we bought the Galapagos trip. He's one of Dan's main backers."

"Really?" He shimmies his legs behind her to lie down again, pulling the comforter over his chest and wedging his pillow under his arm so he still looks half engaged with the conversation. His hair is spiked up at the crown of his head like a Steller's jay's crest; Claire licks her fingers and twists it down into a deep black widow's peak, laughing softly at the effect.

"I think you should talk to him," she says.

Addison shrugs. "I'm happy to talk to him. About what?"

"About money. Investing. What else?" She catches his mildly defensive look and picks up his hand. "He's a venture capitalist, Addison. Lots of biotech, among other things. He might be really interested in vascumab, especially now that I'm connected with the clinic—meaning *you're* connected with the clinic."

He takes his hand out of hers and sweeps his hair back off his forehead. "Claire, I can't just call him up out of the blue and . . ."

"It's not out of the blue. You've met him. I work at the clinic he sponsors. Isn't it worth a try?"

"Honey, I know it sounds simple, but I don't think you really understand how the business end of all this works."

Claire stands up, her voice clipped. "And you're implying you do?" She slaps both hands over her eyes and spins around once. "Okay." Her hands drop to her sides. "I am not going to do this. Look, I have to go to bed." She leans over and kisses him, hard and sure. "Wake me up before you leave. Drive safe."

"Claire," he calls after her as she heads upstairs. "Claire! At least listen to the good news."

She turns around with her hand on the banister and looks down at him, "Okay. What's the good news?"

"I got Jory enrolled in school. She's starting tomorrow. You'll need to drop her off at eight."

Claire feels her body relax, part of her brittle anger giving way. She whispers now, knowing Jory is just behind the bedroom door. "You got her to go? How?"

He lies back down and rolls onto his side. "Bribery. I got her a cell phone."

He does not wake her before he leaves, or if he has knelt at the side of her sleeping body and tried to kiss her awake, the thorny fortress held fast around her. When her alarm goes off she looks down the stairs at the empty couch, and then out the window where his car has left skidding tracks in the snow. But in the bathroom she finds a sticky note curling up from the mirror, printed in the childlike, blocky letters he's always preferred to script:

I'M SORRY
I LOVE YOU

She peels it off and reads it again, wondering if the forgotten period was completely unintentional.

If Jory is angry about school—or terrified, or excited—she isn't giving Claire a hint. She sits as far toward the passenger door as possible and opens it before the car is fully stopped, stepping into the stream of students wearing her UGGS and skinny jeans like she's been part of their circle since first grade. It is the fact that she will not meet Claire's eyes even when she turns to say good-bye that confirms she is scary-close to tears. It's all Claire can do not to call after her, deciding, after a wrenching flashback on her own high school experience, that the kindest thing to do is drive away.

A few snowflakes spiral onto the windshield. Claire looks up the number for the man who plows their drive and punches it in. "Hi, this is Claire Boehning, out on Northridge Road. A moving truck is coming to our house tomorrow with a load of furniture and I just want to be sure we can have the road plowed early if it snows tonight." She squints out at the sky, swollen white and still. "I heard we could get a foot or more, any update on that?"

There is a pause on the other end of the line. Then: "I apologize for this, Mrs. Boehning, but we need another check from you before we can come out."

"Can't you just send the bill after, like always?"

"Well . . ." He clears his throat. "Your last check to us didn't go through."

Claire pulls off the road and slides to a stop. "Didn't go through? Our check *bounced*?"

"Yes, ma'am."

"Well, can you take a credit card number over the phone?"

She hears him chuckle. "I'm sorry, ma'am, I don't have a credit card machine. Basically run this operation out of my house."

She stumbles for a reasonable excuse, assuring him she'll pay any bank fee and interest. Then she calls the moving company. They tell her if they don't deliver tomorrow they will not come for at least ten days. Last, she dials Addison's cell phone but hangs up before he answers. When "Layla" hums on the car seat next to her, she ignores it.

· 14 ·

Most of her patients are women. At first Claire presumes this just reflects the clinic's population, and it's true that more women seek out medical care, or carry sick babies and toddlers in by bus or on foot while their men stay in the orchards and canneries. But after the first few weeks she starts to get it: the men would rather wait for Dan than see her. They catch Dan's eye when he passes through the waiting room, raise their hats and graciously offer their position in line to the female in the adjacent chair when Claire calls out for the next patient. Thus her swelling Spanish vocabulary grows with a feminine shape, plush with words of reproduction and cyclic rhythms, punctured with the language of domestic strife and subservience.

Often the first five minutes of each visit dispenses with the reported complaint on the intake form, and the next half hour is spent teasing out the irritating boyfriend from the abuser, the discontented adolescent from the dangerously depressed, the voluntary undocumented worker from the enslaved. The stories they are slowest to tell are the hardest to hear; the men tell them through scars—machete wounds and bullet fragments and calcified fractures on X-rays. But the women's stories are often invisible—pelvic pain with no organic cause, too many pregnancies for so few surviving children, personal questions hastily diverted and difficult subjects changed.

Patients' charts are now stacked a foot deep on her desk, most of them labeled with Spanish surnames Claire's accent still cuts sharp corners into, the graceful curls of Ulribe and Flores, Aranda and Osario. She keeps a sheet of notebook paper folded inside the dictionary Frida gave her, jots down unusual words, some because they are hard to remember and some simply because they are beautiful to her: *alborozar, pensamiento, incertidumbre.*

Dan, Frida and Anita try to shunt the most straightforward complaints and the best English speakers to Claire, but she still slows the day down. She has to ask Dan for help with any specialist referral—she doesn't know any of the orthopedists or ophthalmologists or general surgeons in the valley. A list of county doctors is pinned to the bulletin board above her desk, but there is an unwritten code of pleading and negotiating to win the few slots they can afford to donate. She has to catch Dan between his own patients to help her sort through the pills and potions brought up from Mexico or Honduras or Guatemala, purchased in *tiendas* or *farmacias* on the advice of lay healers and grandmothers. Often they are drugs no one's used in the United States for a decade or more. Her patients come from a place where doctors are rare and illness is common, where purified and illicit drugs alike pass through poorly regulated channels, and cures might be sought in the roots of plants or the bark of trees, the dung of cows or the fangs of snakes.

By six o'clock she has seen twelve patients and Dan has seen twenty-two. Frida is already standing by the back door with her coat on. Dan comes out of the last patient's room and disappears into the storage closet, emerges a few minutes later with two pairs of metal forearm crutches in different heights. He sees Claire and asks her to follow him.

Jorge Iglesia, a man of twenty or so, is sitting in the chair. He stands when Claire comes into the room, gripping the side of the exam table to pull himself upright. His left leg stops just below the knee. Dan has him try out the crutches and adjusts the height of the pair with the closest fit. He introduces Claire as "the new lady doctor" and asks the man to show her his shoulders. Jorge unbuttons his shirt with an embarrassed smile and turns around, rotates both arms in front of him and then extends them fully out to each side, tensing the muscles in his back. His left scapula flares away from the spine like a broken wing.

Dan thanks him and hands him his shirt. "What's your diagnosis, Dr. Boehning?"

"It's a winged scapula," Claire answers. "Isn't it?"

"Remember the cause?"

She cocks her head for a minute. "He's damaged his long thoracic nerve. The crutches, probably."

Dan smiles like he's been teasing her with this spontaneous quiz, but she also spots, maybe, a hint of pride in the set of his mouth. It passes quickly enough but suddenly she feels a little less overwhelmed.

Dan picks up a worn-out pair of crude wooden crutches from the floor. "He found these at a Salvation Army store but never got them fitted right."

After Jorge leaves Claire asks Dan how he lost his leg.

"Tried to jump a train coming up through Nogales and fell under the wheels. A Border Angel found him and took him to a hospital."

Claire is speechless for a moment. "Someone found him in the middle of the desert before he died? That's incredible. What are the odds on that?"

Dan nods and studies the toe of his boot. "Yeah. Lucky. Not too likely to find work here as an amputee, so he'll be back in Mexico soon. But he's not too likely to find work there, either." After a solemn pause he looks at Claire and shrugs his shoulders.

As much as Claire had resisted letting Jory get a cell phone, she's called her on it six times in the last two days. Yesterday, Jory's first day of school, Claire left work early to be there when the students were let out. But it's clear that is an impossible daily commitment, and equally clear that Jory would walk home through a blizzard before she would take the school bus. Today, they struck a deal. Jory would walk into Hallum and do her homework at the bakery until Claire could pick her up, though when Claire looks at her watch and the pile of work on her desk it's clearly magical thinking to say she can be at the bakery before it closes. She calls Jory again.

"Hey, sweetie, how did it go?" She inflects her voice with all the time in the world, as if her whole day has been on pause until she returned to motherhood.

There is a moment of empty space before Jory says, "Hmm. Okay." Claire listens hard to those three syllables, cupping the receiver against her ear with the palm of her hand wishing some trapped echo might tell her what Jory means.

"Well, that's great! Second day! It'll get easier and easier after this." Jory is stone silent now, leaving Claire's upbeat words bouncing alone between Hallum and some orbiting satellite. She tones it down. "I'm running a little late. How about you walk over to the grocery store and pick out something you want for dinner. I'll call and give them a credit card number."

"It's dark."

"Honey, the store is just across the street. I'll be there in half an hour. Buy a treat for yourself, too." Little more than breath comes back to Claire through the phone. "Please?" She hears Jory mumble something. "I'll be there as soon as I can. Promise."

She makes notes on her last two patients but accomplishes little else, pushing her chair away from the desk to survey the chaos. Dan and Frida seem to thrive on it—or at least stay unflustered. Dan runs the clinic no differently than medicine functioned when he was in his own residency—handwriting all the notes, the only computer so old it chews up more time than it saves. She pulls open a filing drawer and flips through journal articles and pharmaceutical brochures that are so out-of-date they are useless, if not dangerous. Whoever replaces her here, once Addison is back at work, should have a talent for organizing as much as for healing. Maybe that is the gift she can leave them—hire some young doctor who's energetic and fresh, who speaks Spanish and knows how to set up computer transcription and spreadsheets. One who can live on a shoestring. And is board certified.

She flicks off the overhead light and is zipping her coat when she hears a knock on the gate between the hallway and waiting room. Anita, probably, though the bigger she grows the more often she leaves on time, and more than once has scolded Claire (at least it felt like a scolding) that she'll be no good to anyone, in the clinic or at her own house, if she burns out quick as a match.

But it is not Anita. It's a patient. With a surge of both sympathy and impatience Claire imagines asking someone who's already waited this long to go home, imagines Jory watching the grocery's door for her rescue. As soon as the gate swings shut, though, she recognizes the petite shape in the nylon ski cap and the jacket that Addison wore to Huskies football games twenty years ago.

"Hello! *Buenas noches! ¿Su amiga está aquí, tambien?*" Claire looks around the room for the girl who had been with her at the last visit.

"*No. Ella esta mejor ahora.* Better now. I speak some English, okay?"

"Of course. I'm sorry. I can't remember your name?" Claire raises her tone at the end of the sentence, a question of translation more than content.

"Miguela Ruiz."

"Ruiz. Miguela." Claire's repetition overlaps Miguela's introduction, making them both laugh, making it a little easier to stand in this empty building, in this half-lit room.

Miguela lifts her hand in a gesture toward Claire's coat. "You are going home?"

"Well"—Claire glances over her shoulder at the dark hallway leading to the exam rooms—"we're closed. *Cerrado.*"

"*Cerrrrrrado.*" Miguela moves her tongue exaggeratedly against her front teeth, clarifying the sound that has no equal in English. Then she smiles, her lovely brows lifting.

"I can't examine you now, with no one else here, but if there is a problem . . ." Claire sees a puzzled look flicker across Miguela's face and repeats it all slowly.

"Ah! No. I am not sick." She takes her cap off and shakes her head, heavy black waves of her hair fall loose over her face and she combs them back with splayed fingers, a gesture Claire can tell is part of her physical language, as unconscious as breathing. "I came for a job. To work for you."

"For me? Here? Doing what?" Claire is tempted to turn around and look for anyone else Miguela could be referring to. The note of perplexity in her voice sparks an embarrassed look on Miguela's face; her dark eyes pull back a little. "I didn't mean . . ."

"No, no. I am sorry." Miguela shrugs Addison's jacket higher on her narrow shoulders. "Thank you."

She turns to go and Claire reaches out to stop her, brushing against Miguela's fingertips before settling on the rolled-up sleeve of her own husband's coat. "Señora Ruiz, what kind of job do you want? I can talk to Dr. Zelaya tomorrow. What work do you do?"

Miguela shrugs but doesn't move to pull her arm away. "Cleaning. Washing. Anything you need." She smiles at Claire, forgiving any awkwardness. "It's okay. I will come another day." She leaves then, with a small wave through the glass panes after the door swings shut behind her.

Claire starts to lock the door after her but opens it again and leans out, "Miguela, I'll talk to him. Okay? Come by in a few days. You never know."

Jory is standing outside the grocery store stamping from one foot to the other in a manner guaranteed to make Claire feel guilty. "Why didn't you wait inside the doors?"

"Why didn't you get here when you said you would?" She dumps the grocery bag and her backpack in the rear seat and climbs into the car, cupping her hands in front of the heat vent. Claire gives her a minute to declare her mood, which turns out to be more conversant than her frigid glare had implied from the curb. "They have crappy food at this school."

"Don't say *crap*, please."

"Okay. Shitty food." She shoots her mother a schmaltzy smile and laughs. "I'm kidding, Mom. Not about the food, though. Fried cheese sticks?"

Claire pulls onto the highway with a glance at her daughter's profile. "So, tell me something good about the school."

Jory lifts a shoulder and stares at the road. But after a minute she says, "There're some okay people, I guess." And then, harshly: "God, Mom, watch out for that guy on the road!"

Claire focuses through the snow looking for headlights and then spots the red plaid jacket walking between the dark track of wheels and the wall of plowed snow that obliterates any shoulder. She turns the wheel to the right and the car shimmies and slides when it crosses the frozen stripe down the middle of the lane, stopping with the front tire scythed up onto the churned white waste. Jory's hand braces against the dashboard and she stares at her mother openmouthed when Claire gets out of the car and calls out to the figure picking her way across the broken blocks of compacted snow.

"Señora Ruiz?"

After a mix of confused Spanish and English Claire persuades her to get into the backseat. They are quiet while Claire rocks the car forward and back until it catches friction and rolls safely into tracks of bare pavement. She's getting better at driving in the snow, she thinks, developing an instinct for the way the car will respond in the myriad concoctions of water that cover the roads and change by the hour. Claire feels Jory's eyes flashing on her, checking for some sign as to who this woman in the vaguely familiar jacket is.

"Where do you live?" Claire asks, glancing at Miguela's face in the rearview mirror.

"The orchard. Walker's Orchards."

Claire turns around for a moment to face Miguela. "You're working at the orchard? What kind of work do they have you doing in winter?"

"I clean—the offices, the house." She falls quiet again, stares out at the snow. After a moment she asks, "Your child is here?"

Claire introduces Jory, who gives Miguela a quick, shy smile before she unleashes a raft of hair from behind her ear so it falls over her face. Miguela slips toward the middle of the seat and leans forward, patting the backpack on the cushion beside her. "You are in school? You must study very much." Jory doesn't answer this but Claire sees her tuck her chin deeper in the collar of her coat. "I am a teacher. I *was* a teacher. Before I am here."

"A teacher?" Claire asks. She is caught off guard by this. Teachers, shopkeepers, secretaries—these, the tiny, emerging middle class of the developing Latin world, did not come to the United States to work.

The laborers came, the carpenters and field pickers, the waitresses and laundresses and factory workers who were the cheap and renewable engine of goods and services for the 10 percent who lived in luxury. Their poverty was so endemic, so unrelenting they were willing to be smuggled in the trunks of cars or nailed into shipping containers or herded across deserts by some minion at the bottom of a cartel, whose only motivation to keep them alive was full payment on delivery. "Where are you from?"

"Nicaragua. Near Jalapa. In the mountains."

Claire focuses on the road as she slows for an oversized pickup approaching from the other direction, the oncoming lights blinding after miles of uninterrupted winter darkness, a spray of slush spattering her door. "How did you end up in Hallum?" She scans for Miguela's face in the rearview mirror when she doesn't answer, sees her looking at Jory. *Contemplating* is more the word that comes to mind. Jory's blond hair often caught the eye of people for whom such a thing was rare.

"I followed a person," Miguela finally says. "What do you study?" She leans farther forward as if that might persuade Jory to turn toward her and sweep her hair back, reveal her whole beautiful face. Miguela's accent, now that Claire pays attention to it, is different from that of her Mexican patients. Something in the way she drops her *s*'s.

Jory looks across the front seat at her mother, as if she needs permission to talk to this woman in the back of their car, rescued off the side of the road from a frigid winter night. "I'm in ninth grade." Claire smiles at her and Jory goes on to list her classes, even volunteering an opinion about her math teacher—more than she has told her mother to date.

Claire is almost embarrassed to acknowledge how little she knows about Nicaragua. If she had to find it on a map it would take a while, sorting out Panama and El Salvador and Honduras and Guatemala— the blur of countries between Mexico and South America that always seemed to be starting or ending a revolution. "I didn't know anyone from Nicaragua was living in the valley," Claire says. But, really, there could be a whole orchard full of Nicaraguans living in Hallum. How would she know? Jory has been gradually angling her shoulders around so she is half facing Miguela; she whispers something, then clears her throat and says it louder. Through a whip of hair pulled across her mouth like a veil she asks Miguela why she had become a teacher.

Her father had been a teacher, Miguela explains—and so, of course, he joined the revolution when Pedro Chamorro was murdered. She pauses before going on; Claire imagines Miguela waiting to hear, *"Oh, yes, I knew that many Nicaraguan teachers had joined the revolution,"* or, *"Oh, yes, Chamorro."*

"Did your father speak English?" Claire asks her.

"A little. He died when I was a small girl. But he showed me to read." She rests her hand near Jory's on the seat back between them. "Do you like poetry?" She waits for an answer. Jory looks at her mother, either for reassurance or even, perhaps, the answer—Claire can't see her eyes. Miguela laughs softly. "All Nicaraguans are poets. Even the presidents!"

Before Claire can comment Miguela points out a speckle of light on the hills above them. "There, the orchard. I will walk now."

"No, no. Way too cold for that," Claire says. She slows enough to pick out the unlit driveway cut through the bank of snow; the tires slip once then grip and carry them up to the house and cabins.

"Your father is dead?" Jory asks. Claire shoots a look at her, but Jory is staring at Miguela.

"In the war. He was in the school and a contra bomb . . ." She claps her hands and flutters her fingers in the air in lieu of the word. "When I am twelve."

Claire can feel Jory turning this around in her narrow world, scanning for some similarity in her safely padded life. A few divorces had already occurred, one errant girl sent off to a boarding school. The first time she'd seen a homeless man she had listened intently to Claire's gentle explanation and, after a moment of consideration, asked if that meant he had to eat in restaurants every single night.

"Here. Here is good." Miguela points to the nearest in a row of identical white cabins backed up along the driveway. No lights are on in any of them. Claire reverses the car so the headlamps shine through the narrow corridor between the first two, waits for Miguela to wave her away.

Walker's employee housing is better than most; anyone would agree with that. Anyone who gives a second glance at these particular pickers' cabins, strung across the hillside below his orchards like a train of boxcars. The first time they'd driven through the valley, when Jory was quite young, she'd delighted in the idea that some farmer with many children had built playhouses for each daughter, with curtained windows and front doors with real metal knobs and latches. She had spotted one with a green painted flower box not far outside of Wenatchee, and every trip she would turn off her movie and hover at the car window looking for that particular house, checking to see if the flowers appeared tended and watered. She had made up a name for the girl who played there, Aurora, and could spot any change to her cottage—a curtain left half open, a single jelly sandal forgotten by the door.

Claire loved hearing Jory intensify this imaginary friendship every time they passed the cabin. When she was driving, Claire would slow the car down and look for signs of life, almost believing in Aurora as vividly as Jory did. But the houses were always abandoned, the work being seasonal and the migrants only there to sleep between the long hours of pruning and harvesting.

Thinking about it now, she couldn't remember ever telling Jory the truth—explaining the purpose of the clapboard shacks, their economic role in an agrarian community. Of course, Jory knows all that by now, but Claire has never asked where or how she learned—when she had finally given up and transfigured the child Aurora into the adult Jose, or Gabriel, or Manuel.

After Miguela is out of sight and they are back on the highway, Jory asks, "Where exactly is Nicaragua?"

· 15 ·

The moving truck finally arrives on Saturday, pulling down a driveway freshly plowed thanks to a cashier's check carved off Claire's first earned salary in fourteen and a half years.

It feels like Christmas—like the Christmas that was virtually canceled when they sold their house. Addison had stonewalled the buyer about the holiday, maybe because it was the last thing he felt he could still control. "We gave up half a million dollars to these people. I will not give them my Christmas on top of it," he fumed, venting to Claire until she could only sit and watch him pace, watch him funnel his rage—every cursing word of blame he'd held in check when he'd faced the review board and sacrificed his dream drug—onto this one symbolic day of peace.

The buyers threatened to walk until he galled them into silence with a week of exorbitant rent so that his own family, Jory and Claire and he, could sleep on air mattresses and open their few presents in the middle of a bare living room. The house had looked enormous after the movers took the last of their furniture away. The blank walls echoed, the floor danced with floating ghosts of dust and hair; only the lit-up Christmas tree held any cheer—not even that, it was just a little less sad than the cheerless, vacant space that now belonged to another family.

Jory watches the truck turn around and back up to the door, stomping her feet against the cold while the drivers unlock the metal doors. She looks truly excited for the first time in a month; as if she is waiting to find her life inside there, hoping that the enormous van will disgorge everything she's missed along with her white and blue bedroom furniture, then swallow up her loneliness and haul it away to some distant state, some other kid's misfortune.

Despite all they have sold or put in storage the room is too crowded once the van is unloaded. Their contemporary furniture looks ridiculous in this old farmhouse, if Claire is honest with herself. She sits on the arm of Addison's leather recliner, which they'd discovered on a trip to England—the shipping cost had almost exactly equaled what she earned in a month at the clinic. Every wall is lined with stacked boxes; the dining table and kitchen counters are buried under crates of things they have no space for. She should have left half of it behind.

She gets up and peels the plastic tape off a cardboard container—kitchen items: a fruit dehydrator, a pasta press, an espresso machine; a set of Christmas dishes she'd ordered from Denmark and never used. She sinks down into the oversized chair and wraps herself up in a silk and wool throw that had perfectly matched the wallpaper in their library. The fabric and leather, even the tang of forged metal bracing, exude an odor of home—the scent of a place that is still identified in her mind when she speaks the word, *home.* Maybe, in time, in patience, it will seep into the plaster and paint and wood of this house. Or the next house. The house they will reward themselves with when this is over. So she will *make* this Christmas, of a sort. It surprises both Jory and her that such familiar items can feel so new after five weeks of eating and sitting on garage sale castoffs. The last thing the movers lower from the truck is a jaggedly cut slab of concrete, which Claire tells them to put at the bottom of the porch steps.

"What is that, Mom?"

"Your footprints. From when you were five and we had the new patio laid in the garden."

Jory stares at them for a contemplative moment. "Does Dad know you chopped a hole in the patio before the new people moved in?"

"I'm sure they'd rather have their own kid's footprints in their cement."

As soon as the movers have wrangled her bed frame and dresser up to her room Jory hunts down clean sheets and pillowcases, sweeps the pine floor twice before she unrolls her rug. Claire carries a box of Jory's summer shorts and swimsuits upstairs and Jory looks almost embarrassed to be caught arranging books and various kitsch collected from fairs and parties, investing her heart in this room, this still-opposed home.

"It looks nice in here! Your furniture fits pretty well, don't you think?" Claire says, but she feels a catch in her chest remembering Jory's window seat overlooking Lake Washington. Claire had painted the walls with blue and white flowers and yellow kites, hung a sheer curtain over the opening so Jory could hide in her own safe, secret world.

"Do we have any window cleaner?" Jory asks.

Claire stifles her amazement. "Sure, under the kitchen sink. Don't use all the newspaper, we need it for the stove." She swings the closet door open with her foot and drops the packing box on the floor.

Jory lets out a small cry. "Wait . . ." At the same moment Claire notices a plastic storage box in the corner of the closet. She pulls the chain on the overhead lightbulb; the top of the container is pierced with dime-sized holes. The sour smell hits her the second she pries off the lid. "Jory! How long has this been here? You can't keep a mouse as a house pet! What? Did you rescue it from the Havahart? What were you thinking?" Her voice heats into a white anger, igniting every retort she has stifled in the last weeks. Jory feels it, is already crouched on the other side of the large box, grabs the rim as if her mother would destroy the small, terrified creature cowering in a mound of shredded flannel. Claire stands up and Jory's fierce grip jerks the container hard enough to flip it onto its side, jar lids of water spill across the floor and the mouse disappears under the door in a flash of fur.

Claire looks at the filth of wet rags and food and excrement and, suddenly, the task of cleaning it up seems as monumental as unpacking every box downstairs, or heating this freezing, desolate house, or stretching her paycheck from today until Addison announces he has signed with Novartis or Bristol-Myers Squibb. She sinks onto the floor and braces her back against the wall, staring at the upended bin.

The room splinters with silence after their altercation. Then Jory

heaves one single, pleading sob. "I was lonely. I was just . . . lonely."
Claire reaches over and takes her hand, pulls Jory to her chest and waits
for the earth to settle.

She stays up past two in the morning clearing a path to the refrigerator,
poking through random boxes and listening to cassette tapes on an old
Sony Walkman that had miraculously escaped the trash pile. She makes
a cup of hot chocolate and spikes it with peppermint schnapps, loses it
in the forest of boxes and finds it again, multiple times.

Their Seattle house had started life as a 1960s rambler on an·over-
sized lakefront lot; it came on the market only months after Addison
sold Eugena. By then it was dwarfed by the new, hotel-sized homes on
either side of it, smaller than their neighbors' garages. Addison and
Claire were still too flush with the shock of unanticipated wealth to
buy anything ostentatious, anything that didn't demand sweat equity.
They had agreed they would go slowly, cosmetic fixes only until Addison could get his next blood test to market. Claire would eventually
finish her residency and take her boards, as soon as Jory started all-day
school, so she could bring in at least a part-time salary. And the house
was sweet in its humble, squat proportions, Claire thought. The three
of them could move about the low-ceilinged rooms with enough personal space to breathe and grow and create, but still sense, always, the
other two. Room for independence without isolation, privacy without
secrets.

They painted the shingles, put a swing set in the fenced yard and
moved in on July fifth, the first official day of Seattle sunshine. But by
early winter the drafty windows and warped doors and claustrophobic
kitchen were getting to them. Addison said they were heating half of
Lake Washington. They might as well invest in a sound structure. And
by early spring the stock they'd collected in exchange for Addison's biotech start-up had split and risen and split again. They started to feel
safe. They started to notice their neighbors had all gotten newer cars
and taken more exotic vacations and built new additions onto their
already massive homes. They started to spend.

They hired an architect. Claire collected file drawers full of magazine pages and tile samples and paint chips. Their dinner talk lingered over notions of how a house can affect productivity and mood, how space and light can transform the language of private life. As the stock rose and split and split again they luxuriated in unfettered choices about windows and ceiling heights, curved walls and arched doorways—stone and plaster and wood made intimate, plotted out in blueprints and billed by the hour. Jory had been only four at the time, but they'd bought Lego sets and doll furniture and encouraged her to build the bedrooms and play spaces and closets of her fantasies while the architect took notes. They ended up taking the house down to the studs. The whole remodel took two years and cost more than any new house in the neighborhood. And now it was owned by someone else.

On the last night before the movers came to haul their belongings away, with boxes stacked so high the house looked like a cubist representation of family memory, Claire had walked out onto the dock that jutted into Lake Washington from their stone retaining wall. She stood under the cold, fixed stars and listened to the silence, felt the cold, damp air, as fresh as any wilderness lake. She had promised herself, when they'd moved in, that she would do this every night— take ten minutes, five minutes, two minutes, to walk from her warm house onto the dock, taste and smell the water and sky that she had paid millions of dollars to "own." She tried to remember the last time she had opened the doors to the porch after dinner, stood suspended above the lake and looked into its black mirror for falling stars. It had been years.

She hunts down her hot chocolate one final time—gone cold with a skin of milk floating like an island in a brown pond. The kitchen sink is still hidden under boxes; she walks out the front door and steps barefooted into the snow, taking a queer pleasure in the stinging cold. There is no lake at this house, no dock to allow her to walk over the water. But there are stars, even more brilliant in the middle of winter, in the middle of nowhere. She cranks her neck back and searches for the north star. The cassette tape hisses between songs and then Joni Mitchell is singing, *"Still I sent up my prayer/Wonder-*

ing who was there to hear/I said "Send me somebody/Who's strong and somewhat sincere."'

She listens until her feet hurt too much to stand it any longer, and flings the contents of her mug across the snow. Then she pulls her arm all the way across her body and hurls the cup out as hard as she can, hearing no sound when it sinks into the snow.

· 16 ·

"How is Gretta?" Jory asks from the backseat. She is dancing a small hand mirror in front of her face trying to put mascara on as the car jounces up the rough driveway.

"If you want me to drive you, you need to get up on time. You're going to put your eye out with that thing." Then, with a sharp glance over her shoulder: "She's fine. What makes you ask?"

"I heard you talking to her last night." Jory snaps the compact shut and stuffs it in her backpack. "It's a small house."

A truck loaded with cattle is grinding up the long hill at the junction with the main road, the animals calling out in low, plaintive wails. Claire clears her throat. "She sends her love." Then, after a pause: "What did you overhear?"

"Mainly you promising we'd be back in Seattle soon. So am I meeting you at the bakery again? You'll get there before they close tonight?"

"I'll try, babe. I think we need to split the week, half on the bus, half I drive you." She waits but Jory is staring out the window, silent until they reach the school. "You know, you could take a friend with you—to the bakery or home in the afternoon. I could drive them back to town after dinner."

Jory hikes her backpack onto her shoulder and unlatches the door. "Yeah. Well. We're just moving again. Aren't we." She pauses with the door cracked open, looking at the crowd of kids through the fogged window. Claire turns toward her, sees her glossed lips tense for half a second before she steps out. "Love ya, Mom."

It distresses Claire that Gretta is the only example of a grandparent Jory will clearly remember. Her love is genuine enough, but it is, somehow, always . . . *waiting*. Waiting for the best moment to show itself. Waiting until times are better. Claire's father had tried to explain his leaving with many words, all forgiving and hopeful and reassuring. But it was a single sentence about Gretta in his very last letter to Claire that finally caught it: "She's worn a rut of worry in her mind so deep and comfortable she doesn't know how to be happy anymore. Nothing's ever good enough."

Anita is finishing her coffee when Claire slips in the back door. "Frida's looking for you. Waiting room's already packed. Drink up quick." She rinses her cup and pours one for Claire but pauses with the coffee suspended between them. "You okay?"

"Yeah. Just . . . a teenager."

She studies Claire's face, maybe assessing how much consoling is needed, balancing it against the schedule. "Like they say, toddlers step on your feet. But teenagers, they step on your heart. Dan wants to see you before you start—back room."

The door to the urgent care room is half closed; Claire hears Dan talking with another man, a conversation interrupted at moments by a soft laugh, and the voice of a woman, too, all in the rising tones of friendship more than business. She raps on the wood and steps in.

"Hey! There she is." Dan leans forward to push himself up from his chair, an arrested instant as he transfers his weight that makes Claire wish she could see his face, want to grasp his arm. And then he is introducing her, though she could have guessed who both people are.

Evelyn Zalaya looks like her name, tall and lithe, like her body has never gotten in its own way; a narrow, slightly arched nose and finely wrinkled skin that must have been flawless in her youth. Her eyes are a clear, unflinching blue. She must have heard a lot from Dan already; she holds Claire's hands as if she's known her for months, asking about Jory and Addison and the old house.

The man with them is Ron Walker. He'd been in a tux when Claire had met him at the fund-raiser, of course, and even then she could tell that he was not a formal man, uncomfortable in his starched collar and stiff patent leather shoes, as if maybe he had dressed up only to earn more money for the cause. It had made her feel at ease with him, and the wrinkled khakis and somewhat ratty sweatshirt he's wearing today make him look more like a patient than a donor. He takes her hand, loosely at first, with a question that she sees catch and connect the second he places her, then grips with a firm shake until the bite of his ring pinches. He is taller and thinner even than Dan, but with a soft fullness to his ruddy face, a dense, glowing web of veins over his cheeks and bulbous nose that gives him a perpetually happy look—which could be a hindrance or a convenient ruse in locking up a business deal, Claire decides.

"Boehning, Boehning. Eugena, right? Addison Boehning—went to Harvard before he came back for his doctorate."

"How do you remember that?" Claire asks.

Walker breaks into a wide grin. "I remember the *Newsweek* article. I like talent." He focuses more closely on her then, like he's separating Claire from his memory of her husband. "How'd we get lucky enough to hook you up with Dan here?"

Claire flushes at this, her ease abruptly discomfited by a scramble to explain why she is now in Hallum as a resident instead of a tourist. She feels Dan watching her and he taps Walker on the arm. "That phone call you made hit a gold mine, by the way. Got enough antibiotics to purify the whole valley. Come take a look." He escorts them all into the tiny pharmacy where unopened boxes of sulfonamides, penicillins and cephalosporins are stacked high enough to block the window, and, after some general talk about the clinic and a suggestion for dinner together, Claire slips away, back to the packed exam rooms.

The hallway is filled with green flags, needy people in disposable paper gowns hoping for experienced advice. Claire looks at the charts propped in clear plastic bins beside each room, wondering if the thickest, most frayed folders would be harder because they are stuffed with recurrent illness and unsolved complaints or easier because the pa-

tient might speak English. Frida walks in from the waiting room, the
swinging gate whapping against the wall with her determined stride.
She takes one look at Claire's face and says, "Start in two. White girl,
first time here. I brought a spinach lasagna for lunch." Then, under her
breath: "Sick of damn peanut butter."

The girl is eighteen. She sits on the edge of the exam table fully
dressed in clothes that are a size too small, wearing pancake makeup
so thick it's impossible to judge the natural color of her skin. Her eyes
are ringed with black liner; Claire focuses on the play of light reflect-
ing in her iris and pupil, trying to read her reaction to Claire's greeting,
to her white coat. It takes twenty minutes of oblique questions about
vague complaints—headaches and dizziness and fatigue—to maneuver
the girl into saying why she's here, allow Claire to touch her body and
see what's hidden.

By the time Claire finishes her exam and steps into the hall they
are so far behind the waiting room has run out of chairs. She pulls Dan
into the office and shuts the door. "I don't know if I should call the police? Or send her to a women's shelter?"

"The nearest women's shelter is two hours away. The police won't
touch the boyfriend unless she wants to press charges." He takes a
folder out of the file cabinet and hands Claire a page with two names
and addresses typed on it. "These are the counselors in the valley
who'll see her for free, but good luck getting an appointment this
month. Or next."

Frida comes into the office, looks at the names in Claire's hands
and says, "I figured—soon as I saw her. Tell it to me." She drops a stack
of lab slips on her desk and listens with her arms crossed and her head
bowed, then takes the piece of paper, scans it quickly and gives it back.
"Too young for Medicare, too rich for Medicaid, too broke for Blue
Cross. Totally sucks." She walks out to get the next patient ready, but
stops with her hand gripping the doorjamb, turns to look at Claire with
her lips in a set line over her bold white teeth. "Get her to make a regular appointment with you. Keep her talking." She looks uncharacteristically depressed by the girl's plight, even though Claire knows she's seen
the same or worse a dozen times—like she's as sad for Claire as for the

girl herself. "You're not going to save them all. You know that, don't you?" She tilts her head slightly to the side when she asks this, letting Claire understand it is not a rhetorical question, that she will wait here until she gets a response.

By the close of the day her feet are aching but she has nearly kept up with Dan, thanks to a run of bilingual patients. She finds him sitting at the table in the urgent care room, bent over his knees so the ripple of his spine shows through his thin shirt. He looks up when she comes in, maybe just startled, but she sees a glint of discomfort before he changes his face for her. "Hey," she says. "Everything all right?"

He smiles. "Old age. Things start to hurt. Put it off—that's my advice."

Claire laughs. "Yeah. I'll do my best." She sits next to him and leans on her elbow, holding his eyes long enough to test him. "You're sure? You'd let me know if you needed anything, wouldn't you?"

"You're doing it. You're here." But now it is his turn to test, and she finds it hard not to look away. He puts his hand over hers with a sound of dry leaves. "Just give what you can. While you can. That's what I need."

Frida raps on the office door and hands Claire another chart with a blank progress note page in it. "Hey. Last one—that lady who only comes in before we're open or after we're closed. Only wanted to see you. Room two."

The mild irritation Claire feels at having to interview even one more person disappears when she sees Miguela sitting on the end of the exam table. "Hello! I was thinking about you the other day—something on the news about Nicaragua. Did you find any other work? Outside of Walker's Orchards?"

Miguela looks puzzled and holds her thumb and first finger up an inch apart, as she had done the night Claire first saw her outside the grocery store. "*Más despacio, por favor.* Slower."

Claire tries her Spanish. "*¿Encontrado trabajo?*" Miguela shakes her head, but Claire can't tell if she's referring to the work or the words. She decides to start fresh, doctor to patient. "*¿Cómo puedo ayudar?*"

"Ha *encontrado*," Miguela gives her a clear, encouraging smile. Her teacher's smile, Claire imagines. "*Es más correcto.* A better way to say." They finally settle into a mix of slow, clearly pronounced Spanish and English, a blend and rhythm that works for both.

She has come with a variety of complaints—a sore throat, a mild stomachache, a cough, blurry vision. Claire's questions only bring up more disparate symptoms instead of narrowing the possibilities down, until she finally asks when Miguela last had a complete physical exam. "*Todo? Nunca.* Never." She shakes her head, raising her eyebrows as if to express that even visiting a doctor could be considered a luxury. Claire is struck, again, by the sweep of her brows, the large, almond-shaped eyes—so disproportionate within her otherwise diminutive features they verge on anomalous, but instead combine to a strangely distinctive beauty. There is something else there, too. Something irrevocable and determined behind the lush lashes, the rich brown irises. The thought flashes through her mind that Miguela is a woman rarely surprised by life anymore, or—worse maybe—beyond disappointment. Like she has no more trust to let go of.

"Well," Claire says, after a moment's pause. "Why don't we do that today?"

She runs through the long list of standard questions that builds a record of a patient's physical life: when Miguela was born, her child-hood illnesses and immunizations, when she began menstruating and with what regularity, how many pregnancies she has had and how many children borne. A list of injuries and surgeries and broken limbs, eating and exercise habits, allergies and medications. And throughout, Claire laces in questions about Miguela's parents and siblings and partners, her schooling and jobs and interests, almost forgetting the late hour of the day, forgetting that Frida and Jory are both waiting.

Then she begins the physical exam, starting at Miguela's head and gradually moving down, studying her body in systematic sections—the texture of her hair, the clarity of her lenses and reactions of her pupils, the pearly surfaces of her eardrums, the size of her thyroid gland and the hollows of her neck. Her throat is slightly erythematous—probably a minor virus. Claire listens to the sounds of her heart and pounds her fist down Miguela's spinal column and over her kidneys. She looks at her nail beds and skin and the straight, true lines of her long bones. She helps Miguela lie flat on the table with her knees slightly bent and presses gently on her abdomen, hunting for the edge of a swollen liver or spleen. Then Claire asks her to wait while she gets Frida in to observe her pelvic exam.

She guides Miguela's feet into the padded stirrups and warms her hands and the speculum under water before inserting the blades, then twists the metal stem of the gooseneck lamp to illuminate the cervical os, readjusts the light and looks again.

Claire starts to ask Miguela a question but stops herself, glances at her notes open on the counter beside her—pregnancies: zero; gestations: zero; abortions: zero; wondering if their mixed languages have gone wrong. "I'm sorry. You said you've *had* a baby? *Tiene niños?*"

The answer is the same, stated slowly and clearly pronounced in English and again in Spanish. "I have no children." But the opening to her uterus is in the shape of a linear slit, rather than the tight circle of a nulliparous woman. It is obvious that Miguela has delivered a child.

Frida leaves the room after Miguela sits up. Claire asks a few random questions again, only so she can repeat the questions about pregnancy more innocuously, leaving room for different answers that still don't change. She strips off her gloves and gives Miguela her blouse before labeling the swab and slide from Miguela's Pap smear.

"Dr. Boehning, how do you think when you are afraid?"

"What?" Claire turns around. Miguela hasn't moved; the blouse lies creased across her lap. It's such an oddly personal question—it flusters her, coming out of the blue. From the sound of her voice Miguela could be asking about something as simple as where she grew up, what food she eats or books she reads. She puts the glass slides and cultures carefully into a plastic lab bag and sits on the stool. There are hidden problems buried inside many patients' questions—it is hard enough to tease through them without the barrier of language. "When I'm afraid of what?" she asks.

"Well, only you can know."

Claire thinks about it for a moment. She had been afraid the night

Addison finally told her the truth about vascumab, but, really, that had been less fear than a slow, sinking despair. She had been afraid for Jory when her labor came too early, when she had just finished her pediatrics rotation and seen the consequences of premature birth. There had been a car accident in a rainstorm once, the weightless instant of spinning across the wet pavement until time stopped at the moment of impact. She shakes her head, turning the question around to discern Miguela's need, the root of *her* fear. "Are you asking how I make a plan when I'm afraid?"

"No. When you feel danger—for your life. What do you think then?"

When her life is in danger. How can she answer that? No one has ever shot at her, she has never run from traffickers, or rationed water in 120-degree heat, or struck back at an abusive boyfriend. An answer comes out quite spontaneously, before she can thoroughly consider, but she knows it's true. "My daughter. My daughter and my husband." She would think about how much she loved Jory and Addison, and how much she would miss them, how much more she has to do for them before the end of her life.

Miguela's eyes are in soft focus. After a moment she says, " '*Cuando quiero llorar, no lloro,/ . . . Y a veces lloro sin querer. . . .* ' 'When I wish to weep, I cannot,/and at times I weep without wanting to. . . . ' "

"Did you write that?"

Miguela laughs, and Claire is struck by how it changes her, realizes there is a quality of sorrow that underlies Miguela's quiet face, a trace of it even in her laughter. "No. That is Rubén Darío. The greatest poet of Nicaragua. The greatest poet of the world, my father would have said. But I thank you for your compliment."

Claire studies Miguela, wanting the pieces of this woman's life to make sense. "And now you," Claire says. "Your turn. What are you afraid of?"

Miguela slips her arms into the sleeves of her blouse, watches her fingers push the buttons through the stitched holes so that all Claire can see are her navy black curls. "The same as you. Being alone."

· 17 ·

Jory has packed two grocery bags with Newman-O's, white bread, Annie's mac and cheese and ice cream. "Can't you eat anything that isn't white?" Claire asks. "And don't tell me the chocolate half of the cookie counts." She sends Jory back inside for a minimum of three vegetables and a fruit. Claire can see her through glass doors, grabbing a net bag of oranges. There is no learning curve with one child, every mistake Claire learns from raising Jory can only be applied to Jory, all over again. By the time she has figured out how to be a working, often single parent—which arguments to bite back, which to dictatorially win—by then Jory will be gone. She knows that thought is ridiculous, still, something in her chest twists so tight her eyes sting and she clenches her teeth to keep from crying. Miguela had it, didn't she. When you are naked in fear, when you wake up screaming in the night and see the lightning flash on what really matters, it is so simple: it's the people you love. Jory. Jory *and* Addison.

She watches Jory cross the aisles inside the store, probably running over to grab iceberg lettuce or canned peas. What part of a child is mother, father, or their very own recycled soul from heaven? "Just another question to ask God someday," Addison would tell her. He has always seen both God and science in his test tubes, marveled at the miracle of biochemical truths. But even test tubes would still miss the very true fact that Jory's life had made an unbreakable knot between Addison and Claire, too, as much as if the blood of the three ran in a circle instead of only through the heart of the child. Claire wondered, sometimes, if getting married with Jory already in form, though unviable and symbiotic, had made them a different family, in a way she could not define. Maybe stronger, because three people had entered into that original union, even if only two were voluntary. But maybe weaker because their union had this unplanned influence, like the invisible pull of a distant planet, imperceptibly but definably skewing their orbit.

Claire was actually in the middle of her obstetrics and gynecology rotation when she discovered she was pregnant with Jory. She'd worked so many days in a row that time had blurred, and it wasn't until she noticed the stamped date on her milk carton had expired that she actually thought about the time of the month. Addison was still sound asleep in her stuffy attic apartment when she called him from the hospital. "What are you doing on July eighth?"

She could hear the bedsprings creak as he rolled over, imagined him tangling the sweaty sheet around his naked waist, the tufts of hair standing out over both ears like windblown flags. "What time is it?" he mumbled. "Oh God. I have to be at the lab in twenty minutes. Did you reset the alarm?"

"Yes. You probably shut it off in your sleep. You didn't answer me."

She heard him sit up. "Try me again."

"July eighth. What are you doing?"

At last he began to sound awake, appropriately curious. Hopefully worried. "Ummm. Celebrating your graduation from residency?"

Claire was tucked into a corner desk on the labor and delivery charity ward; a sliding glass partition separated her from the room filled with new mothers and their wailing newborns, six of them crowded into one echoing space with thin curtains separating the beds. She slid the window open and held the receiver out so Addison could hear the squalling, catlike cries of day-old infants.

She had been horrified when the little pink plus sign materialized on the test strip. With fifty thousand dollars of medical school debt accrued and eight months of residency to go she had no room for this . . . this . . . fluke! How could it be anything else? She repeated the test three times using kits they stocked in the outpatient clinic.

And then, of course, the miracle overtook her. The shock of waking in the middle of the night, struggling to incorporate this drugstore test result into her perfectly planned life, into a body that felt absolutely the same as it had two months ago—*completely normal!*—began to alter, became less a shock and more a fire of anticipation, slowly consuming everything else she once considered important.

Addison, on the other hand, slept with his hand fixed over her abdomen from the first night onward, as if he might miss the budding of an ear, an arm, a toe without sustaining the nearest connection he could achieve.

How could she not love that in him?

And their calls still reliably conclude with "I love you," repeated each to the other. The words are said sincerely, refer to something honest and valuable, but those three words—subject, verb and object—have morphed and morphed again since they were first shared like priceless gifts.

Maybe that happens for everyone, she thinks. Maybe those three words can mature and grow old just as the union itself grows old, no longer pristine and fresh but still vital. Maybe it proves that love is like any living thing—capable of almost unrecognizable change over the decades, scarring over astonishing wounds, so the words can still be true, just not true in the way they began.

Claire doesn't even hear his car. She wakes up to Jory's shouts and the door slamming hard, and then the two of them laughing, interrupting each other over and over. She lies on her back and stares at the ceiling, focusing on a water stain over the bed that seems to be expanding week by week, finding hidden shapes in the serpentined brown lines and blotches. One of them looks remarkably like a dollar sign. She tries to predict from the pitch of his voice if this will be a good visit.

They move into the kitchen area, and Claire hears them through the thin floors—the clatter and bang of pans, the slam of the refrigerator door. He will be frying up eggs-in-a-hole for Jory, her favorite breakfast. And there is Jory's voice, the almost continuous, unfiltered stream of her thoughts. She rarely talks that freely to Claire anymore.

Jory's conversations with Claire seem to have already been edited before they leak out during dinner or housework. Claire will see her take a breath to start a sentence, then twist her tongue and lips into altogether different words—it's worse than whatever the truth might be. Once Claire banged her fist down on the table and shouted, "Just say it!" hearing how ridiculous she sounded even before Jory started laughing at her. And they do still laugh together, she reminds herself. Out of the blue a fierce hug and "I love you, Mommy" can startle her out of dinner preparations or reading. But it seems like those moments are happening less often the longer Claire works at the clinic, the less she's home. Time travels faster for a forty-three-year-old than a fourteen-year-old.

There is another outburst from downstairs. For the space of a heartbeat she considers putting a glass cup to the floorboards and pressing her ear soundly against the bottom. Then someone turns on the radio and the volume of their conversation drops too low, only episodically pierced by Jory's shriek or Addison's guffaw. Claire climbs out of bed and goes into the bathroom for a long shower.

When she comes downstairs Jory is cross-legged on the floor, knees splayed apart with a dancer's flexibility. Addison is on the couch, tapping out a fast and complicated rhythm on the coffee table while he talks, one half of his brain a combustion of musical energy and the other half a fully focused parent, so engaged with Jory she clearly forgives his absence. "Hi. You're here! We didn't expect you until later in the week," Claire says.

Addison stands up and slips his hand into his pockets, as if he is embarrassed about his coffee table rock band. "Hey. Turned out the best people in San Francisco were the ones I'd talked to in Chicago, so I decided to come home." She recognizes the dark plea in his eyes, and doesn't ask why there is no need to follow up with any of the investors who have heard his pitch. Instead she crosses the room to meet him, places her arms around his waist and lifts her face. It almost surprises her, the sensation of his mouth on hers again. He pulls her into him and she yields, aware that Jory is studying them for clues. In the chilly room the temperature of his body feels dramatic, her chest and stomach warm, her back exposed. She starts to pull away and, for just one moment more, he holds on.

"Jory, you should get your stuff together. Bus'll be here soon," Claire says.

"What time?" asks Addison, turning to face Jory with a fresh-scrubbed smile. "Hey, how about I drive you? I want to see where you spend your days."

By the time Claire gets home that evening, Addison and Jory have completely rearranged the living room, pushed the dining table so it fronts the living room windows and turned the sofa so it faces the windows overlooking the orchard in the back instead of the television set. Addison has carted all the packing boxes still stuffed with possessions they will never use or need in Hallum out to a dry corner of the barn.

"What do you think?" Jory asks, still sweating from the labor.

Claire hangs her coat on a hook and looks around. "Where did the other armchair go?"

"Dad let me put it in my bedroom. By my window. We wanted all the furniture to face out, like, to face the view." She sweeps her hands along the perimeter where the windows are all black as coal after the winter sunset.

"I love it," Claire says, loving Jory's happier mood. "Where's Dad?"

"Shower." Jory scrapes the metal legs of the love seat around to face the TV again, leaving a white arc along the wooden floor. She clicks the channels until she hits a rerun of *Friends*.

Over dinner Claire says, "Dan and Evelyn invited us to dinner this weekend." Addison looks up from his attentive carving of the roast chicken and she sees a flash of reluctance before he smiles, genuinely enough. She is annoyed to think that he might be hesitant to meet them, but then wonders if he's only afraid of the questions they'll ask.

"Great. That's nice of them," he says, ferrying a thigh to her plate.

Jory, on the other hand, has no second thought. "I don't have to go, do I?"

Claire is about to remind her that Dan is responsible for the food on their table, but then Addison rests his hand on Jory's knee and she whips her hair behind her ears, puts a forkful of potato in her mouth and muffles, "Okay. Fine. Whatever."

It is the first night since leaving Seattle that Addison and Claire have slept in the same bed, and when Addison moves a chair in front of the door they can feel one another's shyness, as awkward as a first, tentative coupling. Only it's worse, Claire thinks. Because tonight they feel awkward and shy about what is lost between them, the memory of what had been so easy and instinctive. They undress, shivering, and are easily drawn to each other's warmth underneath the down comforter. But within moments she stiffens, every part of her mind above her limbic drive crowded with questions; wondering if she would even recognize the words that could destroy their marriage in the blink of an eye. And so in midstroke they fall apart, Addison exhales one cryingly sad sigh, then kisses her temple and rolls onto his side, pulling her arm around him so her cheek rests against the broad rise of his shoulders. Neither of them speaks, allowing the history of fifteen years of marriage to absorb the silence.

In the morning he walks her out to the Audi with a mug of his favorite oversweetened chai tea wrapped between his hands for precious heat. He is still in his pajamas and has shoved his bare feet into his best Italian loafers. The sun is barely over the mountains and a mist rises up from the valley floor, a sheer pink and yellow veil lofting slowly into the palest blue sky. It is Claire's favorite time of day, Addison's least, and so all the kinder of him to ruin his loafers in this muck just to walk her to the car.

"What a sky. Free art. And we don't even have to find the wall space to hang it on," Claire says.

He hugs the mug close to his body and shivers, squints to look out over the fields. The aspens at the edge of the property are faint as a memory through the mist. She scans the sky for a forecast encrypted in the clouds, but the morning seems full of the anticipation of warm weather. A quiet settles between them and the calls of birds rise up, ravens and magpies, the piercing scree of a red-tailed hawk, the throaty rumble of blue grouse—the first she has heard this year. Addison watches her with worry in his eyes, his mouth working at a smile. She can't read him right now. "Can I meet you for lunch in town?" he asks.

"Sure. Who wouldn't want to play hooky on a day like this? Some-place cheap." She grins. "I guess almost everything in this town is cheap, isn't it?" He kisses her, then goes back into the house. Halfway up the drive his foot breaks through a skim of ice and she hears the loafer suck and pop out of the mud.

· 18 ·

It is not a busy day—Anita attributes the lull to a couple of Border Patrol cars spotted in town the day before. Claire parks herself in a sunny exam room window to catch up on consultants' letters and lab results, ripping open envelopes and putting her initials on the bottom of every page, stacking them up to be filed in patients' charts, trying to decide which abnormal results are so serious she has to track down the patient for more testing. In another clinic she would pick up the phone, or wait for the next scheduled visit. But she learned weeks ago that most of the phone numbers Anita takes down for their records are made up, half the addresses, too—even when she promises they don't give out information to Immigration.

Claire rips open another envelope and scans the numbers, her pen poised to scribble "C.B." in the corner and file it away. But this slip makes her put her pen down and walk to the files behind Anita's desk to find the chart. She has to read her note again to see the patient's face, a meek twenty-one-year-old who'd come up from Michoacán last year, a boyishly thin mustache on his upper lip and two missing fingers on his right hand after a carpentry accident, which, he'd told Claire, had made it harder to get hired. She rereads her notes until he comes back to her clearly, the way he'd conscientiously used English words here and there with a shy question mark in his voice after each of them, the feeling she'd had that he was growing the sketchy mustache hoping he might be able to hide behind it someday. His main complaint had been nausea, but the only thing her exam had shown was a little tenderness under his right rib cage and a few bruises—all of it vague enough to be anything from pesticide exposure or viral hepatitis, to depression or too much tequila.

But the lab slip is more alarming. His liver enzymes are abnormal and his pro-time and INR, a measure of blood-clotting proteins made by the liver, are high. They don't tell her anything about the cause—there are dozens of possibilities. But it is the kind of information that will send her driving from orchard to orchard to track him down, chewing up the evening hours she wants to be home with Jory.

She is copying down his listed address when something scratches against the window. She jumps, then smiles at Addison's face pressed up against the glass, a wool cap pulled down so that his ears stick out. He mouths something she can't decipher, and when she shakes her head he cups his hands around his mouth and talks into the pane. "There's a 'closed' sign on the door," he says. His breath leaves a circle of fog in which he inscribes a heart with a frowning face.

She pushes open the glass front door. The smell of the air he sweeps in with him is tinged with spring, a faint curl of green caught up in white winter, dissolving almost before she can identify it. "Hi. Sorry. Come on back. I'll give you the blue plate special tour."

Frida walks out of the office and makes a blindingly quick appraisal of the two of them before she breaks open her all-eclipsing smile and takes Addison's hand, cocking her head, Claire is convinced, just to shake her sprocket of curls. "Dan left early for an appointment—I guess Anita decided that meant we were all on a vacation," Frida says. She is looking at Claire now, a friendly neutrality in her eyes that admits she understands more than she has been told, and will ask for nothing more than Claire wants to share.

"Dan left early?" Claire asks. "That's a first."

Frida shrugs. "Bonus on top of the stock options and soaring wages here. Take a two-hour lunch."

Claire laughs. She leads Addison around the corner. "Lab is back here. The microscope is only half as old as me." She sees him lift his eyebrows when she opens the door to the glorified closet that functions as the clinic's lab. She looks around the room herself, more objective about it seeing Addison's reaction. The nearly obsolete centrifuge for hematocrits, the box of microscope slides that is so old the embossed cardboard has yellowed. It looks like a makeshift medical museum. Most of the equipment was donated to Dan when he opened the clinic fifteen years ago, when it was already too old to sell. But she's proud of it all, in a way—discovering that for the first time as she pulls out a paper towel and wipes a splotch of blue dye off the sink. "Every time we do a test here for free we save the clinic money for rent or salaries." Addison starts to ask a question but she cuts him off, shows him the pharmacy stocked with drugs donated by the industry giants he's been pitching vascumab to for the last three months.

He picks up a package of Augmentin and flips it over, studying the box as if a roll of million-dollar bills might fall into his hand if he opened it. Claire watches the change of light on the curves of his face. After a moment she says, "They turned you down in San Francisco, didn't they?" It is out before she can stop herself, but then she is glad, decides she's tired of whispering around the subject, willing even to see the wound in his pride.

Addison puts the box back on the shelf, nudges the corner into perfect alignment with the row so it looks untouched. "I couldn't even get an appointment." He puts his hands in his pockets and scans the racks and cabinets filled with drugs. "It'll happen someday. Vascumab, or its twin, will get approved. Maybe not by me . . . but it's too close to perfect." Now he turns and looks at her, matter-of-fact about the whole enormous issue. "I'm not talking about profitability, you know. Should start a clock—count how many colon cancer patients go down before it finally gets to market." Claire nods. He had done that with Eugena. He had actually had a clock custom made with annual deaths from ovarian cancer, the twelve o'clock position ready to designate the first day Ovascreen was made cheap and easily available.

He breaks out of the mood and nods toward the exam rooms. "What's down there?"

Claire takes his hand. She turns on a light in the first empty exam room and gives him another tour of the modest supplies and equipment, like a new mother showing off her baby's room. "Take off your jacket. I'll check your blood pressure. Free."

"I can check it free at the drugstore."

"Yeah, but you won't. When did you last have a physical exam, anyway?" She wraps the black sleeve around his arm and twists the valve shut, puts her stethoscope in her ears and watches the dial while she slowly releases the pressure. The needle arcs smoothly around the perimeter until it hits 140 and then it makes a tiny jump every time his heart beats. She looks at his face and listens as the thudding dies away to silence. "Addison. You're hypertensive. Did you know that?"

He pulls the bell away from his arm and whispers into it, jocular again. "Since I saw you wearing that white coat."

"Seriously." She loops the stethoscope around her neck and unzips the Velcro wrap around his arm. "I mean, I guess I shouldn't be surprised, but if you were my patient I'd be on you for this." She flicks her middle finger over his belt line. "Do you always have to go out for steaks and martinis after these meetings?"

"The size of the investment correlates with the size of the fillet. And the size of the olives. It's a proven statistic—Harvard Business School did a study on it. I heard sex brings down blood pressure." Even as he says it he blushes, remembering their passionless night in bed. Sunlight streams through the small window facing him. In the full white light his face is ageless, as if he has all the time in the world to remake himself. Contrary to Claire's first impression when she met him nineteen years ago, she knows he *has* been aging well—despite the gentle decomposition of his body over these last stressful months. His hairline, which had begun receding at the age of twenty, has arrested itself in a pleasant lolling W, exposing pale swatches on the crests of his brow; fine blue veins serpentine along his temples, maybe flowing right this minute with the effluvia from some neuronal tempest that might, just might, lead to the next cancer-curing miracle. If he had money to back it.

"I can get you a new microscope. Newer than the one you've got, at least," he says. A cloud slides across the sun, and the lines around his eyes and mouth stand out again. He brushes a strand of hair off her face and his fingers linger along her cheek. "You're doing something good here, Claire."

By the time they sit down in The Rattler, a café that converts to a cowboy bar at night, they are both peeling off layers of clothing, the day making good on its hint of spring. Addison's hair stands straight out after he plucks off his cap. Claire reaches across the tabletop to smooth it down. They order coffee, which comes in thick white mugs stained and chipped in a timeless, comforting way.

The waitress comes over to get their orders and they each pick up the menu for the first time. Addison asks the waitress how the cheeseburger is, whether he can add grilled onions and how much extra that will cost. She doesn't answer immediately and he says, "Well, if the raw onions add on fifty cents . . ."

"Seventy-five," she answers.

"Okay. Seventy-five, and it takes a tablespoon or two of oil, that's about a nickel, and four or five minutes to cook them—how much does your cook get?" She pointedly looks at the full tables waiting for her and shrugs. "Well, for sure more than you, right? Let's say twelve an hour and a share of tips, so . . ." He takes the pencil out of her hand and scratches a number on his napkin. "So say a dollar twenty—let's be generous—a dollar twenty-five. Plus seventy-five plus a nickel. We could add something for cleaning the pan, but if he's cooking on a flat grill the cleaning really shouldn't count, do you think? So, Two oh five. For grilled onions. Tell you what. I'll have a plain cheeseburger with relish. Claire?"

Claire sets her coffee mug on the oilclothed table and stares at her husband for a minute. Then she looks up at the humorless waitress and smiles. "Toast, please." As soon as the waitress walks off Claire kicks Addison's shin under the table. "She could be a patient of mine, Addison. Please. I live here now." The smile slides off his face. Claire drops her head back, grips the edge of the tabletop so hard her fingers blanch. "We. *We* live here now. *For* now." He pulls his hands closer to himself, as if he might stand up and walk out. She starts to reach for him—an automatic urge to make peace; instead she crosses her arms and leans across the stretch of checkered cloth to tell him in a constricted voice, "I didn't mean it that way. You know that!"

They don't say much for the rest of the short meal, though she can see the gradual turning in his eyes from defensive anger to regret. She listens while he talks about Jory's school, and the car, and her mother; listens for the light of him to come back for her, unwilling to tell him she needs it, wondering if they should have a little clock made for *this,* to measure out the time it takes each small battle to end, to watch it lengthen. They would need two clocks, though, she thinks, "His" and "Hers," before they might know for certain who is moving toward and who away.

Addison leaves the waitress an embarrassingly large tip. On the walk back to the car they stop in front of a local art gallery, pottery and handblown globes and clay speckled with bubbles and bumps. A pair of earrings catches her eye, deep blue glass beads with a gold wave twisting down the center—a bright fish in a frozen sea. "I wonder how they get that gold inside the glass?"

He leans closer to the window. "Pretty. They'd be pretty on you, with your eyes. You want to see how much?"

A cloud covers the sun and Claire wraps her arms tight around herself, feeling cold again. "I don't need them." She moves down a few feet and examines some pitchers and bowls. "Kind of funny how people pay more for all the mistakes when something's made by hand," she says.

"What?" Addison sounds more distracted than actually confused.

"Well, I mean, if a bowl or a vase is machine made we want it to be perfect. No flaws. But if it's made by hand . . ."

"I love you, Claire. You know that."

Claire shudders briefly, fixes her gaze on a paper cup spinning in a gust of wind behind Addison's feet. "Yes. I know."

"And all of this"—he gestures around himself, around both of them, without looking at anything, not even Claire, taking in the melting piles of muddy snow, the broken curb, the wind, the cup—"All of this is . . ." He stands still and his hands drop to his sides. He looks into Claire's face and lets his eyes trace the curve of her jaw, the arch of her cheek. "I don't know why I lied to you." His voice is utterly plaintive— even if she didn't understand the words, she would hurt for him.

"It wasn't a lie, Addison. Not to me, at least. You hid things. All right. But you never . . ."

"It was a lie of omission. It was still a lie."

Claire tries to find an answer, something she can say that will take the pain out of his eyes. But then she sees that he isn't waiting for anything from her—he would be more wounded by any palliative assurance. He just needed to say it.

She glances at her watch. "I have to get back. Anita probably opened up again. What should I pick up for dinner?"

"I'll make dinner," Addison says, taking her hand and walking toward the car. "I'm in the mood for grilled onions."

She finds two notes taped to the door when she gets back: one for her, telling her to have a nice afternoon and get out of here; the other for any patients who might show up without an appointment, giving them directions to the hospital and instructions for 911.

Claire takes the address out of her purse, unfolds the paper and hunts for the street name on the map she keeps in her car. Her patient lives at one of the smaller orchards, twenty miles or more west of town. His chart didn't list any cell phone number, and calling the orchard office would necessitate giving the patient's name to whomever answered the phone, making a public link between him and this clinic. So instead she puts more gas in her car and drives.

The fields are still dormant under thinning snow. But there is movement now, a rousing of the earth almost invisible in the still gray and white landscape. Flocks of phoebe and towhee and dove pushing the cold ahead of them. The river teasing back what it had relinquished, pushing, scouring through ice. Even half aware of it, Claire feels the power, like a surge, a resurrection.

She looks at the paper again and turns off the highway up a muddy road to a few dozen acres of bare, espaliered apple trees. There is a ranch-style, wood-sided house that appears to be the office, and behind it are two long aluminum box trailers that must house the workers. She hesitates for a minute, feeling more comfortable knocking at the house, but more certain she could confidentially find her patient in one of the trailers. After she parks, she can tell the closest is uninhabited, its door torn away and the roof caved in from snow. But the second has a light on, and as she approaches she can hear Mexican music.

The man who answers looks at her suspiciously, first glancing past her to scan the yard. He relaxes when she tells him she's come to find someone else. Señor Rubén Aguilar. ¿Lo conoce?"

He opens the door wider and stands on the folding metal stair, starts a flurry of Spanish and gestures out across the fields, squinting into the setting sun. Claire finally puts her hand up to stop him, a gesture she is used to now. "No comprendo! Más despacio, por favor!"

He nods sympathetically and starts to talk louder, as if she were deaf. But she is able to grasp that Rubén has moved on to another orchard. Walker's. She thanks him and starts the thirty-mile drive all the way across the valley, wishing she'd just started at Walker's in the first place. Even if it wasn't Rubén's given address, Walker's employed so many people someone would have known his whereabouts.

She is discovering that the entire migrant community shifts shapes and places—like holographic figures, more or less solid depending on how visible Immigration patrol is that month, or how desperately they are needed back home, or how much money has been paid or held back by employers who have skirted H-2A and are governed by no code more rigorous than their own conscience. It is especially true of the women, who can become as untraceable as this morning's mist. They dissolve across borders on the heels of husbands and boyfriends to take leftover jobs, or care for babies in tents and discarded trailers. And when they leave, it might well be alone, without the man or child that made them risk everything in the first place.

The only time she has driven all the way up the private road to Walker's was when she dropped Miguela off, well after dark. Like many big orchards in the area, Walker's offices are lodged in what used to be the original landowner's home, built before agriculture became so corporatized, probably before this land was even cultivated. This home is a rare find in the valley, built of large granite stones with a chimney on either end; rough wood windows set deep into the walls—larger than the windows in other houses built around the same time, as if the owners had valued light more than insulation. At the east end a set of French doors opens onto a tiled patio nested under an arbor of dead vines. She can see why Walker bought it. It is seductively romantic, even if the business never earns a cent.

A carpenter is cutting planks across the backs of two stout saw-horses in the yard. Men walk in twos and threes up from the or-chard, carrying trimmers and ladders. The sun cuts low over the tops of the trees, breaking beneath the visor rim so that Claire is momentarily blinded. She pushes herself higher in the seat and scans the yard, the cabins, the orchard, the faces of the Latino men who propagate this white man's enterprise. No one looks familiar. Scents of sawdust and burning applewood come to her as soon as she gets out of her car.

She almost expects Ron Walker or his wife to open the front door when she knocks, greet her with an invitation to dinner—the place has such a look of home. But a minute or so after she rings she is ushered into a rather bland, purely functional office by the foreman, offered a seat in a folding metal chair beside his desk. He is a politely busy man, and hesitates for only a moment when Claire says she is looking for Señor Aguilar on a personal matter. He has her write the name down and carries it over to a bank of scarred metal filing cabi-nets pushed against a lovely stone wall, the keystone of an arched fire-place barely showing behind them. While the foreman looks through the drawers Claire studies the room, imagining how she would pull it together if it were her home, wishing she could see the whole house before she leaves. He pulls a file out and turns toward her, skimming the first few pages. Claire is already on her feet when he shakes his head. "I'm sorry. We don't have him listed as ever working here. Is it important?"

"Oh. That's not him, then?" Claire says, pointing at the file.

"Lot of Aguilars. Garcias, Mendezes. . . . Lot of workers over a lot of years."

"Well, this would have been just a few weeks ago."

The foreman flares his empty hand open, a magician proving his innocence. "Wish I could help. Lot of 'em go south for strawberries and asparagus before coming back up with the cherries. You could check back in May or so."

It will be a matter of waiting, then. Hoping that the inflammation in Rubén Aguilar's liver is spurious, something that will either resolve on its own or cause him enough symptoms, early enough, to force him back to her or some other willing doctor before the organ fails.

The boxy white clapboard pickers' cabins appear mostly empty, probably won't fill until the real work on next fall's crop begins in a month or so. She drives past them slowly, scanning the narrow passageways and yard for Miguela. Near the bottom of the road a young man, about the same build and age as Rubén, is clearing out a blocked trench that's damming the snowmelt into a muddy pool, hacking at the rocks and roots so hard he has taken off all but his undershirt and splattered jeans. Claire stops to wait for a passing truck and decides to make one last try, if only to ease her conscience. She rolls down the window and calls to the man, *"Discúlpeme. ¿Conoce Rubén Aguilar?"* He looks up, then glances over his shoulder—like they all do, she thinks. All of them waiting for deportation. He walks nearer, wiping the sweat off his forehead so it leaves a dirty streak. His pickax is slung loose in one hand; it is thickly calloused—she can see the cracked lines of dirt even from her car.

"Rubén Aguilar," Claire pronounces it for him again, ready to turn onto the highway as soon as he shakes his head. He looks like he wants to answer her, wavering. *"Soy la doctora de la clínica,"* she adds, and this time she is rewarded with a wide smile.

"Ah, sí, sí, Señora. Es mi amigo, pero él no vive aquí ahora. Ya regresó a la casa en Wenatchee."

Claire puts the car into park and gets out the paper with Rubén's name. "What house in Wenatchee? Do you know his address?"

"Sólo teléfono." He lets the pickax fall to the ground and digs deep into his pocket for a cell phone, punches in some letters and lets Claire copy the number off the screen. She reaches through the window and shakes his hand, feeling illogically ebullient, in a way, as if she had cured Rubén Aguilar herself. But it's not completely unreasonable to feel relieved, she decides on the drive home. If he were getting sicker

his friend would probably have said something about it. And the best medical care around here is in Wenatchee.

Unless he went there because he was getting worse, she thinks, slowing the car down. She pulls into a riverside park and gropes for her phone, practicing the Spanish words that might explain why he needs to see a doctor. She punches Rubén's name and number into her growing list of patients. But a woman's polished voice answers with the name of some company. Claire apologizes and hangs up, checks the number again and reenters it more slowly. This time when the same voice answers she at least asks for Mr. Aguilar, thinking maybe he is working in a Wenatchee business office now—as if the receptionist is likely to know the name of an undocumented immigrant who cleans the bathrooms or weeds the gardens.

Claire is almost curt when she thanks the woman and hangs up, frustrated at losing her patient so late in the chase. Frustrated with the wasted evening. Despite it all, she drives back to Walker's and looks for the worker who'd been friends with Rubén, drives all the way up to the deserted, locked offices, the empty cabin yards, before she gives up and goes home.

· 19 ·

Sunday morning Addison brings her coffee in bed. Claire, soft and swollen with sleep, props herself up against the headboard. As soon as she takes the cup he holds up a bowl of sugar and she scoops out two spoonfuls, then a third, stirs the coffee and licks the spoon. "Bad new habit," she says, hunching back against the pillows.

"Vices are endearing. Handy it's a cheap one," he answers. "Jory's saying she needs new tennis shoes and I just melted the pancake flipper thing. I thought we'd drive over to Walmart later today. Want to come?"

Jory sits in the backseat plugged into her music and Addison spends the hour-long drive telling Claire about his newest strategy. If none of the bigger pharmaceutical companies will invest, he'll look for another biotech company working on similar molecules; form a partnership and build a new consortium of private lenders. He drives with his left hand dangled over the top of the steering wheel and sketches numbers out on the dashboard with his right index finger, as if Claire can read the untenable sums he seems convinced are ready and waiting once people understand the potential in vascumab. More and more, she is noticing, he gives her such details only when he doesn't have to look straight into her eyes.

After ten miles of it she closes her hand around his outstretched wrist and stops the invisible calculations. "How is this a 'new strategy'? Aren't you just trying to convince the same investors to give you a second chance?"

He glances at Jory in the rearview mirror. "It's spreading the risk over a larger group. I want to take it bigger—look for some mezzanine lenders."

"Some what?" Claire asks, a hot tingle creeping up the back of her neck.

"*Mezzanine.* Just like it sounds. Sort of between a bank and a venture capitalist."

Claire knots her fists between her knees, thinking that it isn't faith in vascumab that was damaged when human trials were denied approval—it is faith in Addison, who had taken all the blame as head of the lab. After a minute she says, "You know, I met Ron Walker the other day. He came to the clinic." Addison keeps his eyes fixed on the pavement. "Why are you so resistant to talking to him?" she asks.

"Why are you so convinced I should?"

She gestures at the road with one hand, as if the answer were painted down the middle of the highway. "Maybe because at least some of the profit might end up at Dan's clinic. Maybe because he's the only rich person I know who's still talking to us. What? You don't want me to have any input on where the money comes from? Like the last time?" Claire sees his cheeks flush and waits for a backlash, but he checks his mirrors and drives on, the small twitch underneath his eye the only sign he's wounded. She has to swallow hard not to cry—not here, with Jory in the car.

Inside the vast concrete box of a store, Jory takes off to look at the electronics section and DVDs, forgetting, apparently, that she has come here for shoes. Addison and Claire wander through the kitchen section. Addison stops in front of a combination microwave-convection oven and pops the door open and closed until Claire heads down toward the utensils. Neither of them mentions the matched sets from Williams-Sonoma they had sold in the garage sale. Until the car ride today they've avoided any discussions about money during this visit. The debts are still so unfathomable it feels pointless to Claire. What difference would a microwave-convection oven make when one page of disputed data had evaporated seven million dollars? If anything, it felt satisfying to argue about a plastic spatula versus an aluminum one. That's three dollars they can carry around in their pockets.

She sees it clearly at this instant—the rush to salvage what was left of their wealth, to save Addison's magic molecule, has been the perfect excuse not to talk about how it was lost in the first place. And here is the fallout—a marriage crumbling under the weight of silence. They end up abandoning their empty shopping cart and walking down the aisles with no purpose other than distraction.

Jory is nowhere to be seen. Addison looks in Entertainment while Claire goes toward Shoes. She is starting to comb the dressing rooms when Jory tugs on the strap of her purse. "Come look at this, Mom."

"Where've you been? The store closes in half an hour."

"They never close. I found *the* most beautiful necklace. Who would have thought—in Walmart."

"What happened to tennis shoes?"

Jory charges off to the jewelry section, which is at least in the direction of Shoes. The clerk smiles when she sees her coming and opens the case, takes out a necklace with a pendant of minuscule diamond chips clustered over a gold-fill heart. Jory holds it around her neck and the clerk angles a large standing mirror toward her.

"It's pretty, honey. Very pretty on you. We need to get your shoes."

"Mom, it's only two hundred dollars."

Claire nods. "It's beautiful, Jory. I wish I could buy it for you. We don't have two hundred dollars for a necklace. Let's get your shoes. Thank you," she tells the clerk, and walks away.

Jory meets them ten minutes later in the shoe department, takes the first pair without so much as a word, and stares out the window on the drive home, her iPod idle in her lap. She disappears upstairs mindful not to stomp, but the small house shakes when she slams her door.

"Leave it," Claire says when Addison starts up after her. She puts a pot of water on the stove to boil for pasta and pours two glasses of wine, signals for Addison to come into the kitchen so her voice won't resonate directly up to Jory's bedroom. "Does she tell you anything about school? Ever mention any friends? She isn't even talking about dance lately."

Addison pulls a chair in from the dining table and straddles it with his arms crossed over the back, turning his glass so the light glows jewel-red through the wine. Claire remembers a party they'd held one summer on their deck, a wine tasting at which each guest had to describe their mystery vintage in a poem created from a vintner's list of words. Addison had won hands down, their friends in hysterics over his "luscious, insipid geraniums, flabby but foxy in their noble finish." It helped that they were on their tenth bottle by the time he read. The kitchen warms and steam fogs the windowpane. Claire dumps a package of tortellini into the water and pulls a second chair in to sit beside him. "The more I'm alone with her the less she talks to me. I hate leaving her here by herself so many evenings."

He shifts in his chair, rests his chin on the wooden ladder back. After a moment he turns his head toward her again, with his cheek nested in the crook of his elbow. "Have you told her everything?" He whispers the words, maybe to keep Jory from overhearing, maybe because he doesn't trust his voice.

Claire whispers back, "No. Not about Rick's data. She thinks the study stopped because the lab ran out of money. And I haven't said anything to her about the personal loans." She sees the muscle in his cheek twitch. "Addison?"

"Yeah?"

"Do we need to see a counselor?"

He hesitates, clears his throat softly before he answers her. "Probably. But I don't know how we'd pay for one right now."

Evelyn Zalaya's salt-and-pepper hair is pulled back in a thick chignon that would look old-fashioned except for the magnificent silver and turquoise barrette pinning the weighty coil at the nape of her neck. Her earrings match, twisted silver with embedded blue stones. Sculptural art, really. It would seem affected on another woman, Claire thinks, but somehow on Evelyn the unusual pieces look more like a celebration of craft, a complement to the artist more than an adornment. When she opens the front door Addison lags behind on the porch steps; Claire can practically hear him struggling to find his act, remembering to smile a beat too late. She has always been the more social one, floating from group to group in a party, smoothing over gaps in conversations until

Addison clicked with someone and ended up in a corner, diving into protein encoding or small molecule arrays or Janis Joplin. But when Claire introduces him, Evelyn ignores Addison's outstretched hand and gives him the same assured hug she had given Claire, and in that one gesture sweeps away his fear that he will be called upon to justify why he is not supporting his family.

Assessing the size and quality of the house and furnishings, Claire has to wonder where two doctors have put their incomes. It is modest even by the standards of full-time Hallum residents, little more than a double-wide dressed up with shingles and strips of wood trim. As soon as she breaks from Evelyn's embrace and looks past her into the main living area Claire sees that they have turned their home into a personal museum of folk art. Brilliantly colored textiles woven in playful geometric patterns cover the chairs and throw pillows—*huipiles* and ponchos and rugs. Paintings hang above the faded red twill sofa and overloaded bookcases, around the bricked-in woodstove, are propped two and three deep against the wall along the floor, as if they'd been bought that very day and await the right mood or the right sunlight to properly set them in the ideal spot. Most depict tropically colorful village or farm scenes painted in the saturated hues of a hot climate, unrelenting sun and humid air intensifying the greens and blues and reds. Jory is immediately drawn to the vivid, miniature worlds and Evelyn points out half-hidden figures—a naked boy being chased by a dog, an old woman bathing in a metal tub.

Dan stands up from the sofa when they come in, and for the first time Claire sees that he is not actually any taller than Addison; it is the lean, straight lines of his face and torso, the clear definition of his bones showing through his clothing that has made her see him so. She catches the slightest waver in his balance when he holds out his hand to take her husband's. Addison shakes Dan's hand tentatively once. Claire feels a sudden catch in her breath at his awkwardness, as if she had blinked and seen the world from inside his wounded ego for an instant. She has told Dan and Evelyn next to nothing about Addison's lab; only general comments about investigational cancer drugs and the cumbersome necessity to master business skills and salesmanship in order to fund his passion. Dan would pause after any such mention, give her all the chance she needed to tell him more, then head off to see the next waiting patient after an agreeable if indecipherable nod. Moving closer now, she hears him start an easy conversation with Addison about the remarkable trout fishing to be had on the stretch of the river near this house come summer.

They eat a stew that Evelyn calls Serrano Pork Chili, her own recipe, hot enough to bring tears to Claire's eyes. Evelyn and Addison eat heartily, unfazed by the peppers. Jory takes one bite and from then on stirs the bowl and brings an empty spoon up to her mouth. Dan hardly touches his own, but when he notices that Claire is washing every bite down with ice water he gets a beer for her. "Water just makes it burn more." He puts a bowl of chocolate chip ice cream in front of Jory and she pushes the chili aside with a meek "Thank you."

"Who's the art collector?" asks Claire.

"Evelyn," Dan answers. "She worked with Doctors Without Borders for a long time, traveled all over. Africa. But Central and South America mostly. I tagged along. She teaches painting up at the town museum now that she's retired from medicine. Took her seventy-three years to work at her real passion," Dan says.

Evelyn adds, "Medicine was a passion, too. A rich life needs more than one passion."

Dan stretches his arm across the back of Evelyn's chair. "Art. Medicine. Last comes me." He winks when he says this, apparently a running joke between them.

They must have been a handsome couple, Claire thinks. Both sort of noble, in an unassuming way. Evelyn looks younger than Dan and still has a graceful fluidity about her. They are *still* handsome together, she amends. "I haven't ever been to the museum. You're talking about the one across from the grocery store?"

"Oh, you must come!" Evelyn claps her hands together, as if the idea of introducing someone to this prize of hers is a present. "You must. All of you. Half the time it goes unstaffed, but if you let me know I'll take you through. We have drawers full of old photographs. I've seen some of your place."

"Our house? The Blackstocks'?" Addison asks.

"You know it was one of the first homesteads around here. There was a log cabin that burned to the ground around 1890, exactly underneath your current house. A lot of that barn is original."

"I'd heard about the cabin." Claire says. "We found a photograph of two children, 'Robin and Marilyn,' probably taken in the fifties. I always meant to find them and mail it back."

"They were Blackstocks. Those kids died in the polio epidemic just before the vaccine came out." Claire stops eating with her spoon halfway to her mouth, surprised at the degree of emotion that comes over her, a tinge of shock as if their deaths affected her life in any real way. Evelyn reaches over to pour more beer into Claire's glass and catches Jory's sidelong look at her mother. "At least that's the story people tell."

Evelyn goes on. "There've been a couple of fires out there—that aspen grove over the rise behind your barn burned about twenty years ago, after a power line blew down. Lot of history out there. Your house used to be the grandest thing around here." She laughs in a quick burst and adds, "Long before I got to Hallum!"

"How long have you lived here?" Addison asks.

"Forty-eight years, if you count from the time we moved." She puts her hand over Dan's. "But only about twenty-five if you subtract our travels."

Claire and Addison and Jory had traveled a lot as well. Every year until this one they had taken some trip—England or Hawaii or the Bahamas. Claire is about to bring up the museums they visited in London two Christmases ago, but the grand galleries and halls seem banal to her at this moment, surrounded by these meticulously painted scenes and the photographs of Dan and Evelyn in front of squat, windowless cement blocks with red crosses painted over the doors, lines of children waiting to be weighed and immunized.

Evelyn begins picking up dishes from the table. Claire and Addison get up to help but Evelyn shoos Claire back to her chair. "Keep Dan company. He needs it. Jory can scoop ice cream and tell me something about dance."

A portable CD player on the bookshelf plays Spanish-language folk songs, a guitarist and female vocalist, words that Claire only intermittently understands: "If you were looking, if you dreamt of freedom, . . ." something else she can't translate. She sits on the sofa, one leg crossed underneath her and her arms splayed out along the back, feeling the muscles in her shoulders and neck ease. The smell of woodsmoke and garlic and yeasty bread, the deep sagging seat cushion, the music—all of it blends, calms, like someone stroking her hair or rubbing her feet. Dan rocks back in his chair and presses a hand over his abdomen.

"You didn't eat much. Frida says you're losing weight," Claire says.

He smiles and adjusts himself in his chair, resting his hands on his knees. "Evelyn's peppers. She's burned off all her tastebuds. Steven Perry says he wants to take out my gallbladder—must need a new fly rod. I'll tell you if you need to worry." Then he gives her that look she has grown to enjoy, like he is keeping some secret wrapped up in tissue paper and ribbons, ready to offer it at precisely the right moment. "Thanks for not quitting yet."

"Well. Thanks for not firing me. Yet!"

"Do you ever think about going back to finish your residency? Taking your boards?"

Claire rakes her hair back from her face, gives herself a moment to answer this. "Oh, I don't know. It's been so many years. I can't even imagine it right now. I'm still just trying not to drown. Or hurt somebody." She rolls her eyes when she says it, proving it is at least half a joke.

Dan laces his fingers together on the table; Claire can see the stiffening in his hands, the swelling of his knuckles. "Hell. I shouldn't even bring it up. Take your boards and somebody else'll hire you away."

She sits up, remembering Rubén Aguilar. "I meant to ask you—I got some abnormal labs back on a patient I saw a few weeks ago and I can't track him down."

"What labs?" he asks.

"His liver enzymes were high. I want to get a hepatitis screen, but he didn't come back for follow up. It's Rubén Aguilar." She pauses for a moment, looking for recognition in Dan's face. "Well. I don't think you ever saw him. Anyway, I drove out to his orchard, but he'd moved. Could it be pesticides?"

"Early for that. We don't usually see much pesticide exposure till later in the summer. Which orchard?"

"Johnson's—a small place, way east of the highway. But they told me he'd moved to Walker's, and then somebody at Walker's, another worker, said he'd moved to Wenatchee, and that turned out to be a dead end."

"Nobody in Walker's office knew where he'd gone?"

Claire shakes her head. Then she scoots closer to the table and leans forward, lowering her voice. "But speaking of Walker, do you have a phone number for him?"

Dan seems to consider Claire's question before he answers. "Walker's not likely to know any of his workers. Kind of stands back from the day-to-day in his businesses. The Money God, if you will."

She smiles at his assumption. "No, no—I wasn't going to ask him about Rubén. I want Addison to talk to him. About a business deal."

As if he had been listening for his name, Addison steps out of the kitchen and Claire sees the change on her own face register in Dan's expression, a mix of empathy and angst, and . . . something else. A memory, maybe. He has had almost twice her years to collect them. Three times her years living a marriage.

Addison has a soaking-wet, hot-pink apron tied around his neck, and his hands are gloved in suds. It would be funny but for the expression of betrayal on his face. It makes her want to turn away—not with shame for anything she's said, but because it is so clear that her husband is prepared for her betrayal, is only waiting for a hint of proof as minor as this mention of his name with Walker's.

· 20 ·

On the drive home Claire can practically feel Jory's eyes moving from one parent to the other, waiting for someone to break the tension. It was only a few months ago that a moment like this would have ended with one of them erupting in laughter, teasing the other out of the mood, letting Jory witness one way to resolve an adult argument. Claire turns away from the prejudiced set of Addison's jaw to watch the night landscape pass by her window, feeling the interior of the car close in around her, silently shouting her side of the fight they can't have. The worst of it is that tonight she was genuinely trying to help. It was his pride that was making him twist it all against her, his assumption that she is trying to manage his business.

A flash of red and white light shows up ahead and Claire tells Addison to pull into the *ampm* so she can pick up milk—anything to break the tension. He wheels into the parking lot without a word and she is out before he's fully stopped, slamming the door behind her. She squints under the store's bright fluorescent lights, irritated, now, by their harsh contrast to the dark car. The low-pitched buzz of the coolers, the red eye of the security monitor, the watchful gaze of the night clerk—it feels like a jury is observing her family conflict. She pulls a Darigold carton off the refrigerator shelf and carries it to the cash register, only at the last minute realizing she has no cash. She pulls her purse off her shoulder and starts plucking quarters and dimes out of

the pockets and seams, finally looks up to ask the cashier what the minimum purchase is for a credit card.

She stops, speechless. The woman putting the milk into a small
brown paper bag is hers—her patient—the woman who'd been
hunched at the end of her exam table just two days ago, hiding bruises
underneath her thick pancake makeup and, even worse, beneath her
clothes. "I'm so sorry. I mean, I don't have enough money. Enough
cash," Claire stutters, the first words that come to her, tumbling ahead
of what she wants to say: *I tried to find someone to help you. You didn't
have to hide from me.*

The woman . . . no, it is a girl, really. Only little more than a girl.
She stares down at the bag, pays careful attention to folding the top
of the brown paper in a crisp, unwrinkled crease before she pushes it
across the counter toward Claire. "It's okay, ma'am. Just pay the rest
next time."

She shuts the door quietly when she comes back to the car, fumbles with
the buckle on her seat belt. Addison pulls out on the highway slowly,
cautiously. The silence in the car, she can tell, is now there to guard her,
and she looks at these other two Boehnings, trying to guess what was
said while she was in the store. When she can't stand it anymore, Claire
turns to Addison and chokes out in half a sob, "I'm just trying to help.
To help you. To help *us!*" She sees the quick twitch below his eye; the car
holds steady, fixed for home. "So I have to live with the consequence,
but I'm not supposed to have any say in how to get out of it. Is that it?
Is that how you want us to be?"

Without a word to this Addison slows the car down, steers onto the
shoulder just emerging from the melting snow. He shifts into Park and
stares at the road ahead as if he could see it still moving underneath
them. "All right," he says, his voice alarmingly calm. "All right. I'll call
Walker when I get to Seattle. If that's what you want."

Long after they are asleep Claire startles awake, listening for whatever
threat broke into her dream; the house and land are still except for the
whip of wind in the aspen grove. Addison is softly snoring. She blows

across his neck until he shifts his body and falls quiet; the dimly lit folds of his chin and full pout of his parted lips make him look untroubled as a child. She bends over him, waiting for him to feel her eyes. "I'm scared," she whispers. "I don't know where we are anymore."

He has always been such a lucky man, had been born believing in his own luck. He'd warned her, when it was clear they would marry, Jory still without formed digits—a tailed frog floating in a dime-sized salt bath—warned her about the genetics of his lineage, the twisted gifting of his luckiness. When Jory was eight or nine she had asked Claire (it seems almost prescient now), "Is Daddy very much like Granddad was?" She had met her paternal grandfather so few times before he died she couldn't have any clear memory of him, and Claire is half glad for that. Addison's father had nearly gambled himself into homeless shelters by the time he was diagnosed with lung cancer. The more money Addison gave him, the faster it disappeared.

"Well," Claire had finally answered, "you've seen his picture. They look a little bit alike. Of course, Daddy's more handsome."

Jory had tucked this fact into a corner of her emerging self and continued, "What did he do? I can't remember."

Because we never told you, Claire thought. "He was in the military for a while when Dad was little. And after that, well, he was kind of an investor."

"What do you mean? What did he invest in?"

"Various things. Kind of a financial risk analyst."

So maybe it was Addison's inherited chemistry that convinced him his solitary signature, borrowing against their communal property, was justified by the profit he expected to count into Claire's trusting hands. His conviction that vascumab *deserved* production, *deserved* its market share and more. The return, in fact, should hardly matter. What mattered was the drug. The patient. The cure. And maybe that was part of what she'd fallen in love with—not the luck itself but Addison's blissful, gullible belief that with any luck at all fate would ultimately be fair.

He'll go away again tomorrow, put on his pressed suit and tie and stride into the offices of billionaires with all the numbers and practiced spiel they should need to believe their next chart-breaking product could be vascumab, a pale yellow liquid, the targeted poison that might shatter all the nearly imperceptible gains most new chemotherapies tout as success. Before his own project had imploded Addison relished in scoffing at the two, three, six extra weeks of life manufacturers were using to justify "improved" drugs that cost a thousandfold more than the current standard of care. "And the side effects *still* ruin any quality of life," he would say, following Claire around the kitchen with the latest *Clinical Oncology* journal rolled up in his hand, whapping it on the counter to make his point. She'd gotten used to it after the first few months, realized it was an exercise for him to share the rush he got from his work, the humming conviction that vascumab was a unique, critical leap in cancer care.

Claire had realized he was on the brink of a personal miracle even before he did. He'd come home late from an international pharma meeting, with that distracted manner he got with all of his incipient ideas, the germ of it clustering and dividing deep in his cortex—a peculiar restlessness waking him in the middle of the night to hunt for notes, tracing the dim scheme onto an imaginary whiteboard with his forefinger, like a sleepwalker who couldn't be startled awake. It reminded her of labor, this ineluctable struggle that overtook him as the seed bloomed into a viable molecular answer. *Gestating*—it came to her now as the perfect word to describe his invisible amalgamation of facts and hypotheses into an idea ultimately too huge to contain. It was almost as if the project happened *to* him, not because of him, as if his brain had been tapped by the stars to bear this infant of pharmaceutical progress.

She had awakened at four one morning to an empty bed and found him sketching out molecules on the back of an envelope at the breakfast bar, target proteins and ion channels. It was winter and she had on a thick cashmere robe with the collar turned up around her throat. Addison, too, was in a bathrobe, so engrossed in the lightning burst of what became vascumab that his thick green fleece had fallen loose, exposing a wide V of pale chest and belly. "I can't believe it," he said, tapping, tapping the point of his pen in the center of the paper so that a cluster of blue dots broke through the surface like Braille. "I have to try it." He looked up at her for the first time since she'd come into the room; his expression implied that she knew exactly what he was referring to, as if the bald crown of his head were made of glass.

Claire shivered and waited. It was like trying to anticipate an earthquake, a volcanic eruption—a shifting of space and ground that would change everything in unpredictable ways. She had been through it before with Addison, when he had first conceived his ovarian cancer test. She'd held her breath, grabbed hold and ridden the wave with him, never fully understanding the science he explained, but trusting that if she clung tight enough he would carry Jory and her to higher, safer ground.

Addison says good-bye to them after dinner Monday night. He has been back just long enough for Claire to get used to both sides of the bed being warm, used to the rock and sway when he rolls over in the night, and the pocket of cold air left in his wake. In their other life she would move into that space, press her body against his; more often now she only wraps the comforter tighter around her neck. Without wanting to, she admits some balance has shifted; having him away is the routine, at home he is the guest.

Jory clings to him in the doorway, then returns to her homework and instant messaging. Claire walks him out to his car. A wind has come up and the sky is brushed with the thin white cirrus clouds of changing weather, maybe the last surprise snow of spring before the greening.

Addison stands with one foot propped on the runner, one arm cocked up on the open door. "I have this great idea for a new business."

"Okay. I'm ready," Claire says.

"Telemedicine."

"That's not new, Addison."

"No, just listen. I'm going to call it Dial-a-Doc." Claire narrows her eyes. "You call an eight hundred number with, say, a skin rash. And it puts you through a menu: 'If your rash is itchy, press one. If your rash is oozing, press three. Bleeding? If you've soaked more than two towels, press two. Abdominal pain? If you're vomiting, press four.'"

She laughs but can't hide the sarcastic bite spurred by their arguments the day before. "Maybe you should just start selling Laetrile!"

He puts his hands on her shoulders and gives a little shake, bends his knees to bring his eyes down to hers. "Claire. It's a joke."

Her eyes start to fill and he pulls her against him so the world is swallowed up inside his damp wool coat. "It's gonna be okay. We'll make it. *I'll* make it okay." When she finally breaks away he reaches into his pocket and hands her a small white box. It is the earrings, the blue glass earrings with the golden wave she had seen in the gallery window. "Not exactly Tiffany's."

"Thank you," she says, but it comes out as a whisper. "You already did Tiffany's." She pushes her hair back and slides the wire loops into her ears.

He kisses her and gets into the car, stops a few feet down the drive and rolls down the window. "Remind Jory to check our Lotto numbers. I taped the tickets to the fridge." And then he is gone. Again.

When Claire goes back inside Jory is at the computer holding up a fan of tickets she and Addison had bought the week before. She shrieks, "Mom, *MOM!* Come look at this. I think we won! *COME LOOK AT THIS!*"

Claire reads the numbers out loud one by one while Jory checks them against those displayed on the computer screen. They match, all six of them. Jory falls off the chair and kicks her legs out in a split. "Whooey! Seattle, here I come!"

"One problem, hon. Look at the date."

Jory sits up and snatches the ticket out of her mother's hand. "You mean he picked the right numbers *one day too late*?"

"No. I mean he bought a ticket on Thursday with Wednesday's winning numbers. To make you laugh. Why don't you call him as soon as you're ready to laugh about it. Better start your homework."

Claire sits at the dining room table with her laptop open to their bank's website, and this month's bills laid out in categorical columns. Her pay stub is parked at the top, as if it might rain money down in some fair distribution to every waiting envelope. She sits with her hands jammed into her blue jeans and stares at a vague point in the middle of all the papers. She's tried three variations, the first time arranging them according to balance due. Then she reversed the order, hoping that paying off the small debts might bolster her courage to write the bigger checks. Third was by order of importance: Would it be easier to lose their lights or their propane? Their car insurance or Internet access? Telephone or next week's groceries? In that go-round the Internet had started on the lowest rung, but she knew Jory would run away from home if they lost that contact with her world. She loosely sums the debts in her head and subtracts them from the red number highlighted on the computer screen. It's almost funny how meaningless the digits can become if you stare at them long enough. She plays around with putting all the zeros that used to come behind the final tally in the front, moving the decimal place around randomly. It doesn't really change what they're going to eat for breakfast tomorrow morning, after all.

She digs deep in her pocket and places another item on top of her pay stub—the diamond ring Addison gave her eleven years ago when he sold Eugena. He'd had it custom designed to sit flush with her plain gold wedding band, but other than that it's quite simple—a standard gold circle with four prongs holding a standard brilliant-cut stone. Your average two-carat GV VS1 diamond.

She opens her cell phone and calls Anna, her closest friend in Seattle. "How've you been?" Claire asks, pushing away from the table so the bills are not in her direct line of vision.

"Claire! You must have read my mind. Sherry and I were talking about you yesterday. We want to come out for some skiing. Or is the season over?"

"They stopped grooming three weeks ago."

"Then we'll just come out to see *you*—help you plow the back forty for spring planting."

Claire forces a smile, hoping she might sound like she finds this funny. "It's okay. We're still buying our vegetables at Food Pavilion." She rakes her hair back from her face. "Wait till the weather's better. Kind of mud season now."

"So how's the job?" Anna asks.

"Pretty good. I'm starting to feel like I'm helping more than just slowing the whole clinic down. I saw a case of measles the other day. Dan, my boss, had a case of malaria."

"God, Claire. It sounds like you're practicing medicine in Africa."

The remark stings, for some reason Claire can't pin down. She is already wishing she had not called, wishing she could blurt out her request without any more empty banter. "Yeah. Right here in the middle of America. How's your house remodel coming?"

"You won't believe what they've done now. The new doors were just installed and they screwed up the finish on the thresholds." One of Anna's children is practicing piano and Claire hears the ding and click of a computer near the phone. "The color at the side door is different than the front door—it looks like it came from a different manufacturer or something."

"Can't they just swap it out?"

"Contractor says because we wanted a custom-made door for the front the same threshold won't fit. Or something. He says we have to live with it. Forty-five hundred dollars and he says we have to live with it!"

"Well, how different do they look?" Claire asks her, scooping the diamond ring onto her Bic pen and dancing tiny rainbows across the white bills and envelopes.

"Different. One has more brown in it. They look different."

"Are the doors next to each other?"

"They're on opposite walls. Okay?" Anna hits a more direct note. "Okay. So most people won't see it, I know. But it's the principal of the thing. I want what I ordered. Total headache."

Claire looks around the living room, the wallpaper from 1960 peeling from the corners of the ceiling, the neon-bright kitchen cabinets Jory and her friends had painted. "Maybe you need to find a new hobby, Anna." She intends it to be a joke but Anna must have heard the cut. She is quiet for a minute. Claire sighs. "Did that sound bitchy? I'm sorry. God, you're the only friend I talk to anymore and I can't even be nice."

"Don't worry about it. Me and my stupid thresholds."

The laptop's screen saver kicks on and a slide show of family photos starts; almost all of them are Jory. Blinking her childhood away before Claire's breaking heart. She shuts the lid and turns the chair to face out the back windows of the living room. "Anna, I'm kind of in a jam. I want you to do a favor for me. If you can."

She can practically hear Anna biting the inside of her lip the way she does. Finally she asks, "Is it about Nash's investment?"

Claire stands up and walks to the window, presses her forehead against the cold glass. "No, Anna. That's between Addison and Nash." Even as she says it she is hit by the memory of a quarrel that sprang up when she had warned Addison about mixing friendship and money.

She can hear the apology in Anna's quick reply. "I shouldn't have . . . Of course. I'll do anything I can to help you, Claire."

Claire strolls over to the stairwell and rests the phone on her shoulder for a moment. It is quiet upstairs. "I want you to sell my diamond ring. There's no place out here to even try. Take it to Fox's and see what they say."

She hears Anna close a door and the background noise dims. "Are you and Addison okay?"

She wishes Anna would make it easy for her, wants to shout at her to just say yes, not punish her with sympathy. "Addison's in a difficult place right now."

"Yeah, I know. But are you okay?"

Claire lets out a hard laugh. " 'You' the plural or 'you' the singular?"

"Well, by this point in a marriage, is there a difference?"

Claire tips her head back for a minute and tries to relax the muscles at the back of her throat. "If I send it by insured post, will you be there to sign for it? You can say no, Anna. I don't want to put you on the spot."

"You know I will. Anything."

Before she seals the box, Claire takes the diamond out one last time and slips it onto her finger, holds her hand splayed in front of the woodstove so the fire refracts through the crystal. The mantelpiece above the stove is crowded with framed photographs Jory had unpacked and arranged all over the room, even before the moving truck had left the driveway. For the first time Claire notices the one that is missing, almost certain it had been there the week before. Forgetting the ring, she pushes every picture on the mantel aside—her wedding portrait, birthday parties, Santa's lap—searching for that very first picture they had taken of Jordan Lillian Boehning, weighing 2.8 pounds, still attached to all the tubes and wires that ended up binding their three lives together.

· 21 ·

No one, in theory, should know the exact reason Addison's drug trial was aborted. His corporate lawyers had worked overtime to insure that, and billed for every minute of it. But Claire knew proprietary information clauses and injunctions couldn't stop the gossip at El Gaucho steak house or the Seattle Tennis Club. Her shame—their decision to leave Seattle, her excuses and obfuscations—probably fueled even more rumors.

She had been so determined and stoic in those first weeks after Addison confessed everything to her, adamant that they could not look backward. She found a Realtor immediately, a woman recommended by friends when Claire explained that she and Addison were looking for something farther out of town, a little more space for Jory. Acreage, maybe. A paddock for a horse someday.

The Realtor walked through the house with Claire on one of those rare brilliantly sunny afternoons that kept the whole city from moving south in late fall. Notepad in hand, she opened closets, ran her finger along the custom-wrought metalwork of the banister, unlatched the French doors onto the capacious tumbled-brick patio that overlooked Lake Washington.

Claire finally stopped narrating the tour and fell back a step to let this broad-backed woman in a pink wool crepe suit lead her through her own house. Pinky, as Claire began to think of her, slowly pivoted in the library, absorbing the handblown glass globe over the hanging light fixture. She assessed the imported Spanish tiles around the fireplace, catalogued the carved wooden chess set that Addison had carried home from India on his back when he was nineteen, the shelves of rock-and-roll history and the biographies in which he lost himself when insomnia struck at two or three in the morning. She put a price tag on all of it. The experience reminded Claire of one of those dreams where you are caught in a public place wearing only your underwear, a discount brand at that.

"Beautiful woodwork. And the view, obviously. Good closet space," Pinky had said.

Claire didn't know if she was supposed to respond to this. The words had been vaguely addressed out into the room as if Claire were invisible, a hired attendant. It forced her to look at her own house through the eyes of this detached appraiser or some anonymous buyer. On such a bright morning the impartial sunlight exposed how long it had been since they'd painted the walls or refinished the floors, shadowing the gouges in the woodwork, the scratches in the kitchen appliances.

Finally Claire spoke up. "We were planning a kitchen update soon. And the master bath. We'd already had the architect draw up plans—those could be included in the sale. We spent fifteen thousand dollars on them. The plans, I mean. They're very complete."

Pinky flashed a smile over her shoulder. "Kitchens go out of date so quickly, don't they? We'll want to stage it." It must have been the royal "we" she referenced—Claire had no desire to stage anything. She wanted to sell the house to someone who loved it as she loved it, and then be gone and never reconsider. She wanted it to happen overnight. Today. Before she could panic and padlock herself to the garden gate.

Pinky went on. "People want to come in and imagine their own things in a house. Not yours." She gave Claire an insider's smile. "Not that yours aren't beautiful—but no photographs. Clear the room out some, freshen it up. Sort of . . . *generic*—you know. It's got great potential being right on the lake. In a different market you could ask almost whatever you wanted."

In a different market. Claire heard the echo as *the market in which*

Addison had borrowed all the house's equity. And in truth, Claire realized, as she prepped for the first public showing, people didn't want to see how the Boehnings lived in the house. They didn't even want to see how they themselves would live here. They wanted to see how imaginary people lived. Perfect people. With no clogs of hair in the shower drain, no piles of laundry, or overstuffed Tupperware drawer. They were hoping to find a house that would not just shelter them—it would transform them.

Out on the lake a group of scullers beat by, the coxswains chanting in harsh rhythm with the slender white wake stirred by the oars. The Realtor stood at the window watching them, looking at the distant towers of Seattle's skyline across the water. "Pity I didn't have this listing last year. I had the perfect client and nothing to show him."

Pinky (even Addison called her that by the time they listed), furrowed her powdered brow and asserted that nobody would buy a house between Thanksgiving and Christmas. But Pinky did not know what Claire and Addison knew. The news about the aborted drug trial was leaking. The bridge loans Addison had taken were overdue and no one was willing to extend. So he had borrowed against their personal brokerage accounts. And then the stock market fell. Addison was getting margin calls and there was no more cash to meet them.

Even now she could almost understand his bad judgment. There had been so much money—money in stocks and bonds. Money in CDs and treasury bills. Money in test tubes and fragments of DNA. Claire had stopped looking when she signed credit card slips. She had stopped complaining about unreasonable return policies, or outrageous interest penalties when the payment was a single day late. Last year she had actually given away a laptop that froze up rather than spend two days reformatting it—an excuse to buy the one with a bigger hard drive and sleeker case. The memory of it shames her now.

The list of needs when their house was empty and beckoning had mutated into a list of wants, and then blurred until she forgot how to distinguish the necessary from the desired. Even the translation between time and wealth began to warp. She could fill a day scouring galleries for the perfect glass bowl to set upon the sofa table, just so, where the sunlight caught fragments of color that matched the paint and the upholstery. And that was to be its only purpose—a bowl intended to hold . . . nothing. Air. Reflected light. After years of such forays and purchases the niches were filled with hand-enameled trays and Santa María pottery and spun-copper baskets. The floors were plush with Tibetan carpets and tribal throw rugs. The perfect eclectic mix of primitive and midcentury European paintings hung on every wall. Shelves were laden with art books, cabinets bloated with crystal, closets burst with coats and suits and gowns and boots. In the space of seven months, from the time Addison discovered the toxic liver tissue in one strain of mice to the day they sold the house short, most of it ended up auctioned off or sold for a fraction of its purchase price.

They took the first cash offer on the house. Two weeks later they held an estate sale. The doorbell rang at six fifteen, the sun not even up on a rainy winter day. Claire answered it in her bathrobe, still half asleep, expecting some urgent warning from the police, some locked-out neighbor or kicked-out teenager. A slumped, tobacco-stained gentleman stood on the soggy mat holding a torn bit of newsprint. A misread address, perhaps. Should she be worried about a robbery? Who brought a newspaper to a robbery? Claire knotted her hands into the fleecy neck of her robe, her breath puffed in little cloud balloons.

"We're here for the sale?" Out in the circular drive a woman and child watched from a brown car with no hubcaps.

"What?"

"Is this 4352 Lake Crest Circle?" The man stepped back and looked above the doorway to recheck the address. Two other cars pulled up to the curb.

Claire propped the door open with a garden stone and padded back upstairs to her bedroom. "Addison. People are already coming. Get some clothes on."

"What?" He bolted upright in foggy panic. "Here for what?"

"The sale. Get up. They're down there now. Roaming through our house. I told you we should have let the auction company handle all of it. Oh God. Why didn't I at least set the coffeemaker!" She pulled on blue jeans and a sweatshirt, ran a hot washcloth over her face and a brush through her hair before she went back downstairs.

"How much is this?" a woman asked her.

"Everything should have a tag on it." Claire turned the silver pitcher over. "Twenty-five dollars."

"Is it sterling?"

"It's plate," Claire said aloud, thinking, It was a wedding gift from my cousin, who was too young at the time to know plate from sterling, who ended up marrying a journalist and moved to somewhere in Indonesia. If it were sterling it would be two hundred dollars.

By ten o'clock her living room had more people in it than when she'd hosted the fund-raiser for ovarian cancer research. Now she was host to a party of strangers, people of varied clothes and varied colors, bargain hunters who had gotten up before dawn to drive across town to a rich person's distress sale, spotting opportunity in the fine print of a classified ad. And it was only at that moment, watching the general populace haggle over the price of a silver-plated cream pitcher, that she recognized how deserving she had grown to feel.

The best of their belongings had already gone to an auction house and would be brought up to a public stage in chunks over the next few weeks. Addison had half joked and half consoled that he might hit the jackpot before their furnishings hit the block, and they could buy it all back. And Claire had laughed. Laughed because she was determined, grit-teethed, that she would not cry during daylight hours about the loss of property. In the hours and days after Addison showed her the numbers she realized the material wealth they'd amassed was dissolving like a sugar cube castle in a summer rainstorm.

Claire knew they must jump together onto some new marital foundation, if they were going to survive. It should be no more difficult than leaping back to the solid ground on which they had begun their married life. There had been no money then, only hope and some reassuring groundwork—his almost-finished doctorate, her medical degree, his brilliance and charisma, their youth and an infinite faith in possibility.

In the crucible of their financial implosion Claire felt vitally bonded

to Addison. After a day of sorting and packing their remaining possessions Addison would open a bottle of wine and tell her more; justify his
decisions by explaining the smudged zones of judgment around bell
curves and P values, how questionable data might be thrown out as
statistical "noise." The wine would loosen him, and Claire would see the
shrewd scientist crumpling as the overwhelmed businessman scram-
bled to keep his lab intact once Rick Alperts left.

Claire was appalled at herself for ignoring the signs for so many
months, and perhaps for that reason alone she was determined to be
Addison's most strident defender. She alone knew his secrets, just as she
knew the folds of his neck and the curl of his navel and the crests and
waves of his ears. His secrets gave her power; power that had flourished
inside the flushed and scented skin of their early marriage, and then
almost imperceptibly diminished over time. He depended on her again
now—depended on her to know his blackest truth and keep it safe. She
felt the fierceness of it: a claw sunk into her heart that made them blood
brothers as much as husband and wife, it made it easier to divorce sen-
timent from the house and the cars and the clothes. For a while.

The last night in their home he slept close to her, curled so that
one arm snugged her to him, his hand grasping her belly. She was
conscious of the loose flesh there, where Jory had stretched her until
crescent moons blossomed just below the surface of skin. And she was
conscious that he didn't care; that he loved their girl, and loved her and
loved the flesh that made all of it.

Then one bright flash before the moment of sleep revealed how
much the illusion of his superiority mattered to her, and how much it
was anchored by trust. Until all of this, until all was stripped bare, she
had not seen it. She took his hand, flaccid and warm, and brought it
up to her mouth, not realizing she would bite into the palm until she
tasted his sweat.

· 22 ·

Claire sleeps in the new earrings Addison gave her before he left. Twice during the night she dreams, rouses, reaches toward
Addison's vacant space, then touches the smooth polished glass. The
last spring snow falls that night, and when she wakes up in the morning
almost five inches cover the ground.

She builds a fire and pours milk into a pot for hot chocolate, then
goes back upstairs to wake Jory, who is still deep in the enviable coma
of sleep unique to infants, teenagers and addicts. Claire sits on the edge
of the bed. Jory's hair is a torrent of spun gold curling down her back.
When she was a baby Claire would sometimes pull a chair to the side of
her crib and sit for hours, watching the stripes on her thin cotton gown
ripple in time with her breath. After so many precarious months the
miracle had been too fragile to trust.

She strokes Jory's back to wake her, and her fingers catch in another
strand of gold. Claire untangles it from Jory's hair, traces it around
until she finds the diamond-studded heart pendant.

She walks back downstairs and calls Addison's cell phone, doesn't
wait for more than "Good morning." "Did you buy a necklace for Jory
yesterday?"

"Does this mean it's not a good morning?"

"Just . . . Sorry. No. I don't know yet. Did you buy her a necklace at
Walmart?"

She hears a deep sigh and knows the answer, then she is back up-

169

stairs shaking Jory awake, tugging at the thin gold chain until it threatens to break.

"What?" Jory mutters, then sits up and grabs her mother's hand around the pendant.

"Where did this come from?" Claire asks her, barely reining the accusatory edge in her voice.

Jory hugs her knees to her chest in a barricade. "You know where it came from."

"Did you steal it? Did you?"

Tears are already streaming down Jory's face, her lips blushing red. "I didn't steal it! I bought it."

"Bought it with *what*? Where did you get two hundred dollars?"

Jory throws herself onto her stomach and yanks the comforter over her head. Claire yanks the comforter completely off and throws it onto the floor. "Get dressed. Now. We are going for a drive."

She calls the clinic to say she can't come in until this afternoon. Frida answers that not many patients are likely to come with the snow, anyway, and makes no comment about the distress in Claire's voice.

Claire smells burning milk and turns off the stove, dumps the contents of the pan into the sink and runs back upstairs to get dressed. Then she stops—paralyzed when it dawns on her—and races back downstairs to her desk wearing only jeans and a bra. She pulls on the bottom drawer so hard it comes out of the frame altogether. Every receipt is filed there by month and she dumps the March folder onto the floor, spreading the receipts out so she can spot the grocery store logo. She lines the last four up side by side, a picket fence of spent money, half of it borrowed, to buy milk and eggs and toilet paper and soap.

Every one of the receipts gives Jory away. Every receipt has a fifty dollar charge for a Visa gift certificate on it. Enough to add up to a necklace and more, but not enough to be glaringly missed.

Claire makes herself take five deep breaths, then five more. Five more still before she goes back into Jory's room, picks up her cell phone and her iPod from the dresser and locks them in the file cabinet. "We are leaving in five minutes. Get your boots on. It snowed last night."

"I'm not coming."

"Fine. I am taking the grocery store receipts and this necklace to the police. I'm sure they'll have an idea about how you can pay it back."

The roads are terrible but Claire is too mad to care. Jory radiates her own fury from the backseat. Three times Claire starts to lecture her but clenches her teeth together instead; still, the rage screams unchecked in her mind. She guns the car at a stop sign and feels the tires shimmy over the fresh, wet snow. She almost turns back at the pass; the snow plows haven't been through, but a glance at Jory's defiant face in the rearview mirror keeps her on the road. She can see the crest and it is only another twenty-minute drive down the other side—when the roads are dry.

She digs her cell phone out of her purse and tosses it back to Jory. "Call your father. Call him and tell him what's going on."

"He's probably in a meeting or something," Jory says, her voice congested with tears.

"Yes, and I am supposed to be at work, too. I am not a single parent. Not yet."

"There's no signal here," Jory says, flipping the phone shut.

Of course not. Claire feels like she is choking on her thoughts, they are rushing through her brain so fast. Jory would never have worn that necklace to bed unless she wanted Claire to find it. Worse. *Needed* her to find it. That stab of guilt makes Claire mad all over again. At herself, at Jory, at five inches of snow in late March, for God sakes. She wants to drive all the way to Florida and get on a boat headed for a hot place where nobody knows her name. "Give me the phone," she says.

"There's no signal. I'll call him on the other side."

"Hand me my phone!"

"What? You think I'm trying to steal your stupid phone, just because you stole mine?"

Claire whips around to face Jory, and at that moment the road edge, buried by fresh snow, cuts under the right front wheel. The car shoots forward and Claire has the sick sensation of falling. She jerks the wheel to the left and the car spins halfway around, the clouds and trees and mountain all flashing across the windshield at the same instant in time. The car skids across the highway and bounces off a guardrail then back again to the other side. A white blast hits her in the chest and the car stops with a jolting snap.

The backseat is quiet and for one fraction of an instant Claire reels past all the anger of the last year, pleads with God to save her baby and cries out for Jory.

After another instant of shocked silence Jory answers her. "Way to go, Mom."

Claire covers her face with her hands; her cheeks are wet. She turns around and reaches for Jory. "Are you okay? Does anything hurt?"

Jory shrugs, then shakes her head, and then she starts to cry.

"Okay. Okay." Claire holds her breath to slow her pulse down, her fist over her chest. "So, we are both okay." She turns the ignition key and the engine starts, but when she puts the shift into reverse and presses lightly on the pedal she hears a harsh clatter that makes her lift her foot as if she'd been slapped for presuming the car would move. "Stay in the car. Try the cell phone again, will you?"

Her door has smashed into the guardrail, and through her window she sees a freefall down the mountain, eight inches and a ripple of metal away. She unbuckles her seat belt and crawls across the seats to step into the snow, gets on her hands and knees to look under the car. The mysterious spaces beneath the frame and body disappear into black shadows. She takes the flashlight out of the glove compartment and gets onto her back to wriggle underneath the car. Ice is impacted between the tire and the axle and she slams at it with the butt of the flashlight until it cleaves away. With a surge of relief, she shines the light over the braces and bars and bolts of metal four inches above her face. And then she sees that the fender is jammed into the rubber grooves of the tire.

She shimmies out from under the car and rests beside the front wheel, combing chunks of icy mud out of her hair. Her lips are chapped from breathing through her mouth. After a moment she stands up, her legs shaking. The view from here is actually quite spectacular. She's driven across this pass four or five times and never really paid much attention, always too intent on getting there and back. She pulls a few calming words together in her mind to break the news to Jory that they will have to start walking.

Jory looks at her in amazement, as if she has been told to fly. "It's ten miles to anybody's house!"

"Downhill. But we need to start now. We'll probably see another car soon." Claire says this at the same time she admits to herself they had not seen a single car on the drive up. The back of her jeans are soaking wet; she shivers in the light breeze. "The snowplow should be coming by sometime." Jory's door takes an extra jerk from the outside, but finally pops open.

They haven't gone half a mile before Jory stops. "Why aren't there any pay phones out here if they know there's no cell service?"

Claire keeps walking, not even looking back. "There aren't any stores up here. Or houses. Who's going to use a pay phone?" A half mile farther, Jory sits down in the middle of the road. Claire finally turns around and comes back to her. It's beginning to snow again, lightly. She squats in front of Jory and grasps her hands. "Honey, we have to walk. We have to keep moving. It's the only way out of here. I cannot carry you."

Jory stares hard at her mother, as if with enough fight she could bend the truth to her liking. After a long moment she says, "One of your earrings is gone."

Claire reaches up to her right earlobe and feels the blue glass pendant, then touches her left earlobe. Empty. She collapses to her knees and starts patting the front of her coat, running her fingers through her hair, twisting in every direction searching the snow for the earring she knows is lost underneath the mangled bumper, buried deeper and deeper with every falling flake. "Did I have it on in the car? Did you notice?"

Jory shakes her head. "So. I guess *you* wish they'd put pay phones up here, too, now?"

Claire lets out a sob and Jory looks ashamed. Claire slaps her bare, freezing hands into an inch of wet snow, sits down flat on the roadway until her legs burn. Finally she looks at Jory, aware that her expression must be alarming to her child, knowing she should try to scrounge up some comforting optimism. All she can do is scream out the only truth she is sure of right now: "There is no *'they,'* Jory. Get that through your head before you go any further in your life. There is no *'they.'* Nobody is going to rescue you every time you fuck up. We are on our own out here."

· 23 ·

They walk a little over two miles before a snowplow radios for the state patrol and they get a lift all the way back to the house, which makes Claire feel better about having paid their taxes. Jory barely spoke to her before they were picked up, stomping ahead with her eyes on the road whenever Claire stopped to take in the vista of snow across the freshly plowed fields, spread like a diamond-studded washboard miles below them with the river whipping hard and silver down the middle of the valley floor.

The shared warmth and safety of the house finally shakes Jory loose again—that or the fact that the necklace is at this moment being towed to a garage, and who knows if they'll retrieve it before the return date expires. She fixes a plate of cheese and crackers and brings it to Claire. "We could see if the store has another pair," she says. Claire looks at her quizzically and Jory adds, "Another pair of your earrings."

Claire nods, trying to act like it's as simple as that. She builds a fire in the woodstove and upends their wet boots on a bench to catch the heat before she starts a dinner of baked chicken and rice. Jory turns the stereo on. If there is any unintended benefit to locking up her iPod, Claire figures, it is that she can hear the lyrics of her daughter's music. Jory comes into the kitchen and fleetingly rests her arm on Claire's shoulder before asking if she can help.

Claire hands her a tomato and a knife. They work side by side in silence for a moment. "You'll have to pay us back, Jory," Claire says. "You understand that?" Jory rinses the cutting board and starts slicing the tomato, focusing all her attention on the task. Claire tries to recollect all the other cries for attention she's been too busy or preoccupied to address. "Leaving Seattle has been tough. I know."

Jory interrupts her, blurts in a high voice, "Mom!" She blinks and looks away for a minute. "Can we please not talk about it right now? Please?"

Over dinner Claire starts with something safe. "So who's on Facebook tonight?"

Jory is lining up grains of rice between the tines of her fork, neatly filling up the empty spaces. "Shannon. Wyatt. Brenna broke up with Eli and Emma's not speaking to her anymore."

It's like walking into a movie at the halfway point over and over again. "Why does Emma care about Brenna breaking up with Ian?" Claire asks.

"Eli. Because *she* talked Eli into asking Brenna out in the first place."

"So, where do they go when they 'go out'?" Claire asks.

Jory shrugs. "The movies, mostly. Hang out at the mall."

Claire puts her knife down. "There isn't a movie theater here. Or a mall."

"These are *Seattle* friends, Mom. I don't chat with anybody in Hallum." She pours salt over everything on her plate and takes two bites, then pushes it aside. "My toe shoe ripped last week." She lifts one shoulder when she says it, either in acceptance or defeat. Claire can't read her.

She reaches across the table for Jory's hand. "Babe, until we move back I don't think we should get new pointe shoes. They cost over a hundred dollars." This she says, but does not say, *and all you can do with them is dig a deeper hole in the corner of this living room floor.* She doesn't feel hungry anymore. "Jory. Look. What if we go to the jazz teacher's studio this weekend. People say she's really good. It isn't ballet, but . . . Just take a look." Jory stands up and carries her plate to the kitchen, washes it carefully and puts it back in the cabinet.

After dinner, Claire calls Frida and arranges to be picked up in the morning. Then she dials Addison's cell phone, which rings through to his message. She listens to the whole recording of his name and professional title, followed by the phone number for his secretary if the message is urgent. The secretary, of course, has long since taken a new job. His title, Claire credits, is a matter of definition and imaginative spin—CEO of a shell game, the elusive die always one sales pitch ahead. Listening to the recording now, she hears the change in his voice. The Addison that drove away from Hallum two days ago seems to have forgotten the man who made the message.

She hangs up, not yet decided how to tell a cell phone that she has wrecked the car. She practices a couple of variations and then dials him again. "Hi. I wrecked the car. Long story, nobody's hurt." After she hangs up she pushes Redial and waits through the message again. "Forgot to say I love you."

Jory's light is already out when Claire comes in to say good night. She lies on the bed and rests her cheek against Jory's, wishing the world could be condensed into this sensation. Jory stretches her arms above her head and rolls onto her back.

"Were you asleep?" Claire asks.

"No. It's okay."

"Need another blanket?"

Jory pulls Claire's arm tighter around herself. "No." She is quiet for a while, then, "Mom, you remember that lady?"

Claire is lost. "Who? The jazz teacher?"

"That lady from Nicaragua. With Dad's coat. We drove her out to those cabins." In the dim light Jory's face looks even younger. She pulls away from Claire and props herself up on her elbow. "She's at the bakery sometimes."

"Miguela Ruiz? Did she recognize you?"

"Sure. We talk. A lot."

Claire feels a defensive instinct rising in her. "What does she talk to you about?"

"I don't know. Snow. Birds. Volcanoes. She taught me a poem. She's nice, Mom. Quit looking like that."

"Like what?"

"Like that. She's nice. She's teaching me Spanish."

Claire sits up and combs her fingers through Jory's hair. "She seems nice to me, too."

Claire kisses Jory and starts to leave the room. Just before the door shuts Jory calls to her, "Mom?"

"What?"

"I will pay you back."

Claire's phone doesn't ring until she is almost asleep; the memory of the accident floods back when she hears Addison's voice. "You're sure you're both okay? You don't think you should see a doctor?" Then, even before she can answer, "Is the car totaled?"

"Well, since we only have liability insurance on it, I couldn't say. If it still moves I'll still drive it." She can picture him sitting on the edge of his bed at the Four Seasons, leaning over his knees with his head in one hand. She rolls over on her stomach and looks out the window, a three-quarter moon setting over the patchwork of snow in the fields. "Do we have any money in the savings account?"

"Not enough for a car. Why were you driving over the pass if the roads were snowed in?" She tells him about the necklace and the stolen Visa cards. "Well. They weren't really *stolen*," he says. "She charged them to us."

"Then she was stealing from *us*!" Claire pauses a minute, wanting him to agree. When he is quiet she says, "I'm worried about her. She's here by herself too much."

"What can we do about that? She's too old for babysitters. Can she take the bus to the clinic after school? Wait for you there?"

"There is no school bus to the clinic. We should get a housekeeper or something."

His voice grows agitated, "Oh God, Claire. Maybe this whole move to Hallum just isn't working. Maybe we should rent something in Seattle."

"We need to put the money into your meetings. Are you giving up on vascumab?"

"No. But at the end of the day, all I really have to sell is my brain. Maybe I should get a job in somebody else's lab."

At the end of the day. Claire is irritated by the trite phrase, as if disasters of any proportion could be wrapped up by sunset, in time for drinks and dinner. She blurts out, "Who would hire you if they knew everything?" But she hates herself as soon as she says it and stumbles toward an apology. He only makes it worse when he tells her she has a point, the defeat in his voice sounding both pitiful and infuriating. After a long silence she says, "Look. We're both worn out. Can we talk about it later?"

She spends the night tangled in half-formed dreams, hearing Addison confess how hard it is to be optimistic in a meeting of skeptical venture capitalists, to keep explaining the life-changing possibilities of his molecule to people who only ask about profit and cost.

She has kissed Jory awake and started out the door to wait for Frida's car when the house phone in the kitchen rings; she answers it ready to convince Addison that he can't give up. But the call is *for* Addison rather than from him. As soon as she hangs up she dials his cell phone to give him the message, "The Super 8 motel in Chicago called to say they found a pair of your pants in a drawer." Addison doesn't say a word. "Not quite the Drake, Addison. Does this mean even your business account is empty?"

He sighs so deeply she can almost feel his breath traveling to her from across the mountains. "I was just trying to save money. I didn't want you to worry."

Claire remembers the last time Addison had said he didn't want her to worry. She had picked Jory up after school on the one afternoon she didn't have a ballet class. They'd planned it for weeks—find Dad's Christmas present together, separate long enough to choose something for each other, then dinner at Il Fornaio, Jory's favorite. They made a game of it, hunting through the men's department for a hot-pink tie, a jingle bell sweater, a rhinestone and blue velvet cuff link case, a green plaid beret, imitating Dad's appalled reaction and faked pleasure on Christmas morning. Claire finally suggested they'd do better at Fox's Gem Shop, since he'd hinted around about a TAG Heuer watch. But as soon as they stepped past the windbreak of the building her umbrella was whipped inside out. Jory pulled her into Gap, where a stack of mini Totes were piled at a cash register.

The salesgirl zipped the magnetic strip down the card reader slide and waited. Frowned. She held the card up, flipped it over and pulled it through the reader for a second and third time. Claire smiled at her. She was probably only a couple of years older than Jory. "They're finicky sometimes. Do you want me to try it? Or if you have a plastic bag—sometimes if you wrap it in a plastic bag it'll read the card, I have no idea why."

A couple behind her in line moved to the next register. Another woman rested her bags beside Claire's umbrella on the counter. "It's so exasperating," she offered. "We were in Vancouver a couple of months ago and I bought a new purse. Two hours later we couldn't charge dinner. They'd frozen the card. I had to stand outside in the parking lot on my cell phone convincing somebody in New York I hadn't stolen my own account number. Security's gone too far." Claire finally gave up on the umbrella and paid for the parking garage with quarters and dimes scrabbled out of the glove compartment and her coat pockets and seat cushions.

When she pulled into her driveway Addison's car was already under the porte cochere, the house ablaze, the stereo throbbing to David Byrne. He stood in their kitchen wearing a Santa Claus apron over his white shirt, suit pants and loosened tie, rocking the steel blade of a knife in an arc across the cutting board. His face was flushed. She thought he might be chopping bones and gristle violently enough to break a sweat, until she noticed the tumbler beside him.

"You're home early." Claire picked up the tumbler and sniffed it. "Scotch? Rough day?" Jory, still upset about the spoiled shopping trip, tossed her book bag on the breakfast table and disappeared into her room.

"*Mais oui!*" he quipped. "Come and give me *le* juicy whomping kiss I deserve," all poured forth in a lugubrious French accent. She slid her purse off her shoulder onto one of the counter stools and leaned against him, pushed into the solid muscle of his arm and pressed her mouth into the warm, fragrant gully of his throat.

It was a scene familiar to the evening ritual of their coupling. But it was occurring two hours earlier than it should, and the music was a decibel too loud, the tumbler a finger's breadth too empty, the smell of his sweat tinged with the edgy musk of anxiety. And now Claire knew the credit card rejection was not a fluke. Some silent and majestic turning had occurred, was becoming discovered in the filamentous cracks before their glass house shattered.

She straightened her back and watched him for a minute, studied the mute victims of his knife. "What is it?"

"Homemade salsa."

"No. I mean, why are you home so early?"

He lifted a shoulder without looking at her and scraped the cilantro into a porcelain bowl, the cutting board bleeding green juice across the granite counter. He cracked the lid off the picante, stirred it into the cilantro with a fork and held the tines up to her lips. She turned away, and so he put the fork into his own mouth, followed it with a swig from the tumbler and began chopping a fresh bunch. Claire watched his hands as he worked, the knuckles blanching each time he pressed the weight of the knife deep enough to scar the wood, taking a quick breath each time he swung the blade above flawless ruffled leaves. She winced when the steel crushed the bright herb.

She turned the stereo down and asked him, before she had intended, before she had readied herself, "Did the credit card company call today?"

She wanted him to act surprised, at least. To huff and blame it on the new laptop he bought yesterday. She wanted him to gesture toward his coat, slung across an armchair, gesture casually with his chin or elbow and tell her to grab the Master Card or his own Visa until he had a chance to track down the mistake.

He placed the fork in the sink and rinsed and dried his hands, took off the apron and poured her a glass of wine. "Sit down," he said.

He grasped her lightly around her wrist and led her into the dark living room, started to sit next to her on the long sofa, then was up again, pacing along the walls. He ran his hand across the stone mantelpiece, fingered their embroidered Christmas stockings, aligned the

corner of a recently purchased landscape painting, flicked the tiny an-
gels on a candle carousel into a shimmer of brass bells that quickly fell
silent.

She waited. He stood at the wall of windows facing the patio, and
stared out at the lake, ink in the early winter night. Someone, probably
the housekeeper, had plugged in the Christmas tree, and the multicol-
ored bulbs lit the broad plane of his half-turned face, made his cheek
look ruddy and young so that she wanted to pull him next to her and
slip her hands beneath his sweater, warm them against his warm skin
and pretend this evening was no different from any other.

Addison gestured toward the lake with a shoulder. "Fenster was
smart to put this patio off the living room. Remember how we argued
about that? Works, though."

The digression put her more on edge. "Addison, just say it. It isn't
just the charge card, is it?"

He turned, stumbled on the edge of the carpet and bumped a crystal table lamp, which teetered until he grasped it, settled it and held
both palms up like a traffic cop, cautioning the lamp to stay put. Then
he sat down at the other end of the sofa. She could hear the sound of
alcohol in his voice, and fatigue, and something else, something she
hadn't heard before. Something forlorn and defeated that made the
room feel big and cold.

"Did I ever tell you about PT Barnum?" Addison asked.

"Sure. When you sold Eugena. Barnum lost everything, didn't he?
More than once?" Claire waited for him to go on, to look at her or
move closer. It felt like the kind of moment when they should be sitting
snug up against each other, gripping each other's hands, she thought.
But she didn't move, either. She cleared her throat and started to ask
him something but couldn't get any words out, bit her lip and began
again. "Is that what you're about to tell me? We've lost everything?"

He didn't answer. Her brilliant, manic, silver-tongued husband, the
shooting star of Seattle's biotech millionaires, had no answer for her.

Claire started to laugh. It was the first emotion that overtook her,
she couldn't think why. To break the tension, probably. Or simply that
the concept was too ridiculous; there was too much money tied up in

this very room to fathom "losing everything." Later, much later, she would think about it and recognize that she had known on some level for months, sensed some drastic storm in the rare air they had come to accept as their due. She had sensed it in the longer and longer hours Addison spent at the lab, the nights his side of the bed stayed cold and empty. She had heard it in the false cheeriness on his phone calls to investors and employees, and the office door he swung shut if she walked by. So maybe that was why she laughed. Maybe it was her apology to him for the complicity of shameless self-deception.

Still, the outburst embarrassed her, even with her husband of fifteen years. Addison turned to look at her, his eyes playing over her face and his head cocked a bit to one side. For a minute she thought he might laugh, too, turn it all into a joke and get up to set the table and call Jory for dinner. And then the space between them seemed to yawn dangerous and wide, and she held her breath, picked up his limp hand in both of her own, held it tight against her chest. "Okay. Tell me everything."

It was serendipity, really, that brought it to light. If Rick Alperts's bicycle wheel had not caught the end of a stick in precisely the position to drive it through his spokes, and thus send Rick arcing through the air onto the pavement, Addison would never have checked the mouse cages and done the blood tests himself. And if Addison had not checked the cages, vascumab would likely have marched straight through Institutional Review Board approval and into phase 1 human testing as scheduled.

Rick Alperts had been Addison's third major coup. The first, obviously, was the bright light of his initial concept, the two altered moieties on the leading antiangiogenesis drug that led to vascumab. The second coup had been Anna's husband, Nash, the last crucial investor to come on board, who understood that the risk in the biopharmaceutical industry was high but the enormous start-up costs could be a tax write-off. And the third coup was Rick. At thirty-two he knew more about VEGFR-2 drug development than anyone in the country. Addison hired him out of a California lab, promising Rick a share in the company. Addison had returned from their last courtship meeting saying he probably hadn't even needed that incentive—when Rick saw Addison's structure he'd been speechless for a few minutes, and then practically begged Addison for the job.

Almost every step had gone fluidly forward after that. Vascumab's pharmacological activity matched all the computer models Addison had worked on for two years. The tissue cell cultures showed tumor clearance and no sign of toxicity. And the mice. Three different strains of mice were infused with no discernible organ damage. They tried it in two primates and the side-effect profile was nil—better than that of any competitor on the market.

The FDA application for Investigational New Drug status was well past the thirty-day mark with no objections raised, and the review board had been considering their protocol for ten days. Approval was expected within a month or two. Two pharmaceutical companies were already talking offers. If the human trials went as well as Addison and Rick predicted, they could license the drug for a high premium within a year.

The day of the bike accident Addison was waiting for Rick when he came in, four hours late with his arm in a sling, jocular about being a little high after one Vicodin. Rick had a small abrasion on his cheek, Addison recalled, which made him look that much younger, a schoolkid roughed up on the playground. But from the look on Rick's face Addison knew immediately these two weren't the only sick mice. They were just the only sick mice Addison knew about.

"It only happened in one strain," Addison told Claire. "The rest showed no problem. Four mice out of fifty-two. Rick was ready to repeat the test on them—he was convinced it was a fluke and we shouldn't interrupt the board's review until we knew for sure." He slumped against the back of the sofa so that she could hardly see his features, the winking Christmas tree lights flickering on his cheeks. "We had so much data already—more than we needed." He paused before he said what was obvious to her. "So I didn't report it."

Claire waited through some silence until it was clear he didn't know how to go on. She prodded him. "But the review board found out anyway. And then they denied your trial protocol?"

Addison looked directly at her then. "They found out because I told them. But when they found out I'd waited four weeks they withdrew approval."

He seemed to physically deflate, as if telling Claire had been the worst moment in the entire cascade of the debacle. She was too stunned, still, to know how she would feel about this tomorrow, next month, at the end of their lives. Too stunned even to listen to the part of her that knew the most critical thing for their family at that moment was to recognize how fragile Addison was. So she asked him, "Where is our money in this?"

"I took some bridge loans to repeat the mouse trials. Rick left— there were delays." He pressed the heel of his hand against his eyes, first one and then the other. "I had to back the loans, Claire." And then he listed all that was gone, all he was able to sign away without ever telling his wife. Without ever asking.

· 24 ·

Frida arrives to drive Claire to the clinic. "You own all this land?" she asks, bouncing the clutch to get her old Volvo started up the driveway. A flock of starlings startles and swerves when the engine grinds.

Claire looks out the window. The new snow is already melting away, the pale, smoky green tops of the sagebrush show where even the deepest drifts had covered them a few weeks ago. Swaths of brown grass lie flattened against the earth in the wake of retreating winter. "It's in an easement—it can't be divided. Otherwise we'd sell some of it off."

"Nice to have so much privacy."

Claire nods, thinking that the privacy has become a burden of loneliness in these last months. Then she turns to Frida, "I need to find somebody to be with Jory in the afternoons. Sort of like a house-keeper . . . but with no housekeeping."

Frida thinks about it for a minute. "Well, you're not exactly on the 'road most traveled' out here. She getting into trouble?"

"Close enough." Claire shrugs and wraps her arms tight around her body, not ready to go into the story. "She's not happy out here."

The car tries to stall in the steep curve just before the drive meets the county road. Frida ratchets the gear down and guns it through the turn. "A lot of people move to the valley thinking it's the same to live here as it is to vacation here. Broke up my marriage."

"I didn't know you'd been married," Claire says, immediately feeling bad that she'd brushed by so much of Frida's personal life. Had she left so little room for it in all their small talk? "Was it recently?"

"Eight years ago. Eight and three-fourths. It was his idea to move here." She tilts her head for a second and then squints at Claire, as if only now reaching a conclusion. "I think he couldn't stand *not* being anonymous. No place to hide in a town of four hundred people. Kind of funny, though. Once the word got out, I had more people offering me food and company than any other time or place in my life."

Claire is quiet, drifting back to the day before they left Seattle. By then most of her friends knew the move was anything but voluntary. The doorbell had rung at seven thirty in the morning, echoing in the empty marble entryway. When Claire opened it she found Sherry, Anna's neighbor, standing outside with a foil-covered casserole in her hands, the first person on that doorstep in a week, besides the moving men. Her eyes kept darting from Claire to her car, where Sherry's daughters sat dressed for church. "I can't stay, just wanted to drop this off." She'd lifted the corner of the foil like she was reminding herself what she'd cooked. "Chicken-corn chowder—the recipe said put in celery salt, but I didn't have any. So I just used salt and celery," she had laughed, talking too rapidly for Claire to add a word. "I don't even know what celery salt is—me and my cooking!" Then she had handed the casserole over and offered Claire a quick kiss on the cheek, waving behind her as she ran back to the car, late for church. "Keep the pan, sweetie. Call when you're settled."

Frida has her gaze steady on the road, but Claire can tell she's tuned in to her mood. She says, "So you just let me know if I need to be bringing you any food and company."

Frida drops Claire at the garage to pick up the Audi. "She runs," the mechanic says. "Don't look so good. I put the bodywork estimate in the envelope there." Claire had never cared too much about cars but, still, it's depressing to see it so battered. The towing fee and unavoidable repairs had cost almost twice as much as the necklace, which is nowhere to be found.

She parks outside the clinic and calls home, hoping the unanswered rings mean that Jory got herself to the bus stop. When she hangs up she sees Miguela sitting on the metal railing of the wheelchair ramp, watching her car. As soon as Claire gets out Miguela jumps off the rail with a little huff, a scratch of gravel. *"Doctora. Buenos días."*

"Hey." Claire drops her keys in her purse and walks to the bottom of the adjacent stairs. "You okay? *No estas enferma?"*

Miguela waves a hand in front of her face once, then sweeps her hair back, the curls immediately rebounding. "Yes. I come to ask again for a job. I see your car. It's okay?"

Claire flares her hands open, wishing she knew what the gesture for acceptance might be in Nicaragua, feeling like so much of her communication with patients here is boiled down to an approximation at best. "Dan would have to decide—it's his clinic. But it's okay with me."

Miguela's eyebrows dart together but then she smiles. "No. Your car. It does not look okay." She points to the mangled front fender. "But you and Jory—you are okay?"

"Oh! Yes. Fine. Thank you. Jory said she saw you at the bakery."

Miguela glances out toward the road, then back, with a look on her face somewhere between apology and hope, or so it seems to Claire. "She is very smart, Jory. She's learning Spanish." The look intensifies and she adds, "I only talk with her there. At the bakery."

"It's all right. It's good—I don't know, you may be her only friend out here so far. We should get you on Facebook." She says this quickly, almost to herself, and can't tell if Miguela understands but decides to let it go. "Well. I am late." She gestures at the clinic door, the shift of colors blurring behind the glass as patients move between the chairs and desk and exam area.

Anita puts a stack of incomplete charts in her hands as soon as she walks down the back hall into the office. "These are all coded wrong. Dan's not coming in today so you better get to work." Her ankles are so swollen in these last six weeks of pregnancy she is wearing tennis shoes with the laces undone, the backs folded under her heels.

"Get your feet up," Claire says. "At least during lunch. Did he say why?"

"He said he and Evelyn had to go to Wenatchee on business. Looks like everybody but me is coming in late or not coming at all."

Claire drops the charts on her desk chair, the only clear surface. "I saw Miguela Ruiz outside. She's looking for a job here."

"She already talked to me. She wants to work for free? Then we've got a job." Anita sways down the hall toward her desk, flipping all the exam room flags out to prove she has filled them.

It is a hard day to be short staffed. Claire has to send two patients to the emergency room across the pass, the first with obvious pneumonia, and the second by ambulance (the spinning red lights stunning the waiting room into silence) when his "acid indigestion" clarifies itself as myocardial ischemia. She doesn't start sorting through all the incomplete charts she'd thrown on her desk until well after six o'clock.

She reaches for the phone and knocks an elbow against the pile, sledding a cascade of paper onto the floor. But she feels too overwhelmed to do more than sit back in her chair and stare at the mess, as if some genie might sort it out if she gave up and went home. She can't even remember if she told Jory to wait at the grocery store or take the school bus—reconsidering, now, who is being most punished by the confiscated cell phone.

"I hope you feel better than you look." Frida is leaning against the doorframe eating a pack of gummi bears.

Claire holds out her hand for one and bites down on it, loving the rush of saliva, feeling her hunger. "You like to surround yourself with Kool-Aid colors, don't you," Claire says, propping her feet on the top of the open bottom drawer. She reaches for another piece, choosing orange this time, enjoying the almost forgotten sensation of candy stuck on her teeth.

"Only my food and my hair bands." But then she remembers more and waggles one foot in its sandal. "Socks, too, I guess."

Claire swivels so she is facing Frida, briefly rejuvenated by the burst of glucose. "I don't actually know for certain where my daughter is right now."

Frida sits down in her own chair, the tops of their desks so close the blizzard of paper makes them look continuous. She spreads open a brochure on STDs and pours out the rest of the package of candy, sorting through to collect the green ones. "Any more thoughts on the housekeeper?"

Claire lifts one shoulder. "I don't have any money to pay one."

"Room and board might be enough."

"You didn't see the inside of my house. The only space is an over-sized closet off the kitchen." Claire stands up to put on her coat, deciding even without calling home again that Jory trumps the paperwork.

Frida leans over the desk on her elbows, pushing charts and lab slips and phone memos into random piles. "It's still probably a lot nicer than where some of these folks live." She waves her hand around the whole cluttered office, referencing every charity patient on their unprofitable books. "Somebody here would be happy to sleep in your kitchen."

They walk out to the parking lot together, the sky a steely blue that is neither night nor day. Frida stands with her car keys in her hand and squints down the valley, where the paler twilight remembers the sun. She takes a long breath, rolls her shoulders up to her ears and then drops them, stretching her arms behind her. Something in the motion reminds Claire of her favorite birds, the blue herons that used to roost in their trees on Lake Washington, hunting along the shallow shore with elastic necks, walloping into the air on ragged wings with pterodactyl cries.

Frida takes her time absorbing this magnificent sky, then turns to Claire. "You don't seem quite so gun-shy around here anymore."

"What do you mean?"

"I mean . . ." She tilts her head up, like maybe there is an answer floating by. "I mean when you first started working here you seemed like you were afraid you were going to break somebody. Drop some patient on the ground and shatter him to pieces."

Claire feels a surge of pride, quickly chased by a surge of embarrassment, like she's taking credit for something she hasn't earned yet. "At least I'm speeding up. You didn't hear anything from Dan, did you?"

Frida shakes her head. "You're worried. Aren't you?"

Claire stares at a pin of light hovering on the horizon above Frida's shoulder. An airplane coming at her or moving away. Or Venus. "He wouldn't tell us, would he?"

"You'd have to pull it out of him like an old bullet." She's quiet for a minute, then adds, as if it were clearly connected, "He's seen so many patients by this age he almost has a second sight about sickness—I sometimes wonder if that's how he can run this place on next to nothing. Line up a room of people and he can smell which one is really sick."

Frida could have no way of knowing how that remark twists in Claire's plexus, remembering her last week of residency, that night in the emergency room. She can still see the woman's face. All the residents knew her—she came in three or four times a month wanting narcotics. "Well," Claire says. "I won't be matching that."

Frida lets out a low hum. "That man taking TUMS for his heart attack today would disagree, I think." She opens the door to her car, seems to make a point of dropping the subject. "Go get your girl. See you tomorrow."

She drives slowly past the grocery store, scanning the white-lit doorway where Jory usually stands, calls the house one last time and gets no answer, then parks and searches the store without finding her. But as soon as she turns the last bend in their driveway she sees that every light in the house is blazing; the music is so loud she can hear it through the closed windows of the car. The door is locked; Jory doesn't hear her knock so she lets herself in, she drops her keys and purse on the table. Jory is dancing, oblivious and invisible, her eyes closed so that all she sees is the slow, swaying rhythm, moving her body in places Claire knows a human is not hinged. Near the end she opens her eyes and freezes, abruptly aware of her mother.

Claire smiles, wishing she'd stayed outside and spied through the windows. "So, you like Bill Withers now?"

Jory twists a strand of hair into her mouth and Claire can barely understand her. "I guess I like that song. That 'Sunshine' song, with all the 'I knows.'"

"Twenty-six," Claire says. "There are twenty-six 'I knows' in that song."

Jory turns off the stereo and the room seems colder in the silence. "You counted them!?"

Claire stands still for a minute. "Ask your Dad about it someday. When did the bus get you home?"

"Two and a half hours ago. Actually, two hours and forty-five minutes."

"Think we're safe enough to turn out a few of these lights yet?" Claire sees Jory blush, a little surprised that she's so sensitive about it. "I'm sorry I was late, sweetheart. Bakery tomorrow, okay?"

Claire fills the rice cooker and rests with her back against the sink, looking into the alcove that juts off the kitchen. It had probably been converted from an attached woodshed—at least that's what she remembered the architect telling them. The ceiling slopes so steeply there is only a four-foot corridor along the living room wall with enough headroom to stand up. There is a closet-sized toilet stall that none of them ever uses—Claire hasn't cleaned it for months. A washer and dryer stand beside it. The floor is covered with cracked linoleum and the only light comes through one small window above the laundry area, too high to see out. No question, it is the gloomiest corner of the house, the place to hide all the junk nobody has time to pick up. Its only saving grace is the clean scent of laundry detergent. But they could put in some sort of door, some paint, a carpet. It could work, if Miguela wanted it to. Maybe better than where she is now.

The rice cooker clicks off and she lifts the lid, filling the kitchen with a starchy floral scent. Jory is vigorously whipping Skippy, sugar and tamari into her own version of peanut sauce. Claire puts her hand on Jory's, arresting the whirl of her fork, and she looks up with a half-expectant, half-defensive expression. "I saw Miguela today." Claire pauses, considering how much explanation she should give. "How would you feel about having her stay with us. Just for a while," Claire asks.

"Like, stay with us *where*?"

"Here. I'd put a door on the alcove." Jory sucks her cheek in and Claire gets ready to hear her protests, practicing responses for each of the tumbling reactions she sees in her face.

"Is this about the necklace?"

"No. Not just about the necklace. It's . . . I have to work late a lot."

Jory's jaw rocks back and forth and her eyes fix on a spot somewhere near the alcove entrance. She shrugs. "Sure." Then she picks up the fork again and whips the white, tan and brown goo into a blended whirlpool.

· 25 ·

They spend the weekend trying to turn the alcove into a passable home. Claire lets Jory choose the paint colors and bed-spread, a few throw pillows and a poster of a dancer's muscular legs in ragged warm-ups and frayed toe shoes. The room doesn't actually have a bed in it yet, only an inflatable mattress. But then, it doesn't have a tenant yet, either.

"So when are you going to ask her?" Jory asks, her hair streaked with turquoise paint.

"I have to find her first. She's always found me. Maybe you should tie your hair back." Jory looks at the blue ends and tries to peel the paint off with her blue fingernails. "Or paint the other side so it matches."

"Speaking of, Mom, can I make a suggestion?" Claire tries to make her face look open, since she knows she will hear it whether she agrees or not. "If you're going to use the drugstore dye you should add in some highlights." After a pause she adds, "That didn't hurt your feelings, did it?"

Claire draws a strand of hair in front of her face. "It washes out. I think I'll just highlight it with gray." Jory seems to find this joke hysterical. "*Now* you're hurting my feelings!" But it has been a long time since Claire has seen her laugh so unself-consciously. Not since her father was last home.

Addison had been quiet on the phone for a long weighted moment when Claire told him her decision about Miguela. "It's an awfully small house, Claire. And you don't know that much about her."

"No. But Jory likes her. We don't have a lot of options at the moment; everything is so up in the air." She'd waited, then, to hear him contradict her, part of her was always waiting, fatigued with waiting, for the screen to go black and the lights to come up at the end of this movie.

"Well," he'd finally said. "I guess it's better than having her stay alone so much."

And maybe only because of the rush of disappointment his agreement stirred, she asked him, "Did you call Ron Walker?"

"I will. I'm still planning to."

Jory had been watching a music video while her parents talked, a blond babe crooning for her Romeo so she'd never have to be alone. After Claire hung up the phone she walked over and shut it off, telling Jory to do her homework, but wanting, really, to cry for all the trouble that still lay ahead in her daughter's life. Wanting her to find love and to be loved and wanting to warn her all the same. And in the end, wanting most of all to smash the money machine that produced these videos that made Jory long for love before she even knew herself.

Claire looks around the freshly painted room—and it feels more like a room now, less like a laundry alcove. "It reeks of paint in here," she says. "I like the color, though. What do you think? Should I talk to her next week?"

Jory stretches to open the small window above the washer and in only a moment the air feels fresher. Claire sees a new stripe of turquoise paint on the other side of Jory's hair—maybe she'd taken Claire seriously. "Why not find her tomorrow?" Jory asks.

There is no cell phone number in Miguela's medical chart, or in Anita's database. Claire drives to the orchard after work and parks near the cabins, wishing she knew which one Miguela inhabited. After twenty minutes the car is getting cold, and she decides to ask the foreman where Miguela lives.

She rings the bell, a little nervous about how he'll react, how much he'll want to know. But it is Miguela who opens the door, with a mop in her hands. She accepts Claire's offer without even asking the salary. The foreman shows no more annoyance than a shake of his head when he writes out Miguela's last paycheck. The strangest aspect of it all, Claire thinks, is the feeling that she and the foreman are brokers for this woman's labor.

Jory is upstairs when they get back to the house, but a flowered bedsheet has been tacked up in front of the alcove and a glass jar with the earliest wildflowers, bluebell and yellow bell mixed in with the dark spiny leaves of Oregon grape, is sitting on the washer.

"We have an air mattress for you. *Una cama,*" Claire says.

Miguela smiles, lifts her dark brows, suggesting as much a confidence in Claire's intentions as any delight with her new quarters. But then she sets her pack down and opens the door to the toilet stall, picks up the jar of flowers and puts it down again, runs her hand down the flowered bedsheet. "It's good," she says. "*Perfecto.*"

When they come out of the kitchen Jory is sitting on the stairs hugging her knees to her chest. Claire sees a blush of color in her cheeks. A small crush, she thinks, like she has a little crush on Miguela. But then it's gone, and Jory jumps up, remembering something, leads them both back into the kitchen and shows them the little hook she has made for the bedsheet out of a broken coat hanger, so the curtain can be held open for more light. Jory takes Miguela on a tour of the house—the two bedrooms upstairs, and the bathroom, making it sound like they have always considered the utility alcove a spare bedroom, once even taking her hand for a moment as they start back down the stairs.

Claire unpacks the air mattress from its zippered bag and plugs in a hair dryer, watches the vinyl bed inflate with soft popping sounds. It fills the small space, leaving only a single foot of room to walk along the opposite wall. When the noise of the dryer stops, she hears Jory talking. She is kneeling on the end of the sofa explaining the photographs on the mantel to Miguela, who points to a picture of Jory at about age eleven, only three years ago. They had gone to Costa Rica for a vacation over Christmas break and Jory had built a snowman in the sand, three half spheres lying supine on the beach under a palm tree, as if the tropical heat had knocked him flat—that or he was going for a suntan. Jory is wearing a bikini that shows her scrawny, prepubescent body, sand sticking to her thighs. It is stunning, really, how recent that trip feels to Claire, how fast her baby has grown up. When they were emptying out the house for the movers Claire had discovered a box of diapers tucked at the back of a linen closet, still sealed up and good as new. She'd given them to the mother of a new baby down the street.

Coming home from work the next day she hears voices through the front door and stops with the knob half turned. Listening. It has been so long just the two of them, mother and daughter. Two women sharing a small space, one still struggling to be in complete control and the other trying to take more control than she knows how to cope with. She doesn't intend to sneak in on them, but still, opens the door more quietly than usual, hangs her coat on the hook without a sound, takes an extra moment to smooth the folds. The room is warm and Claire smells cooked onions and garlic.

Miguela is laughing. Claire hasn't heard her laugh like this before— without a tangling catch in the undercurrent. "*Pero el perro no es perfecto.*" Miguela releases the *r*'s in a light tap, then a snare drum ripple, then a single tap again."

"*Peddddo,*" Jory says, sounding like she has held ice in her mouth long enough to partially freeze her tongue. Claire steps fully into the room now and sees Jory pushing the point of her tongue against the roof of her mouth with her fingertip. Miguela sits with her heels on the rung of her chair, head bowed over her knees and her shoulders shaking. When Jory sees her mother she stiffens like she's been caught with a cigarette.

Miguela stands up and smoothes her hair back, wedges her hands into the pockets of her jeans. "*¿Quiere comer?* I make a small dinner. *Gallo pintó.*" She waves her elbows toward the set table. Two plates are already streaked with bits of rice, beans, and tomatoes. A third, clean place setting is laid out at the other end with a cloth napkin folded under the fork and a pitcher of water, thin slices of lemon floating among the ice cubes like pale aquatic flowers.

The following day Claire comes home after work with a collapsible metal bed frame and twin mattress she picked up at the con-
signment store south of town. She has also bought two new mattress
pads with the hope they might make sleeping on top of a stranger's
nocturnal history more hygienic. It would make Claire sleep better,
at least. She stacks up three plastic milk crates to make a cabinet for
Miguela's clothes and brings one of the narrow bedside tables down
from Jory's room.

Sunday night the wind wakes Claire up from a sound sleep. "Shoulder winds," she'd heard them called, because they swept through at the
turning of seasons, blowing down the valley channel hard enough to
fell trees that hadn't survived winter. It should inspire her with the anticipation of full spring, but they sound too lonely, howling and buf-
feting the house. Now and then she hears the crack of a tree limb, now
and then the clatter of the old barn.

She gets up to make some tea, forgetting that she risks waking
Miguela. But when she steps into the hall she sees a candle burning
on the dining table, Miguela sitting up already, bundled in Addison's
jacket. Claire goes back into the bedroom and finds a bathrobe she
hasn't worn in years, brings it downstairs and folds it over Miguela's
chair.

"I am sorry. Did I make noise?" Miguela asks.

Claire shakes her head. "The wind." She bundles her own robe
around her neck. "Do you want some tea?"

"No." But then she starts to get up. "I can make you some?"

Claire puts a hand on Miguela's shoulder. "I'll get it." She brings two
cups back to the table with a saucer for the tea bags. "Were you reading
a letter?" she asks, indicating a worn envelope in Miguela's hand.

Miguela picks it up, folds it along a smudged crease and holds it in
her lap. "No. Only thinking."

"Are you comfortable enough? The bed is okay?"

"Yes, the room is very nice."

Claire lowers her tea bag into her cup and watches the color bleed
through the hot water, caught in the strangeness of sharing her house
with someone she knows so little about. "I wish I could pay you more

right now. I know you're probably trying to send money home." She leans forward over the table and sets her teacup on the saucer; the sound of glass on glass is jarring. "It's very helpful to have you here right now—with Jory. That's the main thing, just being here with her when I'm at work."

Miguela nods. "It is a hard age for a girl. A special age." Her eyes are too far outside the low light for Claire to see them clearly. "I am not sending money home."

"You said you had a friend here. Someone else from Nicaragua." Miguela shakes her head, either unclear about the question or denying it, Claire can't tell. "I thought you said you'd followed someone here. When I first met you."

Miguela opens her mouth as if she has just recalled the conversation; a flicker of surprise crosses her face, perhaps that Claire would remember such a small detail. "She is not here now." She hesitates a moment and adds, "No one will come to your house."

Claire hadn't meant the question to sound so self-concerned, but feels a tinge of relief at the answer that makes her press on, admit that while she does not need to hear everything, she has to trust what she does hear. "Miguela. I hate to ask you this." She hesitates, not knowing any easy way to put it. "You told me once that you had never had a child. Is that right?"

Miguela's face is perfectly still, as if she is holding her breath, holding her heartbeat. Claire feels a little ripple crawl up the back of her neck, thinks it could as easily be guilt about pressing her on such a personal topic (the breach it requires of a physician's secret, the fierce certitude that women hid births for reasons only God could know) as a revelation that Miguela is quite capable of deception, may even have cause to hide this particular truth from Claire. Another gust of wind buffets the windowpanes and a tree branch tumbles against the roof. Something scuttles inside the wall.

Finally Miguela answers, her voice almost toneless, her face unusually still. "I had a child. But I lost her."

Claire drops her face into her hands, a rush of heat flowing out from the center of her chest. "I'm so sorry." She rubs her palm down her face and looks up. "And I'm sorry I had to ask you." After a moment she stands up and puts the extra bathrobe in Miguela's lap. "Please. This is for you. And if you need anything—we live so far from town here. If you want to go into the store for something . . . tell me. Okay?"

"Thank you, *doctora*."

"Claire. Just Claire."

· 26 ·

When he calls on Thursday evening, Claire hears the change in Addison's voice as soon as she answers her phone. "I want you to come to Seattle, can you? This weekend?"

She walks over to shut her bedroom door. "As in tomorrow? I don't know, Addison. I don't know how early I can leave the clinic. It's been really busy. Plus I *think* I've talked Jory into trying a dance class."

"A dance class?" The way he says it Claire can tell this usurps whatever else has got him so excited.

"Well, it's kind of an experiment. A woman here who teaches jazz— don't get your hopes up yet. Jory sure hasn't."

"But still. I mean, it's a start." Then he seems to recollect what made him call, winding up again. "Drive out later if you need to, then."

Claire sits on the end of the bed, glancing at the clock, the sun breaking over the horizon in a bright rectangle on the floor; she's running late. "What are you so excited about?"

"Hmmm, still up in the air, but maybe good news. At any rate, it would be a nice weekend for all of us." She hears a question mark at the end of this that she knows wasn't planned, waits long enough to catch the rhythm of his breath, wishing she hadn't become habituated to disappointment. "Let me talk to Dan. And the dance teacher." Addison doesn't say anything, holding on until she breaks. She walks to the window to feel the sun on her face, warm for only a moment before

201

it's swept behind a cloud. "All right. I don't know when we'll be able to leave here, though."

The clerk smiles as soon as Claire says "Boehning". He hands her an embossed cardboard folder, gilt-imprinted with the name of the hotel, the Mayflower Park, with two room keys inside. A bellman has already put their bags onto a cart and is headed toward the elevator, describing the services and shops nearby. Jory gives Claire a wickedly happy grin. They pass a small bar off the lobby, a few steps up into a den of wood and brocade, intimate round tables lit with shaded lamps.

The elevator rises past the lower numbers to the twelfth floor, the highest; the bellman keeps his eyes in soft focus on the opposite wall. Claire's temper rises with the car. By the time Addison has tipped the bellman and shut the door she can barely look at him. She stands at the window watching a scarf of white fog draped between the Olympic mountains and the sea. In the Macy's display window across the street a row of identical mannequins in bright bikinis lounge on a plaster beach. Two women push through the double glass doors carrying arm-loads of shopping bags; a startling reminder that people still buy things other than food and electricity.

Addison has unlocked the door between their adjoining suites and Jory already has the television on and the bed stacked with pillows, queen of her private space.

"Warn her not to eat anything from the minibar," Claire says over her shoulder. She hears the door close and a moment later Addison's arms are around her waist. When she does not give he tenses and pulls away. After a minute of silence Claire says, "Adjoining suites? My week's paycheck wouldn't cover one of them. I hope you have some pretty big news."

Addison slips his hands in his pockets. "You haven't even kissed me hello."

She turns around and leans forward on her toes just enough to tap her lips against his, then walks into the bathroom, runs hot water over a washcloth and presses it against her eyelids. He comes in behind her and closes the door, as if Jory could hear through the walls. "It is big. Or it could be big."

Claire takes the cloth away from her face. "It's funny. I'm kind of wishing you wouldn't even mention it until you know for sure."

"I called Ron Walker." She waits for him to go on, water dripping down her cheeks. Addison cups his hand along her jawline and wipes away black streaks of mascara with his thumbs. "He's interested."

Claire sits on the cold rim of the marble tub, feels her heart skip ahead, almost angry that her body will go where her mind doesn't want to. "How interested?"

"Interested enough to be paying for this room. We're meeting him for dinner tomorrow night." He drops his head a minute, and when he raises it again to look at her she sees a lightness playing in his eyes she has missed for months. "He said this is exactly the kind of project he's been looking for."

"I didn't even bring a dress. Why didn't you warn me?" Claire says, letting a small surge of excitement build inside her.

"You look great." He leans over and kisses her, locks his fingers around the back of her neck. "Go buy a dress. Buy some new jewelry to go with it."

"I haven't paid the credit card bill this month." Even before he responds she starts the question she didn't intend to ask him. "Does he know everything about the vascumab trials?"

His eyes grow quiet again. "I don't know how to do anything else but chemistry, Claire. He has all the information he needs to make his own decision. If he's in, we'll be repeating all the animal studies again."

Claire pulls her hands away. After a minute she gets up and steps past him to the sink, picks up the wet washcloth, gone cold now, blushed with the pink and beige of her makeup. Addison keeps talking to her, watching her face in the mirror. "I don't blame you."

"Blame me for what?" Claire asks, hearing the clip of distrust in her voice and wishing Jory would come in unexpectedly, or the phone would ring, or the maid knock—anything that would give her an excuse to change the subject for a while. She turns the water on full until it's hot again and wrings out the washcloth, her hands red, her knuckles white. Addison doesn't answer her, but when she catches his reflection she sees his exuberance dimming. And something deeper in his face, some sadness that snags at the garment of their union.

"Buy a blue dress, will you? Something like that one you got in London?"

She turns around and faces him, because the subject *has* changed, because she wants to have these two precious nights together in their city. "If it makes you happy I'll look for a blue dress."

They make it a good day. Even Jory is careful to stay in the moment of now. She walks between them, sometimes even holding their hands before remembering she could possibly be spotted. They go to the Seattle Art Museum and walk up to Pike Place Market, where Jory is given ten dollars to spend at the bead store and another dollar to have her fortune cranked out of a mechanical gypsy. She shows it to neither of her parents before tearing it into small bits and dropping it through a sidewalk sewer grate. Before they left Hallum, Claire promised her she could visit friends on Sunday, but Jory hasn't called anyone. Claire reminds her and Jory says she'll think about it, giving Claire a please-don't-bring-it-up-again look. And so they become tourists, on vacation in this city they used to own.

Addison takes them into Mario's and has Claire try on every size 8 blue dress, which she turns into a game of America's Next Top Model for Jory's amusement. She finally picks out a simple belted shift at Nordstrom, the color of the sky just before the last sunlight goes. Addison approves although, he says, it doesn't match her eyes as well as the London dress had. By the time they get back to the hotel Claire feels happy, remembers the short-lived thrill that accompanies the unwrapping of new things, like the euphoric taste of chocolate at the end of a fast. She is looking forward to the dinner now; it's been months since she's been to a good restaurant—any restaurant—and not spent more time looking at the prices than the food choices. She takes extra care with her makeup and hair, grooming she has quit giving much attention to in Hallum. The dress looks even better in the flattering lights of the hotel suite than it had under the fluorescents in the dressing room. Addison zips it up the back and pulls out his pocketknife to snip the tag, but she spins around and holds his wrists against her chest. "Not yet. Not till we know. Leave it for a good luck charm."

He folds his pocketknife into his closed fist and brushes her hand against his chin. "You're still not wearing your ring. Even in Seattle?"

She smiles, keeping her eyes at play over his face. "It's in a better place."

Ron Walker stands up as soon as they enter the small dining room. "Did Addison tell you Campagne is my favorite restaurant? We used to come here on my birthday," Claire says, taking his hand. The walls are painted soft green and the angled evening sunlight casts reddish gold across the dark mahogany floors. The maître d' pulls out her chair, the waiter stands one step away ready to accept their drink order. They are at a corner table beside the window. In the center of the clean white cloth, a glass vase holds two bloodred tulips. She unfolds her napkin and sits back in her chair, taking in the colors, the guests, the pleasantly abstract paintings on the walls; remembering the pleasure of allowing a meal to fill an entire evening, the luxury of being served.

"You should have brought your daughter," Ron says. "She's here with you, isn't she?"

"She's eating pizza in front of the TV. She's in heaven." Claire pulls the vase close to smell the flowers, but the blossoms are still too tightly closed. Walker selects a bottle of wine. Addison drinks quickly at first; Claire can tell he's on edge, but Walker seems completely relaxed. He asks Claire about the clinic; it's clear he considers Dan nothing less than a miracle worker. "He started that place just for the farmworkers, but then word spread. He's pretty much the only safety net in the valley, until you're dying and the hospital has to take you in." He fills Claire's glass. "Preaching to the choir, I know. I'm glad you're there. Dan likes to think he's going to have this much energy forever but he looks worn out to me."

They are halfway through dinner before Walker finally turns the conversation to vascumab. Addison has said less and less with each course, with each glass of wine, and then Claire watches him visibly expand as they begin to discuss pharmaceuticals—inflating with hope. Or pride, she thinks. Much of it justifiable pride. Walker describes himself as the ideal angel investor—educated enough to bring money to a smart opportunity, uneducated enough to stay out of a bright scientist's way. But from the questions he asks and the industry comparisons he makes, it is obvious he's read every scrap of information Addison sent him.

"Pharma didn't interest me when I was younger. I've seen people make a lot of money in it, but the risks seemed too unpredictable." Addison leans forward to add something but Walker puts his hand up. "Bear with me. You already know a lot of what I have to say, but if we're going to be bedfellows in this I want to say it anyway."

Claire glances at her husband and leans her elbows on the table with her chin in her hands, ready to absorb Walker's point of view, an economic side of this story she's never fully heard.

"I like cancer." He pauses as if he's replaying his own words, realizing how they sound. Then he breaks into a self-deprecating smile. "I like *investing* in cancer. Cancer treatment." The waiter pours out the last of the second bottle, Walker holds a hand across the top of his glass. He goes on. "My first wife died of cancer."

"Oh, I'm so sorry," Claire says.

Walker wipes his mouth on his napkin, folds it carefully before putting it back in his lap. "Chronic myelogenous leukemia at thirty-nine. She might have lived if Gleevec had been on the market then." His focus comes back to the table. "It was a long time ago." He smiles, though a bit sadly. "I've had a very patient and lovely second wife for the last eight years. But I didn't get rich being sentimental, and so that is not the main attraction. Five years ago I put ten million dollars into a cardiovascular drug. Armor Labs in California developed it. Everybody who saw the data was stunned—said it was the best new drug they'd seen in decades. Even the FDA. Demographics projected it could save 200,000 people a year between heart attacks and strokes. Then the FDA decided we had to study it in 50,000 people before it could be approved, which would take more than ten years. Armor went bankrupt in year three."

"I remember that," Addison says. Then he turns to Claire. "Cancer drugs have a shorter time to market since you're studying them in patients with a terminal disease." She nods at him, wondering if he could have forgotten all the times she's listened to him tell her this and more about his work. He's too distracted, focusing on the endgame instead of the moment.

"That was the last drug I put money into. I do own a large holding company that invests in some biopharma research—including several CROs and an IRB—but I manage their business, not their science. He looks straight at Claire, his graying eyebrows lifted. "A CRO is a contract research organization that helps run drug studies, finds the volunteers and runs all the tests. The IRB is the review board that oversees any human drug testing." Claire smiles politely at this, catches Addison giving her a look that clearly means *Please just play dumb.*

Then Walker reaches into a briefcase at his feet and pulls out a thick binder that Claire recognizes as the reams of information Addison has been carting to meetings all over the country. He pushes his dessert plate aside and plants the notebook squarely in front of himself. "I like this drug. I like it, and the consultant I had review it likes it." Addison shifts in his seat. Claire looks at him but can tell he is trying not to meet her eyes, doesn't want to see his own vulnerability in her expression. "Now for my questions," Walker says.

Addison clears his throat and opens his hands over the table like two birds taking flight. "Ask me anything you'd like to. If I don't have the answer I'll get it for you."

"There are a lot of labs working on antiangiogenesis drugs. Many are already at the human trial phase. You had only a provisional patent on this drug, is that right?"

"Yes," Addison says. He flares his hands again then quickly drops them. Claire watches him, recognizing every sign of his anxiety, holding her breath. Addison continues, "I'm sure you know how tricky the timing can be on patent applications—we wanted to protect the basic molecule while it was still in development but not be forced to disclose the unique structure. I wanted that twelve-month window the provisional patent gave us."

"But in the meantime some other lab could be making your drug. Vascumab." Walker's hands are resting on either side of Addison's files, his fingers in a relaxed arch. Claire has the feeling he knows every answer before he asks the question.

Addison clears his throat again and Claire has to lock her hands in her lap to keep from gripping his knee. "I felt—and believe to this day—that vascumab is a singular molecule."

Walker studies him, motionless, like a hunter waiting for precisely the right opening. "Convince me that your patent situation doesn't expose my investment to greater risk." He fans his arm across the table, taking in the room, taking in the whole world. "You have no way of knowing the lab down the street isn't about to put in their own patent application for the same molecule. Beat you to the finish line."

Addison moves his head in a slow figure eight, not a yes, not a no. Claire waits, her mouth going dry. "Science isn't a process that happens in isolation, Ron. It's a ladder of incremental steps that a lot of people around the world are building at the same time. It's very rare—extremely rare—to have one individual or one lab make a huge leap ahead of anyone else." He pauses. Claire can almost hear him deciding how far to go. "But I have. It may look like a small difference in the chemical structure, but it completely changes the binding characteristics. I haven't seen any other lab focusing on that variance. I believe vascumab is going to change the way we treat cancer, not just in the U.S. In the whole world. It is going to change the meaning of that diagnosis."

Something passes across Walker's face, little more than the way the light is reflected in his eyes. He isn't hearing anything he didn't expect; Claire is sure of that. He is testing. Testing Addison. "How confident are you that vascumab can be safely studied in humans within the year?" Walker asks, sitting a touch straighter, little more than the twitch of a muscle. "Your own child. Or Claire, here. How comfortable would you be giving this drug to them?"

Claire sees Addison stall; she knots her hands in her lap. Walker waits, unblinking, clearly knows more than anything printed in that binder, more than any bankrupting legal fees could protect—the silence makes her want to stand up and put an end to all the possibilities right now, collect their daughter and their bags and the tentative purchases they made today on the breath of hope and drive back across the mountains to Hallum.

But then Addison pushes past the question, into a part of himself beyond shame or ego, lets himself be taken over by the same conviction that drove vascumab from a sketch on a scrap of paper to a biologically active compound. "I believe the mouse studies were flawed. They need to be repeated. As soon as they are I would be happy to be the first human volunteer."

Walker still doesn't move, locked on Addison's eyes as if he can see all the way through to whatever heaven or hell has in store. And Addison holds his own with it, stares right back until, slowly, Walker breaks into a grin. He flicks his eyes at the waiter and within a minute there is a bottle of champagne on the table with three glasses. "Well, then. Let's be sure we get it on the market before any of us needs it."

After too much champagne they all walk down to Steinbrueck Park overlooking Puget Sound, the night so clear and moonless even city lights can't diminish the stars. They stand with their heads craned back, testing each other on constellations, listening to the plaintive bellow of the ferry's horn. Claire starts to tell Walker about the times Addison would wait for three shooting stars, but changes it to something less intimate. "Funny to think some of those stars are already dead. That used to blow me away when I was a kid. But it always made me feel like fate had a plan for me—my own light after death, I guess." She drops her chin level with the ground again and stumbles against Ron in a wave of dizziness. "Oh God. Champagne after wine."

Walker has a hand behind his own head, supporting it like a pillow so he can stare straight up. "I don't know. Always made me feel more like an accident. I think you earn your life."

Claire is quiet on the walk back to the hotel. Addison seems lost in plans until he asks her what she thinks about the dinner, whether she is excited.

"Stunned more than excited, I guess," she says, leaning into him and wrapping her arm around his. "And a little drunk. But I'll wake up excited. So can I ask why you were so resistant to calling Ron, or will you get mad at me again?" He should take it as a joke, the way she lets her voice sing. When he doesn't respond immediately she worries the wine has relaxed her judgment too much, the issue is still too ensnared in their balance of marital power.

But his answer falls outside of any subject she'd been expecting. "Because Rick made the same suggestion to me. Just before we split up the team. He thought I should get Ron interested before the mouse data leaked out." Addison takes his arm out of hers and stops in the middle of the sidewalk. "Paranoia, maybe. Embarrassment. You were walking on a landmine."

Jory has fallen asleep across the bedspread in her clothes; the three empty chocolate wrappers from their turndown treats litter her pillow. Claire shimmies the covers out from under her and rolls her between the sheets. Jory sleeps through it all with nonsensical grumbling, but mumbles, "I love you, Mama," just before Claire closes her door.

Addison is in the bathroom. She knocks. "I forgot my phone charger. Where's yours?" The water is running and he doesn't answer, so she opens the top dresser drawer to rummage through his boxers and undershirts and daybook and computer cords. Underneath them all she uncovers the framed picture missing from the mantelpiece—Jory. Jory weighing less than three pounds, a pencil-sized endotracheal tube strapped to her pale rosebud mouth, bunny-shaped EKG pads over her chest and an IV line taped into her scalp. Her head was the size of a tennis ball. Claire clearly remembers the nearly imperceptible weight of it when they'd let her hold her. The translucent skin over her hands and feet was mottled purple and pink, her ribs puffed like the veil-thin wings of a butterfly each time the ventilator cycled. All the tapes and straps holding baby Jory together had sweet pictures on them: teddy bears and stars, as if designing them for the child she might become gave them less austerity, more healing power.

The picture makes Claire's heart turn over—because she has found it again, and because she remembers it all again. Remembers the wooden rocker they let her sit in day after night after day, waiting for Jory's tissue paper lungs to grow, waiting for the fetal channels in her heart to close. Claire had known too much. Addison could stand beside the incubator and talk excitedly with any nurse that brought news of progress, however small. Claire would have traded every second of her education for some of his naïveté.

But Jory is here now, born just across the cutting edge of neonatal miracles. Here they all are.

She puts the picture back beneath his underwear when the bathroom door opens. Addison sits on the bed. "So how do you feel?" he asks.

She sits down next to him, looks at his profile, his cheeks flushed and damp from washing his face. "You first. When do you think we can believe it?"

He shrugs and rubs his face, runs his fingers up through his hair, the smell of scented soap exhaling from his skin. "Not until the lawyers sign." He smiles at her. "Never till the lawyers sign. It could take months, assuming Ron doesn't change his mind. There's a chance things could go faster because he's already connected with a CRO and an IRB. If we could run the drug trials through them."

"That sounds so nepotistic, doesn't it? How can you own the research organization *and* the review board that are evaluating the drug you're investing in? It seems like a conflict of interest."

"He owns the holding company that manages them. I think he's pretty removed. Anyway, he can't vote. He wouldn't be allowed to actually sit on the board. If you think about it, how objective is a traditional academic review board that oversees its own studies—asking faculty to criticize a study designed by their boss? The last thing any investor wants is a lawsuit. They have every incentive to keep it safe. And if you take all the profit out of it, why should anyone invest the half a billion dollars it takes to get a drug to market?"

Claire scans his face with a half smile. "Just testing you," she teases.

He pulls her backward on the bed and rolls over her. "But that champagne felt like the real stuff." He brushes her hair off her face, lets his eyes roam the arc of her brow, the slope of her cheek. "Your turn. How *do* you feel? Really?"

Claire lets her arms fall back on the bed and looks past Addison's face. "I don't know yet." She pauses and adds, "Tired. I'm tired. You know how sometimes you don't even realize how tired you are until the stress lets up?" And that was true for her right now. It reminded her of a story she'd heard from one patient about a badly botched border cross-ing—two people had died within a thousand yards of water. Dan said it happened a lot; they would get close enough to almost smell it, almost see the lights of a house and collapse, as if the most they could hope for was to have their bodies claimed; their souls had fled miles before. She looks into Addison's face. "So what do you think? Do you think we re-ally get the life we earn? Did we earn this life?"

"*This* life?" he says, emphasizing the here and now, making it clear that he can't answer that with a simple yes or no after the precarious ride of the last year. "Maybe." He thinks about it another minute. "Yeah. I have to say I probably earned it. Both the crash and the recovery. If it really comes. You don't?"

Claire turns toward the window, a siren passing in the street below. "I think . . . I think I might have said so before I worked at the clinic." She pauses. "I can't just walk out on them, Addison. Dan's missed two days in the last week, for 'appointments in Wenatchee.'"

"Well. We aren't there yet. You worried Dan's sick?"

She huffs. "He cuts me off if I even think about asking."

"Then I guess this isn't the time to think about it." He moves closer and runs his hand lightly down her sternum, reaches behind to unzip her dress.

They leave the heavy drapes open so the lights of the city and the distant harbor illuminate them both kindly, agelessly. The bedsheets are the soft, expensive kind that Claire used to buy with impunity. In this plush hotel room paid for by Ron Walker, this capsule of hope Ron Walker has inspired, they fuse the present with the best of their past. They roll and burrow and play silently on the other side of the locked door from their sleeping daughter, eventually locking together in naked sleep.

Claire wakes up twice in the night, and holds her breath with her eyes closed while the dream of it all crystallizes into a real memory, into something that will still be there when the sun rises. She thinks about Jory's face, what she might say when they tell her.

· 27 ·

When Jory was nine Addison had taken four days off from work to drive her back to Chicago so she could see her grandparents' graves. Claire stayed behind to help her own mother move into the house they had bought for her, and only later heard the story from the child, and the story from the father—marveling at their disparate details.

Jory told Claire she had begged and pleaded to drive by the house her daddy grew up in. He had driven her around and around, finally parked on his street and let her guess which one was his house. She had looked at them all carefully until she was sure—the two-story white brick box with matching black shutters up and down, and a chimney in the middle of the roof. She loved the way it lined up so neatly with all the other houses on the street, each with a trim square of green lawn. But she couldn't get him to tell her which window had been his room.

After Jory went to bed Addison had apologized, but also defended himself to Claire. He *had* decided to take Jory to his childhood home, had actually driven her down his street—worse now than it was when he was a kid. Then he had seen Jory's expression and kept driving, almost randomly, until he ended up in a safe neighborhood and parked the car along the curb. He had let Jory come to her own conclusions.

Claire insisted it was more critical to show Jory the truth, to teach her how to decide her own destiny and make whatever she wanted of her life. But the subject was still too tender for Addison. His father had been to Seattle only once, resurfacing after a lengthy binge just a few months before he died. He had walked through their freshly rebuilt Lake Washington home, slowly pivoted in the middle of the living room and whistled, "So. You got a rich man's house now. My son is a rich man." Claire had seen the look on Addison's face.

On the way home from Chicago they had stopped for the night in some small Idaho town, a motel where the TV only picked up two stations. Addison had walked down the highway to a Les Schwab tire dealership and brought back two bags of popcorn, then let Jory stay up all night watching a *Three Stooges* rerun marathon. She sat mesmerized at the foot of the bed while Addison leaned against the headboard flicking bits of popcorn into her hair, complaining about the spiders and centipedes in the room. When she finally caught him she poured the rest of her own greasy bag down the back of his shirt.

He had once used the story to sum up his philosophy on life and death to Claire: hell must be an eternity of forgetting about the popcorn tangled in your daughter's hair while you sat on a polyester bedspread in Idaho watching Moe, Larry and Curly live again. In fact, hell, as he saw it, was an eternity of remembering all the parts of your life you didn't know mattered until they were gone, gone.

Jory knows the truth about Addison's family by now, though Claire can't even recall how she'd learned. There hadn't been any traumatic moment of revelation—she'd been young enough that one set of facts was easily replaced by another, as long as she still woke up in the same bed.

Claire and Jory check out of the Mayflower on Sunday and Addison stays in Seattle. Driving back to Hallum, Claire asks Jory if she remembers the trip to Chicago, if for nothing else than to get Jory to take her iPod earbuds out and talk more. "What made you think of that out of the blue?" Jory asks.

"I don't know. Houses. Aren't you excited about the news?"

Jory shrugs. "Yeah. I guess." She is quiet for a long time, then abruptly adds, "I'll get excited when we buy *our* house back from *those* people. How's that?" The earbuds go back in and Claire tries to concentrate on the scenery and the winding mountain road.

Twenty miles later Jory turns to Claire and says, "This man went out to buy groceries and his wife was at home and heard on the radio that some crazy person was driving the wrong way down the highway. So she called her husband on his cell phone and said, 'Be careful 'cause some crazy person is driving the wrong way down the highway.' And he said, 'You're telling me! There's not just one—there's a whole ton of them.'" They both laugh, Claire until she is wiping her eyes. And then Jory says soberly, "I am excited. I am, Mom. I'm just scared it won't last."

Claire would not have described the house as untidy—"not particularly clean," maybe, *that* she might have agreed with—but tidy enough. When they open the front door and flick on the light, however, both she and Jory put their bags down quietly and look around the room, taking in the absence of dust and webs, the scent of lemon and vinegar, the uncluttered surfaces that shout to them now, for the first time, of how desperately they had wanted this attention. Jory walks to the refrigerator. She opens it and turns to her mother, mouths, "Amazing," so that Miguela, presumably asleep behind the floral print curtain, will not hear. Then she bends down and pulls out two plates wrapped in Saran, each arranged with a broiled chicken breast, beans, grilled onions and corn.

They carry the plates upstairs on a cookie sheet and eat on the end of Claire's bed with the door closed. Even this room seems refreshed. There is a small bowl of crushed sage leaves on the bedside table, its clean, savory scent hovering just below the surface, like a window opened in summer. Claire had wondered how it would feel to open the front door and see the same peeling wallpaper, the leaking windows, wondered if the room would overwhelm her with its irreversible decay after their weekend back in the city. But whether because of Miguela's thorough cleaning, or unacknowledged attachment, she'd felt immediately relaxed. At peace. At home.

"She would come with us, right?" Jory asks.

Claire finishes chewing, wonders for a minute if she has missed part of what Jory has said. Then she realizes that Jory is asking about Miguela.

. . .

Within a week of returning to Hallum the dinner with Walker seems less real, less . . . *shiny*. In a way, the diminishing euphoria feels better to Claire. Safer. The very nearness of his money was like a mirror forcing her to relive what she'd already survived. But she still allows herself to play out the fantasy of how it would be different this time: They would budget. They would diversify. This time, it would all stay transparent. She begins to view it as a pact with fate—*Give me this chance, this second lightning strike, and I will show you I can be worthy*. But even inside this cautious realm she is enticed to linger at shopwindows, tempted to put three small steaks in her grocery cart instead of ground meat. She buys the first box of Bing cherries shipped in from a thousand miles away at three times the price she would pay for them next month.

A week to the day from their night at the Mayflower, she stops in front of the same gallery where Addison had bought the glass earrings and sees a pair of dangles made from seed pearls and garnet briolettes, displayed on a black velvet tray with the tiny price tags carefully turned over. It wouldn't hurt to look, she decides. Nothing like the diamonds and rubies she would have considered buying two years ago.

She pulls open the door and the jingle of bells makes the shop-keeper look up—Claire is the only customer, it would be awkward to turn around and walk out. "I wonder if you could tell me how much the earrings are? The ones in the corner window?" And then the woman is unlocking the display case and putting the clusters of faceted gems in Claire's palm.

She turns a mirror so it reflects Claire's face. "They match your hair—lovely with your skin tones."

At first Claire only holds one next to her earlobe, but then they are on, suspended like drops of colored water on gold threads.

"They're only one fifty." The shopkeeper examines the tag again. "But you're in luck today. The artist wants to move them, so I can make an adjustment. Say, one twenty-five? Can I wrap them for you?"

In luck today. And then she feels it. Feels lucky. Remembers how willingly Walker had poured the champagne, the excitement in his smile, how inclusive it had felt. "Well . . . Yes. Thank you." She puts her credit card on the counter and the clerk reaches into a drawer for a box. "Wait. No. No, I'll just wear them."

She checks her face in the rearview mirror driving back to the clinic, enjoying how the sunlight catches and plays in them when she moves her head. But a hundred yards from the clinic she pulls over and calls Addison, who is still in Seattle. "You haven't heard anything from the lawyers yet, have you?"

He laughs at this, though not meanly. "There are still a dozen things that could turn the deal, Claire. I can't even predict how long it might take."

She feels heat rise in her chest. "Yeah. That makes sense."

He must hear the mix of anxiety and desire in her. "It probably *will* work out. But even if it doesn't for some reason, it's still a change in the tide. It means vascumab can still attract an investor. Walker's no fool, Claire." And he must believe that; even Addison is gradually letting "when" replace "if" in his conversations, mentioning the best car to replace the bashed Audi, or a new idea about the house remodel—at least decent insulation and a better furnace.

Even the arrival of spring encourages her. In only a week the season has changed, the trees frosted with tender new leaves, the recently turned fields tinted a pale green, so faint she would miss the change of color but for looking down the length of the planted rows of alfalfa and spring rye. When she drives into the clinic early, farmworkers are already walking down the long, parallel rows of apples and cherries and apricots with sharp, purposeful tools—pruners and clippers and saws and scythes.

There is a noticeable uptick in the number of patients they are seeing. Frida warns her that this is just the beginning; as soon as the California cherries show up on the grocery store shelves in Washington, everybody who picked them will follow: "Heading north for the harvest and Dan's hospitality." Her voice has a complaining wheedle when she says it, but Claire can see that she's energized. She moves from patient to lab to pharmacy to patient with clean efficiency.

Anita is also growing. "How long are you going to keep working?" Claire asks her, taking the first patient's chart out of her hand.

"Until I pop. My sister takes care of my kids during the day. As soon as this one's born we swap. She helps out here and I stay home. I'll tell you the truth—this work is easier."

Dan, though, seems more subdued, more selective about the patients he sees, letting Claire or Frida get the intake history and physical on anyone who is new to the clinic, sticking to the patients he already knows, taking a moment now and then to give Claire a summary of his most complicated cases. Just before lunch she leaves an exam room to discover him waiting for her, propped against the wall by one leg, making notes in a chart. "Do you have a minute?" he asks. The patient he introduces is fifty-eight, a subsistence farmer who'd sliced acre after acre off his land over decades, until he was left with a run-down house and yard. He is sitting in the chair that would usually be occupied by a relative or translator. Dan is on the rolling stool, leaving Claire to lean against the end of the exam table. "Just tell Dr. Boehning the same things you told me, Jim."

Claire sees Jim look long and slow at Dan. "Why would she want to hear about me fixing my fence?"

Dan is sitting forward on the stool with his hands on his knees. He presses his palms down firmly so his elbows wing out, leaning closer as if Jim is hard of hearing. "Go on and tell her. Say exactly what you said to me."

Jim rotates in his chair toward Claire, somber faced. "I have a fence out back that needs paint." He blinks and looks at Dan again, almost like he needs reassurance to keep talking. "Well, I fell. Landed on my back and thought I should have Dan check me out."

Dan nods his head, urges him to go on. "Just like you said it to me. She's a doctor, too."

"All right. I fell a few times last week, too. A few other things."

Dan leads him through a description of symptoms with careful, nonjudgmental questions. Jim complains about not being able to read the paper anymore, about coughing every time he eats. He finds his hands starting to shake sometimes. The longer he talks, the more agitated he gets, looking as if he might break down. Dan stands up and rests his hands on his shoulders, calming him like a parent might calm an upset child. "Tell you what, why don't you wait outside with Elizabeth and let Dr. Boehning and me talk for a minute."

After the door closes Dan says, "I've been Jim's doctor for two years. He's been coming here for one thing or another every couple of months and I only made the diagnosis today. Did you catch it?"

"Based on his fall?" she asks.

"Based on all of it. The fall. What he said, what you saw." Dan is smiling at her now, his unique mix of colleague and teacher and friend, obviously enjoying this game physicians play from their earliest days in medical school, matching the described traits of an illness to the subjective complaints of a patient.

"It's a movement disorder, I think. I can't be sure without examining him."

Dan nods. She sees him narrow his eyes, a look on his face like he has won a secret bet, takes personal pride in her answer. "Parkinson's," he says, matter-of-factly. "Not a good thing to have, but at least we know how to treat him."

Anita knocks on the door, ready to put the next patient in this room. Claire watches Jim cautiously making his way toward the waiting room. Something nags at her, something learned or heard too long ago to say why it has inserted itself into this man's particular set of symptoms. She goes in to see her next patient, an asthmatic woman who seems offended at the suggestion that she has been cooking over an open fire, though her clothes reek of woodsmoke and scorched corn. She's printing a label for the woman's inhaler when Dan walks into the pharmacy and it comes to her. She puts her hand on his sleeve. "I don't think it's Parkinson's. I think it's PSP—progressive supranuclear palsy. He's falling *backward*. And his tremor—it's not a Parkinson's tremor." Dan's face changes from confusion to disappointment and then, gradually, to something near camouflaged pride. "I mean, I could be wrong. There are other possibilities, too. But I don't think it's Parkinson's." She lets her hand fall to her side. "I'm sorry."

"No, no. There's no contest here."

"Oh, I meant I'm sorry it's PSP. It's a worse diagnosis."

Dan nods, studying her like he's weighing it all. "No. I've not seen that disease. But he's lucky, at least he has a good doctor."

She feels a small rush of pride when he says this. But by the end of that afternoon, when she has seen more patients than Dan, and thought more about the quiet sobriety she'd seen in his thinning face, she feels only concern. And when he doesn't come in on four days over the next week—running to Wenatchee for some meeting with their banker, once saying he had to go to Seattle for more clinic supplies—Claire knows it is more than the natural slowing of age.

· 28 ·

On Saturday Claire drives to Dan's house. Evelyn is outside working in her garden. Her lilacs, their leather-smooth limbs as thick as a man's wrist, are lush with purple flowers, just splitting apart a million tiny green pods. Evelyn stands and takes off a gardening glove to hold Claire's hand. "You're good to come by. It's a busy season for just one doctor. Are you handling it okay?" Claire doesn't answer her because the question itself is not what she hears. She hears Evelyn's admission that Dan will not be working at the clinic much more.

"Is he up for visitors?"

"For you? Always. Come on in." Evelyn scrapes the mud from her boots and drops her gloves into a plastic crate filled with garden tools and bulbs, some already sprouting as if ready to walk into the ground. Claire sees her square her shoulders when she opens the front door. "Dan? Claire's here. You decent?" Claire can't hear his answer, but Evelyn holds the door open and waves her inside the house.

The living room is dim; sun stripes shine through the half-closed blinds across the dining table where they had shared dinner just a few months ago. There is a new odor in the room, something faded and organic. Or maybe it's the absence of what she expects—the smell of Evelyn's southwestern cooking, the smell of pine and woodsmoke that has always followed Dan, even into the clinic. He is on the couch, covered with an alpaca throw, and hails her with a firmly raised hand, swings his legs to the floor.

"Hey. Don't get up." She pulls a chair out from the table and turns it to face him. Evelyn sits on the arm of the couch. "How are you?" Claire asks him. As soon as she says it she wishes she'd chosen any other words: *We miss you, your patients send their best, Frida's coffee is worse than yours.* He turns on the table lamp and she sees it immediately, is astounded, even as a doctor, at how rapidly his skin has changed from an aged, sun-spotted ivory that has always jibed with his Hispanic name to the yellow of an aging bruise. The scleras of his eyes are the color of lemon pulp.

He watches her face change as she recognizes the most likely diagnosis. "I hate the itching. Even after all these years practicing medicine it caught me off guard. Need to wear mitts or something," he says.

Claire smiles but feels tears coming. She concentrates on keeping her face still—if she knows Dan at all, he does not want to put up with her sympathy. She starts to talk about her patients, or ask about his walk by the river, but the falseness feels insulting. There is nothing to do but address it outright and let Dan guide her. "It doesn't hurt, I hope?"

He winks at her, and that more than anything threatens to make her cry. "Good thing about being a doc is that you can write your own scripts." He chuckles at himself. "I'm seeing Will Hesston in Seattle. He's generous. Probably try a celiac plexus block next week."

"So it's pancreatic?" It is a moment when knowing too much about medicine imposes its toll. Hesston is the best in the region for pancreatic cancer, and if surgery had offered any hope Dan would have already had it.

"They put in a stent last month, kept the jaundice down until last week. Gonna have to change my wardrobe now. Evelyn says I should stick to yellows so I look like a reflector. I told her with a red hat and green shirt I could be a stoplight. Hallum's first."

Claire breaks out in laughter at this and hopes he thinks the tears streaming down her cheeks are from his pitiful joke. Evelyn cannot seem to stop herself and picks up a Kleenex box from the end table, plucks out a single white tissue and puts it in Claire's hand; it relaxes the tension among the three of them, in a way.

Dan tells her more about his cancer; it has spread into his liver. The symptoms had been so nominal at first he had ignored them. "I got to live in blissful ignorance that many more weeks."

Evelyn excuses herself to start dinner, though Claire suspects it is really to give Dan time alone with her. She sits quietly for a minute, rolling the tissue between her fingers. "You knew when you hired me, didn't you. That's why you called."

He lifts one hand feebly off his stomach, reaching for another excuse, maybe, then lets it drop again. "I got the CT scan results a couple of hours after you left." He moves his tongue along his upper teeth behind his lips and then smiles at her again, a gleam of a dare in his eyes. "I've put you in quite a bind now. Are you mad at me?"

She tilts her head to the side and tries to look like nothing more than an exasperated parent. "Well, I would have been picking your brain a lot faster if I'd known."

He is quiet for a minute, serious at last. "You're better than you know you are, Claire. You love it more than you know." She feels blood rush into her face. Dan is watching her closely. "So once Addison makes his bazillions back, don't walk away again. Even if you don't stay in Hallum."

She wishes that she had already told Dan about Walker. The fact that he has guessed so much makes her feel false with him now, at a point when there is too little time to fix it later. "I guess I still think of myself as being 'in training.' Waiting to see what happens."

"You've been a curiosity to me in some ways, you know," Dan says. Claire lifts her eyebrows, half expecting him to finish with one of his jokes again. But looking at him she thinks he is only taking advantage of his mortal diagnosis—if there can be any advantage at all—to say exactly what is on his mind. "You never seemed to me like the kind of woman who would quit on something you'd worked at for so long. Not out of convenience, anyway. Not for money. Not unless you had some reason to think you'd made the wrong choice in the first place."

Claire looks down at her hands; she has rolled the Kleenex into dust. She fills her chest and holds her breath for a moment, releases it in a sigh. "It was more than money. More than Jory, even." He waits for her to go on, waits until she is ready, almost as if he needed to hear this to fully understand his decision to hire her. "I missed a diagnosis."

"That's part of learning medicine. Will be through your whole medical career," Dan says, his voice totally calm, his yellow eyes without judgment.

"I missed an ectopic. A heroin addict who came to the ER every week with one pain or another. I discharged her and she bled to death underneath a bridge." She sees Dan take a breath. "I never checked a pregnancy test." She doesn't take her eyes from him when she says it, sees the quick pull of muscles at the center of his face. She is grateful that he makes no effort to console her.

Evelyn comes out of the kitchen to walk Claire to the door. From the look on her face, the careful placement of her palm on Claire's back, she knows Evelyn is thinking less about her own well-being at this moment than Claire's. "He wouldn't even consider chemotherapy," Evelyn says.

"You'll call me for anything, won't you? Anything you need."

Evelyn doesn't answer. She wraps her strong slender arms around Claire and hugs her fiercely. When she pulls away she keeps both hands fixed on Claire's shoulders and says, "You know what he wants you to do."

Claire feels something wind up in her chest again, tries to keep it out of her face. Her voice is lost now; all she can do is nod.

"You need to think about it carefully." Evelyn smiles, a bit weakly. "You're a little young to give everything up for a charity mission."

Jory and Miguela are not inside when she comes home. She scans the field and walks around the back of the house to look in the apple grove. The craggy overgrown boughs are massed with blush-colored buds nested in young green leaves, it takes her a moment to realize the electric hum in the air is ten thousand bees. She calls Jory's name and listens, almost glad for the solitude before she has to pretend everything is fine. A gust of wind carries their voices to her and she follows the shoulder of the hill down below the aspen grove, farther onto the land than she's explored in years, to an escarpment cut by a shallow stream where they've waded across to a bank of flat rocks still lit by the nearly horizontal rays of evening sun. When Miguela sees her she gathers beach towels, shoes, an empty box of Ritz and starts up the path of trampled grass toward the house, ahead of Jory.

"We found some flowers." Jory has a mayonnaise jar filled with lupine and balsamroot, the first of this spring. She puts an arm around her mother's waist and Claire is suddenly overtaken by a sob. She pulls Jory tight against her chest and feels her body yield like a kitten lifted at the scruff of its neck, suspended and trusting; and then Claire turns it all into a game, squeezing her in tight bursts until she laughs and twists free. They are almost back to the house before Jory stops talking about her suntan and the highlights she wants to add to her hair. "Mom? Are you okay?"

The sun is dying in Jory's face, a gasp of red and orange that burnishes her skin an Indian bronze. "Sure, baby. I'm just a little sad about a friend who's sick."

"One of your patients?"

"No. Not someone I take care of. Someone I care *for*." Claire smiles. "I guess those are the same sometimes."

Jory studies her face for a moment, then looks down at the jar of flowers, as if she's consciously sparing her mother's privacy. They start back through the damp grass and her hand slips into Claire's. She says in a near whisper, "I'm sorry, Mom."

Addison comes home that weekend, and Claire sees a visible change in him: the burn of self-confidence in his eyes that had been so much a part of him when they had fallen in love. More than what *she* loved in him, it was what he loved in himself—the application of his mind to a task he was uniquely designed for, witnessing the manufactured products of his dreams change flesh-and-blood lives.

Claire leads him into the kitchen to introduce Miguela, but the flowered bedsheet has been pulled over the alcove entrance with not a breath of movement stirring the folds. They go upstairs, careful not to talk in full voice until the bedroom door is closed. He drops his bag and waits for her to come to him and rest her forehead against his chest before he places his hands at the small of her back. Some of the sexual ease they had rediscovered at the Mayflower has already slipped away, she can tell, like a pendulum rocking back toward the centering force of gravity.

"Where's Jory?" he asks, breaking away to heft his bag onto the bed and pull out his toilet kit.

"At a dance class, believe it or not. A friend is driving her home after. She likes the teacher—at least she hasn't said she *doesn't* like her. Three classes so far."

"I thought about buying her new pointe shoes in Seattle."

Claire sits on the bed and crosses her legs. "Buy her modern dance shoes. A lot cheaper."

"Can you get them over the Internet?"

"You get them from God. Modern is done in bare feet. So is this a sign you're still optimistic?"

"No reason not to be." He is putting his razor and toothbrush away and catches her face in the bathroom mirror, turns around and stands in the doorway, watching her. "You haven't talked to Dan about it yet, have you?"

Claire shakes her head. "Not Frida or Anita, either. We're advertising for another doctor—maybe we'll get lucky and find two." She sweeps her hair back from her face and presses her fingertips hard against her temples. "I don't want to say anything yet. What's the point of saddling Dan with this, too, until we know?"

The front door slams and Jory calls out, having seen her father's car in the driveway. His face changes instantly and he is down the stairs, scoops Jory into his arms and spins her in a fast Lindy pretzel. She is wearing gym shorts and a V-neck tank top; her hair catches in her mouth every time she spins. But even in play she is all dancer, sensing Addison's moves before he knows them himself, as if her muscles alone could calculate the laws of physics.

Claire stands on the bottom step and flashes back to the first week they'd had Jory home from the hospital, barely weighing four pounds. They had bought a food scale and every day Addison would dress her in a single dry diaper and baby blanket and balance her in the middle of the plastic tray with his hands hovering on each side, waiting, his face frozen with anxiety until the flashing orange LED display settled and stopped. The day she broke five pounds he had carried her down the hall of their apartment building, knocking on neighbors' doors with the news.

Addison flops onto the couch, sweating, but Jory seems to have barely warmed up. She plugs her iPod into the stereo receiver and pushes the table against the window. "Okay, wait a sec. I've been working on something." She puts her hands on her chest to catch her breath and bends over her knees with a singular self-conscious laugh. Then she dials to the song and counts a beat of eight with her eyes closed before she pushes Play and begins to move in slow, fluid turns, long lines of arm and leg and neck.

Claire looks at Addison as soon as "Ain't No Sunshine" starts, and suddenly she can't breathe, as if every soft part of herself between her mind and her heart is wrung tight. He must feel her looking at him; she sees his face change even in profile. Or maybe he remembers it himself. He should—this song has often enough been the inside joke that breaks through any argument. And just as suddenly she doesn't want him to look at her, doesn't want him to look for the same passion that had made this child to this song fifteen years ago. Doesn't want to see him questioning, as she is, how much Ron Walker's money can resurrect.

· 29 ·

The first night Addison is home, Miguela takes her dinner into her own room. Claire finds her with her plate balanced on her lap, eating on the side of her bed. Claire squats in the corner of the alcove against the washing machine, her knees folded inside her crossed arms. "The house feels smaller now, with my husband here. I know."

"Señora . . ."

"Claire."

"Señora Claire, I should go back to the orchard." She says it so quietly it's almost hard to understand, even sitting this close. Miguela continues to eat, but Claire has the feeling this is only so she won't have to look at her.

"We want you to stay. Mr. Boehning will be going back to Seattle again, probably. It's made a big difference to have you with Jory in the afternoons. She really likes you, Miguela. You're her friend."

Miguela looks up at Claire. For one flash her eyes seem naked, on the verge of taking Claire into her history—gone in a blink. "I can stay for Jory, if you need me. For a while. But I have something to ask you . . ." They are interrupted then; Jory unabashedly pushes the curtain aside and asks who wants ice cream, scooping a spoonful directly from the carton into her mouth.

Claire gives Miguela an apologetic smile and struggles to stand up on tingling feet. "How about my husband makes you a door before he leaves?"

It is finally Addison, though, who draws Miguela back to the dining table. He is rocked back on the rear legs of his chair proofreading an essay Jory has written for English, his shoulders almost imperceptibly swaying with the words. When he's done he places the paper on the table and nudges it toward Jory. "So how much do you know about *arribadas*?"

Jory sucks the last taste of ice cream off the spoon and drops it in her bowl. "It's when the sea turtles come out of the ocean to lay their eggs at night. Sometimes they come in these huge waves, like, thousands and thousands of them, laying millions of eggs." Her arms draw circles over the table, as if she can see the turtles swimming up to the beach. "Nobody knows what signals them. But after they hatch, almost all of the baby turtles die trying to cross the beach to get to the ocean. Miguela told me about it."

Addison glances at Claire, who makes a perplexed face.

"Cool. What else do you talk about?"

Jory drops her eyes too quickly at the question, Claire thinks, instinctively alert to what her daughter *doesn't* say as much as what she says. "Jory? Dad asked you a question."

But Miguela answers her from the kitchen doorway, her unexpected voice making them all turn in unison, Jory with a startled intake of breath. "My father took me to see the turtles laying their eggs, when I was young. Much younger than Jory. I have always remembered it. I thought Jory would like to hear."

Addison looks embarrassed; the tops of his ears take on a pink glow that Claire usually notes as a cue to change the subject. He stands up and rests his hands on the back of his chair. After a minute, when Miguela still hasn't moved, he clears his throat and says, "Please. Please sit with us." He seems completely unaware of Jory's fidgeting, how she remembers a math test she still needs to study for and takes her books to the corner of the living room.

The night is so warm they can open their bedroom window; the ratcheting cadence of crickets is slow and hypnotic in the deep grass. It reminds Claire of the steady patter of rain in Seattle, how it tapped the roof like worrying fingers rippling over and over on a wooden table; nature at its least threatening. Dependable. Repetitive. "You've been home three hours, and you know her better than I do," Claire says.

Addison is lying on his back, one arm angled across his forehead so his fingers swing just beside Claire's face. "Well, you have to admit it's pretty amazing," Addison says. "Her father was a Sandinista revolutionary? Killed by the contras? That all seemed like it was happening on another planet when I was in college. And now it's living in our laundry room."

Claire starts to laugh and Addison rolls up on his elbow, bunches the pillow underneath his arm. His dry-cleaned shirt is turned back at the cuff. She smells the starched white cotton, the Tom's deodorant, the oils in his hair and the slightly smoky sweat under his arms, all of the blind scent that would be Addison and only Addison in a room of a thousand men. "Good thing you were born when you were. A few years earlier and you would have been bombing public buildings," she says.

"Me?" He breaks his gaze for a second. "Nah. I might have been designing *cleaner* bombs, but never setting them off."

Claire is lying on her back staring up at him, aware, from this position, of how his jowl pouches along his jawline. "I have a lot of patients like her. What they've left behind . . ." She closes her eyes. "It makes those turtles sound lucky."

"Claire?" He waits, almost rhetorically, it feels to her. Like he's waiting to see the fight going on in her boil itself out. "You still have time here. You've already helped a lot of people."

When she doesn't answer he undresses, throwing his clothes on the floor at the foot of the bed. He turns out the light and lifts one drowsy hand, stroking her cheek before he tucks it under his pillow and folds his knees up, the place he always starts in sleep.

"You trust him, don't you? Ron, I mean?" Claire asks.

"Trust him how?"

"I mean, it's more than just the money. You think he really believes in vascumab? What it can do for cancer?"

She can tell this pulls him a step back into his daytime world; he sighs with a tinge of impatience. "Yeah. I think he believes it's a good drug. But right now I have to mainly trust his business sense. Just getting vascumab ready for phase one trials again is going to cost ten or fifteen million. He can't take that kind of risk just to be a good Samaritan."

She tries to make out the details of his face in the darkness. "Have you called any of the lab team yet?"

"The *team*?" He says it with such bite she knows she's hit a sensitive point. Rick had been the key player, when it came down to the irreplaceable brains. "The *team* is all otherwise employed."

She puts her hand on his shoulder. "I'm sorry. I just meant . . . God. What did I mean? It's just the uncertainty of it all."

They are both wide awake now. After a minute he sits up, naked, and stares at her, then flops his half of the covers off and climbs out of bed, unzips the top compartment of his suitcase and squats in front of it. He comes back with something in his hand, a small blue velvet box, which he places on the comforter between them, then tucks his crossed legs underneath the sheet again.

Claire doesn't touch it.

"Go ahead," he says. "Open it."

"Addison, I'm really glad you have faith in Ron, but I'm not ready to spend invisible money."

"Okay. Then I'll open it." He holds the box between his hands and pries the hinge back. Sitting on the puffed satin bed inside is a square of cardboard with a pink thread attached to a small gold safety pin.

Claire laughs. "Thank God. I thought you were going to give me something too gorgeous to return. What is it?"

Addison plucks the paper out of the cleft intended for a jewel and holds it in front of her—the tag from her blue dress. "I'm at least sure enough of the deal to cut the tags off."

"Okay. I guess it's unethical to take it back at this point anyway." She kisses him. "Thank you."

Addison makes a grand gesture of snapping the hinged box closed again, then holds it up in front of her face and shakes it. Something rattles against the cardboard sides. "Hey, maybe I forgot something. Better look."

Now Claire's eyebrows draw together. "Please, Addison. I don't . . ."

"Just take it, would you?" She reluctantly reaches for the box, holds it for a moment before she opens it again and pulls the satin-covered cushion out. Underneath it is her diamond ring.

Addison waits for her to move, finally takes the box out of her hand, dumps the ring out and puts it on her finger, turning it so that it matches flush against the wedding ring it was designed for. "Anna called me. She didn't have the heart to sell it."

He makes love to her that night almost too consciously, too carefully, the exuberance she'd seen in him before dinner tamped down— by caution, by her own hesitance, or because they'd watched their beautiful grown-up girl recall for them a night that is gone. It is not a thing she can ask him to explain. Hours later, sleepless, she goes into Jory's room, rests the palm of her hand on Jory's forehead as if checking for a fever. Jory sleeps through the touch, deeply, utterly vulnerable, the way only the protected can sleep. Jory. The true sunshine of their lives. Conceived to Bill Withers and twenty-six "I knows" played over and over until Claire could count it right, or stop laughing long enough to try. It's almost funny, she thinks, that the only babe to take and hold was conceived out of wedlock, like a proof against righteous laws. Twenty-six "I knows" and this house still ain't no home anytime he goes away.

· 30 ·

It feels good to be in a pattern of two parents and a child again. The balancing of who scolds and who consoles, who pays and who withholds is healthier when it is split between them—the tried-and-true strategy of good cop, bad cop, but no one has to be stuck in either role too long. The first few days Miguela has to be coaxed to the dinner table with them. But Addison's uninhibited interest in Nicaragua's turbulent history brings out another facet of Miguela: the teacher, the daughter of a revolutionary idealist. And it is Jory, remarkably, more often than Claire, who ends up translating the missing words for Addison.

Addison spends his days on the phone with his lawyers and accountants and a few technicians from his dismantled lab who might be willing to come back to work for him.

But at the clinic, for Claire, a glass bubble seems to have wrapped itself around questions of moving back to the city. Every time she makes a follow-up appointment with a patient, every time she sits at that wobbly card table with Frida and Anita eating peanut butter sandwiches, she pushes the moment she needs to talk to them one day, one week, one month farther. They have cohered as a group, in the same way she had cohered with her interns and residents in the middle of brutally long call shifts during her training, under the pressure of too much work for too few people. It was friendship fired in shared strife, richer and more dependable even than friendship born of shared neighborhoods or social tiers.

On good days Dan comes in for an hour or so, sits with his feet up and listens to Claire talk about the patients he knows better than she ever expects to. He starts with specifics: Juan Rivas is likely sending his steroid pills back to his wife in Mexico for her arthritis, so if his poly-myalgia is worse, tell him you'll give him more but he has to take his own pills, too. Dean Grauer's father had Huntington's and he'll come in every two or three months about a rash or a pain in his knee, but what he really wants to know is whether he's showing symptoms—don't write any of this in his chart because if he ever gets health insurance again it could be a preexisting. She takes meticulous notes the first two or three times, then one day he takes the pen out of her hand and tosses it in the trash. "It's the forest we're going for here, Claire."

Late one evening Claire comes out of an exam room and Frida puts a chart in her hands. "I can't even get this guy to talk to me. You try." Claire starts to counter that Frida's Spanish is still twice as good, but Frida's already walked in to see the next patient.

Gabriel Sanchez, a small Chiapan with a thick accent who has lived in a tent since arriving in Hallum two weeks ago, is here to see the doctor about a rash. Claire introduces herself as Doctora Boehning. He hesitates a second and looks at the closed door, then takes his hat off and crumples it into his lap. The imprint of the canvas band has left a dent in his forehead that continues right on around through his thick black hair. He nods. "*Señora.*"

Claire sits on the stool so her face is the same height as his. Slowly, practicing every phrase in her head before she says it, she asks him when the rash had first appeared. What part of his skin is affected. Does it itch, or hurt, or weep? Is it bumpy or raised? Splotchy or smooth? Has he been exposed to any new lotions or sprays? Mr. Gabriel San-chez—his first name that of God's messenger, his last a name older than America itself—won't look at her, keeps his eyes on his cap, turning it in his hands as if feeling along the rim for some essential tactile detail.

She finally asks him to show her his rash. "*Senora. Perdon. Dr. Ze-laya no está?*"

"*No. No está aquí hoy. Sólo yo. Soy su doctora.*"

She sees him stifle a grimace and worries her Spanish is still flat out wrong at times and she's missed something. After passing the Spanish–English dictionary back and forth it becomes clear that his rash is in his crotch, and the exam he finally allows her to perform, with one arm thrown over his pinched-shut eyes, confirms that he has crabs. It takes another fifteen minutes of stumbling Spanish and the shared dictionary, she opening it to words in the front half and he searching for words in the back half, to hopefully convince him that all his tent mates must use the special shampoos and lotions, too, and they must wash their bedrolls at the Laundromat in hot water, not the icy waters of the river they are used to.

She drops a store-bought pie and rotisserie chicken off with Evelyn and gets home long after her own family has eaten dinner, so tired she falls asleep before she's changed out of her clothes. She wakes up after midnight to discover Addison has put her book on the nightstand, taken her shoes off and covered her with a light blanket before he slid under his half of the bedspread. She peels her jeans off, flips her pillow over and buries her cheek in the cool fresh cotton.

And then she hears a voice—Jory, calling out in her sleep. She stops her breath and listens hard enough to hear the hum of her pulse. Nothing. Then footsteps. She slips to the door in bare feet and cracks it open. Jory is sitting at the dining table in the wavering yellow light of an emergency candle stuck inside an orange juice glass.

"Why are you still awake?" Claire hisses, upset enough to scold but not wanting to wake Miguela. Jory sits bolt upright—the sudden, defensive move spurs Claire to put on her bathrobe and come all the way down the stairs. "What are you doing? It's a school night!"

"I had to look something up for a test tomorrow," Jory says.

Claire scans the empty table. "So if you're studying for a test, where are your books?"

Jory stands up with her arms crossed tight around her slender body. "Okay. I'll go to bed." She starts to walk by Claire and something metallic hits the floor and skids across the room.

Claire turns on the overhead light, blindingly bright after the candle glow. "What's going on, Jory?"

"Nothing."

"What did you drop?" Claire folds her robe close around her legs and starts searching the floor, walking nearer the table and along the wall. She sees a glint of gold beside the table leg and squats down; Jory lets out an audible cry. Claire has to crawl on her knees to reach it, a dull gold locket about the size of a half dollar, hinged on one side. She picks it up, grasping the edge of the table to balance herself in a wave of vertigo. The first thing that flashes through her mind is the diamond necklace—the discovery she made a month ago while trailing her fingers through her sleeping daughter's hair that Jory was capable of such a lie—the lie of such a theft.

She holds the locket out on her open palm in front of Jory's horrified face. "Where did you get this?" Jory shakes her head once and then seems to freeze. Claire's voice drops from a shrill accusation to a harsh plea. "You didn't steal it, did you? Jory, please tell me . . ."

After a minute of tense silence Jory starts to cry and Claire wants to apologize to her, wants to hold her in her lap, wants to shake her and accuse her all over again. Her shoulders sag. "Jory . . ." she says forlornly. But Jory has already walked into the kitchen doorway and is standing next to Miguela.

"She did not steal it. It is mine," Miguela says.

Jory is looking at Miguela, imploringly. Beseechingly. The anguish on Jory's face makes Claire feel like part of her own flesh is being pulled away, a deep thudding certainty that some critical secret has been shared without Claire's protection. "Jory, I want to talk to Miguela alone for a minute. Wait upstairs, please."

Jory immediately sits on the closest chair and locks her hands under the seat, as if her mother might still be capable of physically carrying her out of the room. Claire closes her fist around the locket and sits down solidly in her own chair, looking from Jory to Miguela, weighing the choices. "All right. Okay. Miguela, sit with us, please. We'll *all* talk."

Miguela's hands are knotted in her lap and her head is bowed. Claire wants to reach over and lift her face up, make her show her eyes. After a long, uncomfortable pause Miguela looks at Claire and says, "The locket belonged to my daughter, Esperanza."

Jory lets out a cry of betrayal. "You don't have to tell her!"

Claire starts to get up, but it is Miguela who addresses Jory now. "Your mother needs to know, Jory." Miguela looks exhausted, like the act of breathing causes her physical pain. But right now, in this house tonight, Claire is not Miguela's doctor, not even her friend. She is only Jory's mother.

Claire flicks her eyes between Miguela and Jory—Jory looks like she's ready to grab Miguela's hand and run out the door. "Why is this a secret, Miguela? You told me you'd had a baby," Claire says.

"Yes. But I did not tell you how she died." She pauses, seems to struggle for words. "I did not come to the United States for money. I did not come to the clinic for a doctor. Or a job. I came to find who killed my daughter."

Claire is silent for a minute, trying to decide what to say. "Your daughter was here? In Hallum?"

"Esperanza left Nicaragua when she was fifteen. Three years later she came home, so sick I did not know her. A stranger found her in a bus and drove her to me. To Jalapa. She was pregnant. She died four days later."

Jory is silently crying, tears running down her immobile face. Claire realizes it is the first time she has seen her daughter cry in the manner of an adult, suppressing every other controllable sign of grief. Claire moves her hand to the middle of the table, where Jory can reach it if she wants. "I'm sorry," Claire says. "I'm so sorry, Miguela. Do you know why she died?"

Miguela shakes her head, more in hopelessness than as an answer. "She came home with only this." Miguela puts an envelope on the table. Claire recognizes it as the one she'd been reading the night she moved in. "Go on. You look," Miguela says. She slides it across the table. It is so worn the paper has the texture of flannel at the creases. Inside are two pieces of paper. The first is a check stub from Walker's Orchards, and the other is an appointment card for Dr. Dan Zelaya.

Claire turns it over in her hands, hoping for a revelation in the few words and numbers. "Every time I saw you at the clinic, you came in before we opened or when we were closing. When Anita wasn't at her desk. Were you looking for her records? Her medical chart?"

Miguela nods.

"Why didn't you just ask me? Even after you moved in here. With us. You didn't think I would help you?"

Miguela looks out into the middle of the room for so long Claire starts to repeat her question, but Miguela breaks in. "Esperanza went to a special house to live. The men at the orchard sent her. *They* made her sick—they put medicine in her and made her sick. She had bruises." Miguela runs her hand over her arms and face. "Bruises everywhere."

"Are you sure she was pregnant?" Claire asks.

"Her stomach was this big." Miguela holds her arms out in front of her abdomen. "I wanted her baby to live, but it did not move. Never."

Claire's mind is flying through the possible complications of pregnancy and the confused translations that had stretched across four thousand miles, two cultures, and the contorted delusions of critical illness. "Maybe the house was a hospital—someplace to have her baby?"

Suddenly Jory speaks out, her voice sounds edgy, almost desperate. "Tell her about the needles they used on her. Esperanza wasn't sick before the people at the orchard sent her to that place. It wasn't a hospital."

Miguela looks worn out, like she doesn't have the reserves left to convince Claire of anything. She snaps the locket open and looks at it, then passes it to Claire. Inside the small gold frame is a picture of a girl Jory's age, with Miguela's eyes, Miguela's hair. "Here is all I know. In Nicaragua, if you are born with nothing, you will live all your life with nothing." Her eyes are glistening but her face is composed, the purpose of her life crystallized inside the unexplained events that transformed the girl in this snapshot into the pregnant woman who came home to die.

Claire can't find any words.

After a long silence, Miguela says, "I know. You can't see it." She sounds both plaintive and resigned, as if faced with an immutable injustice that she is deciding not to fight anymore. She searches Claire's face like no language in the world could translate their separate lives, an expression of such sophic compassion that Claire feels exposed.

"What?" Claire asks. "What can't I see?"

"You cannot see what you have."

Claire waits for Addison to say something. She has tried to stay as clearheaded as possible, repeating not only what Miguela has told her tonight but all the odd occurrences she's noticed since Miguela showed up in front of the grocery store out of nowhere; how they had all just seemed like cultural or linguistic quirks until they exploded inside this weird story. She's trying to fathom how she could have invited someone into their home, into Jory's life, based on trust alone, when she knew so little about her.

Addison is lying on his back, naked underneath the sheet, his arms crossed over his chest and his eyes closed. She leans over him, finally taps her finger in the center of his forehead. "Are you listening?" He reaches up and closes his hand around her own. "I'm listening. I'm thinking. Go on."

"I don't feel like you're taking this seriously."

"Why? Because my eyes are closed?" He rolls up on his side, props his cheek on the angle of his wrist and stares at her. "I really am. Listening. I'm trying to figure out what part of this has you so upset— her daughter's death or the fact that Jory knows more about it than you do."

"I just . . . I wouldn't have thought she could lie to me."

He gives her a thoughtful, questioning look. "Well, did she lie to you? Or just not tell you the whole truth."

"Why would she hide it from me, though?" Claire falls onto her back now. "This story about her daughter being poisoned in some house . . . do you think she could have been part of a prostitution ring? On drugs?"

"That's not unimaginable given the stories you bring home. Maybe Miguela's hiding it because she's scared. It sounds like she thinks someone in Hallum is responsible."

"Addison?"

"What?" he finally asks.

"Walker's not the type to do something like this, is he? Get a teenager pregnant and send her out of the country? Or worse—send his workers into prostitution?"

He lofts the sheet and turns onto his stomach, pulling his pillow under his chest. "This is the same man who funds your charity clinic. As far as I know he's happily married." His eyes are blinking heavy and slow, they drift closed for a moment.

"Since when does money and power keep a man from taking advantage of people who work for him?"

He rouses again with this, "It's two AM, Claire. You're not making sense." He blinks again, waiting for her to answer or go to sleep. "You want to believe her, don't you? That's why you're so upset."

Claire nods. "Yeah. I want to believe her. Believe *in* her. I feel responsible for her. But it's him, too," she says.

"Him who?"

"Walker. I need to believe in him, too."

· 31 ·

Anita is due to deliver any day, and her sister, Rosa, has been coming in most afternoons just to lighten her load. When the volume picks up in the afternoon the four women fall into a rhythm of patient triage and flow—symptoms and vital signs, medication lists and wound care pass between them like relay batons, each of them kindly, efficiently cutting to the quick of the complaint. Even the patients seem to catch on that there can be no unessential requests or the last in line will get no care at all. They all go forward as if Dan might come back to work any day, because none of them can imagine this place surviving long without him.

Other than putting an advertisement in the newspaper, Claire hasn't brought it up. She and Frida are at the clinic until after eight thirty each night, dividing up Dan's messages and lab reports, trying to guess what his patient care plans would have been, delaying as many follow-ups as possible so they don't have to call him at home.

"So, where would they go?" Claire finally asks, her lap filled with crisscrossed stacks of pathology slips and radiology reports and pink phone call memos. "Would Kit or Hale or the hospital take up the slack?"

"How could they? They already see plenty of people for free," Frida answers. Then she dumps every paper on her own lap into her black plastic in-box and puts on her windbreaker. Buttoning it up quite deliberately, she circles her chin around the room, at the dangling lightbulb, the cracked window over its flimsy chicken-wire mesh, the broken linoleum squares on the floor. "I don't know! How much can you worry about where all the water goes after a flood? You just swim harder while it's high. This place is falling apart as it is." She walks out through the swinging gates and then walks right back in before they've stopped moving, points her finger at Claire and says, "You need to get home to your girl. That's who needs you most. Don't you let her daddy raise her without a mother."

It is an unusually light morning. Frida says it's because they are starting to harvest; too much money is hanging on the trees for workers to leave the fields for any reason. Anita blames it on *La Migra,* the border patrol, circulating through town again. Claire listens to them both and says Hallum must be a pretty pure place, because if there's any season an orchardist would be enticed to bribe the law it would be for the picking of fruit. Half the crop would rot on the ground without the migrants.

An hour after everyone else leaves, Claire turns out the lights in the waiting room and walks to the bank of file cabinets behind the reception area. She has a name, she has a birth date, she knows the season in which Esperanza was seen. There is a grant proposal sitting on her desk right now to hire a part-time person to digitize their files, but Dan had always eschewed any need for more than their one aging computer; all the records in the clinic are still written and filed by hand.

Esperanza Ruiz's clinic chart is almost pristine, the cream-colored folder unblemished. Claire sits down at Anita's desk and flicks on the light. From the story Miguela has told her she suspects Esperanza died of some complication of pregnancy, probably toxemia—a poorly understood biochemical backfire between fetus and mother. She had been only seventeen, young enough that toxemia was more likely, and it could also explain the bruising and swelling and confusion Miguela described.

Dan must have seen Esperanza a few months before she went back to Jalapa. The single page inside her chart, dated early October, sketches a typical intake history and physical. Her chief complaint was nausea and vomiting, her physical exam remarkable only for some slight swelling in the ankles, a heart rate a bit faster than expected. Her last menstrual period was reported as August, but there is a question mark beside it, and if Dan did a pelvic exam, he didn't put his findings on the page. Esperanza's height and weight show that she was a stout girl, unlike her mother. Dan's impression, at the bottom of the page, lists a differential of pregnancy, viral gastroenteritis or hepatitis and an order for some blood work—a hematocrit and white cell count, a chemistry panel and pregnancy test. He could have easily gotten a urine pregnancy test in their own makeshift lab, but if he was drawing blood anyway, if she hadn't been able to give him a sample, he might have just tagged it along with the blood he sent to the hospital lab. For whatever reason there is nothing else in the chart except the typed-out page of demographics that Anita must have recorded. Esperanza's address was Walker's Orchards.

Claire closes the chart, disappointed. She had hoped for a definitive answer, some solace for Miguela, if there could be any comfort in pinning a confirmed diagnosis to her daughter's cause of death. Claire opens the folder one more time and flips to the back of the brass-tabbed pages looking for the lab results. Nothing. Which meant nothing. Esperanza might have walked out the second someone came in the room waving a needle at her. But the fact that Dan had been checking a pregnancy test was enough. The diagnosis of toxemia fit. At least she might convince Miguela her daughter had not been murdered or part of a sex ring.

She tries to imagine Esperanza traveling by bus on rutted dirt roads through the mountains of Nicaragua, pregnant and sick, her illness escalating toward seizures and inevitable death if she couldn't be delivered. If she had stayed here, she and her baby would most likely be alive.

She waits until Addison and Jory are upstairs to talk to Miguela, tries to ease into it by asking her to repeat what she remembers again, anything that might explain more than Claire found in the single page of Esperanza's chart. Had she had a fever, any rash, had the baby still been moving? Did any doctor see her before she died? Was she *sure*

Esperanza was pregnant—Dan had not been certain only three months earlier.

Miguela seems worn out by the questions. "The doctor in Jalapa said it was too late."

"I think, from everything you've told me, I think Esperanza had a complication from her pregnancy. It's called toxemia. Without being in a hospital, without a C-section—*cesárea,* you understand?—without that there is no way to save the mother's life."

Miguela's face looks like Claire is pronouncing Esperanza's death for the first time. She is struggling against such a final conclusion, Claire can see it. As if she's come too far tracking her daughter's death to accept it as an unpreventable consequence of nature—needs to identify some perpetrator other than God and poverty. "But what about this house? She told me she was there many weeks."

"The address in her chart was for the orchard. Toxemia makes the brain swell—I think Esperanza might have been confused. Maybe the house was the orchard office. Or the clinic."

Miguela is quiet for a long time. Finally Claire asks her if she wants to be alone.

She puts her hand on Claire's sleeve. It is the first time, Claire realizes, that Miguela has ever touched her. "*Doctora* . . . Please. I need to see myself. I want to go to the clinic."

Claire is used to the clinic on Sundays, a quiet peace that helps her work or study. A sense of time and disease arrested. She locks the door behind them, knowing that the lights might attract any passing patient with a complaint. Miguela seems hushed, intimidated by the vacancy of a place usually filled with waiting patients and the noise of illness and injury. Claire leads her through the swinging gate into the records stacks. Even for so small a clinic they are impressive, with floor-to-ceiling shelves of coded charts on two rolling metal frames. She walks down the row of *R*s until she finds Esperanza's, slips it out and puts it on Anita's desk.

Miguela seems hesitant to open it. Claire pulls out a rolling stool and sits beside her. "It's okay. She was your daughter." Miguela runs her hand over the smooth manila cardboard of the chart. Claire watches her, sees her take in a breath and sit up straighter, then, at last, lift the front cover open. Claire asks her, "Can you read it?"

Miguela nods but stares at Dan's note without moving her eyes, maybe just absorbing the fact that these words are the closest she will ever come to her daughter's life in this country. After a few minutes she turns the single page, as Claire had done, looking for more, scanning the typed facts of age and address, the country of origin. Then she pushes the chart away and stands up. "Thank you. You are kind to bring me here when everything is closed." Claire picks up the chart and walks back along the row of Rs to find its place. She hears Miguela start to leave the waiting room. But then Miguela takes a step back toward Claire and asks, "Why would they not use her whole name?"

"What?"

"Why did they only use part of her name?"

Claire stops, turns the chart sideways to read Esperanza's name in bold type along the edge of the front flap. She looks at Miguela, puzzled. "Esperanza Ruiz. Isn't that . . . Wasn't that her name?"

"Esperanza De Estrella Ruiz. Her father's name was De Estrella."

"Her father's name was De Estrella?"

Claire knows it is the common custom in Latin America to use both parents' names—often enough it has caused confusion with their medical records. "Did she go by both names after she left Nicaragua? Do you know?"

Miguela shakes her head. "Will you look? Please?"

Claire pushes one rolling rack down the length of its tracks and stands on a footstool to reach the Es. She flips through them, pressing her thumb against the edge of each chart, saying the names under her breath: "Escada, Escondido, Estonce, Estrella." There are multiple Estrellas. None is Esperanza. She steps down. "She's not there. Probably she went by Ruiz in the clinic."

Miguela takes a hesitant step forward, then walks up to the shelves and scans the letters lining the protruding flaps. She is ahead of the Es, reaches up to push a few charts forward and pulls one slender volume out of the rack. ESPERANZA DE ESTRELLA RUIZ. It had been filed under the letter D.

The date on it is late November, less than two months later. It's no thicker than the other chart; the two combined are only five pages. It is the contrasts between them rather than the similarities that are disturbing, the numbers marching in a column down the last sheet that refute the diagnosis she was so sure of half an hour ago. Some of the labs could be consistent with toxemia—the elevated liver enzymes, the anemia, the low platelet count—*if* they had been discovered late in Esperanza's pregnancy. *If* Esperanza had been pregnant. Her pregnancy test result in the laboratory section is negative. Claire looks at it twice, even runs her finger across the page from the chemical term, Beta HCG, to the negligible measured quantity. Dan's note on the lined progress paper consists of a single word scribbled during Esperanza's follow-up visit, *hepatotoxicity,* underlined and followed by a bold question mark.

"She wasn't pregnant. Something was wrong with her liver. *Hígado.*" Claire translates when she sees Miguela's confusion. "It can make the abdomen fill up with fluid—enough to make a woman look pregnant."

Miguela seems almost afraid to open this chart, touches it once and then moves her hand away. "Why? Why would she have this?"

Claire starts to list the possibilities—viruses and cancers and alcohol, toxins and Tylenol, sclerosing ducts and impacted stones—but all the medical words sound coldly clinical, untranslatable even if she knew the Spanish words. "There's just no way to know from these labs." She hates the finality she hears in her voice, relaxes her posture so that her face is nearer Miguela's. "I'm sorry. I'm so sorry."

Miguela covers her eyes with one hand; the other is pressed into her abdomen like her body might fly apart if she let go. Claire can't tell if she's crying. "Can I get you anything? Some tea?" she asks.

Miguela looks at her like she hasn't understood this, either. "It's because of the medicines they gave her, isn't it?"

Claire flicks on the small desk lamp beside Anita's computer. "Miguela, there's nothing in her chart that indicates she was given any kind of medicine. Dan's note doesn't . . ."

"Other people lived in the house with her. She told me. If we could find them they would remember."

Claire studies her face for a minute, notices the shadowy hollows underneath her eyes, the grim set of her mouth. Every smile Miguela has shared in the last month seems like a sad, strained pretense now. She lowers her voice, trying to hide her frustration. "Her address was the orchard. Walker's Orchards. Where *you* worked. She was confused. You said that. Remember?"

"Yes. She worked at the orchard. But then someone took her to this other place, where they hurt her."

Claire doesn't know what to say anymore. Logic, reason, any rational counter is doomed because it will always end with the same tragic fact of Esperanza's young death. She opens the chart again, ready to show Miguela anything more measurable than her grief-tainted memory. "These numbers, here: Esperanza's INR and her pro-time. They measure a protein made in the liver that helps blood clot. They were too high. It means her liver was very sick. That is why she had bruises."

Miguela looks bewildered; maybe Claire's explanation has been too complicated. But something in Miguela's unashamed, questioning gaze cuts to the mother in Claire, begs her to admit she would do the same—push and push until she found an answer. "Let's go home. We'll eat something and we'll talk about everything you remember. Maybe we can find someone in Hallum who remembers her. Maybe I can talk to Dr. Zelaya." She opens the back flap of both charts side by side on the desk, unclasps the brass tabs that hold the pages together.

Miguela watches her intently, possessively. "Why are you taking them apart?"

"To combine them, so everything will be together." Claire stacks the pages of Esperanza Ruiz and Esperanza De Estrella Ruiz into their new order, thinking it all through one more time: a young girl living in a house where someone was giving her medicine or drugs, using needles on her. How many thousands of immigrants ended up trafficked for sex, or addicted through choice or coercion? If that had been Jory's irremediable fate she might not even want to know about it.

She aligns the punched holes and slides the pages onto the opened brass flanges. But now the front page, the one with the factual demographics in Esperanza's mistaken name, is wrong—should, in fact, be torn up, Claire decides. She lifts it off the tabs and the two pages with their two different names are side by side in front of her. And for the first time she sees that the name is not the only difference in the typed data that Anita must have taken from Esperanza at this very desk.

Miguela has obviously noticed her reaction. Claire feels caught, wishes she had just left the charts as they were.

"What is it?" Miguela asks.

Claire hesitates, then turns on Anita's computer and opens the patient database they keep, little more than an Excel spreadsheet; scrolling through the Rs and then through the Ds she finds the same duplication—two Esperanzas. With two different addresses.

Miguela sweeps the pages into her lap, scanning the boxes of information. "The addresses are different. She is in Wenatchee here."

Claire sees the change in Miguela's face, sees her back away from releasing all of this—almost relieved that her obsessive hunt can résumé and delay the insurmountable fact of Esperanza's death. "Miguela, there could be another reason." Claire starts talking, tempted to take the pages away from her. "I'll ask Anita on Monday. She might remember something."

"Call the number."

For a moment Claire thinks that Miguela wants her to call Anita right now. "Call?"

Miguela picks up the desk phone and holds it out to Claire. "Please. Call the number in Wenatchee."

Claire dials the number and waits through six rings, about to hang up when a woman answers. She listens for a moment and clicks the receiver down.

"What is it?" Miguela asks.

Claire shakes her head. "It was some company. A business." She brushes her hand across the page, as if the numbers might magically appear more clearly or change altogether into an obvious solution she should have put together from the start. At least, she thinks, it's unlikely a brothel or drug house would hire such politely professional office staff. "Maybe I dialed wrong. Or the phone number could have changed since Esperanza lived there."

She dials the number once more; this time the woman answers after only three rings. Claire's finger hovers over the button ready to disconnect the call; she's crazily embarrassed about disturbing this complete stranger again. But now, when the woman answers and states the name of the business, Claire recognizes it.

She hangs up and walks back to the record shelves, this time hunting through the *As* until she finds Rubén Aguilar's chart. She already knows the contact phone number and address are out of date, doesn't bother to compare them to Esperanza's. She is looking for the single, loose slip of paper she had scribbled his address and new number on, riffling through the pages, shaking the chart upside down with no luck. Miguela is watching her, visibly restraining herself from interrupting. Claire stops to think for a minute, tries to slow her mind down so she can remember.

Miguela reads the name off this other patient's chart. "Who is this man?"

"I think he was there. At Optimus. I'm sure that's who answered the phone. . . ." She stops, remembering at last where she'd put it. She pulls her cell phone out from the clutter of her purse and punches in the first three letters of Rubén's last name. The same number they have just called pops up in the screen.

She turns to Miguela again. "Tell me. One more time. Tell me what Esperanza said about the house."

Miguela begins to repeat what she has said before, glimpses of something like a hotel or a boardinghouse, confused with memories of medications and needles and blood, all of it mangled by Esperanza's illness, by Miguela's grief, by an imperfect translation between Spanish and English. It's a senseless history if you listened to it rationally or considered it skeptically, degenerating more every time she tells it. Claire can see that Miguela is distraught.

The computer screen has already gone dark, but jumps to life as soon as Claire touches the mouse. She clicks onto the Internet and types in *Optimus*; a dozen different companies fill the page. Then she refines the search, adding the words *research* and *Wenatchee, Washington.* The screen goes white while the slow clinic connection filters through to a new list—the top link connects directly to OptimusRe-search.com, a blue and white scheme with the words *Optimus Clinical Research* in bold letters, slanting across a broad band of graduated color. Above the company name a man and woman in white coats consult over a clipboard. The man appears studious, handsomely graying with a stethoscope looped around his neck; the woman is blond and smiling. Underneath the logo a string of quotes float by, like banners pulled by a prop plane across a blue sky:

Fastest track to FDA approval in the U.S. market
Safe, Secure, Efficient
Optimus brought our drug to patients in record time at half the cost.

"What is it?" Miguela asks.

"It's a clinical research organization."

"I don't understand."

"Research. Like a laboratory. *Laboratorio.* They help drug developers test new drugs." She closes both charts and holds them in her lap, creases the empty cardboard folder labeled ESPERANZA RUIZ and puts it into the trash can under the desk.

Miguela's eyes are closed and she is sitting very straight and still, as if she is blinding herself to the world. As if she's praying. Claire remembers the first night she saw her, how terribly cold she must have been. "Miguela, let me take you home. I'll go see Dan. At least, maybe, we'll find out what made her sick."

· 32 ·

By the time she drops Miguela at the house and drives to Dan's it is after six thirty. She hesitates a minute, wishing she had stopped at the store for a gift—food or flowers. Then she picks up both Esperanza's and Rubén's charts and walks up the driveway, passing Dan and Evelyn's old Buick, rusted in spots along the bottom from years in this climate. Evelyn's purse is sitting on the driver's seat. Claire lifts it through the open window and rings the doorbell. The lilacs are in full bloom now, exuding a sticky-sweet scent, swarming with bees.

"Did I leave it outside again?" Evelyn asks, pushing open the screen door.

"In the car."

"Yesterday it sat on the front porch half the day before I tripped on it going back out to the store. Lucky we live in a safe town. Come on in, he's on the sofa."

"Is he up for a visit?"

"Tired. We spent the last two days in Wenatchee getting a new stent—I try to stack up the doctors' visits so we only have to make one trip a week. Really wears him out."

The usually neat gray weave of Evelyn's chignon is feathered with wispy tendrils escaping the clasp of her painted leather barrette. The smells of the house have altered—something sharp and medicinal is in the air. Evelyn touches her shoulder and heads toward the small kitchen, murmurs something about tea. It takes Claire a moment to find

Dan in the dimly lit room. She tries not to react to the change in him.

"Hey there," Claire says softly.

Dan stirs and opens his eyes. When he sees her he pushes himself up on the sofa so that he approximates a sitting position, waves his hand at her, a gesture that should appear casual and lithe but instead looks like the static moves of a stick man. "Hey yourself. You're starting to stop by pretty frequent. Should I be dusting off my black frock coat?"

"Not unless you know somebody who's getting married," Claire answers, pulling a chair around to face him, determined not to let him see how alarmed she is by the weight he's lost in five days.

"You just getting off? Whole point of working in that podunk clinic is to get home at a decent hour."

"It's Sunday. I was trying to clear my desk."

"Sunday," he repeats, pausing with a shake of his head.

"Anyway, Frida's already ratted you out. I know you never got home before seven until you hired me."

Dan smiles at her and straightens up a bit, one hand guarding his abdomen. Evelyn brings in a tray with a porcelain teapot, cups already rinsed with steaming water in the English way, a saucer of ginger cookies, a pitcher of cream, and a jelly jar lid filled with pills and capsules. She pours tea for Dan and hands him the jar lid. He lifts his cup in a mock toast and throws the medications onto the back of his tongue one at a time, chased with a swallow of tea. He wipes his mouth with his sleeve and Claire sees his hand tremble.

"I left a mess for you to clean up. My apologies." He laughs once. "I always planned to get better organized."

"We're making it, Dan. Rosa and Anita are both working part-time. We've told Anita she's not allowed to have her baby till Christmas. And Frida can take care of most patients on her own, you know that. I just cosign her scripts."

He nods, his gaze fixed at some distant point out the window. Then he turns to her with a completely focused look, a resilient voice. "I want you to call me with any question at all. I'm leaving so much undone— that's the worst of it all. Call me. At least I can tell you where to go for money when you run out."

Even with this perfect opening Claire finds it almost impossible to ask him about Esperanza. It sounds ridiculous when she starts piecing the questions together in her own head. Could Dan know anything about Optimus Research? Is it purely coincidence that two patients who used to work for Ron Walker had the phone number for Optimus listed in their charts and then turned up with liver damage—fatal in Esperanza's case? She should call Optimus again herself, ask them flat out how long they've even had that number. "I mainly need you to convince the men I'm trustworthy." She looks down at her hands, running one thumbnail under the other, suddenly awkward about the transition, however tangential, to his mortality. When she looks up, though, she can see in Dan's face that everything will be all right, whatever she needs to say to him. "We put an ad in for another doctor."

"'Bout time!"

"Yeah. Anita wrote it as 'salary commensurate with experience,' but Frida said we should change it to 'salary commensurate with the depth of your gullible, bleeding heart.'"

Dan laughs with his head thrown back, a sound like something rusted breaking free. Claire feels lifted by the ring of it, risen to a place where she can see beyond her tense, circuitous guessing game with Miguela in that deserted office, over nothing more than a sketch of facts and her own dread that Ron Walker—Addison's golden parachute—could be tainted.

Dan wipes his eyes with a napkin from the tray, settles back on the sofa with a relaxed smile on his face. "I need to go to the bank Monday. I'll do it during lunch, if you'll meet me there. I need to make you a cosignatory on the account." She would have trouble meeting his eyes now, except for the matter-of-factness in his manner, as if he were telling her where to buy new business cards or thermometers. "Ron will give you whatever you need."

It's jarring to hear Ron's name now, like Dan has been reading her thoughts all along. Another example of the multiplying coincidences that truly *can* occur in a small town. Claire wonders when Ron learned about Dan's cancer. Before their dinner together? Was he so capable of separating his charity from his business he hadn't given a clue away? Or was it pure professionalism, respecting her option to move in a different direction than her husband?

After a few more minutes of conversation she sees Dan's eyes begin to lag. "You're tired. I'll come back. Or I guess I'll see you Monday, won't I?"

"It's the morphine. I'd make a lousy addict."

Evelyn must have been listening. On that cue she comes out of the kitchen and walks Claire to the door, keeping the conversation roving around Jory and cooking and her garden, breaking off a heavily drooping branch of lilacs for Claire to take home. Only when Claire bends to kiss her cheek does she clutch Claire's shoulder, fiercely, quickly, the flash of distress gone almost the moment Claire feels it. Then she stands with her perfect, elegant posture and tucks the lilacs into the top of Claire's purse, hundreds of tiny purple petals scatter through her brush and wallet and loose change. Evelyn gestures with her clasped hands at the manila folders under Claire's arm. "Do you always take patient charts with you when you visit your friends?"

"Oh . . ." She gives an awkward laugh. "I had a question. It's not important."

Evelyn puts one hand under Claire's chin; her fingers are warm and soft. Claire remembers a moment a decade ago when her own mother had stroked her face in comfort after the last miscarriage, when she knew she couldn't bear to try again. It was the last time she had truly felt like her mother's child. "Claire? If you need to ask him anything, you should do it now."

Claire sits on the dining room chair again, with the two charts on her lap. "Dan?" She whispers his name with her hand resting lightly on his knee, sees him struggle to open his eyes.

It takes him a moment to focus, but then he smiles. "Monday already, huh?"

"I'm sorry. If you're not too worn out, I *do* want to ask about a patient. You only saw her twice, I think. You may not even remember." He grins, as though he remembers every patient who's come through the clinic, year after year, a flood swelling and ebbing as they follow crops like a tidal current of human labor—anonymous, undocumented, infinitely replaceable.

"What's the name?"

"Esperanza Dela Estrella Ruiz."

Dan is quiet. For a moment she thinks he has fallen asleep again. But then she sees him nod, just a tuck of his chin. He squeezes her hand once.

"I found her chart. Charts, actually. She had two, under different names." He waits for her, seems to want her to lead. "She's Miguela's daughter. I promised Miguela I'd try to find out what happened. That's the real reason Miguela came to Hallum."

He sighs, a raspy shudder of breath. "What did you find in the chart?"

"You thought she was pregnant. She had a little edema, nausea. Her period was late. You ordered some labs and a pregnancy test."

Dan's blink is slow, drugged, or maybe just worn out, but he is quick in his response. "I ordered liver functions and a hepatitis screen."

Claire considers how to put the story together so Dan might comprehend how it's impacted her. "She came back a couple of months later, weeks after you'd scheduled her follow-up."

"And the lab results showed a negative pregnancy test. Her liver enzymes were all high. Bad high. But her hepatitis screen was also negative. Albumin was down, platelets were down, red blood cells were low." It's as if Dan is reading the eight-month-old lab results from the page.

"Your note says . . ." Claire starts.

"It says she had hepatotoxicity. Liver damage. Probably drug-induced." He stops again, a crease of worry between his eyes. Or maybe pain. Claire glances at his hands to see if he presses one against his abdomen, the way he had for so many weeks before she'd learned why.

"Do you know what drug?"

He frowns briefly, then looks at her and shakes his head. "I didn't have a chance to run any other tests on her. Could have been anything from pesticides to Tylenol."

"I know." Claire nods and licks her lips. "I know." She takes the other chart in her lap and opens it on top of Esperanza's. "But I had another patient, too—Rubén Aguilar. I told you about him a few months ago. He had the same picture—liver damage, viral hepatitis screen was negative. He must have moved away after I saw him; he missed his next appointment. The weird thing is, he and Esperanza had the same address for a while. Or at least the same phone number. I called—it's a clinical research organization. Optimus Research. The kind of place that runs investigational drug studies. They *both* used to work at Walker's Orchards. And then they both ended up at this Optimus place. Both ended up with liver damage."

After a long pause Dan says, "Maybe I'm not following you here. Are you trying to connect Ron to this research outfit? He's the biggest employer in Hallum. Half the migrants in the valley work for him at some point." He winces when he says this, a look that could be mistaken for annoyance if Claire didn't understand what he was going through, didn't fully comprehend how much he owes to Ron. He seems distracted by the pain for a moment, then scans Claire's face, something deeply personal in his eyes. "Why did Miguela come to Hallum to find Esperanza?"

"To find out what happened to her. Miguela's convinced someone is to blame—that it was intentional. She thought Esperanza was pregnant when she got back to Nicaragua. I guess she had enough fluid in her abdomen—ascites—to look pregnant. From Miguela's description, the bruising and swelling and confusion, I assumed it was toxemia. It was a miracle Esperanza made it back to Nicaragua at all." She pauses, leans forward a little. "It wasn't until I found the second chart with the lab results, found out she wasn't ever pregnant, that I knew she'd died of liver failure."

The change in Dan's face is immediate. Claire realizes that he has been listening to this story with some degree of hope, now completely upended. "Oh, Dan! I'm sorry. You didn't know she died."

"No." He covers his face with his long, thick-jointed fingers, pulls them down his cheeks so she hears the brush of his cracked skin across his beard. He lets out a small gasp and rocks back and forth once. "No. I guess I knew it on some level." He sighs again and struggles to collect himself. "Esperanza didn't get to Nicaragua through any miracle. When she came to see me the second time she was pretty sick. Jaundiced, swollen. Too sick for a clinic. I drove her to the emergency room.

Stayed with her until they told me they were admitting her. I expected she'd be in the ICU within another few days if it didn't turn around, she looked that bad to me."

"What happened?"

"I went back the next day. To see her. They told me she'd left."

Claire sits up straighter in her chair at this. Dan almost seems to be waiting for her to tell the rest of the story. She tilts her head. "How could she have been discharged if she was that sick?"

"You really don't know? No guess?"

Claire shakes her head.

"They stabilized her and put her on a plane. They bought her a ticket back to Nicaragua because it was cheaper than hospitalizing her."

"I don't believe it. They would send her home rather than treat her?"

Dan pulls the blanket closer about his waist, shifts his torso like he can't get comfortable. "My dear, the only positive thing I have to say is that I'm thankful such a thing still surprises you."

· 33 ·

The sun is already setting when she reaches the top of the long driveway. A forest fire has been burning out near Chelan and a south wind pushes the smoke their way, the sunset bleeds strange and thick with unnatural purples and reds.

Claire parks and sits in the car, watching Addison move between the windows like panels on a movie screen. He's getting dinner on the table, opening a bottle of wine, pointing to something Jory is reading. Nothing comes to Claire, no clear way to talk to him about Optimus. Not even clarity on the rightness or wrongness of Walker's possible involvement.

She picks up the medical charts and her purse and gets out; the air smells of burning wood and scorching earth, a primitive impurity in it. The silhouette of the old barn looks as if the first summer storm will knock it to the ground. But it has stood long enough—through a world war and polio epidemics and a burned-down aspen grove that has already grown back dense and strong. That barn had outlasted the Blackstocks and will outlast the Boehnings.

She opens the front door and hears Addison reading another Web-generated quiz aloud with Jory, leaning over her shoulder and laughing. As soon as he sees Claire his face changes, the playful father replaced by something more serious. Is this the effect she has on him now? How she tips their triangled balance?

"Hi, guys," Claire says, shutting the door with her foot. "Smells good. Chicken again?"

Addison puts his hands in his pockets. "Cook what you know how to cook, I guess."

Jory seems exuberant. Oblivious. "Mom, answer these questions and I can tell you what kind of animal you are. If you were an animal, I mean."

"Can it wait, honey?" She drops the charts and her purse on the table and kisses the crown of Jory's head. "I need to talk to Dad about something. Would you mind giving us a minute by ourselves?"

Jory starts upstairs but stops halfway. "I'm fifteen years old next month. When are you going to make me part of this huge family secret?" Addison gives Claire a frantic look. "I'm going. But would you please look for a house that has more than one shared room—not including the bathroom?"

After her bedroom door shuts Claire asks Addison, "Where is Miguela?"

"Out walking. What's going on?"

Claire pulls two dining chairs into the kitchen, what has become their unspoken code for an impending argument. Scraping the legs of the chair over the scarred wood onto the cracked linoleum, Claire remembers the parallel tracks from the vacuum that would often mark the thick carpet in their formal dining room for weeks because no one entered it. She sits down; Addison lags behind, then adjusts his own chair a few inches closer to the door before he sits, his legs straddling the laddered back so that it rises like a gate between them.

"Did Miguela tell you what happened? About the charts?" Claire asks.

He lifts one shoulder. "It didn't make much sense to me. She said you went to talk to Dan."

"So she didn't tell you how Esperanza died?"

Addison cocks his head, as if this unexpected topic upends his defensive wariness. "I thought it was a problem with her pregnancy."

Claire rakes her hair off her forehead and starts to say something but stops before any words come out.

Addison asks, "What? Was it AIDS or something?"

She takes a breath. "Esperanza was never pregnant. She died of liver failure."

He scans her face, blatantly puzzled about the relevance this has for his own family, why Jory shouldn't be allowed to overhear. "Why did Miguela say she was pregnant?"

"She must have had ascites—enough fluid to fill her abdomen. It could all look like toxemia—the swelling, the bruising, the confusion. But it was all because of liver failure."

"Are you sure?"

"I saw her labs." She waves one arm at the dining room table where Esperanza's chart sits on top of Rubén's. "It's all there. Dan remembers her clearly."

Addison rocks his shoulders from side to side and leans over the back of the chair, almost provocatively. "Okay. But you still can't bring her back to life. So, tragic as it is, why are we having this conversation?" He circles his forefinger in between them and hisses, "*In here?*"

Claire pauses for a moment, knowing what she's figured out will sound crazy when she says it out loud. "I think Esperanza was involved in a drug study. I think she died of drug-induced liver damage because she was a volunteer in a new drug trial."

Addison looks blatantly skeptical. "Based on what?"

"I had another patient with liver damage. I got his labs back the day you bought me those earrings, do you remember? I drove all over the valley trying to find him but he'd moved. They had the same phone number listed in both their charts, for a company called Optimus in Wenatchee. I looked it up; it's a clinical research organization."

He pulls his head back and the crease between his eyebrows deepens. "Well, does Dan know the name of the drug? I should have heard something about it if any study volunteers got that sick—that kind of thing travels fast in the industry."

"I don't know if it was ever reported. Dan took Esperanza to the hospital and they put her on a plane back to Nicaragua. Nobody in the U.S. would know she died." She can see the doubt creeping into his face even before she tells him the rest—the worst. She gets the charts from the dining table and puts them in his lap. "Read the labs yourself. It's right there—look at the last sections."

He opens both folders, turns through the few pages, skimming over the numbers. Then he flips them closed and hands them back to her. "You're right. It looks like liver failure. But where are you coming up with the theory about a drug study?"

She opens Esperanza's record again and shows him the demographics page. "This phone number; it's the same for both of them. Call it now, if you want. Look it up on the Internet—they have a Web site."

Addison's eyes flick back and forth across Claire's. She sees the small muscle in his cheek twitch. After a long-evolving silence he sighs. "I'll find out what I can. If any patient died they would have stopped the study, Claire."

"Sure. If they knew about it." He makes a move to stand up and Claire puts her hand on his arm. "Addison, both Esperanza and Rubén worked for Walker's Orchards before they went to Optimus."

Addison settles back into his chair again, waiting, a hint of defensiveness creeping back into his face. "What are you suggesting now? That Ron is funneling illegal immigrants into drug studies?"

"No. I don't know." Then, almost in a whisper: "Maybe."

Addison gets up so fast the chair falls over backward with a loud clap. "I thought you were as excited about this deal as I am. Are you *looking* for a way to make it fall through? You like living this way?"

"No. This has nothing to do with the deal. I just . . . Walker told you he had other biotech companies. Even a research organization. Didn't he imply you could run the trials on vascumab there? In his own CRO? I *like* Ron. I *want* to like Ron. But if he's doing something illegal I want to find out now. Before."

"His holding company owns some CROs. Along with about thirty other businesses. And there's nothing illegal about enrolling undocumented workers as volunteers in a drug study, Claire—just for the record. As long as they fully understand the consent. They probably get better food and better housing than they do on a farm or in a factory."

"Well, how 'voluntary' can it be when half of them have no other place to live? And would be too terrified to call the police if something goes wrong?"

Addison leans against the refrigerator, his head resting on crossed arms. Claire sees his ribs expand under his T-shirt with each deep, slow breath. Finally he says, "Okay. All right. I'll ask Ron."

"Ask him what, exactly?"

He turns to face her, his cheeks blotched with emotion. "I'll ask Ron if he's intentionally poisoning the same people he supports at your clinic!" His voice is full of sarcasm, but something more distressed, too. Doubt. Teetering on the edge of a lost dream.

"That's not what I'm saying!"

He raises one hand toward the ceiling, like it might catch the thread of Claire's unspoken thoughts. "Then what are you saying? Just tell me. What do you want me to do?"

And suddenly it is clear to her what she wants, for the first time since she'd seen the same phone number in both Esperanza's and Rubén's charts. "I want you to find out who owns Optimus. I want to know if it's Ron's CRO."

He puts his hands on his hips and stares at the black square of the kitchen window. When he faces her again a shiver runs over her skin. "Fine, then. I'll go to Seattle tomorrow and talk to Ron. I'll talk to his lawyers, too. But even if he does—even if the worst of what you're suggesting is true, Ron has done nothing illegal. I explained this to you that night at the Mayflower; it's legal to invest in the contract research organization that's testing the drug you are funding, and it's legal to have the whole shebang ethically reviewed by the IRB you own, as long as you don't vote. It's also legal to enroll migrant farmworkers as drug study volunteers with informed consent." He crosses his arms and pauses an instant before he goes on. "*And* it's legal for the hospital to buy a migrant a ticket home before they get so sick they are required to admit them and pay for a month in the ICU."

He goes upstairs. The house is unusually quiet for a long time, and then she hears another door open. Jory is standing at the top of the stairs with her hands on the banister. She looks like a Dickens waif, with her hair dangling in a tangled mess over her faded nightgown. "You're fighting again. Aren't you?"

Claire shakes her head, but then pinches the bridge of her nose and holds her hand out. "Come down. Sit with me awhile."

Jory walks down the stairs so slowly Claire can tell she's considering going back up with every step. Claire pulls out the nearest chair, but Jory sits in the farthest and hunches forward over her knees, wrapping her arms around her body as if it were still winter.

"Are you and Dad getting a divorce?"

"Sweetheart, it's not . . ."

"Will you just answer me? Are you?" Jory asks, tears making her voice hoarse.

Claire hears Addison moving around in their bedroom, the closet door creaking open and something hitting the floor. She walks around the table and kneels with one hand on Jory's back, the other on her knee, feels her body tense. "That's not what either of us wants."

Jory's lips are in a tight straight line. She nods her head once. "So then you won't. If you don't want to, you won't."

There is such a decisive tone in her voice Claire knows she doesn't want a verbal answer. After a moment, Jory goes up to bed without even looking at her mother.

When Claire goes upstairs Addison's suitcase is open on the bed. He comes out of the bathroom with his shaving kit and puts it on top of the dry cleaner's bag holding a freshly pressed suit.

"Can we talk about it more before you go?" she asks.

He doesn't answer, moves past her to the closet, close enough to brush the sleeve of her robe and—does she imagine it?—pull ever so slightly away. She sits on the bed, watching him move from the suitcase to the dresser, into the bathroom again and back to the closet. She discovers she's counting the items he's packing to guess the days he'll be gone; irrationally, *ridiculously,* she tells herself, but then she watches for his heavy fleece robe, his bulky electric razor, his favorite stereo headphones—items he has always left at home. After enough silent minutes she can't even remember who should be apologizing first. She grips his wrist as it wrestles the zipper around the over-stuffed case. "Addison?"

He doesn't answer at first, maybe waiting for her to go on. But after he latches the metal prongs on the lock he looks at her face and his shoulders sag. He sits down beside her so his own weight shifts her body against his.

"Yes, Claire. I'm coming back."

· 34 ·

Claire had not appreciated how rapidly the clinic would swell with patients once the cherries began to ripen. The stream of human hands required to pick and pack the delicate fruit flowed north from the citrus groves of Texas and the California vineyards and the Oregon strawberry fields to saturate the orchards around Hallum. Almost overnight her patient population changes. More men come to see her now, not because Dan is gone but because this seasonal wave of transient pickers often left their wives and girlfriends behind when they crossed the border. They crowded into rusting cars and one-room cabins and trailers, eager to work the fourteen- and sixteen- and eighteen-hour days offered them before the fruit fell worthless onto the ground. Over the winter Claire had been primarily a gynecologist and obstetrician, a pediatrician and marriage counselor. Now she is an orthopedist and surgeon, treating the strains and stress fractures of hard labor, the sprains and broken bones of ladder falls and cracking branches, the lacerations of saws and pruning shears. She is a pulmonologist and dermatologist, diagnosing the asthma induced by inhaled pesticides and the rashes inflamed by fertilizers.

By five o'clock on Thursday Claire has already seen thirty-eight patients and every exam room is full. Frida looks like she has burned through her last inch of patience. The crush always comes at the end of the day because no worker wants to forgo paid hours, and so they have hobbled on after being injured until the pain or wheezing or immobility drives them out of the trees. By that time their wounds are encrusted with dirt and sweat and the makeshift bandages of torn T-shirts are more a source of infection than protection.

She is examining an ankle, so swollen she is almost certain there is a malleolar fracture, hunting down the X-ray order forms they can't keep in stock. Frida opens the door without even knocking. "Would you come to the urgent care room, please. Now."

When Claire walks in she takes in several facts immediately: the young man with blood all over his T-shirt and torn jeans is looking at her like she alone in the world knows the only magic that might save him; he is breathing too quickly; he is perspiring in a room that is cool. She can tell he has nearly consumed the last breath of energy a body reserves for escape—knows this from the way his face changes as soon as he sees her white coat. It makes her want to look over her shoulder to find Dan standing behind her with his reassuring and unflappable calm.

The man is sitting up on the gurney with his interlocked hands supporting his quivering thigh. His left foot has been severed across the metatarsals, cleaving off all but the great toe, which juts at an unnatural angle. Someone, a friend—hopefully, please God, not his boss—has tied an elastic band around his ankle to stop the blood flow, but Claire can tell from the doorway that this is strangling what remains of his foot. It is colored a dusky blue-gray. A fine red spackle fans over the white paper stretched across the vinyl mattress.

"*Buenas noches, señor. Me llama Doctora Boehning. ¿Cómo se llama?*" She walks up to him as if this were the most normal of days for both of them, the most typical of injuries. She puts her right hand over his right hand and then slides her first two fingers over his radial pulse—his heart rate is decidedly over 100, probably a combination of blood loss and dehydration and pain. "*¿Habla ingles?*" He shakes his head and she continues in Spanish. "*¿No será más cómodo acostado? ¿Cuántos años tiene?*" She is hoping that he will tell her he is under eighteen and eligible for Medicaid.

Frida brings over IV supplies and a bag of lactated Ringer's solution and puts a blood pressure cuff around his arm. "How did he get here?" Claire asks, just as glad now that the patient can't understand her.

"Two guys carried him in through the back door and got out as soon as they saw me. Ambulance is already on the way."

"Great. Can you get the ER on the phone for me? Even better, the surgeon on call. I think it's Perry."

Claire slips an elastic tourniquet around his arm just below his elbow and looks for veins. He is so dehydrated they are slow to fill. But his youth, his lean build, his years of manual labor have blessed him with easy targets for her IV. "Veins thick as steel pipes," Dan would have said. She scrubs his skin with alcohol, hits the bright red flash almost as soon as she enters the skin, advances just far enough to withdraw the needle and slip the flexible catheter into the lumen of the largest vein running along his forearm. Then she moves down to his ankle and slowly loosens the constricting band. He whistles with a sharp intake of breath and his leg goes rigid.

Frida hands her the phone. "Ambulance says five minutes. Perry's on hold here. How much morphine do you want?"

"Start with two. Put some oxygen on him. Thanks, Frida."

Steven Perry doesn't seem fazed. It is, he says, just the beginning of the picking season and the accidental intersection of farm equipment and human flesh will keep him busy until late fall. By the time the medics come the patient is somewhat comfortable and his pulse is down to 70, but his foot is still an ugly color from the ankle down. Frida has already started clearing out the waiting room when Claire comes back; it's almost seven o'clock. Rosa has rescheduled anyone who wasn't urgent, and sent anyone who looked too sick, or even just too anxious, off to the emergency room, where they could wait all night to be seen.

Claire sits in one of the empty chairs while Frida locks the doors. It occurs to her that she has never actually sat in a chair in this waiting room; she's never looked this closely at just how scarred the walls are and how pitiful the faded health education posters look tacked up to the walls. "These chairs are really uncomfortable," she says when Frida sits down in the orange plastic chair next to her. "We should get some with cushions. Well, after we pay last month's electric bill."

Frida pulls her stethoscope off her neck and coils it in her lap. "So when are you going to tell me who this 'we' is? For real, I mean."

Claire searches Frida's face for a clue about how much information she's ready to hear. "What do you mean, 'for real'?

"I mean, who exactly is going to be working here by the time they're harvesting apples and we have twice the patients we saw today. Are you still planning to hire someone?"

Claire raises her eyebrows and sighs. "Sure." She looks at Frida with a wry smile. "Why? You see a line of applicants somewhere?"

"Course! That ad we put in the local paper has the phone ringing all day long."

Claire nods, too tired to put all the pieces together and laugh. "I've got another one ready to go in the journals and medical bulletins. Offering the same whopping salary we get. Maybe I should troll the mortgage foreclosure list looking for homeless docs, huh?"

Frida doesn't laugh this time, fiddles with the stethoscope in her lap for a moment before she says, soberly, "You know what I'm asking you."

"Yeah." Claire pushes up from the chair and starts shutting off the lights and the computer. "Let's go get some dinner. Can you?"

"Nobody waiting at home. Nobody at all."

They find a table in the corner at the same dark bar they'd shared a beer just a few weeks or so after Claire had started at the clinic. This time, though, Claire recognizes some of the faces at the tables. The waitress, Vicki, has a daughter in a dance class with Jory; she drops the menus on the table and sits down for a minute, asking Claire about a popping sensation her daughter gets in her knee every time the teacher has them do a specific kind of turn, which neither Claire nor Vicki can remember the name for.

"Jory's making friends, finally," Frida says after Vicki leaves.

"She is. A couple of girls from dance."

"That's critical—especially being an only child. Means you drive about a hundred miles a day, everything's so far away. But kids out here who don't stay busy get in trouble."

"I see one boy showing up on her Facebook page pretty often. Not so wild about that."

"Who?"

"Zach somebody. Mentions baseball a lot."

Frida nods. "Zach Avery. He's okay. His dad owns the bakery."

"How do you know that?"

Frida shrugs and leans away from the table when Vicki brings over a beer for Frida and a glass of wine for Claire. "If you weren't moving back to Seattle, you'd know everybody, too, in a couple of years. At least by name."

Claire squints at the menu in her hand, discomfited that Frida would address such a flammable topic so obliquely. "So that's what you've heard?"

"I didn't hear a thing. You come back from your weekend in Seattle all buzzin' and chirpy and now these last few days you've been so preoccupied I figured you'd won the lottery and decided not to share it." She scans the menu, tipping back in her chair for all the world like she is talking about what flavor cake they should order for Anita's baby's christening party.

Claire lets her own menu fall flat on the tabletop. "You're kidding. You guessed all this?"

"You're not as subtle as you think." Frida takes three consecutive swallows of her beer and wipes her mouth on her napkin, rests her forearms against the edge of the table. "And then there were those Seattle Windermere and Coldwell-Banker ads that kept showin' up on your desk." She drums her fingers on the varnished wood tabletop and regards Claire with a taunting smile. The waitress comes back just at that moment with a plastic basket bulging with curly fries dusted in an inorganic hue of barbecue-orange.

"I'm sorry," Claire says, genuinely contrite now. "So you've been working with me for the last month waiting to hear I'm quitting."

"Not at all. I've been waiting to hear you're quitting since you started, six months ago."

"Frida, does being so damn blunt about everything always work for you?"

"Sure separates my friends from the pretenders."

Claire stares at her for a moment until Frida bursts out laughing;

a spray of orange fries lands in the middle of the table and she slaps a hand across her mouth, laughing even harder.

"Yeah, well, I guess you could separate them by spitting on them, too." Claire drapes a paper napkin over the flecks and plants the basket of fries on top. "I probably deserved that, anyway. So how do you know I haven't just been protecting you from my own horrific dilemmas until I have them sorted out?"

Frida laughs again. "I don't need all your pretty manners. You know me better by now."

"I stopped showing you any manners the day Dan left. But okay. Here's the thing." Claire picks up a tightly wound coil of fried potato and pulls one end until it breaks in the middle. "Addison's in Seattle. He's been in negotiations with an investor about his drug." It makes her uncomfortable to refer to the man who has funded both their salaries so anonymously, but for once Frida's perceptive ability to slice through bullshit doesn't seem to pick up on it.

"So he's already gotten that far?"

"Well. There's a chance he'll be backing out of it. It's gotten complicated." She pops half the fry into her mouth and chews it thoroughly, suddenly craving more of the salty-sweet fat. "So I guess tomorrow I'll find out if we're going to be have money and choices again, or stay broke."

Frida cocks her head and uninhibitedly studies Claire with a curious look, maybe trying to guess why she's finally telling her this, maybe wondering what else has gone unsaid for so many weeks. "And if you stay broke . . . ?"

"I don't know. I guess we stay just where we are. I do, at least."

Frida freezes for an instant, then says, "Well. I haven't seen life stay in one place for quite so long as you seem to be expecting. Nothing in the middle, then?"

Claire uncoils another fry and twists her mouth into a forced smile. "The ugly truth is that when you've been as well off as we were the middle can feel pretty broke."

"And how about the middle with you and Addison? Or does staying together also depend on whether you're rich or broke?"

Claire's stomach knots up and her appetite disappears. Then Vicki walks up with their food, carrying a circular tray big as a side table on one hand. She kicks the folding metal brace open with the toe of her shoe, as smooth and practiced as any dance move Jory has perfected, swings the tray off her shoulder so it balances precisely across the parallel bars. Claire is thankful for the interruption, too stunned by Frida's remark to acknowledge she heard it. Claire veers into the first fresh subject that comes to mind. "Well, thanks for the thumbs-up on Zach, the Baker's Kid. At least when we were teenagers our parents could hear one half of a phone conversation. Now I just hang around waiting till Jory forgets to sign out and read whatever I can. I get tempted to pretend I'm her and start a chat session sometimes. It's scary being a parent—you can't imagine."

Frida seems to take Claire's cue and starts talking about Anita's baby boy, born five days ago and already Anita is saying she wants to come back to work. "She's just tired—he's still feeding every three hours. Those first few months are too precious to miss, though. They go fast enough. I guess it's harder to remember that after you have more than one."

Claire nods. "You're right. Especially with Jory being so premature—I didn't want to miss a minute."

Frida is unusually quiet for the rest of the meal. Claire picks at her food and tries once or twice to reopen the topic of staffing, whether they should advertise in the whole five-state region. She promises, again, that she'll stay until someone new is settled, says they should both visit Dan next week and talk about writing another grant, maybe they could afford a nurse practitioner in addition to an MD. Everything she says feels false.

After dinner they walk to Frida's car first, the nearer one. Claire leans over to hug her, wanting at least their physical contact to bring them closer again. She can't blame Frida for feeling the threat of desertion despite all her reassurances, if indeed that is what made her lash out. But the arm Frida puts around Claire feels stiff. When Claire starts to pull away, though, Frida gives her one last intense squeeze and holds on to Claire's hand, exhales like she's been holding her breath for too long and says, "When my husband walked out eight years ago he took my little boy with him. He was ten. His name is Andy. I haven't seen him since."

A cry escapes from Claire and she covers her eyes. "Oh my God. My God, Frida. You never told me."

"You would have heard someday. Everybody in town remembers it. Reason I stay here is because it's the only place he'd know to look for me—if he ever tries."

Claire finds it hard to make any words come out. "I'm . . . I'm so sorry—I wish I'd known."

"I stopped talking about him two years after the police stopped trying to find him." She steps off the curb and unlocks her car door, looks almost afraid Claire will try to touch her again, console her. Like the smallest thing might unleash the terror in a new way she hasn't figured out how to fight.

Claire puts her hands in her pockets, her arms and hands and facial expression awkwardly posed in self-conscious shame, and she's ashamed even of that—of being focused on her own irrelevance in the face of what Frida carries with her every day.

Frida sticks one hand out of the window and gives a little wave above the roof of the car. Then she backs out and stops, rolls down the passenger window and waits until Claire steps near enough to hear. "Maybe I shouldn't have told you that tonight. At least some of it was meanness. Or frustration. My own selfish way to shake you up. But maybe I just want you to know the middle isn't so bad if you're not there alone." She turns her head away briefly, then says, "It's not bad at all, Claire."

It's still light when she gets home. The payback of short northwestern winter days is this gift of indolent summer twilight, time to linger in the subtle drama of shadows and purple sky.

Miguela is in the kitchen putting the dinner dishes away. She had asked Claire to repeat everything Dan remembered multiple times, going over some parts of the story with a dictionary in her hand until the unlucky truth settled in and replaced the tortured murder she'd envisioned. Even as the discovery of Esperanza's cause of death is threatening to tear Addison and Claire's future apart, it seems to be piecing Miguela's life back together. She has not said this in so many words—if the blend of languages they have made together even contains such possibilities—but the hum of secretive purpose that was always part of her, moving around her like an aura, has quieted.

Claire knows Miguela is leaving soon, knows it through the precise pronunciation she is demanding from Jory during their Spanish lessons, and the recipe she writes out for *gallo pinto*, the Nicaraguan dish Jory has come to crave. For the last week Claire has opened the door to Miguela's room each morning just far enough to check whether she is still in her bed, her clothes are still on the shelves.

And then Miguela asks Claire for permission to take Jory on a picnic by the stream, just the two of them. When they come back it is obvious Jory has been crying. She eats dinner in silence and excuses herself as soon as the dishes are done. Claire follows her up to her room and quietly shuts the door. Jory is sitting at her blue wooden desk, the one Claire had painted with butterflies to match her walls in the Seattle house. The window is open and the cyclic song of frogs swells up from the bog near the aspen grove, then the solemn hoot of a distant owl. The bookshelves and walls are still filled with pictures of Jory's Seattle friends, but there is a Hallum sweatshirt draped over her pillow and a photo of one new friend on her bedside table. Claire sits on the bed, waiting for a signal. Finally she asks, "Want to talk about it?"

Jory won't look at her. "Did you ask her to leave?"

"No. You're the only one she's talked to about it. You're her best friend here." Jory doesn't move. Suddenly Claire feels like she is looking down a ladder of all the trials and separations Jory will face in her life, all of them crowding into this blink of time with no space to recover, one crisis hurtling right into the next. It would be a curse to know the future. She aches to reach inside Jory's young heart and hold the pieces together.

"She just said it's time," Jory finally says. "Why can't she stay with us? She could live better here."

"Nicaragua is her home. She cares so much about you, Jory. You know that."

Jory wipes her face. "She gave me this." She hands Claire the worn red cloth-covered book of Rubén Darío poems Miguela has been using as Jory's primary Spanish textbook. "She asked me to come to Nicaragua sometime."

"We'll all go. I'd love to go. And now you'll be able to speak the language a little." They sit in silence, then, until it is clear Jory wants to be alone. Claire kisses the top of her head and starts to leave.

"You know what her name means, don't you?" Jory says just before Claire opens the door.

"'Miguela'? No. I didn't know it had a meaning."

"'Esperanza.' Her daughter's name. It comes from *esperar*. It has two meanings. It can mean 'to hope' or 'to wait.' Both verbs in one word, even though they seem so different."

Two days later Claire and Jory drive Miguela into Wenatchee to catch the bus for Seattle; from there she will fly to Managua, Nicaragua. Claire watches Jory for a signal about how prepared she is for this good-bye. Her conversation is almost giddy at first, a pressure of nervous, disconnected thoughts. But the resilience of adolescence takes over by the time they arrive and all she talks about is the visit to Jalapa she has thoroughly planned.

They have to wait more than an hour for the bus. Miguela has never been on an airplane; she keeps checking her pack and her ticket, jumping between Spanish and English, halting her conversation altogether every time another Greyhound arrives or departs. She seems unconvinced that she will be in Nicaragua by tonight—laughs about how easy it is to get *out* of the United States.

Just before she gets on the bus, Claire puts an envelope into Miguela's hand. "A little piece of America to take home."

Driving back to Hallum, Jory asks her what was in it. "A thank-you," Claire says. "Something she can turn into what she needs."

· 35 ·

She hears Addison's car pull into the driveway after midnight, hears the dinging sound of the alarm while he gets his bag out of the trunk, the car door slamming, then the front door opening and closing behind him. She tries to guess from the pace of his footsteps, the energy or defeat in his weight hitting the stair treads what he will tell her. Their phone calls this week have been studiously openended. Utilitarian. Safe.

He opens the bedroom door with one hand gripping the edge, as if that might hush its usual creak.

"I'm awake. It's okay," Claire whispers.

He stands still for a minute, then picks up his bag and carries it to the closet, sits on the side of the bed to take off his shoes, all without saying a word.

"So, I guess it isn't okay. Is it?"

He takes off his tie and belt, loosens his pants and lies down next to her. "No. Not okay."

Claire pulls the sheet up to her neck, holding it there with both hands. "Does Ron own Optimus?"

"His holding company owns it. Ron's not very involved with the daily business. But yes. His money runs Optimus."

The room is suddenly very hot, as if a silent explosion has gone off in the middle of her and is consuming them all. She wants to loft the sheet over her body like a fan, and at the same time she must

275

keep the sheet clutched tight around her. "Did Ron send Esperanza to Optimus?"

"No. He'd never met her. He had no idea any of his employees, Esperanza or Rubén, were enrolling in the drug trials. I won't say it was coincidence—there's a grapevine effect. The trials pay a little money and this study gave them meals and a bed for a month."

Claire waits for him to go on, certain from his mood alone, the tone of his voice, that there is more, that she cannot let herself feel relieved. After a minute she asks, "What's wrong, then? If Ron didn't know about it and he's done nothing illegal . . . Surely you got the drug trial stopped."

Addison crosses his arms under his head; the shifting of his body seems to sink him deeper into the mattress, as if a weight were pressing down. "The drug trial went through just fine—it concluded two months ago with Esperanza and Rubén categorized as 'lost to follow-up,' meaning they drop out of the statistics altogether. The other volunteers were all Caucasian; none of them had an abnormal reaction. It's possible there's a genetic variance that affects Hispanics. Without their results the drug looked safe. In fact, the drug would probably be moving right through FDA approval if Ron hadn't notified Optimus and the review board."

Claire rolls up on her side now, so her face is above Addison's in the darkness. "Ron did everything he could, then. Even Optimus, didn't they? It shouldn't affect vascumab. Why are you still acting like something's wrong?"

"What's wrong is the drug they were studying. The sponsor is a biotech company in California. They've been working on antiangiogenesis drugs for years—long before I was."

"So it was another VEGFR-2? Just tell me, Addison. Are you worried it was the same kind of liver problem you found in the mice? Is this drug similar to vascumab?"

He shakes his head once, then sits up and smiles with a pitifully ironic twist of his mouth. "The drug *is* vascumab, Claire. Identical. I saw the design; it's my molecule."

"How is that possible? You have a patent . . ."

"We have a provisional patent. On part of the molecule. The company testing the drug at Optimus is the same one Rick worked for before I hired him. He went right back to them after he left Seattle, last spring. Remember the bike tour Rick and Lilly bought at that auction? Walker's charity thing?" He waits for Claire to react, stares at her frozen face for a moment before he goes on. "The medical director at Optimus was on that trip."

Claire explodes in righteous outrage. "Rick signed a confidentiality agreement! All those proprietary information restrictions . . . he couldn't take your idea out of your lab!"

"Yeah, I guess I could sue them. Rick could counter that they were working on the same drug all along. And who knows, Claire? Maybe they were. Should I spend a few hundred thousand dollars trying to save the patent on a dangerous drug? The only thing that matters is that vascumab is the reason Esperanza is dead."

In the morning Claire wakes up and reaches for Addison. The sheets are damp where his body had lain; his dreams must have tossed him into a sweat. She sits up. The window above the bed is open and the day is fresh with rising dew, a pink and baby-blue day before the sun burns across the field.

It is so quiet here—even six months after leaving the city she is surprised to hear nothing on the land that she wouldn't have heard a hundred years ago, a thousand years ago. No cars or sirens, rarely even planes; the only sound of urgency is in the competing calls of the birds, the howls of coyotes, the abrupt silencing of an animal caught and killed. A magpie flushes out of the wild mock orange below the window. She hears Addison cough and a moment later he steps into her view.

He looks small from this vantage: the tail of his wrinkled white button-down shirt hangs loose over his baggy gym shorts; his hair is a halo of black fluff. In the morning light the full blow of last night's conversation rushes back to her. She holds her breath with her eyes squeezed shut until her pulse sings in her ears, praying he is down there waiting for her to wake up, waiting to tell her he has already seen the solution.

She scratches her fingernails on the screen. "Hey."

"Hey." He searches out her face under the shadow of the eave.

She goes downstairs in her bathrobe and a pair of rubber flip-flops, sits down on the top step of the porch. Even this early in the morning the day is already hot. "Did you sleep at all?"

He shakes his head but doesn't turn to look at her.

She waits a moment before she says, "It'll be okay, Addison." Still he doesn't answer. "It'll be okay. You'll figure something out. A new molecule. Or a new cancer test."

He scans the horizon with his hands loose at his sides, his posture relaxed. Without seeing his face it could seem like he didn't have a concern in the world. Finally he turns around and sits at the other end of the lowest step. "I'm sorry I did this to you, Claire. To you and Jory. I was stupid to risk our own money." She wants to move nearer to him, sit close enough to feel the invisible connection that has always kept them together through the worst of their arguments. But something in his face holds her back. "I don't know if I've actually said that to you before—out loud."

"You didn't need to."

He lets out a little huff, almost a laugh, that makes her feel ashamed for saying something she doesn't believe.

"Okay. You do need to," she says, suddenly angry at his feckless apology coming so late; flooded with a storm of frustration more than forgiveness. He doesn't respond and she slaps her hand on the wooden step. "Well, do you want me to scream at you? Hasn't there been enough of that?" She hates the bitterness in her voice.

Addison sits splay-legged with his elbows on his knees, not once turning to face her; so detached it feels like he's goading her on. He rips a long stem of weedy grass out of the dirt and peels it into fine green curls.

Claire has an urge to wrench it out of his hands. "All right, then! How could you do it? Borrow against everything we owned without even talking to me? Rob our family of every safety net?" Claire's voice breaks apart now in a single harsh sob. She grits her teeth against it. "Oh God. I'm just so tired of putting a good face on everything. Promising Jory it's all going to be okay." She drops her head into her hands. "I'm terrified, Addison." Part of her aches for him to come to her, feels safer in their simmering anger and blame than the aftermath of what they are doing.

He doesn't move.

"Claire, where did you think all the funding came from for Eugena? You think a line of investors were begging to give me money? I walked us right out to the ledge for it. And you didn't even know, did you? And I won. *Women* won—all over the world. You know how many women won't have to die of ovarian cancer because of Eugena? And vascumab . . . God! The difference I thought it could make!" He throws his head back with an audible groan. After a long moment he shakes his head, staring out toward the aspen that fringe the cusp of the hill. "By the time Jory was three or four you stopped even pretending you were going to finish your residency. And I didn't care. Even before we sold Eugena. Even when we were broke, I didn't care if you ever finished. Whenever we had a discussion about money you seemed to take it as a judgment—like I was pressuring you, making your decisions for you. So I dropped it. It was like you'd rather pretend everything worked itself out through magic.

"You remember when I sold my dad's car? Told you a Mustang collector had seen it on the street and called with an offer? I sold it to a lab tech so we could pay the rent that month. And then, after we sold Eugena . . ."

He didn't even need to finish. Claire knows. After Eugena, money had gone from being a perpetual strain to being a miracle, a blessing. And within a few years it had completely melded into the background of their lives, becoming familiar to the point of being expected; stealthily seeping into the fabric of every choice they made until they forgot there had ever been limitations.

It feels as if the earth is moving out from under Claire. Like a fundamental property of nature she has trusted to the point of neglect—gravity or air or light—is disappearing. Is this how a marriage dies? she wonders. The deepest wounds torn open again and again by the forgotten apology, the neglected thank-you, the complacent assumption that love will sustain itself. How do you finally decide that all you can hope to save are the disunited hearts, because the union itself is irreparable?

"I'm not a good businessman," Addison says. "Never wanted to be. I'm a biochemist. I needed to raise money for my project and I found a way. I never told you how I was financing the lab because you never asked." He looks at her again, his anger spent. "And that probably still makes it all my fault."

A noise from the window over the porch hushes them and a minute later Jory walks outside. "You're fighting again," she says. "Something's gone wrong, hasn't it. With Dad's job offer." Addison's head drops and he glances at Claire. Jory raises her voice. "Quit hiding this from me. I thought somebody was buying Dad's drug and everything was going to be fine again."

After an awkward silence, Addison turns around and motions for Jory to sit between them. "I'm sorry you feel like we're hiding things, Jory. Yes. There is a problem with the sale."

"What? What's the problem?"

"The problem." He ties a knot in the long stem of grass he has been worrying, tosses it onto the dirt and plucks another, giving himself a moment. "The man who was going to invest his money in my company believed he was buying a certain asset. My drug, vascumab. You know what an asset is? In business terms?"

"Yeah. I don't know, maybe not. Something that's good."

Addison nods. "That's right. An asset is something that has value, something that's worth money to someone else. In this case vascumab was the asset he was buying, essentially. But some new information was discovered that means my drug isn't safe to use. That means it's not worth any money. So now I have nothing to sell him. It's sort of like you had a nice car or a beautiful diamond ring and someone offered you money for it. But if the car didn't run right or the ring turned out to be fake, you'd have to give the money back."

Jory looks like she has heard only half of Addison's explanation, or maybe the question she wants answered is not what he's assumed. "I thought you were working on a cure for cancer. How can that not be worth anything?" She sounds more hopeless than a fifteen-year-old should be able to convey.

Addison is quiet for a long time, his face unnaturally still. He throws the grass away and gets up. "Yeah. That's a good question, Jory." He walks inside, letting the screen door slam behind him.

Claire scoots closer and runs her hand along Jory's temple, twists a heavy strand of her hair through her fingers. "It's complicated, sweetie. But it's . . ."

Jory grabs her mother's hand, stopping her. "Did this have anything to do with Miguela's leaving? Did she leave because Dad isn't getting the money?"

"No. In fact, what Dad learned about his drug made it possible for her to go home, which is what she wanted."

Claire expects Jory to contest this, argue and blame them again. But Jory's eyes are moving over her mother's face much as they would when she was years younger and Claire would try to explain any difficult fact of life—why her best friend could be so much more hurtful than people she didn't care about; why a grandfather could love her but forget her birthday. Explanations that made little sense at the time but which, Claire knew, she would turn and shape until they budded into something useful and comprehensible, ready in the place and time she needed them.

Jory looks out over the field, the sun high enough now that prickles of sweat glisten on her upper lip. "At least tell me when we're going to go back to living normally."

"Do you mean move back to Seattle?" Claire asks.

"I don't know. I don't even know if I want to go back to Seattle anymore." She pivots her body away, maybe afraid of tears. "I just mean *normal*. Like we used to live."

Claire rests her cheek on Jory's back, hears the thrum of her heart through her thin shirt, her skin. She remembers a day when Jory was so tiny she barely stretched from wrist to elbow along the bones of her mother's arm. A lab technician had pricked her wrinkled red heel with a lancet and squeezed until a drop of blood oozed down a capillary tube for her bilirubin test. Jory, so premature her eyes were incapable of focus, had searched the universe for her mother's face and cried out in wonder that the world could hurt her. The cells violated fifteen years ago didn't even exist anymore—already sloughed and replaced, forgotten as thoroughly as Claire's heartbroken consolation. It makes her breath feel short to think of it now, to wonder if all these years of protecting Jory have only made her more vulnerable.

She turns Jory's face toward hers. "What we had, the way we lived in Seattle—sweetheart, that wasn't *normal*. That isn't how most people live."

Jory swallows twice and asks in a strained whisper, "Well, do you think this is normal? Are we going to live like *this* forever?" She looks up at the rotted Victorian trim work, the cupped and peeling porch boards. She looks at the door her father slammed shut between them a few moments ago.

Claire takes both of Jory's hands into her own and holds them firmly in her lap. "No. Not like this. Maybe not like we did—but we'll be fine. We'll be okay."

Addison calls out the screen door that he is making pancakes, if they're ready to come inside. Jory looks at her mother, and then at the sketch of color behind the screen that is her father. She pulls her hands away and stares at Claire with such maturity it startles her, like she has aged five years in a heartbeat. "Mom, don't you get tired of saying that to me?"

· 36 ·

The first time Addison and Claire came to Hallum
Valley was only four months after she met him in the emergency room
where he worked as an orderly. Four months after their first date: the
last D in ADCVANDISSLD. It was Memorial Day weekend, and one of
Claire's med school friends had invited a group—anyone who wasn't
on call—to spend the three days at her grandparents' old log cabin.

Addison had met her friends a few times: a dinner after an afternoon
lecture, at the Comet for a beer once. But Claire had been circumspect
about fully including Addison in her tightest circle. Other boyfriends had
come and gone during the first two years of medical school and she'd
dragged them to every party without a second's thought about anyone's
opinion. And what was there not to like about Addison? He was smart—
already accepted into the PhD program even before he'd finished his
master's degree. He could make people laugh, once you got him off the
subject of polymerase chain reactions or monoclonal antibodies. He had
a better music library than anyone she'd ever known. And he was cute,
kind of. Cute in a different way than her other boyfriends. No full head
of hair, a little extra tissue in places the others had been all muscle, always
saying he was going to start working out as soon as he finished his next
set of exams.

She was only beginning to admit to herself that the real reason she
was on edge about a weekend spent in a small cabin with her closest
friends (who would all be giving Addison the closest if most consider-

ate inspection) was the sense that she was floating in a small boat far out in the ocean, coasting up the side of a larger-than-average swell on a calm, blue day. But gathering underneath her was the mass of a tidal wave, a natural force that would change her life quite permanently if she allowed it to. She was old enough to know there might be other chances if she let him go. But nothing like this. Not like this.

He picked her up on that Friday morning in his ancient pickup truck—her more reliable car wasn't big enough to carry the barbecue grill they'd promised to bring. The traffic was horrendous leaving the city, but horrendous in an oddly happy way, a million people having an enormous party, trapped on the I-5 bridge watching boats weave drunkenly through the Montlake Cut. Addison rolled his window down to change lanes, the grill blocking his view, and the blare of boat horns and rock bands gusted into the cab like so many invisible flower petals shaken loose by a spring breeze.

The truck held its own in the stop-and-go traffic up the highway, but the gradual climb up the western slope of the Cascades sent occasional puffs of dark smoke out the tailpipe, the engine whined steadily higher until they were both tense, as if even the weight of conversation might burn it out for good. Clouds pulled in, covering the broken blue that had been a rare enough May gift for Seattle. They massed up against the peaks until a misty rain turned the charcoal powder on the grill's hood into rivulets of black grime, and Addison's frayed windshield wipers beat blurry streaks across the glass.

But then they reached the summit, and in one of those moments when the geography of the Pacific Northwest manifests all its magnificence, the clouds stalled just below the snow-covered caps, and on the other side the sky shone so bright Claire's eyes stung. The truck practically coasted down the eastern slope, making it all the way to the turn-off a few miles from the cabin, where it met a solemn, peaceful death.

They got out and walked. With the persistent tension about the truck's reliability resolved Claire was in a surprisingly happy mood. Unencumbered, even if on foot. Addison was, too, she could tell, though she knew the cash to repair the truck would be hard to spare.

It was hot on this side. A mile from the cabin the road veered next to the river and they waded out to a large rock near the middle, the water just melted from snow and their feet bright red by the time they climbed up. The flat area was so limited they had to sit back to back and hook arms for balance.

She knew the turning point was coming for them, expected that after a weekend immersed with Addison in this group who knew her so well, the building wave would have to break, one way or the other. They had shared many things already: dinners in the small cheap restaurants on Broadway; hours and hours of studying; her bed. The requisite facts of their lives had been conveyed. Addison knew Claire's parents had divorced when she was in high school; she knew his parents were together but shouldn't be—enough facts to trust this was not a dead end. But each of them, too, had held back. When Claire thought about it later, it seemed clear to her why: it was only these retained secrets that still offered either of them a way out.

Addison dipped his hand into the splash and rubbed it over his neck. "My mom loves water. Rivers. She would take us into Chicago to walk along the river. And she can't swim."

Claire turned her head so she could see at least a part of his profile. "Really? She can't swim?"

"Nope. Grew up in a little Midwest town without a drop of swimmable water. Got married at eighteen, and my dad sure wasn't going to teach her." They didn't talk for a while after that. The river must have swept away the odor of their human presence finally, and on the bank animals and birds began to go about their gathering and hunting without a perception of threat. "There were a lot of things my dad never taught my mom. It was almost like he could see the future—she would have left him if she'd had any means. I think. I hope."

"I'm sorry. It must be hard—knowing they're unhappy."

He looked back up the road toward where they had abandoned the truck. "Well. It didn't have to be that way. They could have made other choices, I think."

"You mean about who they married? Or staying together."

"No. Maybe that, too." He picked a flake of rock away and skipped it over a calm pool. "I mean about how they live. They fight a lot. Dad works for a while and then he hits the card tables, convince he was a day away from rich. I think if they'd lived when you could just barter for stuff they might have been okay." A raccoon appeared from behind a Douglas fir just yards away, waddling like a cat with a broken back to the edge of the water, where it washed some scrap of food. They were quiet until it moved out of sight. Then he asked her, "What about your parents? Why do you think your dad left?"

Claire started to give the usual explanation of differing interests, the fights that happened behind closed bathroom doors or inside the parked car, maybe thinking Claire wouldn't know any better. But then she boiled it down to the source. "The same, really. My mom worried all the time. I think she believed all her problems would be fixed if they could get a bigger house or take better vacations."

She'd felt his body change against her then, the taut muscles that were keeping him from sliding off the rock loosening enough to curve into her own more closely. Finally he slid his hips around so he was beside her, both of them facing upstream. He took her hand into his lap. "I'm a lab rat, Claire. I want to do bench research. It's never going to pay me very much."

She felt the wave beneath them rising, lifting, hurtling them forward and interlaced her fingers with his. "I know." She had laughed then, out of relief and terror and exhilaration, and because they agreed without even spelling it out. "And I really tried to like a specialty that pays better than family practice."

They had gone through the weekend closed inside their brand-new world after that—a transformation blatantly obvious to all of Claire's friends. There were too few rooms or beds to divide up as couples, but those were the last nights Claire and Addison lived apart.

It is the building wave that makes Claire think of that day now. Not the odd fact that their love had gone in such a geographic circle, and not the portentous conversation. Not the heat. It is the sense memory she has of a silent and monumental force carrying her smoothly, steadily up and up, only menacing because it gathers stealthily enough to be missed. And the deadliest consequence of a tidal wave, she knew, was if you failed to see it in time and rescue what is dear to you.

Jory goes up to take a shower after she bolts her food, and Addison and Claire carry their plates out to the porch, where at least the hope of a breeze seems cooler. Addison unbuttons the top of his shirt and pulls it out from his belt; yellow jackets swarm over his plate and feed at the rim of the pooled syrup, unfazed by his waving hand. He finally puts the plate under the porch steps. "It's been two years since I walked more than fifty yards from this porch," he says.

Claire twists her hair up, pinning it to the top of her head with one hand and fanning her blouse with the other. "The stock pond was full a month ago. It must be lower now. Miguela used to go there a lot, I think."

"Show me."

"The pond? Now?"

He looks like he is challenging her, wants to push her to a new place. "Yeah. Why not?"

It amazes her that the grasses have grown so high in such a short time, already brushing against her calves, their braided wheat tips like soft whips. Small golden crickets, invisible among the golden stems, buzz like a rattler's tail when she steps across a gully, snapping her focus onto the bare earth for the ripple that might be a snake. Addison sees her freeze and takes her hand, leads her slowly, cautiously around the low hill and the bright green and white aspen to the water. They can hear the stream when they stand still, even though the grass hides all but a single silver stripe where it curves into the wide, slow circle stalled behind Jory's rock dam, and beyond that the deep pool of the stock pond.

The water level has dropped a foot or more since Claire was here with Jory and Miguela. The shallowest edges are dense with cattails and reeds, but the huge flat rock still juts into the clear center. Claire dangles her sandals from the fingers of her right hand and slides her feet along the mossy rocks, shifting her weight from one tremulous balance point to the next. When she reaches the rock she makes a single flamboyant leap from the last large stone and waves her sandals above her head with a whoop.

From up here the rolling slope of yellow green grasses looks like an untouched prairie, patchworked with snowberry and chokecherry and elderberry, the way it must have looked when the Blackstocks grazed their cattle or the Indians traded skins and beads, or even a time before any human had seen this land. The heat gives it all a magical, shimmery quality and she finds herself unwilling to think about anything but the beauty of this day. She does a dancy little spin and plants her hands on her knees, then dances again, this time because the stone is almost too hot to bear against her naked soles.

"Dare you to jump from that rock." She points to one farther away than her own launch site.

Addison takes off his shoes and tosses them onto the higher ground behind him, rolls up the legs of his khakis. "And what's the bet?"

She sits down, tucking her sandals under her buttocks. "Seven million. I'll bet seven million. Give or take a few bucks."

He studies her for a minute, like he's trying to decide which way to respond to this figure, equal to their lost savings. The heat makes his face shimmer, like the grass and the long blue sky behind him. It blurs the edges of his shape so he looks like some transient spirit that might disappear if she turns away.

"I have a better idea," he says.

"What?"

He wades out to the middle of the shallow stream, wobbling like a top with each alternating foot, and then, after rescuing himself from each of those possible spills, he puts his wallet in his shirt pocket, loops his belt around his neck and sits down in the water. "Come down here and meet me."

His pants are already soaked, and water is wicking up his shirt. Claire strips her T-shirt off over her head and tosses it onto the rock before she climbs down in her bra and shorts. The water cools her whole body instantaneously and the blistering temperature becomes a pleasure. She tips her head back, not caring what the sun will do to her skin.

Addison spreads his palms flat against the surface of the water, fingers splayed to catch the leaves and bits of grass pushed along by the slow current. "Has anyone answered the ads you've put in for a new doctor?" he asks.

"A few. It's early still. I don't want to rush it. Evelyn said she can help out while Dan is still strong enough to be alone."

"You've liked it, haven't you. You bring that home with you. I can see it."

She floats on her back for a moment, suspended on her hands so only the prominences of toes, knees, hips, breasts break the surface. "Are you asking me if I know how to swim?" Addison looks confused and she smiles, glad that the reference was missed. "I'm not sure what you're really asking me."

"Well. Me neither. So I have another question for you." He trails his fingers along her left arm until they reach her hand and he grasps it, tipping her off balance. He holds her left hand up between them. "Where's your ring?"

Claire looks at the solitary wedding band on her finger as if the missing diamond surprises her. "Hmm. Not there! In a good place, though. Trust me."

He is suddenly less playful, holds her left hand in his right and twists the gold band in a circle. Then he looks at her closely. "Did you give her the ring or the money?"

Claire answers in nearly a whisper. "I didn't think she could sell it in Nicaragua." She pauses, waits for his reaction to become clearer in his blank face. "I kept some for us, too. Are you furious?"

"Furious?" He shakes his head. "No. It was yours. Your choice." He turns and walks down the stream, still holding her hand, almost as if he's already forgotten it.

They reach a broad delta just before the stream flows into the pond and sit down again. "Okay, my turn," Claire says. "What are the chances you can fix vascumab? Figure out what caused the liver damage and try again."

Addison takes a minute to answer, submerges his face until all she can see is a pink glob underneath the clouded water, marked by an explosion of bubbles just before he comes up and wipes the water off his face. "About seven million to one. With any luck at all."

There is nothing in this that surprises Claire. The differences between vascumab and the multitude of other failed drugs was minuscule to begin with. She had hardly realized she still hoped for it until now. And even within the disappointment, part of her welcomes the end of the waiting, the space it opens up. But still, the blow of hearing him say it makes her turn away. She stumbles to her feet again, almost slipping on the slick, river-polished stones. She hears Addison splashing behind her, falling once with a groan of surprise and possibly pain but she doesn't wait. The bottom becomes muckier sand and she wades in to her knees before he catches up and turns her by her shoulders to face him.

"Claire, what matters is that we stopped this drug. Stopped *my* drug. If you hadn't learned what happened to Esperanza and Rubén it could have hurt a lot more people."

"I know. That's good. More than good. So now you spend another twenty years of your life trying to invent another cancer test? Another vascumab?"

"No. I go back to doing the work I'm good at and see where it leads. Ron is willing to help me start something in Wenatchee."

She scans the burning white blue sky. "I knew better than to think it might still work out."

He is quiet for a long time, then: "We have to both decide what it is we really want to still work out, Claire."

She turns to him, sees the solemn look on his face and feels the blood rush out of her head, feels the surge of water rising, swelling underneath them. "Are we really there? Is that something you're trying to decide?"

"No." He shakes his head. "No. I know what I want. But what I want isn't behind us. I can't take us back there."

She is about to cry, holds her breath for a moment to fight it. "Then we won't. We won't go back there."

Addison's eyes are filling now, a thing she has only seen twice in their marriage—the day they wed, and the day Jory was born and almost died. "Okay. I heard the word I needed to hear."

"What?" she asks, too emotional to even remember precisely what she'd said.

"*We.*"

She lets out a small laugh that turns into a choked sob, waits for the surge of anchoring security that should follow—the attaching force between them, as reliable as gravity, that has always followed their impassioned reunions after discord. Waits and knows at the same time that she can only expect half to come from him. "So is it too soon to talk about where we *can* go?"

He shrugs, but after a pause adds, "No. Not too soon. I have a great idea." He strips off his clothes and wades into the middle of the stock pond, and when the water reaches his pale white chest he dives under, comes up and shakes the water from his eyes. "It's perfect. Come on."

Claire tosses her bra and shorts and panties on the nearest rock and wades in after him. When she moves, the ripples spread in such a way the rocks appear arranged in perfect, concentric circles, some miraculous natural order, until the water goes clear again and they settle into chaos before her. The pockets of colder water break against her skin, the muddy bottom oozes between her toes until she tucks her feet up and swims to him. A small fish nips at her leg and she screams, then screams once more when she realizes it's Addison's hand. He wraps his body around hers, their naked skin sliding slick and smooth, impossibly young again. And when his hands begin to move over her, without thinking, without planning, they are both surprised, as seduced by the illicit setting as teenagers. They have stumbled through confessions and apologies for eight months trying to claw their way back. Only now, at this inevitable point of giving up, does she understand how these new, raw surfaces bind them. As if the wounds torn through both of them might, finally, scar their flesh together.

Acknowledgments

A book doesn't really come to life until someone besides the author opens the cover and steps inside the dream. I am grateful to you, the reader, for spending hours inside these pages, and to the booksellers who helped bring us together.

If there is any task more daunting than writing a first novel, it is the work of writing a second novel. The scope of research for this book stretched far beyond the eventual storyline, and many people contributed time and information that isn't written in these pages but which still shaped the characters and plot. Indeed, the most valuable lesson I discovered by talking to people on opposite sides of such complicated issues as immigration, healthcare access and biopharmaceutical research is that the gray zones are always more fascinating and true than the black and white. My eternal thanks for the many individuals who volunteered their valuable time to help me understand worlds well beyond the one in which I live and work.

For their personal and medical experiences and expertise, I thank Siri Kushner and Hector Guillen, Gabriel Solano, Julian Perez and Antoinette Angulo, Ann Diamond, Tamara Merritt (who answered all my endless emails!), Steve Brown and the staff at the Brewster Family Health Center, medical social worker Jeff Harder, Jorge Baron of Norwest Immigration Services, Angela Macey-Cushman and financial consultants Dan Nelson, Rick Thomas and Deb Hiss. Thanks to physicians Anna Beck, Karen Hanten and Dana Lynge. Though I never got to make the visit you so kindly offered, thanks to border agents Daryll Griffin, Mike Fisher and Richard Barlow. For their amazing patience in guiding me through the science, business and regulations of drug development I thank Ann Miller and Alex Burgin (how many times did I promise you both this was 'one last question?'), Nancy Salts, Joe Neal, Chris Bernards, Cheryl Weaver, Mette Peters, Pam Witte Gallagher, Dan Gallagher, Jim Bredfeldt and the thoughtful observations of bio-ethicist Carl Elliott. Thanks to naturalist Dana Visalli for his detailed knowledge of the Okanogan.

To the people of Nicaragua, a country rich in open hearts and open doors: I only scratched your surface and found great friends and natural wonders. I'm coming back! Thanks to the board of BOSIA for building the bridge between Bainbridge Island, Washington and Ometepe Island, Nicaragua.

In this era of ebooks and downloads it becomes easy to assume a book magically zips from my computer straight to the printer or the reader's electronic device. Nothing could be further from the truth. Innumerable people have invested time, creative guidance and wise advice to carry this story from my imagination to yours. My great thanks to my editor Marysue Rucci, who recognized the heart of this novel long before I did, and my publisher, David Rosenthal. Thanks also to Kerri Kolen, Kate Ankofski, Sophie Epstein, Jonathan Evans and Judy Steer, Julia Prosser and Leah Wasielewski, and the many others at Simon & Schuster working behind the scenes. Thanks to my agents at Inkwell Management, David Forrer and Kimberly Witherspoon. You gave me critiques, opened doors and held my hand when I needed it.

Dennis O'Reilly gave me the honest feedback I needed through more drafts than any human should tolerate. Thank you to the best writing brainstormers I know: Susan Wiggs, Suzanne Selfors, Sheila Rabe, Elsa Watson, Anjali Banerjee. Thanks to the Seattle7writers, laughing with you may have saved my sanity: Stephanie Kallos, Erica Bauermeister, Jennie Shortridge, Garth Stein, Randy Sue Coburn, Mary Guterson, Kit Bakke, Maria Semple. Several brave friends accepted my request to read the manuscript and tell me the truth, not an easy assignment. Thanks to you, Zan Merriman, Pam Shor, Marc Shor, Martha Burkert and Martha McLaughlin.

An entire page should be devoted to my family for their endurance and unwillingness to let me sink into despair, even when my floor was buried in paper and my brain began to blur; even when the cat walked out the door with my sticky notes stuck in its fur. Kathie, Ray, Ellen and Marilyn, thanks for the readings, the research, and the faith. And to the family I have made, Steve, Sara, Will, Julia and Elise, how many hours this took me away from you! The five of you are my center of gravity and horizon of hope. Forever.

If you are interested in learning more about Nicaragua or would like to contribute to an organization working to build relationships between the peoples of Nicaragua and the U.S., visit www.BOSIA.org.